TARQUIN JENKINS
and the
BOOK OF DREAMS

PETER FORD

BLOATED SHAGGANAT PUBLISHERS

Edited by Paul Barnett/John Grant, www.johngrantpaulbarnett.com
Cover Designed by Aaron Ferrara; www.husbandandhusband.net
Interior Design by Woven Red Author Services, www.WovenRed.ca

Tarquin Jenkins & The Book of Dreams/Peter Ford—1st edition
ISBN: 978-0-9950142-0-6

Acknowledgements

In the 12 years it has taken me to publish this book, several people have inspired, helped and cajoled me into writing.

Thanks to Paul Barnett/John Grant for his editing skills, without which this book would never have got off the ground; he took a series of amusing incidents and made them into one rip-roaring adventure.

Thanks to Ger Harley for his editing, Chris Penycate for his pedantry, and all those at Chrons who took an interest.

The beautiful cover illustrations for the book were created by Aaron Ferrara.

For Delilah, and David, our incredible son

Time and tide wait for no man, but they might for a teenager

Table of Contents

WHAT'S COMING NEXT?

Dramatis Personae

Tarquin Seebohm Jenkins	Our Hero
Malcolm Seebohm Jenkins	Tarquin's Father
Charlotte Anne Jenkins	Tarquin's Mother
Aunt Mira and Uncle Harold Tench	Tarquin's Aunt & Uncle
Jeremiah Pharoah Cavendish	Steeple Snoring's Lock Keeper & Wormhole Guardian
Ingeborg Cavendish	Jeremiah's Wife
Julius Ulysees Rigsworth	Tarquin's bohemian Uncle
Professor Thomas Cramdunkle	Surgeon
Rhiannon Patricia Collins	Trainee from the Llangollen Canal
Archibald Campbell	Trainee from the Union Canal
Alice Cooper	Trainee from the Shropshire Canal
Therious/Liam, Madge	Droids
Georgia Blade	Space Pirate
Captain Gruilash Vandergaard, Lieutenant Granwold Burbart, Prince Solace Ruttfarter	Griddlebacks/Putriryosomatidarectem from Putrios
The Shanklin O'Macy Braigetori Big Band	Musical ensemble
Tricky Dicky and his Dancing Cullions, Aquos From Aquaenos	Cabaret performers
The Amazing Angelinas	Dance troupe
Tresore Munroe	Owner of the Bloated Shagganat Night Club
Izal Medicated	Tresore's colleague
Reckitt Vangelos	Leche
The Spectres of Cali	Leche horde

Kartoleons	Aliens
Castor & Pollux	The Time Guardian Twins
Great Aunt Audra Louvenia Doorley Polidori	Tarquin's Great Aunt
Smodius P Munchfumble	Zargoth lawyer
Judge Freelash E. Pompitulary Ginglebaum III	Zargoth Judge
Miss Amelia Hoploosley	Resident of Steeple Snoring
Oleg Tremagenev	Russian emigre
Sergeant Sloth	Steeple Snoring's Police Officer
Cybelle Rain	BIFS Controller
Berbitedge Sludge	Alien
Captain James T Kirk	Captain of the Coldstream Regiment of Foot Guards
Calbhach O'Reilly, D'Arcy Ogrungion, Rhiordan Findus O'Mallerty, Finbar Brennan and Flaherty (The Brothers Grimm), Ardal	Leprechauns
Screwball, Hugh Willard, Merv Mulligan, Dave Moriarty, Big Joe Damanski, Seamus DeWoods Kelly, Paddy	Clurichauns
Boris, Havel and Giorgi	The Russians
Wing Commander Doughton Dogberry Botley, DFC and Bar, Rtd.	Lock Keeper and Guardian of BIFS Northern Hub
Brocca Bogglers	Alcoholic beverage banned on most planets
Wopplefop	Cuddly, furry animal
BIFS	British Intergalactic Foreign Service
TART	Griddlebacks Tactical Armed Response Team

HISTORICAL PLAYERS

Colonel Blood	Irish mercenary
Talbot Edwards	Keeper of the Crown Jewels
Whythe Edwards	Talbot's Son
King Charles II	King of England (1630-1685)
The Duke of Buckingham, Sir Thomas Clifford, Lord Arlington, Lord Ashley, Lord Lauderdale	Advisors to King Charles II
Sir Robert Cecil	Advisor to King James I of England
Lord Monteagle	Cecil's colleague
Guido Fawkes	Tried to blow up the British Parliament in 1606
Nostradamus	Frenchman who predicted the future
Leonardo Da Vinci	Inventor & painter
Nell Gwyn	King Charles IIs love interest
Louise de Keroualle	French aristocrat
Lisa Gherardini del Giocondo	Artists muse
The Beatles	Musical group from Liverpool

MEMBERS OF THE ROYAL SOCIETY

Samuel Pepys	diarist
Christopher Wren	architect
Isaac Newton	scientist & mathematician
John Evelyn	writer, gardener & diarist

CHAPTER 1

THE BEAR NECESSITIES

The sleepy Northamptonshire village of Steeple Snoring was not known for its bears. In fact, nobody at the post office could recall ever having seen one here before, let alone thirty strolling down the High Street.

"I saw what I saw," said Mrs Harbinkle, crossing her ample chest with her arms. "On their hind legs too!" she continued, nodding sagely at the villagers clustered around her.

"They're here for a reason," added her husband, looking warily through the post office's casement window toward the bears' last known position. Standing in the queue for service and listening avidly to the conversations was a local lad, Tarquin Jenkins. A tall boy for thirteen, with a mop of curly black hair and dark brown eyes that shone as he chuckled, Tarquin knew about the bears. In fact, he was due to meet several in the Enchanted Teapot Tea Rooms shortly to celebrate the opening of the new addition to McCauly's petting farm.

"Why? What could they possibly want in Steeple Snoring?" asked the postmaster. He bleakly enumerated the village's vital statistics: a population officially given as 2,769 (although that figure was in need of revision ever since Mrs Tiptree, may she rest in peace, and her mobility scooter had inexplicably shot down Marble Hill and sailed through the bay window of the Four Feathers); two pubs; the church with its famous, crumbling, spiraling steeple; a row of dilapidated shops; the school; the scout hut; the police station; the Enchanted Teapot (unlicensed) Tea Rooms; and the canal, with its double lock and the lock-keeper's cottage. Oh, and the post office, of course.

"Don't forget the petting farm owned by Donald McCauly," added Mr Johnson. The Right Reverend John Ford had delivered several fiery sermons condemning the establishment of the petting farm from his Calvinist pulpit, many miles away in Peterborough, claiming it was Satan's attempt to gain a foothold in the village. He was sure it would bring with it an outbreak or two of divine wrath. Despite this fear, the petting farm had drawn a fair amount of business to Steeple Snoring's shopkeepers, and much-needed funds for the steeple repair.

"That's it!" exclaimed Mrs Harbinkle, jabbing a finger at her husband, "They're off to the petting farm!"

Murmurs of approval and the flexing of aged muscle wobbled slowly through the post office queue.

Tarquin had a party to go to, but he wasn't going anywhere fast. His hand reached for the small gold cricket bat on a chain around his neck. It was the last thing his father had given him before he and Tarquin's mother had died. He looked out of the window. A crow, its wings thrashing wildly in the bright sky, whirled past.

Blast you, Dad, thought Tarquin, just as he bumped into Mr Ricketts, standing in front of him.

"Sorry," mumbled Tarquin. His mood had darkened immeasurably after seeing the crow. Mr Ricketts turned and, recognizing Tarquin, smiled.

"How are you settling in, Tarquin? Can't be easy living with my old school buddies, Mira and Harold."

Tarquin took a deep breath and sighed. Mr Ricketts was right. Ever since his parents had disappeared and left him at the mercy of his aged relatives, his life had become a dead end.

"Okay, I guess. I can't complain," he lied, and reached again for the cricket bat.

"Please give them my regards when you get home. I'll be round later for bridge."

Tarquin smiled weakly. Another fun-packed night in with his aunt and uncle, he thought, nodding.

"My friend saw a wallaby once."

Heads turned toward the far corner of the post office where, propped up against the greeting card display, stood a small, thin man wearing an overly large raincoat and a tartan flat cap.

"She called it Wally," he said loudly, flapping a gloved hand at the villagers watching him. "It hopped all the way down Duston Wildes High Street." Bending at the knees, he demonstrated, albeit slowly and with some discomfort, the wallaby's hopping motion.

"Kenneth!" boomed a voice from outside. All eyes turned to the door. Bustling into the post office came a large woman in a wool coat, headscarf and bright red lipstick, heading straight for the man in the raincoat.

"What have I told you about leaving your mobility scooter unattended! You know what happened to Mrs Tiptree!"

Kenneth had no time to reply. With the skill and efficiency of a dustman lifting a bin, his wife had her arms under his and was carrying him across the floor, his feet trailing. Before you could bat an eyelid they were out the door.

Tarquin felt compelled to break the ensuing silence.

"They're obviously not real bears. They're people dressed as bears. And I believe they're having a picnic in the tea rooms." He was met by the withering glare of the post office pensioners. Unperturbed, he continued. "Probably got lost coming in off the A43," he said. A sardonic smile spread across his pale face. "Take the wrong turn by Bishop's Gate and you'll be on the High Street in no time."

"Perhaps there's a circus in town?" queried the postmaster, ignoring Tarquin's contribution.

"Circus!" shrieked a rotund woman in a maroon tweed suit. It was Miss Hoploosley, spinster of the parish, doyen of the lace-curtain brigade and a pensioner. She had been standing on the periphery of the conversation and was not amused.

"I'll go to the police," she said, waving her Golden Jubilee umbrella high in the air. "We don't have circuses here!" Turning smartly on her heels, she thrust her letters back into her purse, pushed past customers, and strode purposefully from the post office on her way to the police station. All thought of posting her letters had clearly been scoured from her mind.

With her departure, the post office returned to normality, and soon Tarquin reached the counter. He quickly paid for his aunt's stamps and envelopes, and left for the tea rooms.

On his way, he took from his pocket the gold envelope that had been pushed through his letterbox that morning. Taking out the invitation card for the hundredth time, he read aloud:

Rupert Bear and Teddy Roosevelt

cordially invite you to celebrate the recent

extension to Donald McCauly's Petting Farm

Invitation Only

Teddy Bears' Picnic

The Enchanted Teapot Tea Rooms

Steeple Snoring

12:30 PM

Sponsored by the Ideal Toy Company

Nearing the Enchanted Teapot, Tarquin heard the thumping, regular bass of rock music, accompanied by singing and laughter. Two large bears stood in the tea rooms' doorway brandishing bright red plastic machine guns with large silver fins. The one with brown fluffy ears and what appeared to be the Olympic rings strapped to its chest stepped out from the doorway and waved its toy gun at Tarquin.

"You have serious business here today?" said the bear in a thick Russian accent.

"I am invited, see," replied Tarquin, nervously thrusting his invitation into the bear's outstretched paw.

"Excellent!" boomed the bear, stepping aside and pushing open the door. Sickly sweet air that spoke of warm jellies, trifles, custard and cake grabbed Tarquin around the throat as he entered.

"Invitation," demanded another huge black bear, just inside the door. Like the two bears outside, it cradled a plastic gun.

Tarquin thrust his card forward. The bear, naked but for a pair of denim trousers and a Canadian Mountie hat, looked at the invitation closely, eyed him up and down, and then waved him through.

With so many bears inside, Tarquin could go only a few feet before he stopped again. Standing by a table next to the door, he gawped at the scene before him.

Every imaginable type of bear was standing, dancing, sitting, drinking tea, eating and slurping milkshakes through fluorescent bendy straws. There were fast-food-chain bears, children's television bears, comic bears, bear mascots and even beer-commercial bears, which must have rankled the owners of the unlicensed Enchanted Teapot. Tarquin had never seen the place so full. The rock music he had heard halfway up the street came from four bears in evening dress. A drummer, a guitarist, a bass player and a saxophonist set up near the fireplace were rocking the room. Above their heads, hung from the ceiling, was a banner:

CELEBRATING DONALD'S NEW EXTENSION!

As Tarquin watched the undulating, bopping, popping and jiving smörgåsbord of bears, he spotted, sitting at a table on the far side near the toilets, the only person in the room aside from Tarquin not to be in a bear costume. He was a large man, with a one-piece Groucho Marx disguise: thick, black-rimmed glasses, shaggy eyebrows, a false nose and a large, silver walrus moustache above a three-piece suit and a pencil-thin tie. Perched on his head was a deerstalker hat. Tarquin thought his attire more suited to a steampunk convention than a picnic. He was deep in conversation with Rupert Bear. Relieved to see another human, Tarquin waved to attract the man's attention, as any attempted shout would have been drowned out by the music. After a few seconds, the man looked up and signalled him over.

Slowly, Tarquin worked his way through the gyrating mass of fur, paw and claw.

Rupert Bear and the man rose politely from their chairs, and a choking waft of aromatic aftershave filled Tarquin's lungs.

"Tarquin! Glad you could make it," said Rupert, offering a paw.

Coughing, Tarquin smiled and shook it.

Turning to the man, Rupert introduced him. "This is Teddy, Teddy Roosevelt."

"Bully!" shouted Teddy, pulling off his hat and the disguise to reveal a round, ruddy face. He winked and grinned, showing quite a few gold teeth, before grabbing Tarquin's hand and shaking it vigorously.

"You remind me of Mr Cavendish, Steeple Snoring's lock-keeper," said Tarquin, flexing his hand to get blood circulating after the crushing shake.

Roosevelt laughed. "I be United President of the States. I not be old Jeremiah!"

Rupert nodded and added a two-handed thumbs-up.

"Of course," said Tarquin, hesitantly.

"Take a seat," invited Rupert.

Tarquin pulled out a chair and sat down.

"Tea?" continued Rupert, taking a cup and saucer from the tray in front of him. "Milk and sugar?"

"Just milk, thanks."

"It's a fun party, isn't it?"

"Yes. But why are you having a party for a new shed at McCauly's?" said Tarquin, taking a sip of his tea. "And why invite me? I've never gone to the petting farm and probably never will."

Rupert didn't answer.

Teddy picked up a tin of biscuits and offered it to Tarquin. "Custard cream?"

Tarquin took two and was about to ask the question again when Teddy jumped in.

"Speak softly and carry a big stick and you will go far," he said, in a peculiar variant of a Northamptonshire accent.

"That's enough, Teddy," said Rupert, cocking his head sideways and looking at Tarquin. "Why, indeed?" he continued, just as a line of dancing bears snaked around their table.

"Half the village is up in arms about all these bears," said Tarquin. "No one seems to have known the party was scheduled." He looked around the room, "And where's Mr McCauly?"

"Good question," replied Rupert, pointing a paw at Tarquin. "The answer would no doubt surprise and amaze you."

"Surprise and amaze me, then."

"No," came the reply from Rupert.

"No?" Tarquin repeated, startled.

"No," said Rupert firmly, shaking his head.

"Okay," said Tarquin, his voice trembling, "I'm going to leave. I have things to do and my aunt will be wondering where her stamps have got to."

He started to rise, but a large bear paw on his shoulder encouraged him to stay in his seat.

"What's going on?" Tarquin looked anxiously up at the black bear looming over him.

"Tarquin Seebohm Jenkins," said Rupert, "we are related."

"Really!" mouthed Tarquin in mock astonishment.

Slowly Rupert removed his costume head to reveal a grinning, red-faced, middle-aged man with a silver goatee.

"Uncle Jules!" cried Tarquin, slumping lower in his chair.

"Seebee!"

Every family has a charismatic uncle and Tarquin's was no exception. Inventor, world traveller, tea-taster, apothecary, balloon-racer and all-round know-it-all, this was his Uncle Jules—or Jules Rigsworth, as the rest of the world knew him. He was back in Steeple Snoring and causing mayhem.

Again.

"You were right, this is Jeremiah Cavendish," said Jules, gesturing toward the hulk of a man next to him.

"I knew it!" exclaimed Tarquin as Jeremiah smiled and nodded.

Uncle Jules went on, "Jeremiah is an old friend. As you know, he and his wife run the double lock on the canal. He's also my business partner."

"Okay, Uncle, answer the question: why put on a party and invite me? It's lovely, but why?"

"Well, you're getting older and, as we happened to be here for the celebration, I wanted to know if you'd be interested in learning about our tour-guiding business," came Jules's reply.

"Wearing silly costumes and pretending to be famous people to guide tourists around Steeple Snoring? Why on earth would I want to do that?" asked Tarquin, looking incredulous.

"Yer uncle and me thought you lacked adventure," said Jeremiah.

"It would be a great experience," added Jules.

Tarquin took a deep breath, raised himself up in the chair and put his hands on the table.

"Uncle, ever since Mum and Dad … disappeared, you've tried to involve me in your crazy schemes. Do you really think dressing up as presidents, prime ministers or … or bears and going on picnics is adventurous?"

"I am your godfather, and I promised your parents I'd look after you." Jules seemed hurt by Tarquin's reaction.

"I know," said Tarquin, "and I love your madness, but I live in the real world with Aunt Mira and Uncle Harold, in a small cul-de-sac, in a small house, with a small garden, in a very small, boring town."

"Haven't you ever wondered what really happened at the signing of the Magna Carta?" asked Jules.

"Or the Declaration of Independence?" said Jeremiah.

Tarquin shook his head. "Don't change the subject!"

"You love history, don't you?" said Jules.

"If I was that interested, I'd read it in a book."

"Yes, but wouldn't you rather see it first-hand?" said his uncle.

"What?" Tarquin laughed. "Go there and see it happening—for real?"

"Yes," said Jules.

Jeremiah nodded.

"So, let me get this right." Tarquin warmed to his joke. "I'd catch the next number 101 bus to Runnymede arriving in 1215 and chew the fat with King John and his barons?"

He laughed again, but then saw that the two men's humorous demeanours had been replaced by grim, po-faced expressions—the clowns had become accountants, as it were.

"Okay, sorry, that was silly." He looked at his uncle and felt uneasy. "What hare-brained scheme are you working on now? I don't see you for years, and then out of the blue you anonymously invite me to a teddy bears' picnic to celebrate the opening of a shed, and when I get here you spout gibberish. How do you expect me to behave?"

Jules pulled his chair closer to the table and leaned forward, looking right into Tarquin's eyes. "What if you really could go to Rome in 63 CE and see a live chariot race?"

"Or," added Jeremiah, "watch the Spanish Armada arrive off the English coast?"

An icy chill ran down Tarquin's spine. "You're both serious about this, aren't you?"

"Deadly," said the two men together, nodding.

Tarquin searched their faces, waiting for their smiles, the joke, the punchline. Nothing came.

"But," said Jules, pushing back into his chair, and taking a sip of tea, "you'll need some basic training. We can't just send you off into the past without proper training."

"That be dangerous, no proper training," agreed Jeremiah, tapping the table.

The boy looked from Jules to Jeremiah and back to Jules. His day had started surreally in the post office, discussing bears, and now he was debating time travel.

"So," he said, not having the strength to argue, "where would this training be done?"

"On the Silvery Moon," Jules and Jeremiah said in unison.

"The Silvery Moon," repeated Tarquin, raising an eyebrow. "That old canal boat by the locks? Is it like, like a time ship—is it blue, and bigger on the inside than the outside?"

He was finding it difficult to take anything the two men said seriously.

"No, it's not blue," replied Jules crossly.

Jeremiah winced. "Well, actually, it is blue."

"That's not the point!" shouted Jules, staring harshly at his friend before turning back to Tarquin. "There's a wormhole junction by the double lock on the canal. Jeremiah guards it. There are several wormhole guardians in the UK, and Jeremiah is the guardian of the wormhole in your village. He's going to be your teacher." Jules tapped Jeremiah in a fatherly fashion on the arm. "He was a good friend of your mum and dad."

"Wormholes?" said Tarquin.

"Yes. That's how we travel through time," replied Jules.

"And how do you do that? Use trains, planes and automobiles? Or do we grow wings and fly?" Tarquin, struggling to make sense of all this, turned again to humour as a way of coping.

"This is not a game, lad." Jeremiah looked sternly at him.

"Okay, you're right. I'll behave," said Tarquin after a long moment.

"You'll need to do an apprenticeship under Jeremiah's tuition, then we can talk about you going to the year 2340 and joining my Tour Guide School," explained Jules.

"Of course, living in the future makes perfect sense." Tarquin failed to suppress a giggle.

"You really don't seem to be taking this seriously," said Jules, shaking his head, "Perhaps I can persuade you to start doing so."

Tarquin sat back in the chair, crossed his arms and waited for enlightenment.

"Your mum and dad did a lot of travelling, as you'll recall," continued Jules.

"Yes, they did."

"And they brought you presents from their travels?"

"Yes," agreed Tarquin, starting to sober up now that his parents were involved.

"Ever wonder where those presents came from?" queried Jules.

Tarquin shook his head, "They visited antique dealers and had a love of old things and history, like I do. They knew a bargain when they saw one, I suppose."

Jules looked at Jeremiah. They smiled and slowly shook their heads in that annoying way people do when they know something you don't.

"What?" said Tarquin. "Is there a joke you're not sharing with me?"

"No joke," said Jules. "Your parents travelled through space and time and, while gathering intelligence on our planet's enemies, they also collected things."

"They were interplanetary spies," added Jeremiah.

"Our planet's enemies? We're not alone, then? Interplanetary spies, like interplanetary James Bonds?"

Jules looked at Jeremiah and they both grimaced, before Jules turned back to Tarquin.

"Well, sort of."

CHAPTER 2

THE MEETING

Bolts on the large metal door slid back and it slowly opened. Two dull metal spheres the size of soccer balls bounced over the threshold and rolled into the brightly lit room, only stopping when they thudded against the legs of the conference table in the middle of the sparsely furnished room. All but one of those seated got up to get a better view.

A noise like a passing express train filled the air, accompanied by muffled shrieks from inside the spheres. The braver of those standing around the conference table stood firm; their more timid colleagues took a step back. With a searing flash of white light and a cloud of thick smoke, legs, arms and two shrouded heads erupted from the spheres. As the smoke cleared, two thin, eight-foot-tall shapes, hooded and shrouded in black-and-gold cloaks, hunched like vultures over the foot of the table. From the blackness inside the hoods came the sound of wet, throaty wheezing.

The man who had remained seated at the far end of the table finally looked up and slowly shook his head in frustration.

"Each time we meet, you two create an entrance that scares the bejeebers out of everyone. Okay, boys, show's over."

With a swish and a gentle rustle, the cloaks dropped to the floor, leaving two piles of twitching cloth. From within the material folds emerged a pair of pale blue skeletal humanoids, each about half a metre tall.

"Pollux and Castor!" introduced the chairman, sitting forward in his chair to bring the entertainment to a close. "The Time Guardian Twins."

"Can't resist a grand entrance," said Castor in a lisping drone as he and Pollux sprang gazelle-like onto the table. Dressed immaculately in brightly coloured seventeenth-century silks, replete with powdered wigs, pink hose, platform shoes and walking canes, the two epicene fops bowed and began preening each other.

Satisfied with his appearance, Castor sidled forward and brandished a hand full of scarlet-painted fingernails. "We haven't got long. The French Revolution is about to kick off, and we need to get back."

Opening a powder-puff compact, he checked a ridiculously prominent, red beauty spot on his cheek and strutted down the table. He stopped with one hand on his hip, the other turning the cane in small circles on the table, affecting boredom.

"Thank you all for coming," said the chairman, getting up from his seat at the head of the table. "As you all know, we are only a few months away from the fire at the tea rooms. We are down to the last journey Malcolm Jenkins made before his disappearance—his 1666 visit with Jeremiah Cavendish to the London diarist Samuel Pepys. If the Book of Dreams is there, or a clue to finding it, we have a plan."

He waved his hand at a man with a goatee who sat on the right side of the table. "Jules, please take everybody through it."

Jules Rigsworth nodded, got to his feet and cleared his throat. "Without explaining our true purpose, Jeremiah Cavendish will take Malcolm's son Tarquin back to 1666 and visit Pep—"

Before Jules could go any further, a grey-haired woman rose.

"This is ridiculous!" she said, glaring at the chairman. "Why all this cloak-and-dagger malarkey? Why not send one of your agents to 1666 and interrogate Pepys?"

"You know why, Polly. Malcolm was clever. He left a clue that only his son would understand. Tarquin has no idea about clues to a book, or a magical time-bending amulet. We've asked him—without him realizing of course. We suspect the clue Malcolm left will be activated only by another clue. The book is just the beginning of the puzzle he left behind. Besides, we don't interrogate historical figures. Imagine what Pepys might write in his diary!"

Murmurs of approval spread around the room.

"How can you be sure Cavendish won't mess this one up?" continued Polly, still standing, still scowling. "He's a buffoon. As I've said all along, he's not the right choice to mentor Jenkins junior." Her face turned even sourer as she screeched, "He's … he's incompetent!" She rapped her swagger stick on the table. "The moron's already missed half a dozen items that the boy's stolen while travelling!"

Her voice cracked and eventually broke. Quivering with rage, the blood-engorged veins on her temples pulsing like a wriggling cluster of tightly knotted bloodworms, she glared at the faces around the table. Then she thrust her stick in the direction of Jules and, in an attempt to resuscitate her vocal cords, hacked loudly before shouting, "How on God's earth"—yes, her voice was back to its vociferous best—"did he miss that ruddy belaying pin!"

Heads nodded, and again murmurs of agreement spread around the seated suits.

The chairman stood up and raised his hands in an appeal for calm. The murmurs around the table quietened.

"To answer your first point, Polly, Jeremiah may not be blessed with a sharp mind, but he's devoted to his job as a guardian and to mentoring Malcolm's son. He has no idea or interest in a book or an amulet. This is his strength. He can't give away what he doesn't know." The chairman paused, looking at the woman. "And it's true," he continued with an ingratiating smile, "we all failed to notice Pirate Hornigold's belaying pin—"

"Yes, you did!" yelled Polly, waving her swagger stick high in the air like a battle flag. "It could so easily have been one of Malcolm's combination puzzles, and therefore a clue to the whereabouts of the infernal amulet!"

The chairman was not fazed by the hysterical display. He had seen it all before. "But it wasn't, was it, Polly? It wasn't a clue."

For several minutes they stared at each other; only the gentle ticking of the room's wall clock and Polly's rasping breath broke the silence. After what seemed an age, she growled and sat down, her quivering bony hand having crushed the life out of the poor ivory duck on top of her swagger stick.

"Besides," continued Jules, "Cavendish has no idea why he's going back to visit Pepys. He's just been told to pay him a visit as part of Tarquin's time-travel education."

The chairman turned to Pollux and Castor. "You've got this, haven't you?"

"Like hawks," said Pollux with a curl of a six-fingered hand and an extravagant flourish of his handkerchief. "We've checked everything he's brought back."

"Just be careful," reminded the chairman. "No more 'stand and deliver' nonsense."

Castor inhaled deeply. "Needs must, but, I tell you, that boy may not have found the Book of Dreams yet, or any clues to its location, but he's a right time-travelling thief! If he wasn't so tall I'd swear he was a clurichaun!"

The feeling of tension in the room eased with Castor's joke, and several attendees smiled.

The chairman once again raised his hand for silence. "And what of our scaly friends? Have they shown any interest?"

Pollux shook his head. "Not yet, but it won't take them long to figure out we're looking for the book and the amulet."

"So far they've been preoccupied planning something big in the 1960s, but we've got them covered," added Castor, thrusting his nose dismissively into the air.

The chairman continued, "And our French friend with the stolen sedan chair? Harmless?"

Pollux glanced warily at Castor and stepped forward. "Harmless. A mere hiccup. He will soon be back in France, and none the wiser for his adventures."

"Let's hope so," said the chairman. "For everyone's sake, let's hope so."

THE NARROWBOAT

Tarquin Jenkins was running as fast as his legs could carry him—faster, if anything. He grinned, pained at the irony that he could travel five hundred years in a second but fail to be on time for an appointment a kilometre from his house. Miss this time-jump and he might have to wait a further month before travelling again.

He looked nervously at his pocket watch and tried to spur himself to even greater speed.

Friday the thirteenth. It's almost four and I am ruddy late! Why today of all days?

For two years, ever since his first time-travelling adventure with Jeremiah, Tarquin felt he had been in control of time, but today he was chasing it. He reached the Navigation Inn and scurried down the winding path toward the lock-keeper's cottage before tripping over his ill-fitting boots. He pitched forward, steadied himself, took off his baseball cap and shook his mop of curly black hair free before ploughing on.

I feel like I'm the White Rabbit! If Lewis Carroll could see me now! Talk about life imitating art!

His lungs bursting from the exertion, Tarquin careered past the side of the cottage towards the narrowboat that was moored by the lock gates.

"Blast your ruddy photos, Eddy Manet!" he gasped aloud. The curse sent a moorhen skedaddling across the canal, its feet trailing in the water like orange flames from a rocket.

Tarquin's love of history had made him late. He could not leave college without correcting Mr Reynolds, his art teacher, on Manet's use of photographs. It wasn't unusual for Tarquin to correct teachers on some historical issue or other. Some teachers found it very irksome, others a revelation, but all agreed that Tarquin spoke of historical figures as if he knew them personally.

"No need ta run, Seebee. We've plenty of time," boomed a voice from the cottage garden.

Surprised by the voice, Tarquin tripped again and landed in a heap, groaning, just as Jeremiah's familiar hulk rose from behind a small elm hedge, his huge frame blocking out the afternoon sun.

"Jeremiah! I didn't see you there!"

A hand the size of a gorilla's reached over the hedge and grabbed his collar. Tarquin was tall for a fifteen-year-old, but Jeremiah hoisted him effortlessly off the ground and over the hedge, setting him on his feet.

"I'm not late, then?" asked Tarquin, gasping and rubbing his neck. "I wish you wouldn't do that."

"Everything's tickety boo, Seebee. Time were pressin', so as luck would have it I found us another wormhole that will get yer back here shortly after you leave, so I moved your jump back an hour, to five." Jeremiah dusted Tarquin down and gave him back his cap. "I were just picking rhubarb for the missus and feeding me worms when I heard yer cursing." Jeremiah rose to his full height of well over two metres and looked around his garden, pleased as Punch. "It be a fine day for gardening and a-time-travelling!" He ruffled Tarquin's curly hair.

Steeple Snoring's longest-serving lock-keeper might be huge, but he wasn't scary huge. He'd been a professional wrestler in his younger days, the kind that old ladies loved to see win on a Saturday afternoon on cable television. He'd made quite a name for himself, if you believed his stories. Sadly, after an accident in 1985 he had retired from the wrestling game, and with his Swedish wife, "Ingeborg the Invincible", whom he had met in the ring, he took on the job as Steeple Snoring's lock-keeper. It wasn't as glamorous as showbiz wrestling but it allowed him to enjoy his days restoring his beloved narrowboat, the Silvery Moon, raising tiger worms, and time-travelling.

Tarquin wiped his brow and ferreted about in his frock-coat pockets before pulling out two crescent-shaped objects. He grinned as he thrust the blocks under Jeremiah's leathery nose.

"I got 'em!" The boy's coal-like eyes sparkled in the afternoon sun. "I ruddy well got 'em!"

Jeremiah's walrus moustache bristled with excitement as he eyed the objects in Tarquin's outstretched hand. Putting on a pair of chunky reading glasses, he peered through their jam-jar lenses at the ivory objects.

"Oh my suffering slugs!" exclaimed Jeremiah. "You got old Washington's false teeth! No time to waste. Let's get to the Silvery Moon."

He grabbed a dozen sticks of rhubarb and strode towards the narrowboat. Tarquin followed, taking two strides for each of Jeremiah's.

Laughing, Jeremiah looked at him. "You okay, Seebee? You're sweating a lot."

"Fine. It's just that rushing here made me hot."

Under his cream frock coat, Tarquin wore a cable-knit sweater, scuffed leather trousers and, wound around his neck, a bright red scarf that matched the current colour of his face. On his head sat a New York Yankees baseball cap, worn backwards. A "real babe" had given it to him—or so he claimed.

These were not clothes meant to be rushed about in.

The two friends reached the boat and Jeremiah put one foot onboard, offering a helping hand to Tarquin. "Take care, Seebee. I've just polished the old girl."

Tarquin took off his cap and stared lovingly at the restored blue-and-gold narrowboat. He kissed his small gold cricket bat, took Jeremiah's hand, and stepped aboard.

"You make me laugh with your funny little ways," said Jeremiah, chuckling as he opened the topside door. "I'll be with you in a tick," he added with a wink. "Got to give Her Majesty the rhubarb."

Jeremiah hurried from the boat down the winding path towards his cottage, the stems of rhubarb held high and their leaves splayed out like a vast bouquet of flowers. Tarquin smiled. Jeremiah wore his love for his darling Ingeborg proudly on his sleeve.

Descending the boat's steps to the cabin below, Tarquin smelled the familiar odours of beeswax, engine oil, horse liniment and Hai Karate aftershave. They hugged him like an old friend. Looking around, he was yet again startled by the size of the boat's interior; it was so much bigger than it should have been. Jeremiah described it as the "appliance of science". All Tarquin knew was that, even though on the outside the Silvery Moon was an ordinary canal boat, on the inside it was the size of a basketball court.

Little had changed since his last visit in October. With its eclectic mix of beam tetrodes, pentodes, transformers, reflex klystrons, glass balls and two rows of gleaming brass levers on the port side, the room was a strange mix of the innards of a 1950s television set, a diesel submarine and a pawnbroker's shop. On the starboard side, several new items had been added to Jeremiah's collection of Elvis memorabilia: a certified hair lock, a piece of a towel, several original RCA records, album covers, a guitar that Jeremiah claimed Elvis played in the film Viva Las Vegas, and a bobblehead. Alongside the Elvis shrine hung framed pictures of Jeremiah in his wrestling heyday as The Singing Silo from Somerset, a.k.a. The Hay Maker. The pictures showed him dressed in a baggy yellow costume of shirt and dungarees, topped off with a red Batman-style hood, and grappling with past paragons of the wrestling world. In pride of place in the centre was Tarquin's favourite picture of Ingeborg and Jeremiah, dressed in their wrestling finery at their Las Vegas wedding. Tarquin was both delighted and surprised to see the picture finally on display. It had taken a lot of persuading.

Tarquin walked to the centre of the cabin and sat down in Jeremiah's battered leather swivel chair. Swinging the chair around, he looked out of the port-side porthole towards the lock-keeper's quaint cottage and shook his head. Despite two years of time travelling, Tarquin still found it hard to comprehend that Jeremiah's picture-postcard cottage and narrowboat were linked to a network of wormholes that cut through past, present and future. His gaze drifted to below the porthole, where a gaudy gilt frame held a faded pseudo-parchment document:

This Commission confirms that Jeremiah Pharaoh Cavendish
is a Member of the Ancient & Venerable Corps of
Lock and Folly Keepers.

It was Jeremiah's time-guarding commission, displayed proudly above his writing desk. The big man had once let slip that a visiting British Waterways official saw him framing it topside and queried its genuineness. The nosey official was duly "helped off" the boat, starboard side.

Tarquin swung the chair back and lifted his feet off the ground. As the chair spun around, a photograph, disturbed by the movement, floated from Jeremiah's desk. Tarquin stopped the chair and picked it up.

It was a surreal picture of Jeremiah and a bear at a table, drinking vanilla milkshakes through straws. Jeremiah was wearing a Groucho Marx disguise.

Tarquin chuckled.

"The day it all started. Would you believe it?" he said out loud.

"Believe what, Seebee?" said Jeremiah, coming down the steps carrying what looked like two packed lunches. Tarquin was pleased to see that food was on the agenda.

"Time travel," he replied. "Who'd have believed a meeting with you and Jules in the tea rooms on my thirteenth birthday would lead to me jumping through time and space and living through history!"

Jeremiah put the packed lunches on the side. "Don't recall it," he lied.

"Hah!" said Tarquin. "Yes, you do. You're playing with me." He tapped the picture. "You and Uncle Jules were drinking milkshakes through bendy straws and wearing silly costumes. See, that's you. Pictures do not lie!"

"Oh, that birthday." Jeremiah grinned and picked up a book from the side-board. He waved it at Tarquin. "Now, you done your reading?"

Tarquin pulled at a lock of his hair, his habit when caught not having done what he'd been told to. He wasn't good at hiding a lie from his friends.

Jeremiah gazed solemnly at his young friend. "We promised your parents we'd start your guide training when you reached your thirteenth birthday, and that's what we did, but—"

"I know, I know. It's no good if I don't do my homework." Tarquin's voice oozed unenthusiasm.

"We explained it to you, remember? Being a time-guide's apprentice is not easy."

Tarquin certainly did remember. He had learned a lot in the two years since meeting Uncle Jules and Jeremiah at the bears' picnic party in the Enchanted Tea-pot. Time travel was not something you could do without preparation. You had to know what you were headed for, and what to expect.

"Okay, we have some time before the jump, so let's 'ave a cuppa and a lesson." Jeremiah walked to the open-plan galley at the end of the cabin. Ducking his bald head under a crystal chandelier, he squeezed into a faded leather armchair. "Chinese green, or that lapdog sushie-doobrie stuff you like?"

He opened a drawer and took out a small canvas bag and a box of lapsang souchong tea. "I kept the bag from your second trip, remember?"

Tarquin grinned.

"Wen Cheng," he sighed. He unwound the scarf from around his neck. "My Tibetan princess!"

Jeremiah laughed. "That lassie smittened you," he said, getting up to fetch cups and plates. "I sees it plain as day."

Tarquin leaned back, closed his eyes and thought of his Tibetan adventure. Had it not been for Wen's intervention he would still be there—alive, or more likely dead.

"Chinese, please," said Tarquin, coming out of his brief daydream.

"With your usual?" inquired Jeremiah.

"Mmmm, absolutely," replied Tarquin.

"If you'd done your reading properly, you'd have known to look for an earlier wormhole in China."

"That's unfair," said Tarquin, "It was only my second trip without you, and they moved my chair."

"It was nearly your last trip!" chided the lock-keeper.

Tarquin knew Jeremiah was right. If he had done his homework, his returning from 641 CE would not have been by the skin of his teeth and reliant on Wen's help.

"Will I get a chance to go to the year 2340 and enroll at Uncle Jules' guide school soon?" asked Tarquin.

"When we think you're ready."

"I've been jumping for two years. It's time for me to leave here and go to guide school."

"When you are ready," repeated Jeremiah.

Tarquin huffed. He wanted to see the future, now. But there was no point in arguing.

After a while, Turandot's aria "Nessun Dorma" rang through the boat. Jeremiah was happy, so he was singing. In the world of wrestling, The Hay Maker singing an aria was the precursor to a forearm smash, a full nelson double chicken wing, and a submission. Jeremiah's warbling voice had brought a chill to many a wrestler's spine. On the other hand, his classy rendition of Figaro had been kept solely for fighting his two major nemeses, Giant Haystacks and Big Daddy, during their head-to-head battles on Independent Television's World of Sport.

Soon the smell of toasted peanut-butter-and-jam sandwiches wafted in from the galley and distracted Tarquin from his thoughts.

"Tea's ready," called Jeremiah.

Tarquin left the chair and headed to the galley table to join his host. Two steaming mugs of tea and a plate of toasties sat on the table between them.

"Thanks." Tarquin took a drink of tea and looked across at Jeremiah. "Why couldn't I see you as soon as I got back with the teeth?"

Jeremiah looked surprised and shuffled uneasily on his seat.

"You remember, I told you. Inga and me were booked on a month's world cruise. We left that afternoon." He smiled weakly. "Anyways, Seebee, you're here now, ready and raring."

Tarquin knew when Jeremiah was hiding something because his words got muddled up and his accent took on a peculiar mix of Somerset, Swedish and North-amptonshire.

"And I still don't understand why I always arrive back in a different part of Cretins' Copse or Ricketty Field each time," said Tarquin. "I always land in mud or cow muck!"

Jeremiah took a deep breath and, like an evangelist, pointed with both arms at the roof of the boat.

"It's the appliance of science!" This was Jeremiah's response to anything he was hiding, didn't understand or couldn't explain.

"'Science'?" retorted Tarquin.

"Absolutely, Seebee. You clearly haven't done your reading homework. Wormholes don't end back where they start, oh, be nobodies, no! Remember those Apollo looney landings in the sixties?"

Tarquin grinned. "You mean lunar landings?"

"Same thing. They left from land and splashed back in the sea. They couldn't land the same place they took off." Jeremiah shook his head. "Too difficult." Then he beamed at Tarquin. "Same principle with wormholes, see?"

"Hang on," said Tarquin. "I've done some reading, you know. Wormholes are areas outside space and time that link the present with the past or the future. I don't remember there being any reason why a wormhole can't come back to where it began."

"You've been reading that Stephen Hawkwind, haven't you?" Jeremiah cocked his head.

Tarquin chuckled. "It's Hawking. Stephen Hawking."

"A one-hit wonder, whatever his name is."

"Okay, then, Professor Cavendish, how are wormholes possible?"

Jeremiah didn't reply, just rubbed his pate and stared into the distance.

Tarquin smiled. He would save his enquiries about wormholes for Uncle Jules when he eventually got to 2340.

"Did you get my dentist chair back? I pushed the red button," Tarquin asked, changing the subject.

Jeremiah jumped, woken from his contemplation. "Yep." He reached for his tea and took a big gulp. "I found it in the hedgerow next to the lane end of the copse. Now, if Master Tarquin Seebohm Jenkins has finished with his twenty questions, let's be having another look at them treasures of yours."

Tarquin took the dentures from his pocket once more and placed them on the table.

Jeremiah picked up the two crescent-shaped rows of false teeth, for upper and lower jaw, and rolled them around, before putting one on top of the other and centring them. "You did well, Seebee. Can't deny it. It was a job well done." The big man's thick brows meshed into one silver brush. "What else did you take?"

Tarquin looked stunned.

"Come on, let's see," said Jeremiah. "I knows you pilfer things when you go jumping, too tempting not to." He wagged a finger. "Doesn't help our plans for you to be a tour guide, you keep nicking stuff."

Tarquin gulped. "There was, ah, a pocket watch, but I left it at home today."

Jeremiah shook his head in mock despair. "You be very careful, Seebee. One day you'll take something special and cause us all a problem."

The boy nodded sheepishly.

"Now," said Jeremiah, looking at the teeth, "how'd you get them, eh?"

Tarquin warmed to his tale. "Well, I arrived in New York as planned. On my last day, I got into the house through the back door—"

"Getting in were that simple?" Jeremiah sounded surprised.

Tarquin spread his hands. "Mr Washington and his wife were asleep, so I looked around and found the teeth on the bedside cabinet."

"That's magic, Seebee!" Jeremiah cackled and sat back in his chair, clearly imagining the scene.

"Yep! It were that simple."

With a glint in his steely blue eyes, Jeremiah picked up the teeth and jammed them into his wide mouth, balancing them precariously on top of his own teeth.

"Howdy, all. I'm the Presi …" he started to say, before the two crescents of hippo ivory tensed like springs, slipped, and flew from his mouth across the room.

"Jeepers creepers, what did George have for dinner that night?" said Jeremiah, pursing his lips as if he'd bitten into a sharp lemon.

Tarquin scrambled after the teeth, trying not to laugh. "Why did you want George Washington's false teeth, anyway?"

"It was another test for you, Seebee. But enough of that." Jeremiah took the teeth and put them on a shelf above his head. "Name a famous time-traveller?" he quizzed.

Tarquin looked to the ceiling as if struggling to recall a name. "Isabella Mary Beeton," he said smugly.

"Okay, clever clogs, tell me all about her theories." Jeremiah knew that Tarquin knew the answer, but he enjoyed testing his young charge.

Tarquin explained that Isabella Beeton—or Mrs Beeton, as she became universally known—was the matriarch of time-travellers, not just a simple Victorian housewife with a unique lifestyle plan. She understood that wormholes spreading through time and space are, by their very nature, constant and, in certain circumstances, form a repeating pattern. After logging their appearance, she made a jump calendar that followed a ten-year cycle and cleverly disguised the information and other time-travelling nuggets amidst her needlework tips, recipes and housekeeping recommendations. Her books, though written in the nineteenth century, soon became the definitive time-travelling companions. "And," Tarquin concluded, "they're still used by time-travellers today."

"Very good, Seebee. Anything else?"

"Her household-management books hold your three favourite meals: broiled pheasant, jugged rabbit and potted chicken."

"How do you know that?"

"Inga told me. Just after the incident at Donald McCauly's petting farm last year."

"It were a simple misunderstanding, nothing to it," mumbled Jeremiah.

"Misunderstanding? She took your gun away and made you promise never to go there again!"

"Well, it were dark and I didn't see the petting sign. Not my fault the rabbits were loose."

Tarquin saw his friend's discomfort and patted his arm. "It's okay. It was a misunderstanding, just like you say."

There was a brief silence, then Jeremiah shrugged, dismissing the subject. "Where you want to be going today?"

Tarquin took a small leather-bound book from his frock-coat pocket, a book that Jeremiah had given him when they returned from their first time journey together. It was his father's Jump Planner, and it contained, in chronological order, a list of wormholes and their opening and closing times. Against each wormhole was a set of historical dates and places and a short narrative.

Tarquin had marked two pages. He turned to the first of them.

"I narrowed it to two choices. One, we spend a night at Le Rat Mort in Paris. Miss Wholepepper, our sociology teacher, said it was a melting pot of bohemian life and—"

"Heavens to Betsies!" cried Jeremiah. "You don't listen to that Miss Whoever-majig! That's no place for the likes of us!"

"Okay," said Tarquin, bemused. "Or, second"—he turned to the other book-marked page—"write a thesis on Napoleon and Wellington—"

Jeremiah sucked in air through his teeth, shook his head and growled.

"Not so sure, Seebee. Remember what happened the last time you met old Boney?" He pointed at Tarquin's cream frock coat, "You might not be so lucky this time."

Jeremiah did have a point. "Acquiring" Napoleon's coat at Waterloo had been a spur-of-the-moment impulse, and a dangerous one at that. Tarquin would not wish to be stuck in nineteenth-century Belgium if things went wrong.

"I knows you normally get to choose where you go, but I was wondering …" Jeremiah paused. "Well, this new wormhole I happen to have found goes somewhere you haven't been before. What I mean is, I was wondering whether you would be wanting to go on an adventure with me today?"

Tarquin sat up in his chair. After a few early jumps, Jeremiah hadn't accompanied him for over a year.

"Yes, of course!" he said, pocketing the Jump Planner.

"Okay," said Jeremiah, springing from his chair and clattering his head into the chandelier. "Jumping Johonses, if I don't sort that out, it will be the death of me," he groaned, swatting at the elaborate device for the thousandth time. "We need to pick our clothes. Follow me."

"Where are we going?" asked Tarquin, quickly finishing his tea and grabbing the last toastie.

"A wormhole," announced Jeremiah in his best BBC English pronunciation, "is opening up in a London bakery, Saturday evening, September 1, 1666 …"

Tarquin observed religiously the principles outlined in Rigsworth's Recommended Time-Travellers' Diet: An Aid To Flatulence & Indigestion (revised edition) before each journey. It was important to read the revised edition. The first edition had been a disaster, so full of mistakes that jumpers risked returning covered in boils or coming out in a painful rash.

For twenty-four hours before each jump, Tarquin gorged on bananas, custard-cream cookies and plain yogurts. This Friday morning he had taken five spoonfuls of a foul-tasting elixir given to him by Jules. Over his two years of jumping Tarquin had learned that, though not perfect, the elixir went some way to helping his body adjust to the rigours of time travel. Tea and peanut-butter-and-jam toasties were an optional and more pleasant-tasting extra.

At the stern of the boat, Jeremiah passed him a lithographic print. "You choose the gear, I'll sort your time out."

The big man disappeared back through the steel door.

Tarquin looked at the drawing and sighed. "Lace, wigs and hose … again." He turned to face the mirror on the front of the big, ornately painted wardrobe. A pale face with large, dark eyes, framed by shoulder-length curly black hair, looked back.

Opening the wardrobe doors, he found a drawer marked: "Seventeenth-century England." He rummaged through the clothing and pulled out several pieces, comparing his choices to the lithograph.

Finally, happy with his selection, he dressed quickly, looked at his reflection in the full-length mirror and sighed again. He'd never live it down if his college friends saw him like this. All he needed was some ridiculous-coloured lipstick and a sitar and he could be mistaken for his New Age cousin Henrietta!

"What year did you say?" Tarquin said into a wooden candlestick telephone while trying on a wide-brimmed hat.

"1666." Jeremiah's voice squawked and crackled from a tiny speaker in the wardrobe above Tarquin's head.

"The year of the Great Fire of London," mused Tarquin, already visualizing the project he could write for his college history course.

Fifteen minutes later he opened the steel door and walked proudly into the front room.

"Hang, on lad. Be with yer in a mo, just doing the necessary." Tarquin saw Jeremiah planning their journey, hunched over two tattered volumes, Mrs Beeton's Book of Household Management and her Book of Needlework—or The Jump Manual and The Time Almanac, as time-travellers called them. With a scratch of his head, and a "That'll do nicely", Jeremiah closed the books and turned to Tarquin.

"Fire and brimstone, that's amazing, Seebee," he said, grinning at the young cavalier before him, clad in black periwig, hat, lace ruff, breeches, waistcoat and hose. "Right, you know what to do. Collect your knapsack and take the chair. I'll set you off and join you in a tick."

Tarquin nodded, and made for the time portal behind the steps that led to the top deck. In the time room, sitting on the dais next to his own time chair—an adapted nineteenth-century dentist's chair—was a fighter aircraft's ejector seat.

He climbed the dais and examined the time chair that Jeremiah was planning to use. It was American, with the word "Lockheed" on a large metal plate below the black padded headrest. The base and back were also black and padded. Tarquin shook his head. Gritting his teeth, he clambered into his wooden dentist's chair, and held the leather armrests so tightly that his knuckles whitened. His mind full of the journey ahead, he reached for the cricket-bat pendant his father had given him and turned it in his hand, running a fingernail across the inscription on the back.

In his head he recited the words: "If over others you would leap, then in books you must seek," and remembered the day, four years ago, when his father had given the bat to him, and the gloomy omen that had followed soon after …

"Tarquin, Tarquin."

"Yes, Dad?" said Tarquin.

"Come away from the window. The bird will be fine. They're used to high winds."

Malcolm Jenkins, Tarquin's father, was a tall, ruggedly handsome man in his mid-forties with the kind of weathered face that hides an inquisitive mind and a sharp wit. He encouraged his son to be independent and foster interest in everything, especially history and puzzles. Tarquin watched as the crow turned, weaved, and disappeared across the neighbour's hedge.

"Come," said Malcolm, "I have a new puzzle for you to try."

He reached into a leather pouch he was holding and retrieved a cylindrical wooden object about fifteen centimetres long, and passed it to Tarquin.

"It's beautiful," said Tarquin, turning it carefully in his hands, as he looked at the eight discs of different coloured woods, held together by two end discs and a tube that ran through the middle of them.

"I got the plans from a man in Italy before you were born, and made it for you," said Malcolm, smiling, enjoying his son's excitement at something new to understand.

"Another piece of history?" said Tarquin, laughing. Every time his parents went away on a trip they brought back some unusual artefact or antique from the past as a reminder of their travels.

"Custard-cream?" continued his father, pushing towards his son an Egyptian casket-shaped biscuit tin with the words "Huntley & Palmers" on its side.

"Another new biscuit tin?" Tarquin turned the container and admired the Egyptian scenes decorating it before opening the lid and taking three biscuits. His father loved to collect old tins. Tarquin often marvelled that, despite their being so old, each tin was in pristine condition—looked brand new, in fact.

"Yes, your mother found it in London," said his father, taking two biscuits. "Now, to business. The puzzle." His father pointed back to the wooden device. "I wonder if you can find out what's inside. Try opening it."

Tarquin rolled the puzzle in his hands, examining the markings on each dial. The first and last discs had letters, and the other six bore numbers from 1 to 36.

"I line up the combination against the groove to the left?" asked Tarquin. His father nodded.

After turning each disc of wood to his desired combination, Tarquin pulled gently at the puzzle, trying to twist and turn the wooden pieces apart, but they held firm.

"Think the problem through," said Malcolm, sitting back in his favourite armchair. "I'll give you a clue. You are a combination of numbers and letters."

Tarquin's eyes lit up. "Got it …" he said, turning each disc again, until it clicked as the correct sequence of T010300J—his initials and date of birth—was dialled in, and he withdrew a tube.

"Excellent, well done! Now, look inside the tube." Tarquin pulled out a small, gold cricket bat on a chain.

"Keep it safe," said his father.

Rolling the bat in his hands, Tarquin saw an inscription on its face, and read aloud: "'If over others you would leap, then in books you must seek.' What does it mean?"

"Knowledge is everything," said Malcolm, smiling. "It's also a reminder that we love you dearly."

Bemused, but delighted with his unexpected gift, Tarquin grinned at his father, threw his arms around him, and hugged him tightly.

"Thank you! Thank you, both!"

In the garden, the crow had returned, swooping low over the neighbour's hedge. It wheeled towards the house, and spun out of control before crashing into the french windows, falling lifeless to the ground.

When Jeremiah joined Tarquin in the time portal he was dressed in black breeches, a waistcoat filled to bursting and a frock coat of his own. Perched on his head was a rather fetching black periwig. Tarquin smiled. Cousin Henrietta had doubled in size but her dress sense hadn't improved and her face was now extremely hairy.

"You kept that quiet," said Tarquin, nodding towards the ejector seat.

"Well," said Jeremiah, pulling at his waistcoat, "I am not as young as you and I needs me comfort when travelling. You ready for your language helper?"

Jeremiah lifted the lid on a huge wooden barrel next to a desk covered with bottles of various sizes and colours.

Tarquin's smile fell from his face and he nodded reluctantly. It was this gloopy part he detested most—even more than Jules's elixir—but, without being able to speak the right language when you got there, any trip would be unthinkable.

Jeremiah took off his wig and clambered into the barrel.

"No problem with the American dialectical linguisticises on your last jump?" he shouted, his bass voice echoing from within.

Tarquin waited until he emerged, clutching three dusty jars. "I had no problem with the American dialect. The mix was fine," he said.

"Good, then let's begin."

Jeremiah put on his reading glasses, made space on his desk with his elbows, and sat down to gently unscrew the jar lids. "I'll mix a couple of jars to get the dialecticals right. Seventeenth-century English can be a bit of trouble if we're not careful."

He pulled a fireman's brass helmet closer to him on the floor and busied himself pouring and mixing the jars' contents with an old windshield-wiper blade while humming an aria.

The big man had explained the process countless times before, but it was still gobbledygook to Tarquin. The gloopy stuff went inside each ear and two wax plugs kept it there, but this didn't interfere with your normal hearing. Somehow, the gloop helped you hear, understand and speak other languages. There was a different gloop for each language, and to create dialects you mixed them together. Getting the balance right between language and dialect was a skill that Jeremiah guarded jealously. After five days, or when a plug was removed, the gloop evaporated and you were back to normal. Jeremiah insisted that Tarquin always take a spare bottle of the appropriate mixture with him—just in case.

Jeremiah cursed as he spilled liquid from the helmet for the umpteenth time.

"You really should look into getting an electric mixer," Tarquin commented.

"I don't trust them whirly things." Jeremiah scowled. "Anyways, Jules has promised me a proper language mixer, automated an' all."

"Good! You've used that battered relic of a helmet ever since I can remember," said Tarquin with a laugh.

Jeremiah huffed. "It were me dad's. Anyways, I am a busy man an' all. Appointments take organizing. I can't just go wandering off to get machinery. What would Her Majesty indoors say?"

"You don't trust modern things," said Tarquin, "You prefer the old ways. My aunt's the same."

"Just don't like peoples messing with me ways and means," said Jeremiah, taking off his glasses. "I goes all wobbly doodle at the thought."

Tarquin laughed again and lay back in the dentist's chair while Jeremiah returned to his alchemy.

"Okay, here's yer helper," said Jeremiah, walking towards Tarquin and brandishing two syringes full of gloop.

Tarquin closed his eyes and waited. Getting glooped was like having a tidal wave crash and foam inside your head. Twice.

"There, that's not so bad," said Jeremiah, plugging the second ear.

"That's a matter of opinion," grumbled Tarquin.

Jeremiah dropped the syringes into the barrel and pulled a polished brass lever.

With a hiss and a series of jerking movements, two tubes and a box fell from the ceiling and hung suspended on metal tubes in midair. Growling, Jeremiah bashed the wheezing machinery with a bicycle pump until it hummed. Within the box, two glass eyepieces shone an iridescent blue.

"I've got to get you fixed!" he said, admonishing the contraption like a teacher talking to a naughty child.

To the layman, the device might have looked like a submarine periscope. Unlike a periscope, though, it didn't spy on things above the water: it spied on the past. The Look-Sees, as Jeremiah called it, allowed a 360-degree panorama of the time-traveller's arrival area. Using it before setting off was essential to prevent the traveller from suddenly appearing in front of bystanders. That sort of thing could cause all sort of complications. Like the time Tarquin materialized before Napoleon, in his tent that night at Waterloo. Jeremiah claimed he hadn't seen anyone through the Look-Sees in the arrivals area. Luckily, Tarquin had the good sense to jump from the chair and take a photograph of the Emperor with his digital camera. Stunned by both the camera's flash and the abrupt intrusion of an unexpected guest, a gobsmacked Napoleon had stood there, rooted to the spot in his long-johns. Taking advantage of the situation, Tarquin had then snatched Napoleon's signature cream frock coat from where it lay on the Little Corporal's camp bed, hopped back onto his time chair, and disappeared. Sadly, Napoleon's recollection of the incident went unrecorded in the annals of history.

Satisfied with what he had surveyed through the Look-Sees, Jeremiah backed away from the dais and waved his arms at Tarquin.

"Right, Seebee, here we go." He mimed for Tarquin to put on his periwig and hat and collect his cane and knapsack. "Nothing in the jump area. I'll set you off and join you in a tick. Oh, and don't forget Inga's packed lunch." He tossed a greaseproof-paper packet into Tarquin's lap.

With a loud screech, Tarquin's chair rocked back and forth and started spinning erratically. Tarquin clutched his knapsack, lunch and cane to his chest. The chair's speed increased and the jolting, jerky movements eased. Soon the chair was revolving smoothly. Tarquin saw the inside of the boat melt away and then explode into a myriad of coloured fireworks.

As he passed out, his mind was filled with images drawn from the past.

Centuries away, the far end of a wormhole was opening in Pudding Lane, London, on the upper floor of a small house, close to a bakery. It would be there for two hours before closing, not to reappear for four days.

Tarquin stood by the French windows inside his Oxford home, cradling the small gold cricket bat on the chain around his neck and watching the rain lashing against the greenhouse windows. The house was full, a family gathering, but this wasn't a happy party. It was the day of his parents' funeral.

Uncle Jules appeared to be everywhere, dragging him around like a pet's favourite toy, introducing him to dark-suited relatives he had never heard of and friends of his parents he had never met. The sky darkened, and the rain got heavier.

Tarquin shook his head. Death was for old people, not his parents.

He squeezed the bat under his chin and sighed. It was so wasteful.

The day of the accident was on a constant loop in Tarquin's mind: his mother scolding him for leaving his sports kit on his bedroom floor, his father fretting about the time and the weather, and Tarquin standing outside their home in pouring rain, waving them off in the taxi. Then they were gone. Never to be seen again.

Back inside, Auntie Mira fussed about the overflowing bowl of washing up and the state of his parents' hall carpet, while Uncle Harold, now ensconced in Dad's favourite chair, riffled through the many books on the table next to it. Tarquin sighed. How could a plane just disappear? No wreckage; no flight recorder; no survivors; nothing.

"George Gordon, Lord Byron!"

Shaken from his melancholy memories, Tarquin turned to see a stern, weathered face glaring up at him.

"Great-Aunt Polidori! I didn't know you were here!" he exclaimed.

Ever since his Great-Aunt Audra Louvenia Doorley Polidori had first set eyes on his pale complexion, curly black hair and dark, brooding eyes, she had called him George Byron, after the English romantic poet.

"There's an awful lot you don't know," said Polidori caustically. "But," she continued, "that's neither here nor there. Your future is the most important thing now."

"It is?" Tarquin gazed at his great-aunt, all swathed in black crinoline and lace. A frightening vision of a dour Queen Victoria in mourning jumped uninvited into his head, and he shuddered.

"Now, now Auntie," came the calm, reassuring voice of Jules, like a life-belt to Tarquin's rescue. "Let's not concern the poor lad with his future today. He's barely twelve years of age."

The two adults gazed at each other intently, and Tarquin watched their silent conversation.

To his surprise, Great-Aunt Polidori was the first to blink. "Mark my words," she said, emphasizing each syllable with a lunge of her swagger stick that made Tarquin jump. "Time for now is on our side, but it's a demanding mistress. Preparation and education are everything." She looked soberly at Jules before arching an eyebrow, turning on her heels and bustling into the midst of the gathering.

"She's scary," said Tarquin, confused by what she'd said.

"I know," replied Jules. "But she means well. I think. What with your parents' death, she has a lot on her mind. Cake?" he said, changing the subject.

The boy gladly took the proferred fairy cake.

"Wait here," Jules continued. "I need to talk to your Aunt Mira and Uncle Harold. You'll be living with them in Steeple Snoring, a lovely village in Northamptonshire, and you'll attend the local college close by."

He disappeared towards the kitchen.

Of course, no one could replace Tarquin's parents. Looking around this room so full of history, language, puzzles and books, he was reminded of all the long summer evenings spent here with his parents, sharing their great love of history, puzzles, languages and storytelling. Tarquin smiled. Each time they returned from a conference, his parents would show him artefacts from countries and lost civilizations they had found in antiques shops on their travels. Then, over dinner, they would weave wondrous tales around each relic, bringing it to life.

Never again.

Chapter 4

Tower of Trouble

Tarquin wearily opened his eyes. He had materialized inside a cold, dark, damp room that smelt like a drain. He took a handkerchief from his coat and covered his nose.

Slowly his eyes adjusted to the gloom. The only illumination was moonlight coming in through a small window next to his chair's landing spot. Tarquin was relieved to find that Jeremiah had made no mistake with the Look-Sees this time around.

As he slipped quietly from the dentist's chair, the packed lunch fell from his lap. Something brushed his ankle and he froze with fear. On the floor, glistening in the moonlight, were dozens of cold, wet beady eyes, all looking up at him.

"Crikey! Rats!" He shivered. "I hate rats."

Ignoring him, the rats continued scavenging in a wave across the floor.

With one eye on the rodents, Tarquin climbed back onto his chair, hooked his feet under him and looked around.

There was something very foreboding in the decrepit nature of what he guessed had once been a bedroom. Understandably, as this was 1666, it wasn't like any bedroom he had ever seen. In the far corner, past the scorched fireplace full of broken bricks, he could make out a charred and broken chair, leaning on its side. The remains of the front right leg lay splintered and scattered about the floor. A burst cushion sat next to the chair. Against the wall, propped up on shards of roof tiles, were the relics of a bed and, beside it, the blackened skeleton of a small animal, picked clean by the rats.

A recent meal for someone … or something, he thought, trembling nervously. He flipped out a small drawer in his chair to reveal a remote-control device, and pressed the Cloaking button to hide any evidence of his arrival.

At least, that was what was supposed to happen. This time, however, the chair didn't disappear.

He shook the remote and pressed it again.

Still nothing happened.

An eruption of loud snores from the room next door made his heart race. His head, still reeling from the time-jump, throbbed painfully.

Returning the remote to its drawer, Tarquin left the safety of the chair and moved slowly towards the door.

He stepped on a loose and noisy floorboard and froze. Had whoever it was in the next room heard him?

After much snuffling, the snoring fell back into a regular rhythm, but Tarquin still felt vulnerable standing in the middle of the room.

Better wait for Jeremiah. Two heads are better than one when you're dealing with the unknown. And it's also pretty handy to have an ex-wrestler on your side if things turn nasty.

He eased his foot off the broken board and crept to the door. Inevitably, the door creaked as it opened, but thankfully it didn't seem to disturb the sleeper. Crouching low, Tarquin waited nervously for Jeremiah to arrive.

He should be here by now, he thought, checking his watch. Twenty minutes passed and still no Jeremiah.

Tarquin considered the possibilities. Perhaps Jeremiah had missed the wormhole? Alternatively, could he have dropped into the wrong one?

The boy didn't like the idea of staying here any longer. He had to do something.

Cautiously he made his way across the landing toward the room where the snoring was coming from. Taking a deep breath, the young time-traveller peered through a crack in the door, his taut heart knocking against his ribcage.

His eye spied a familiar form.

"What the …?" he whispered.

Stretched across his padded Lockheed ejector seat, cloaked by steaming mist, was Jeremiah, snoring loudly.

Thank goodness! thought Tarquin, stepping into the room.

He gently nudged his friend awake. "Pssst."

Jeremiah sat up with a start and wobbled his head and shoulders as if getting rid of a shiver. When he saw Tarquin he grinned and broke into song:

Tosse the pot, tosse the pot, let us be merry,
And drink till our cheeks be red as a cherry.
We take no thought, we have no care,
For still we spend and never spare,
Till of all our money our purse is bare,
We ever, tosse the pot.

Tarquin groaned and covered his friend's mouth with a hand. Jeremiah had often warned him that, after jumping, the language gloop occasionally went haywire and the traveller would spout gibberish in the new language or dialect.

"Marvellous," said Jeremiah, sleepily squinting at Tarquin as he raised his arms high above his head in a yawning stretch. "Aye, very grand is this travelling malarkey." He opened his mouth wide and yawned as if coming out of a long hibernation. "Let's get on, Seebee, no time to waste."

Tarquin shook his head. "You're unbelievable!"

Jeremiah grinned again and stumbled groggily off his chair. Almost at once he tripped, staggered across the room, and fell headlong to the floor, ending up with his nose against the opposite wall. Raising himself up on his elbows, he sniffed the plaster.

Tarquin shook his head and cowered, convinced half of London must have heard this performance. He hid behind the ejector seat, scanning the stairs through the cracked door, expecting someone to arrive at any moment to investigate.

"This is new. It can't be new!" said Jeremiah, pawing at the wall. "By heck, it is, you know." He looked at Tarquin, sat up and rummaged in his waistcoat. He took out a battered pocket watch, checked the third and fourth hands, and then snapped it shut in frustration and anger.

"We're too friggin' late!" Jeremiah got to his feet and kicked a lump of plaster across the floor, sending it crashing into the wall. He stomped around the room, repeating over and over again, "We're not in 1666? Why are we not in 1666? Why?"

Tarquin finally interrupted, "So, where are we?"

Jeremiah fixed a cold eye on Tarquin. "We're here! The eighth of May, 1671!"

A blood-curdling scream stopped Jeremiah from saying anything more, and sent Tarquin diving back under the ejector seat, displacing a family of rats that had taken refuge there from the singing. He was about to press the chair's red button when Jeremiah signalled him to wait.

The screaming came from the street. Tarquin and Jeremiah crawled to the window. Peering over the sill, they could see, in the moonlit street below, a man writhing on the wet cobbled road. People were running to the man's aid. Tarquin's eye was caught by a coach and horses galloping furiously away down the road; as he watched, it vanished into the distance. Several of the people below tried to chase the fleeing coach, but they had no chance of catching the horse-drawn vehicle.

"The man's hurt bad! Where's a doctor?" someone shouted. "The mail coach broke his legs!"

From their vantage point on the second floor, Jeremiah and Tarquin could see the man's broken and twisted limbs and hear his agonized cries. Blood pooled on the cobblestones. A couple of folk were desperately trying to stem the flow.

The time-travellers ducked down. Tarquin swallowed hard, feeling sick. Despite his years as a St John's Ambulance cadet, he wasn't prepared for this. He had never witnessed such stark suffering.

"What do we do?" he asked, sweat beading on his brow.

"Help them," responded Jeremiah.

The big man took out his chair's remote and pressed the Cloaking button. Nothing happened.

"Strange." Jeremiah repeatedly stabbed his large finger at the remote.

"Mine wouldn't disappear either," said Tarquin.

"We need to hide them somehow."

The pair looked around for anything they could use to disguise the chairs. No luck.

"We'll just have to leave them be," said Jeremiah, shaking his head dubiously, "and hope no one comes in and moves them."

"What about the people who live here?" asked Tarquin, remembering the charred animal bones in the next room. They stared silently at each other for a few seconds before another horrifying scream pierced the air.

"The man comes first," said Jeremiah, hurrying to the door.

The two scampered down to the street and pushed through the crowd towards the stricken man.

"Make way, make way! I'm a doctor!" shouted Jeremiah.

Tarquin took a deep breath and followed his friend through the crowd. Moments later he nearly fell over him.

Jeremiah was kneeling beside the screaming victim. Tarquin could see that the injured man was middle-aged and slightly overweight. The hit-and-run coach had crushed the man's thighs, bursting them like ripe tomatoes. Shredded remains of his britches were all that held the shattered legs together.

Jeremiah quickly pulled off his shirt and ripped it into several lengths. He thrust a roll of fabric into the man's mouth, then looped tourniquets above his thighs. He slowly tightened the tourniquets using his and Tarquin's canes, but the man's upper body continued to heave and convulse, his eyes rolling aimlessly in their sockets as he slipped in and out of consciousness.

"Oh, God," said Tarquin, tormented by the sight of those eyes. Gasping for breath and grabbing at his stomach, he turned away from Jeremiah and retched. The crowd, huddled together, swayed like wheat in a field out of the way of what had once been Tarquin's breakfast toastie.

Finally, Jeremiah staunched the flow of blood, to the accompaniment of thankful sighs and gasps from the crowd. Behind him crouched an ashen-faced and trembling Tarquin, still not up to looking at the scene.

Jeremiah turned, put his arm gently around Tarquin, and pressed his lips to the boy's ear.

"Keep it together, Seebee." Jeremiah gazed at the crowd. Curious eyes were watching their every move. "I really need your help. He's lost a tankful of blood, but we can save him."

Tarquin took a deep breath and nodded, wiping vomit from his chin.

"The bleeding's stopped, but I needs your help in getting rid of this lot," explained Jeremiah, indicating the bystanders.

The big man lifted Tarquin to his feet, took off his coat and threw it over the victim's smashed legs. Raising a hand above his head, he addressed the gathering.

"We must move him inside quickly so that I can tend to his injuries. I need some help."

The crowd, now up to well over fifty, mumbled agreement. A woman stepped forward and pointed to a building across the street. "Take him there. That's my house."

His stomach calming, his St John's Ambulance training finally proving worthwhile, Tarquin organized four of the crowd to help move the injured man. A cart was found and the man quickly lifted onto it. With Jeremiah by the man's side, a group of Tarquin's volunteers pushed the cart slowly to the woman's house.

Tarquin helped the four bearers carry the injured man through the front door and into a large room, with a table near an open fire. Someone cleared the table for the unconscious man to to be laid out on. His breathing was shallow and his face pale and clammy to the touch.

The majority of the throng attempted to follow what Tarquin couldn't help thinking of as a stretcher party into the house to watch. Those who couldn't get in peered through the windows in an attempt to catch a glimpse of the gory scene. Around the table stood a disparate bunch of curious onlookers. Packed in like sardines, young and old, they stood expectant, inquisitive, waiting for Jeremiah's next move, murmuring questions and speculation about the injured man's fate.

Above the murmuring came the deep timbre of a man's voice, followed by a heated exchange of words. The voice's owner appeared in the doorway carrying a cudgel. His large frame filled the entrance.

"Get you out of my house, you morbid bastards!" he yelled, pulling and pushing people from the room. Reluctantly, the crowd thinned. Loiterers were cuffed about the ear, or encouraged to leave by the cudgel waved in front of their faces.

As the room finally cleared, the man walked up to Jeremiah. "I am John Charles, the constable for this section of London. This is my house. Are you a doctor? Is there anything my wife and I can do to help?"

"Thank you, you're very kind," said Jeremiah, turning to the constable's wife. Her eyes were fixed on the dying man's pale face.

"Ma'am, I need you to find me some linen, hot water and wooden splints." She didn't respond. "Please ma'am, I need your help. Now!" Jeremiah repeated firmly.

Her husband stepped forward.

"Elizabeth, this poor man needs our help." Her husband's gentle persistence broke the spell. "And the doctor has sacrificed his shirt. Please fetch him one of mine, alongside the other things he has requested."

"I'm sorry," said Elizabeth, "it's just that this poor injured stranger looks so much like our son." She scuttled from the room, followed by her husband.

Jeremiah was about to say something to Tarquin when a thickset man in a mud-splattered cape and hat walked through the door. They both swivelled to look at the newcomer.

"I'm a surgeon," said the man, nodding to supposed fellow-professional Jeremiah and brushing past Tarquin. He didn't offer his hand to either as he went straight to the table.

No sooner did he reach it than he turned and spoke. "I've seen many a dying man in my time. There's nothing we can do for this one. Best if we let him pass peacefully away."

"If you give me room," said Jeremiah, forcing his way between the surgeon and the table, "I can save him."

The man put a firm but gentle hand on Jeremiah's shoulder. "You're wasting your time. Let him be." The voice was quiet but firm.

Jeremiah stepped back and tried to grab hold of the surgeon's hand but the man pulled it away and thrust it hard into his coat pocket.

It was the last thing he did before crashing to the floor.

Tarquin stood over him, holding the tankard with which he'd bashed the surgeon across the back of the head.

"What the ruddy hell you do that for?" gasped Jeremiah, bending down to the unconscious surgeon on the floor.

"He was going to stab you!" whispered Tarquin, hastily picking up the stiletto dagger that had fallen from the surgeon's hand. Jeremiah stared at the knife, took off his hat and massaged his head. Tarquin's heart sank. He had never seen Jeremiah look frightened before.

"Thanks, Seebee," said Jeremiah at last, taking the dagger and looking at Tarquin's trousers.

"The tankard must have been full of mead." Tarquin felt a clammy wetness on his trousers and blushed.

Groans came from the table. Jeremiah spun round and pointed to the kitchen. "Quick, lock the door, I'll close the shutters. He's coming around. We don't have a moment to lose! When the constable and his wife try to come back in, you stall 'em. I need time to mend the bones and get blood into him."

Tarquin rushed to the door, "There's no key!" he said, as loudly as he dared, running his hands over the roughened wood and the iron lock.

Jeremiah rubbed his hands across his head again as if to control his thoughts. "Stick a chair in front of the door."

Hearing footsteps approaching, Tarquin heaved the nearest chair toward the door, wincing at the scraping noise it made on the stone floor.

"Is everything all right, sirs?" cried the constable, rattling the door handle.

Unsure what to do, Tarquin stared questioningly at Jeremiah. The big man signalled him to speak.

"Fine … Fine, thank you." Tarquin sat down on the chair. "Everything's … Everything's tickety-boo."

It was the best he could come up with under pressure.

"I thought I heard something fall," said the constable. "We're just waiting for the water to boil."

Tarquin grasped the chair's arms and sighed with relief. Preparing the water should take some time.

With a practised hand, Jeremiah dug in the pocket of his coat, put on his glasses and tugged out a small pen-like instrument. He adjusted a combination of numbers on the "pen" before pressing the tip into the man's neck. Then he set to work removing the man's bloodied coat and breeches before steering the device slowly over the man's fractured legs. As Tarquin watched, the blood around the open wounds congealed and flesh started growing.

Nodding in satisfaction, the big man took a silver ball from the knapsack and placed a sample of the man's blood into its centre.

A couple of seconds later, a short tube extended from the side of the ball. Jeremiah pressed it against the man's carotid artery.

"Four pints should do it," he said, pocketing his glasses and pressing a button on the ball.

"Hello? The door's stuck," shouted the constable.

"Hurry!" hissed Tarquin.

As blood flowed into his neck, the man's thighbones creaked, straightened, and fused together. Then, like the bow end of a sinking ship, they slowly disappeared back into his thighs.

"Can we come in? Is the door jammed? What's wrong?" The constable thumped hard against the door with his shoulder.

"I daren't do any more otherwise it'll be thought the Devil's work." Jeremiah stooped over the man's legs to check scabs that were as long as a forearm.

"Jeremiah!" shouted Tarquin, leaping from the chair.

The surgeon—if indeed he was a surgeon—had recovered consciousness and had grabbed a candlestick as a makeshift weapon.

The metal implement arced downward, but Jeremiah, his reactions still swift despite all the years since last he'd been in the ring, grabbed the man's arm and wrestled the weapon away.

Just then the constable burst into the room and, seeing Jeremiah grappling with an unknown assailant, ran to his aid. The two men forced the surgeon to drop the candlestick and twisted his arms behind his back, then launched him headlong into a chair. He rolled over the chair-back and collapsed in a heap, unconscious once more.

"Who the—?" said the constable.

"Your lock must have got stuck," muttered Tarquin pointing to the rough metal and pulling nervously at his periwig, trying to distract the man from his line of enquiry.

"What's going on?" wheezed the constable, gripping the handle of his sword as he hauled in air. "What's this knave doing here and who is he? Did you let him in?"

"He tried to kill me," said Jeremiah, quickly throwing his coat over the injured man's mended legs to hide them from view. "He would have done it if my cousin and you hadn't stopped him."

The constable walked over to where the "surgeon" sprawled like a rag doll on the floor, and examined his clothing. "He's a coach driver. Why would a coach driver try to kill you?" He backed away from the centre of the room, his hand on the hilt of his sword.

"This poor man was run over by a coach," said Tarquin. "I think the intruder is the driver of that coach. He must have come back to finish his victim off—and us if he could—so as not to be recognized."

The constable eased his hand from his sword-hilt and wiped his brow. "How is the injured man?"

"Resting," said Jeremiah, collecting his hat and periwig from the floor.

The constable's wife appeared from the kitchen carrying wooden splints, a bowl of hot water, a bundle of linen and a not-too-clean-looking shirt. She was nearly sent spiralling to the floor by an agitated, grey-haired man who, belying his evident years, bustled at speed into the room and headed straight for Jeremiah.

"Where's my son? What's happened?"

Seeing the unconscious, outstretched figure, he rushed to the table.

"Wythe!" The newcomer gazed for a long moment at the injured man before turning to Jeremiah. "Who are you?"

Jeremiah smiled gently at the perplexed father. "A doctor."

The man looked confused. His eyes darted from face to face searching for explanations. "Doctor? … Doctor who?" he stammered.

Tarquin struggled to stifle a hysterical giggle.

"Er—" was the only word that came out of Jeremiah's mouth.

"Dr David Livingstone, the eminent Scottish surgeon," said Tarquin quickly. "And I am Clint, Clint of Eastwood, his cousin and medical apprentice, at your service." He bowed.

The man looked dumbstruck at Tarquin, then back at Jeremiah. "'Tis good to meet you, Dr Livingstone and Clint of Eastwood." He doffed his hat. "I am Edwards, Talbot Edwards, and this is my son Wythe, home from military service."

Talbot Edwards turned back to the younger man, who was just beginning to show signs of coming to consciousness. "Wythe," Talbot whispered, grasping his son's hand to his chest.

The younger man turned and smiled weakly at his father, colour slowly beginning to return to his craggy, weatherbeaten face.

"They said you were dying, son." Tears welled in Talbot's eyes.

"It looked far worse than it were," said Jeremiah. "A couple of days' rest and he'll be as good as new."

The elderly man straightened himself and cleaned his hands on his jacket before offering one of them to Jeremiah. "How can we ever repay you?"

"Think nothing of it, Master Talbot. We are passing through London and are in need of a bed for the night. If you could point us in the direction of a local inn, we'll wish you and your son well and be on our way."

"Pish and tish!" cried Talbot. "You must stay at my home, as my honoured guests. I'll hear naught else. My carriage is waiting outside. It is the very least I can do in repayment."

Jeremiah and Tarquin struggled to get Wythe as comfortable as possible inside the carriage before clambering aboard. The vehicle jolted off before creaking and swinging its way through the streets of London. After a while it began descending toward the River Thames and a walled group of imposing buildings.

"You know what's over there, don't you?" whispered Tarquin, nodding slightly to his right as the carriage moved forward.

"I knows, Seebee. The Tower of London. We're following in traitors' footsteps."

As the carriage weaved its way through the outer buildings, Tarquin was struck by the casualness with which they were allowed to pass. Only once were they stopped, to allow a guard to look into the carriage. Talbot apologized, saying that the checking of carriages was unusual but that there were tensions between the Dutch and King Charles.

"Here we are," said Talbot a while later. "Be it ever so humble, it's home, sweet home."

Tarquin and Jeremiah got out of the carriage. Tarquin looked up, not quite believing where they were. "The Martin Tower," he said quietly. He knew the Martin Tower was home to the most prized possessions of the British Monarchy, the Crown Jewels.

Jeremiah gently lifted the sleeping Wythe from the carriage in his arms and followed Talbot through a doorway. Tarquin held back a little and looked towards the dark, shuttered windows and the heavy wooden door on the bottom level of the Martin Tower. He was a mere six metres away from the most valuable jewels in the seventeenth-century world.

He quickened his pace and caught up with Jeremiah and Talbot as they started up several flights of steps toward the welcoming light from an open door.

When Talbot reached the door a rotund woman stepped out onto the threshold and stood, hands on hips, silhouetted in the frame. In the cool night air, steam rose from her round, cropped head. She reminded Tarquin of a newly cooked Christmas pudding.

Mrs Edwards greeted her husband and then her eyes settled on the bundle of clothes held in Jeremiah's arms.

"Wythe!" she cried, knowing at once that it was her son. She threw herself at Jeremiah and smothered Wythe's head in her ample bosom. "What happened?" she asked between sobs.

"He had an accident, but he's going to be okay. He needs rest, and is not to be disturbed." Jeremiah gently prised Wythe from his mother's chest. Mrs Edwards grabbed a candle and led the party slowly up three flights of creaking stairs and into their lodgings.

"I am not as young as I used to be," said Talbot, breathing heavily at the top of the stairs and waving a hand at a door ahead. "You can put my son in the room over there."

Jeremiah entered the bedroom and the others followed. Wythe was placed in the middle of the bed. Mrs Edwards was instantly at the bedside, fussing and smoothing his hair.

"I must insist he doesn't move or be disturbed for a day or so, ma'am," said Jeremiah, taking off his hat and wig before rubbing his head. "Just keep him warm, fed and watered."

Tarquin felt Jeremiah's nervousness around Mrs Edwards, and recognized the feeling. His Great-Aunt Polidori had the same overbearing presence, and Jeremiah never knew how to react to her. No one did.

Mrs Edwards nodded without moving her gaze from her son as she sat by his side and fiddled with the bedding. She laid a hand on her son's brow. "Get me some water, Talbot. He's got a fever."

"Would you good sirs like to join me for something to eat while my wife sorts out our son?" said Talbot, his eyes flicking to the door.

Tarquin watched as Talbot and Jeremiah communicated in a silent language of expressions. Despite the gulf of three hundred or so years between where they came from, they both knew never to interfere with a mother tending her offspring, even if he was a middle-aged man back from war.

Talbot motioned with his lantern for them to follow him through the door. "I'll show you to your lodgings and then we can eat."

He led the visitors to the courtyard, then to the right, following the battlement wall to a small building that jutted out from the side.

"This is the Brick Tower," he said, unlocking the small wooden door. They all ducked to go through. Talbot led them up a circular staircase to quarters on the first floor. From the darkness, several small pairs of eyes looked at them, blinked and disappeared. Tarquin recognized the sound of scratching, and shivered.

Talbot settled the lantern on the oak table that dominated the small room. "It's spartan, but with a fire going it'll do you fine for tonight." He picked up some kindling from an iron bucket beside the stone fireplace and set it in the grate. "There's a flint on the table and brushwood by the fireplace. Treat this place as your own. Come back to my lodgings when you're ready. Don't get lost. There are a lot of guards about and I don't want to be going to the guardhouse to collect you every half hour!"

Talbot laughed at his own joke, and Tarquin and Jeremiah joined in. It was good to see the man relaxing after the evening's events.

The visitors dropped their bags as Talbot backed out of the room. Tarquin waited until the door was closed and then rounded on Jeremiah.

"We must leave immediately!" he said, his voice quivering. "I don't want to appear rude or ungrateful, but this trip is getting way out of control." He had never spoken to Jeremiah like this, but he felt scared. "And, you know what?" He pointed a trembling, accusatory finger at his friend. "I don't think you know what's happening either."

Jeremiah shook his head. "Let's not be falling out, Seebee. You knows I wanted 1666, not 1671. Anyways up, we can't leave for another forty-eight hours."

"Why the hell not?" gasped Tarquin.

"Get a grip, Seebee. You knows there's no wormhole ready."

Tarquin sank onto a chair and put his head in his hands.

Jeremiah got out his pocket Mrs Beeton's and sat on the bed. "Found another wormhole," he said after a while, "but it has the same opening time as the last."

"What do we do then? The evening's only going to get worse and we're right in the middle of it."

Jeremiah got up from the bed and walked over to Tarquin. "I'll look after you, mark my words. I'll not let nothing happen to you on my watch."

"Do you know who Talbot Edwards is?"

"Er, maybe?" replied Jeremiah, obviously trying very hard to hide the fact he had no idea who his landlord for the night was.

"Or Wythe Edwards?"

"Oh, er?" said Jeremiah, taking off his periwig and rubbing his head. Tarquin saw the perplexity on his mentor's face. Realizing Jeremiah had no idea what would happen that night, he took pity on his friend.

"I've been here before, with my college. I know all about Talbot and Wythe Edwards. According to the history books, Talbot Edwards was Master of the Jewel House. His son, Wythe Edwards, returned home unexpectedly from military service, and that night raised the alarm when he found a bunch of Irishmen, led by a rogue called Colonel Blood in the guise of a parson, stealing the Crown Jewels!"

"Alarm? With the Tower Guard?" queried Jeremiah.

"Yes, but you see the problem? Wythe can barely raise a smile, let alone a hue and cry!"

"I see." Jeremiah shot Tarquin another perplexed look.

"I knew the date sounded familiar when you checked your watch after you woke up. The eighth of May, 1671. The robbery happens tonight or maybe tomorrow night. Trouble is, by us being here, I think we've changed history."

"You mean … this Colonel … this Colonel Blood is coming here?" said Jeremiah.

"Yes. He has to arrive soon, along with the others—they're all relatives—and announce himself as a parson. And, then"—Tarquin waved his hands for emphasis—"Blood becomes the only person in history to steal the Crown Jewels."

Jeremiah thudded a huge ham of a fist into his palm. "Leave Blood to me!"

Tarquin grabbed his friend's sleeve. "Promise me you'll take care."

Jeremiah smiled at his young charge, "Ah, you knows me. I be a kitten really!"

Tarquin didn't share Jeremiah's optimism, but there was little he could do. He wasn't in control of this adventure and, with Wythe in bed, someone had to stop Blood, save the jewels and get history back on track.

The pair returned to Talbot's rooms and the welcoming sight of a food-laden table. Their host ushered them to chairs close by the fire. Jeremiah quickly tucked into a meal of bread, beef, pottage, cheese and onions. By comparison, Tarquin ate very little, absorbed in thoughts and worries.

Jeremiah had just finished a second helping of pottage when there was a knock on the door. Tarquin looked at his friend, and mouthed, "This is it!"

Talbot got up from his chair and went to answer the door. A warder stood there. Tarquin, straining to hear the conversation between the two men, saw Talbot nod and heard the warder call down the stairs. The sound of heavy footsteps echoed up the stairwell. A tall, broad-shouldered man appeared from the darkness, filling the open doorway. Talbot shook the man's hand and drew him inside.

Tarquin eyed the stranger warily. If indeed this was Blood—and who else could it be?—how were the two time-travellers going to foil his plot?

He grabbed a tankard and gulped down a comforting couple of mouthfuls of mead.

The newcomer removed his heavy coat, all the time eyeing Jeremiah and Tarquin. Talbot took the garment and, after allowing the stranger to warm his hands by the fire for a few moments, guided him to a chair at the table. As soon as he was seated, Colonel Blood started ripping into a roast chicken, dismembering it with terrifying ease.

Tarquin felt his throat tighten. *Is it the mead making me feel like I want to upchuck, or the knowledge that this man would kill me as soon as look at me?*

Talbot cleared his throat. "Dr Livingstone, Master Clint, this is our good friend Parson Blood."

The "parson" sized up Jeremiah and nodded a greeting. Tarquin saw suspicion in the man's eyes. He glanced at his friend and prayed that Jeremiah would get up, make his excuses, and leave the scoundrel to his meal. No such luck. Instead, Jeremiah's face lit up like a firework display.

Tarquin had seen that look a dozen times while watching videos of Jeremiah's wrestling bouts on board the Silvery Moon. Beaming red face equalled "ready for a challenge".

"Parson Blood!" exclaimed Jeremiah with open arms. "Well, knock me down with a goose feather and roll me up in fat and liniment. I never thought I'd get to meet you!"

Blood looked confused as Jeremiah leaned across the table and grabbed his sizeable hand, vigorously shaking it. The two men were of about the same stature as each other, but Blood was perhaps a little broader, with a swarthy, unkempt appearance. All Tarquin could do was sit and watch the sparring.

If there's to be a fight, it'll be a close one, thought Tarquin. *What do I do if Jeremiah loses?*

"'Tis a famous name you have, Parson," said Jeremiah, leaning back in his chair and flexing his upper body muscles.

"Have we met?" Blood took a deep breath and moved slightly backward in his seat.

"Nope." Jeremiah grinned.

Tarquin pushed a slice of onion around his plate, keeping his head down, desperately hoping hostilities wouldn't break out at the table.

"Will you stay a little while?" asked Talbot, looking at the black-clad man.

"Well, I—"

"Of course he will," said Jeremiah, cutting him off loudly. "The night is only just beginning." Again he grinned at Blood.

"Yes, that'll be fine, but I came to see your wife." Blood turned his gaze towards the door.

"She'll be down soon. Our son is home and she's looking after him." Talbot stood and poured Blood, Jeremiah and Tarquin another drink. "Wythe, our son, had a terrible accident, and these kind gentlemen saved his life. God's ways can be strange, can't they, Parson?"

A sickly smile spread across Blood's face as he nodded. Tarquin felt a cold shiver move down his spine.

"You are indeed blessed, Talbot," said Blood, ripping a leg forcefully from another chicken.

A loud rapping on the door made Tarquin jump and knock over his drink.

"Who can that be now?" said Talbot, rising wearily from his seat.

Jeremiah scowled at the back of Blood's turned head, as Tarquin mopped up the mead.

"It'll be my nephew and cousins," said Blood, "They must have been held up by the Tower Guard. We need water for our horses. We've travelled far tonight, so if you would be so kind as to help …?"

"Of course," said Talbot. "I'll see to it."

After talking with the guard accompanying Blood's relatives and their horses, he closed the door again. "Your relatives are going to the stables. They'll be given food and small beer."

Blood was now chewing on the leg of a pheasant. His aquiline nose and constantly shifting eyes reminded Tarquin of a hungry turkey vulture he'd once seen on a wildlife programme on TV.

Chewing open-mouthed, Blood stared at Jeremiah's forearm. "Elvis, the King? King of where?"

Jeremiah hurriedly rolled down his sleeve. "It's nothing, Parson, just an ink drawing I got from a friend."

"This King Elvis, he was carrying a lute," continued Blood. "Is he a troubadour?"

Jeremiah looked vexed. "It really is nothing, Parson. It were done many a year ago, during my youth." He lifted a serving dish and presented it to the man, "Perhaps some more meat?"

Blood scooped roast duck onto his plate and then into his mouth.

The sound of footsteps made them turn. Mrs Edwards had come down from sitting with Wythe. She rubbed her hands on her dress and looked relieved.

"My son sleeps peacefully. Thank you so much, Doctor—"

The sight of Blood stopped her in her tracks. "Oh my!" she said, fussing with her apron. "You're not due till tomorrow night, Parson Blood, so please forgive my appearance. Talbot, you should have told me we had more guests!"

Blood smiled. "I quite understand. You had important matters to attend to. There have been developments, and I have to see your daughter this evening. It is about my humble offer to her of my nephew's hand in marriage."

Tarquin's ears pricked up.

Jeremiah leaned across the table. "Marriage, you say?" He scratched his chin. "This sounds interesting."

Blood calmly took another sip of wine, ignoring Jeremiah's baiting. Mrs Edwards joined the men at the table.

"As we discussed during my last visit, my nephew Rupert would make a fine husband for your daughter." Blood waved elaborately in the air. "I am not well versed in the ways of the world, but I believe a bride price of several hundred pounds a year would be suitable if the marriage were to go ahead." He raised a napkin to his lips and patted the corners of his mouth.

Mrs Edwards looked excitedly at her husband.

"We are keen for our daughter Miriam to be wed, and the money would be useful, but I would need to talk with your nephew about his intentions," said Talbot.

Blood's eyes glinted in the candlelight. "Of course. By chance, he is here tonight with the horses in the yard."

Mrs Edwards, now all of a flutter with the idea of a new source of income and a wedding to plan, busied herself clearing space on the table.

"It is a pity our daughter is attending the Royal Court tonight, but never mind. It's right that we should talk with your nephew first." Talbot glanced at his wife, who nodded and said, "That's fine with us, Parson."

The proposal discussion over, everyone drank a toast to the "ways of the world" as Mrs Edwards scurried from the room with a pile of empty plates in her hands and a huge smile on her face.

When she returned moments later with more wine, Jeremiah wiped his moustache, rose from his chair and offered his hand to Talbot. "Well, we are much obliged to you for your hospitality, and your wife makes a fine supper, but it's time we were off to bed," he said. "We have a long journey ahead of us in the morning."

He turned to Blood and took the man's hand, squeezing hard. "Look forward to seeing you again soon, Parson."

Blood rose from his chair and stood toe-to-toe with Jeremiah, their hands gripped tightly together. Like two prize fighters at a weigh-in, they puffed out their chests and locked eyes as they sized each other up.

Once again, Tarquin knew the look. He put his head in his hands and waited for the first thud of fist on head.

"Come on, Seebee, time we were gone."

Opening his eyes, Tarquin was relieved to see that Jeremiah had released the rogue's hand and was heading for the door with Talbot. He got up and quickly followed.

"You remember the way to your room?" their host asked, opening the door to the stairwell.

"We'll be fine. If we get lost we'll raise the alarm and cause you merry hell." Jeremiah looked at Blood and laughed heartily.

Talbot chuckled, slapped Jeremiah on the back and bade them a good night's sleep before closing the door.

The time-travellers descended the stairs and, on the ground floor, Tarquin stopped. He pointed to a locked door ahead of them.

"I never got to see them on my college trip. Too many people queuing." He went to the door and looked through its window grill. He saw crowns and sceptres glinting in the moonlight. He stood for a moment, mesmerized by the riches.

"Come on, Seebee, we've got to get some rest before it all kicks off."

As they walked along the wall toward their accommodation, Jeremiah kept shaking his head. "Colonel Blood is the parson," he whispered as loudly as he dared. "Would you believe it?"

"One thing puzzles me," said Tarquin. "That nephew of his—the one he said was with the horses—didn't really exist, according to history. I wonder who he's going to introduce to the Edwardses as Rupert?"

"Some flash bugger as crooked as Blood is himself, I'd say." Jeremiah looked as if he'd like to take them both on at once.

Tarquin looked ceilingward. "Oh, let's not stay any longer. Please. Blood's bigger than you. Let's get our belongings and go."

Jeremiah stopped as if shot. His eyebrows meshed and he glowered at his young friend. "What? Bigger than me?"

Tarquin realized he should have kept quiet. Now Jeremiah definitely saw Blood as a challenge he couldn't refuse.

"Nay, lad, we stay. I am not missing being involved in the making of history. Not a bat in hell's chance."

"It's a cat," grumbled Tarquin. "A cat in hell's chance."

CHAPTER 5

SWIMMING THE MOAT

Tarquin jerked awake, struggling to breathe. A greasy, gnarled hand covered his mouth and the barrel of a flintlock pistol dug into his temple. He opened his eyes to find Colonel Blood looking at him, a venomous smile on the man's face.

"Where's the surgeon?" the scoundrel whispered.

Tarquin looked anxiously around the room. Jeremiah was nowhere to be seen. He felt terribly alone. "I don't know."

Colonel Blood pulled Tarquin roughly from the bed and held him tightly as one of his cronies tied the boy's hands behind his back. A moment later Tarquin's legs were kicked out from under him and he landed on the floor with a groan. The crony kicked him hard in the ribs. Tarquin screamed in pain as several bones cracked like matchwood.

Blood crouched down and pulled Tarquin half-upright. "What yer doing here?"

Tarquin gagged as his nostrils filled with Blood's rancid breath. Any sudden movement started a riot of agony from his ribs. He shook his head and got a clout on the ear for his trouble.

"Hmmm, what have we here?" said the fake parson, ripping the gold cricket-bat medallion from around Tarquin's neck.

"Please, no, that's mine," the boy wheezed.

The two men laughed as Blood pocketed the treasure.

"What is your friend playing at?" asked Blood.

"I don't know—" replied Tarquin.

A thwack of flintlock on forehead sent him reeling back, his head bouncing on the stone floor.

When consciousness returned, Tarquin's head felt as if it had been stuffed with cotton wool and sealed in a plastic bag. The pain there competed for attention with the pain from his ribs. All he wanted to do was curl up in a ball.

Struggling to breathe and to comprehend what was going on, with shapes and sounds seeming to flow all around him, he tried to clear his vision. A blurry mass coalesced until he could recognize it as Blood, looming over him.

Their eyes met and Tarquin felt the knot in his stomach tighten again. The man dropped to his knees next to him and grabbed his jaw.

"You're up to something, I can tell." Blood's voice was full of rage. "You and your fake 'doctor' friend are not going to spoil the plan that I've been working on for months."

He stood up and kicked Tarquin again, this time a sickening blow to his head.

The momentum rolled Tarquin onto his side, where he lay unconscious and bleeding.

The next time Tarquin woke it was to a world of nausea, a feeling not helped by the gag over his mouth. Again, he had no idea how long he'd been out. His head and ribs ached from the beating that Blood had administered. The unhelpful swirl and whine of what sounded like a dozen bagpipes seared through his head as he struggled against the pain to gather his thoughts. He could see blood from his nose and face pooled in a large claret circle on the floor.

Terrified, expecting at any moment another kicking, he quickly scanned the room for the "parson" and his accomplice. Mercifully, they'd gone.

Trying to control his panic, he squirmed to the bed, his hands still tied behind his back. Somehow he managed to lever himself up, his eyes never leaving the door in case Blood returned. Panting heavily, with the throbbing pain of someone constantly turning a knife in his ribs, he looked to the ceiling and a flood of tears erupted, washing across his bruised cheeks and nose, stinging the open wounds. His mind filled with questions he could not answer.

How had their adventure gone so badly wrong? Why had Jeremiah left him to the mercy of Blood and his thug? Had he not warned Jeremiah they should leave?

Tarquin felt incredibly alone, and badly betrayed. Jeremiah was not coming back. He was too busy with his dreams of wrestling glory.

A walk down memory lane for him—death for me, thought Tarquin, venting his spleen at Jeremiah. Worse still, Blood had stolen his cherished cricket-bat pendant—his prize possession, the last thing given to him by his father.

Anger, fear and guilt consumed him, but these emotions provided strength and a distraction from the agony. Jeremiah was who knew where. Wythe was only just recovering from his injuries. It was up to Tarquin to warn the guardhouse, to put history back on the right track, and, by any means possible, to recover his pendant along the way.

Gritting his teeth, he realized he had one big advantage. He knew Blood's plan from his history studies at school.

Sweat dripping from his brow, he hauled himself towards the fireplace.

The metal of the grill was roughly forged and, in places, quite sharp. Pressing the ropes binding his wrists against the edge of the metal, he slowly worked his hands up and down.

At first nothing seemed to be happening, but then the outer fibres of the rope began to tear.

After what felt like a lifetime, the rope finally gave way.

Tarquin ripped off his gag and vomited, long and forcefully. With his cracked ribs, the retching was painful and exhausting, but after it stopped and he could catch his breath, he felt a lot better than he had—although he was now desperately thirsty. Wiping his mouth, he looked around the room in search of water.

The morning sun reached the window and flooded the room with light, making him cringe. Rising unsteadily to his feet, he saw two pools of yellow liquid and wax on the floor and silently cursed. His gloop! How was he going to communicate his message to the guards without it?

Seeing a flagon on the table, Tarquin grabbed it and drank deeply, not caring that much of the water flowed down his chest and onto the floor.

Drawing in breath in deep gasps, he went to the window and surveyed the barracks below. He must get downstairs and raise the alarm.

Then his heart sank. A man in tatty clothing—surely one of Blood's cronies—was lurking in the shadow of the Tower doorway.

Blood must already be in the Martin Tower, he thought. Where can Jeremiah be?

He had to find another way out. He went to the window at the back of the room. From there he could see open ground and then the outer wall, with the moat below. If he could get to the wall he could maybe raise the alarm from there.

Carefully easing his knapsack onto his back—if anyone saw it, they'd wonder what it was, but he'd deal with that problem when he got to it—Tarquin put on his periwig and picked up a poker from the fireplace. The pain in his ribcage flared up. He was going to have to move slowly.

Poker in hand, he headed downstairs to the back door and opened it as quietly as he could. There was no sign of Blood's men.

Tarquin crept across the open ground, hoping to find a guard, anyone he could try to tell about the treachery that was in progress. The language barrier was another problem that he'd solve when he got to it.

More bad news. Now that he was closer to them he could see that the buildings towards which he was staggering were only abandoned stores. There was no one about. That was why Blood's men hadn't bothered patrolling the area.

He reached the nearest building and pushed open its door. The indescribable stench of London sewage filled his nostrils, making his stomach lurch. Doubling over, he retched once more, losing much of the precious water he'd drunk. When the heaving stopped he leaned on the wall to catch his breath.

Directly across from him was an open window that led to the moat and the source of the awful stink.

Tarquin bent over and rested his hands on his knees. He needed a minute to compose himself and think things through.

The only way to avoid Blood and his men and raise the alarm was to swim around the moat to the front of the Tower. He knew this; he just didn't want to know it. He hated swimming. Come to that, he hated sewage. But, faced with the option of being caught, it was the only course open to him. In his present condition, swimming was going to be agonizing if not impossible, but he had to give it a try.

And then, looking from the window, he discovered that at long last there was a piece of luck that was going his way.

Moored against the far bank of the moat was a small boat.

How could he get to it? He remembered using pyjama trousers to earn a bronze lifesaving badge at school. What you did was you tied the ends of the pyjama legs in a knot and buttoned up the front. Trapping air in the pants, you gripped the waistband and put the air-filled legs around your neck. This allowed you to float without the need to keep treading water. If it worked then, it should work now. And he had a spare pair of trousers in his knapsack!

Leaving the window, Tarquin walked along the wall of the empty building, looking for a door that would give him access to the moat. After being sick so often, and still in pain from his beating, he had to lean against the stone for support as he shuffled along.

A continuous line of rats scurried down the wall, like shoppers rushing for bargains at the January sales, and disappeared around a barrel in the distance. As he reached the barrel, Tarquin could see the rats squeezing through the rusting grill of a storm drain. It wasn't a door, but it might serve as one.

He scattered the rats with his poker, knelt on the floor, and looked through the grill. The sight and smell that greeted him made him close his eyes and take a deep breath; then he wished he'd done without the deep breath. A potpourri of raw sewage, dead animals and seventeenth-century garbage undulated slowly from right to left, driven by the tidal River Thames. In the distance he could see the boat moored against the far bank of the moat.

All he had to do was break the grill, squeeze through the gap, swim fifty metres or so to the boat, and paddle his way to the Tower front. Simple, really, if it weren't for his broken ribs, his cut and bruised face, his rampant nausea, his fear and exhaustion …

Taking a moment or two to gather what little strength he had, Tarquin braced himself against the wall and gave the grill a hefty kick.

The rusted metal collapsed and splashed loudly into the moat. He closed his eyes and slumped back, listening intently for any indication that Blood's men had heard him. Thankfully, only the chirping of a family of birds and the sloshing of the water disturbed the silence.

Armed with the poker, clutching his knapsack to his chest, Tarquin got on the floor and squeezed through the hole where the grill had been.

He found himself sitting precariously on a damp and decaying ledge a few metres above the filthy moat. Peering over his knees as far as he felt was safe, Tarquin watched the foul water slop against the Tower wall like mulligatawny soup. Mindful he could fall at any moment, he prepared his "life-vest". Trapping air inside the trouser legs, he held them around his neck like a make-shift parachute.

A dead dog drifted past him in the water below.

I have to do it, he thought.

Swallowing back his nausea, and with his stomach seemingly somewhere between his chest and mouth, he waited for a gap in the sewage and dropped into the water.

A cold and wet darkness enveloped him as he sank below the water, the weight of his clothes, poker and knapsack pulling him down. But the air trapped in his spare trousers took him back to the surface, where he bobbed in the water like a fisherman's float. With a cry of revulsion, he spat out a mouthful of foul-tasting water and watched his periwig float away on the current like some alien seaweed. Cursing steadily, he held the trousers tight about his neck and frog-kicked towards the boat, pushing past a rotting sheep.

After a while the pain in his ribs became too great and he lost his grip on the trousers, slipping under the surface. The cold, swirling water numbed his arms, legs and brain, creeping remorselessly into his bones.

In a blind panic, he kicked hard and, after what seemed forever, he surfaced for just long enough to seize the trousers and fill his lungs with air. It was only a moment, and then his head was back under the water again.

This time, when he kicked, his momentum was enough to take him close to the boat. Whooping with exhaustion, he grabbed at a rope dangling in the water and pulled himself the rest of the way to the boat.

Hanging limply at the boat's side, Tarquin sobbed and gulped in clean air. No way was he going to be able to climb in. He was going to have to use the boat as a float as he swam to the Tower gate.

He pushed his knapsack, poker and trousers into the boat and worked his way around to the stern. The mooring rope was loose; one tug and it fell into the water.

Tarquin peered around the side of the boat at the water and garbage ahead of him. He would head towards Legge Mount and the Devereux Tower, then turn left.

At least this route goes through clearer water, he thought, kicking off.

Rounding Legge Mount and the Devereux Tower, the boat picked up a bit of speed as it drifted in the current towards Bywater Bridge and the Middle Tower. If he could just hang on, the route was straight and, Tarquin figured, any guards on the bridge must see him and raise the alarm.

As it neared the bridge, however, the boat shuddered to a halt. Here the moat was heavily clogged with submerged debris, carcasses and fallen branches. The little craft was wedged tight, and no amount of rocking would break it free. On the bridge, in the distance, he could see guards walking up and down.

If only I could get closer to them!

Using what few reserves of strength he had left, he pulled himself partway out of the water so he could see into the boat and find his trousers. He would have to leave his knapsack behind.

Dropping back into the putrid moat, and with his makeshift life-vest once more secure around his neck, he let go of the boat and pushed himself forward through the filth.

Eventually he reached clearer water again, and could float along with the ebbing current towards the bridge. He was moving quickly now.

As he went under the bridge he tried to yell but there was no strength in his voice; his cries were certainly not loud enough for the guards above to hear him.

Ahead, the moat water flowed into the Thames. The increasingly strong current was pulling him away from the moat wall.

Fighting his way back as best he could, he found a series of eddies and calmer water. Keeping to the moat wall, he drifted slowly around the corner toward St Thomas's Tower and Traitors' Gate, where he knew there was a guardhouse.

I'm going to make it! I'm going to make it!

But, just as the gate's steps came into view, his foot snagged on something and he was pulled beneath the surface. In his fright he let go of the trouser waistband and the poker.

Tarquin battled desperately against the current, trying to free himself. Floundering, he gulped in mouthfuls of foul, thick, soupy water. Finding strength in his terror, he kicked wildly one last time.

It was enough!

He broke free, surging forward and crashing against a set of stone steps.

Tarquin screamed from this latest agony but clung like a limpet to the stone.

Despite the swell trying to suck him back into the moat, he managed to claw his way up a step or two and, straining for breath, grip a rusting spike he found there. Each returning swell of water threw him against the steps. The excruciating pain in his ribs made it impossible to haul himself out of danger, and the sucking rise and fall of the water drained his remaining energies yet further.

Then came a rogue swell. It broke his grip and plucked him away from the steps. Flailing haplessly in the water, like autumn flotsam carried on the whim of a fast-moving current, Tarquin knew he was about to drown. He felt no fear, just the urge to relax, close his eyes and slip beneath the water forever.

Then the same tide that had snatched him from safety swirled upward and back, like a cobra ready to strike, and spat him halfway up the steps—and out of danger.

Tarquin vomited what seemed like an entire moat's worth of foul water, then curled into a ball. Drained and exhausted, he drifted into unconsciousness.

He awoke cold and feverish, the sunlight stabbing relentlessly at his eyes. He tried to unfurl himself, but his legs and arms were leaden and unresponsive. He looked up the flight of stone stairs and counted ten to the top. Just ten steps! You can do that!

Steeling himself, he put all his weight onto his legs and, with the aid of one hand, pulled and scrabbled his way up the slippery steps; with his other hand he tried to protect his ribs. Several times he lost his footing and slid painfully back. Each despairing breath drove a hot knife through his chest.

"I can't, I can't make it!" wailed Tarquin aloud, gazing up at what seemed a mountain he still had to climb. Only five steps now from the top, but he had nothing more to give. The sun, for so long in his eyes, disappeared, casting him into shadow. For several minutes he was lost entirely to despair.

And then he heard what sounded like muddled words of English, spoken in a strange accent. Two burly arms hooked under his, and pulled him up the remaining steps.

Hanging helplessly limp, his head spinning, Tarquin briefly blacked out again.

When he recovered he found himself being dragged across cobblestones, his legs bouncing and dancing on the uneven surface like a giraffe walking on ice.

The guards who'd been half-carrying him stopped. Tarquin blearily raised his head. He was at the entrance to the Bloody Tower!

"The jewels, the jewels, they're being stolen!" he croaked. The guards didn't answer. "Colonel Blood is stealing the Crown Jewels!"

The party started moving again and Tarquin was hauled for what seemed ages until he was unceremoniously dropped to the ground.

Groaning, he rolled onto his back to ease the pain in his ribs. His upside-down view showed an open door ahead of him. A burly sergeant-at-arms came through it to speak to the two men standing over him. Without his language gloop, Tarquin recognized only the occasional word: "spy", "traitor".

This didn't sound promising.

Despite the pain, he hauled himself up into a sitting position, which he held with all the uncertainty of a baby trying it for the first time. He pointed toward the Martin Tower, and looked despairingly at the sergeant.

"Please, the jewels," he said, coughing up blood. "Please, the Crown Jewels." Tarquin tapped his head. "The crown, they're stealing it."

The sergeant looked at him and spoke. This time Tarquin was able to make out what the man was saying, even though the words seemed grotesquely twisted, as if someone were trying to strangle them. "It sounds like English, but I don't understand the accent," the man said.

Tarquin desperately drew a circle around his head with a finger.

"The crown, it's being stolen."

"Can he mean the Crown Jewels?" said one of the guards, looking towards the Martin Tower.

Tarquin nodded twice, and then his strength finally gave way. His arm dropped to his side and he slowly keeled over. As the sound of boots running on cobblestones clamoured into the distance, Tarquin's only clear thought, spread-eagled on his back, was how wonderfully blue the sky was.

On an inconsequential planet named Khufu, in a galaxy a billion light years from the Milky Way, Berbitedge Sludge sat in front of his three-metre Vissy Viz screen, holding a Vissy Viz dinner, a pail of Vissy Viz ale and a mountain of Vissy Viz cellulose. Entertainment conglomerates across Khufu constantly scanned the galaxies looking for alien civilizations to laugh at. A probe from one such conglomerate had chanced upon a little planet known to those on Khufu only as E0o/j5 (but known to us as Earth). For two Earth-years the probe from Khufu had been sending back recordings of all manner of events. Now, across time and space, Vissy Viz channels fell over themselves to package and broadcast the thousands of hours of Earth history descending like snowflakes on Sludge's planet.

Friday night on the Human History Channel was the night for his favourite programme. Sludge leaned to one side on his seat, passed wind, and hit the channel selector before belching his satisfaction.

"Welcome viewers," said the presenter, Dorky Dewis, flashing a toothy grin. "Tonight we have a special bout all the way from"—he paused for effect; Dorky always paused for effect—"E0o/j5 year 1671, in little ole England!"

The presenter ran his tendrils through the white tuft of coarse fur on his otherwise bald dome and pointed one of his six hands at the screen behind him. "This is an epic, one-on-one, no-holds-barred contest!"

Sludge's head bobbled from side to side in excitement and his five fleshy chins wobbled in agreement like a chorus of sycophantic terrestrial politicians. He settled back in his shell, scooped up a huge mouthful of ale and gargled loudly, before swallowing, twice. E0o/j5 History World of Sport, and especially its Fight Night segment, presented by the colourful Dewis, was surely the best show on TV. Sludge's five concubines thought him mad to watch aliens grapple but, as a soon-to-be father of twenty or thirty Rinchkats—depending on the currents and prevailing wind—he reckoned Friday night was his time to chill.

On Sludge's screen, someone was on the ground floor of a tower, whacking a large golden ringed object with an iron club. Others, close by, were cramming golden balls and sticks down their trousers.

"Let's go over to the Tower of London," said Dewis with an oily chuckle. "Kent, what do you see?"

"Interesting question, Dorky." Kent always started with the same, unimaginative observation.

Jeremiah waited excitedly at the rear of the Martin Tower. He listened as Blood and his relatives worked inside the jewel room. Suddenly, a loud commotion came from the courtyard in front of the Tower, followed by musket fire. From inside the jewel room came the sound of running footsteps, growing louder.

When Blood appeared in the doorway, Jeremiah stepped out and, singing, "Figaro qua, Figaro la", smashed his forearm into the colonel's face, sending the would-be thief recoiling backwards against the Tower wall.

Blood's cronies, not wanting to get involved in a fist-fight with a man-mountain, raced back into the Tower. As Blood stood panting against the wall, the St Edward's crown, half-hidden within his tunic, tumbled to the floor.

"You bastard, you're no surgeon," growled the colonel, wiping blood from his split lip. With an abrupt movement he drew a pistol from beneath his tunic and levelled it at Jeremiah.

Bang!

The force of the shot knocked the air from Jeremiah's lungs and sent him staggering. He wobbled on legs suddenly gone rubbery, gawping at the torn material on his chest. Then he slowly looked up at Blood and smiled. "Your shot don't seem to have hurt me."

He launched again into The Barber of Seville.

"Figaro la, Figaro su, Figaro gi."

Jeremiah circled his arms above him like a wind turbine caught in a hurricane.

"Bravo Figaro, bravo bravissimo, ah, bravo Figaro!"

Colonel Blood stood transfixed, confused by the fact that his target was apparently unhampered by the shot.

Jeremiah lunged forward and gripped the colonel in a headlock. Though surprised by the ex-wrestler's speed, Blood deftly twisted from the hold.

"You'll not take me!" he shouted, head-butting his foe and kicking his legs from under him.

Jeremiah fell to the ground with a sickening thud. Jumping on the fallen man's back, Blood put his hands around Jeremiah's neck and pulled the lock-keeper's head backwards.

Groaning, Jeremiah went limp.

With the sweet taste of victory in his mouth, Blood eased his hold … and then Jeremiah struck. Shifting his weight to one side, he unbalanced Blood enough to turn him and push him to the floor. In a flash, their positions were reversed.

Placing his not insignificant weight on Blood's back, Jeremiah whispered in his ear, "You've just been siloed."

It was time for Jeremiah to return to centre stage of the La Scala Opera House—in his mind, at least. With an almighty "La la la la la la la, Figaro!" and one hand firmly around Blood's neck, the other gripping the man's arms, Jeremiah began the last, triumphant verse.

As his rendition was coming to an end, a company of yeomen from the barracks appeared, followed quickly by the sergeant-at-arms and his guards. Four guards rushed into the Martin Tower and quickly overpowered Blood's cowering accomplices. Outside, the sergeant-at-arms and the guard stood applauding as Jeremiah rose to his feet, bowed and stepped back, gesturing towards Blood, now groaning on the floor.

"Here's your thieving Parson Blood—or should I call him Colonel Blood!"

"A lowly parson, eh?" said the sergeant-at-arms, puffing out his chest and prodding Blood with his sword. "Good morning, Colonel. Your traitor's breakfast awaits you."

Guards hauled Blood to his feet and took him and his cronies away.

A beaming Jeremiah, chest thrust forward and nose in the air, followed the guards through the courtyard towards the Martin Tower. He was about to take his leave of the soldiers and go to wake Tarquin when he overheard the sergeant talk of a boy swimming the moat and raising the alarm.

Jeremiah grabbed the sergeant by the shoulder. "What happened? Where's the boy you speak of?"

"We left him on a bed in the guardhouse," said the surprised sergeant.

"He looked at death's door to me," muttered a soldier standing close by.

"No!" cried Jeremiah, lumbering headlong towards the Bloody Tower.

"He's upstairs," shouted the soldier, "but he'll be dead by now."

Jeremiah ran as if his life depended on it, two guards in his wake. He reached the White Tower and stopped, gasping for breath. He leaned against the wall for several seconds, and then worked himself around the tower. As he trudged towards the guardhouse, four soldiers ran out, muskets at the ready. Luckily the two guards who'd followed Jeremiah vouched for him, and the trio was allowed to pass.

Jeremiah reached the guardroom door and collapsed, dragging in air. The two guards helped him to his feet.

His leaden feet dragging, Jeremiah found the stairs and pulled himself up, relying on the banister for support. On the first floor he searched all the rooms until he saw Tarquin lying pale and motionless on a bunk.

"Oh, no, no!" the big man howled.

Slamming the door shut, he secured it with a chair-back under the handle before sinking to his knees, groaning.

"I've killed him," he moaned. Tears ran down his cheeks.

He pulled himself to his feet and moved to the bed, staring at Tarquin's gaunt, sallow face with its open but lifeless, unseeing eyes. He fell across the bed and began weeping uncontrollably.

He didn't know how long he cried. Time didn't seem to matter now. His stupidity had killed his young friend. If only he hadn't left their lodgings early. He should have realized that Blood and his relatives would come looking for them.

At long last Jeremiah sat up. He gazed forlornly at his friend, hoping Tarquin might wake, yawn and smile.

But Tarquin remained deathly still.

Rising from the bed, Jeremiah took the chair from the door, sat down and rubbed his bald head. Tarquin, the key to so many questions, was dead. How would he explain this to Jules and Great-Aunt Polidori? Jeremiah thought back to his first meeting with Tarquin two years before. He had seen many boys time-jump, over the years, but this one was special. Jeremiah had jumped with Tarquin's father, so he knew what he was talking about. Time travel was in the Jenkinses' blood.

His selfish desire to test himself against the Irishman Blood on history's centre stage had destroyed his young friend. Tarquin's death was down to the ego of the one man who was supposed to be looking after him.

A soft purring noise emanated from his breast pocket. His medical kit! The device must have been vibrating for some time, as the box was warm against his skin.

He took out the oblong box and shuddered with remembered fear. For a moment back there he'd thought he was a goner. Embedded in the box was the round lead ball that Blood had fired at him.

Jeremiah prised open the box and carefully inspected the damage.

"Jumping Johanas!" he shouted, rising to his feet and punching the air. He shook with excitement, "Oh yes, yes!"

Inside the box, a long pen-like instrument flashed and buzzed. Jeremiah lifted it carefully from the box but it fell apart in his hands, landing in several sections on the floor.

"No, no!" Jeremiah cried disbelievingly, falling to the ground and scrabbling for the pieces.

"How long has he been like this?"

Jeremiah spun round and fell against the bed, rubbing his eyes.

"I said—"

"I heard you, Doc." Jeremiah could hear the quaver in his own voice. He stared wide-eyed at a hologram that had appeared in the room—a hologram of a smiling, silver-haired doctor wearing a white coat and with a stethoscope around his neck.

"You're in hypovalemic shock. You need to rest," the doctor reassured the shaken lock-keeper.

"It's not me that needs help, it's me friend," said Jeremiah, pointing to Tarquin's unmoving body.

The doctor looked at Tarquin, and his smile disappeared. "I can see from your face that you have great affection for this boy." The Doctor came to the bed and began carefully examining Tarquin's body.

"Yes," said Jeremiah with a tear in his eye. "Seebee treats me special."

"It shows. Now, how long has he been like this?"

Jeremiah's face creased like sun-dried leather. "I ... I ... I don't really know."

"He has the remotest of chances, but only if I know how long he's been in this state."

Jeremiah threw open the door and ran down the stairs. Two minutes later he charged back into the room, beet-red and once more gasping for breath, "Hour and a half, give or take five minutes," he wheezed.

The doctor nodded. Taking a small oval object covered in buttons from his coat pocket, he leaned over Tarquin and ran an eerie blue light the length of the boy's body.

Meanwhile Jeremiah knelt by the bed, cradling one of Tarquin's cold hands in his giant paws. "I want you back, Seebee," he whispered. "I've no idea what you've got ahead of you, but I'll be damned if it be a coffin."

The doctor continued to move the light methodically back and forth all over Tarquin, pushed buttons in various combinations, and examined the readings, his every movement watched intently by Jeremiah.

Eventually the flickering figure stood up, patting his brow with a blue handkerchief. He sneezed loudly.

"What's up, Doc?" asked Jeremiah.

"I've caught a virus, nothing to worry about." The doctor shimmered, then coughed. His head went sideways, fizzed loudly and descended to the floor before springing back up and attaching itself to his chest.

"Okay, Doc, you're frightening me," said Jeremiah, getting up and walking warily away from the hologram.

"It's not a problem," insisted the doctor. He pulled a large metal pipe from his coat and thumped himself hard under the chin. This time his head rippled, grew large, then slowly glided back to its rightful place on top of his shoulders. "Now, that's better."

"What next, Doc?" asked Jeremiah, rubbing his head to make sense of what he'd just seen.

"It's tricky." The doctor's expression made Jeremiah feel ill. "But he may have a chance."

The hologram moved closer to Jeremiah and looked at him sternly. "You must follow my instructions"—the doctor's face flickered again—"and you must do this very carefully."

There was a major outbreak of static, obliterating most of the instructions the holographic doctor was trying to impart.

"Er, I missed that, Doc."

"Take the metal syringe with the long thin needle from your kit and, on the base, dial in 31. You need to put the needle into the boy's heart. After precisely 23 seconds, press the green button, then the blue, then the red."

The medic stared at Jeremiah for a few long moments then asked, "Do you believe in a god?"

"That's a peculiar question coming from a hologram," said Jeremiah nervously.

The doctor smiled. "Well, if you do, now's the time to talk to him." The hologram fizzed again, "Don't forget to—" Once more the hologram wobbled.

"What Doc, what?"

The doctor reappeared. His smile had gone, and he looked very serious. "Periods of high anxiety, nightmarish flashbacks." He shook his head. "And heightened senses—"

With a final disconcerting flicker the hologram disappeared.

"Doc! Doc!" Jeremiah waved his hands through the empty air where the doctor had stood. "What mustn't I forget?"

Wiping tears from his face, he looked down at Tarquin. He had to do something. He took out his glasses but they fell apart in his hands. Both lenses were cracked. "Nooooooooooo!" he shouted, looking at the twisted metal and glass shards. Shaking his head, he tried desperately to pull himself together.

"There's nought else for it," he said, picking up the syringe. Holding it at arm's length, he tried to focus his eyes and dial in 31 on its base. It was now or never.

Straddling Tarquin's torso, he checked the base one more time and prayed. With a deep breath, he raised the syringe high above his head and plunged the needle through Tarquin's chest and deep into his heart, breaking the wooden bed and sending them both crashing to the floor.

Two hours passed before the bedroom door opened and Jeremiah made his way slowly from the room. Mrs Edwards stood wringing her hands by the guardhouse fire. As Jeremiah thudded down the stairs, his head bowed, she went to meet him.

"You saved my husband's life and my son's, Dr Livingstone," she said, sobbing, her eyes brimming with tears. "Talbot's taken a hell of a beating but when you insisted he put on chain mail you saved his life …"

At the sight of Jeremiah's tear-streaked face, her words trailed away to nothing. Putting her hand gently on his sagging shoulder, she said, "I am so sorry. There is nothing worse than losing family."

Jeremiah couldn't answer; he was numb.

"Come, sit by me, and we can recite a psalm together."

Mrs Edwards helped Jeremiah slump into a chair by the fire, then carried over the guardhouse bible.

The big man's eyes welled up as he stared slack-jawed at the dying embers of the fire.

"He seemed a fine lad—"

"'Seemed'?" said Jeremiah loudly, as if woken from a stupor. "'Seemed'?" he bellowed, rising to his full impressive height and puffing out his barrel chest.

"The lad's swallowed enough water from the Thames to wipe out a small army, and he's delirious with fever." Jeremiah's face creased into a huge smile and his pallid complexion regained its colour. His shoulders grew even straighter, and his eyes glowed. "But he's going to be all right!"

Clenching a giant fist, he waved it at Mrs Edwards. "He's going to be all ruddy right!"

Grabbing the startled woman by the shoulders, he shook her like a rag doll. "Mrs Edwards, I fancy the largest, strongest drink you have in the house!"

Jeremiah pasted a large soppy kiss on her blushing cheek and, with a devilish glint in his eyes, roared "Figaro, Figaro" at the top of his lungs until everything in the room rattled.

Tarquin woke around mid-afternoon the following day. The pain in his ribcage had dulled and his fever had ebbed. He had a raging thirst. Weak and dizzy, he struggled to sit up. Breathing heavily from the effort, he rested against the bed's wooden headboard and looked about the room. A myriad of different-coloured strings floated, pulsing and undulating before him.

"Cool!" he whispered, extending his arms and feeling the strings wrap around his arms and hands, entangling him. Talbot's wife sat in a chair at the end of his bed, snoring loudly.

Without warning, the strings disappeared, to be replaced by a sharp pain in his chest. He felt a strange lump over his heart, and saw Colonel Blood ripping his gold cricket bat from around his neck. He felt alone and desolate as he gazed towards the window. Blood's face leered back at him.

Tarquin jumped. The face disappeared. His heart was pounding as if it wanted to leap out of his chest.

Is Jeremiah dead? He had to leave immediately and find his time-travelling chair. Dozens of faces filled the room, and he sank back against the headboard. Flash-backs from the previous day came to him, one after the other. He vividly remembered swimming in the moat and almost drowning. He should be dead. He looked at the snoring woman and wondered how she had got there.

"Excuse me, excuse me! Old woman, overweight, big fat woman! Hello!!" he shouted, staring boggle-eyed at Mrs Edwards.

Woken from her slumber, she gaped at the boy in the bed. His hair was on end, his eyes blinked rapidly, and he waved his arms above his head. Screaming, she toppled backwards, landing on the floor like a heavy padded cushion.

"Sorry," said Tarquin, as if coming out of a dream. "I'm not sure what came over me. I didn't mean to startle you. Is my uncle alive?" he asked, dreading the answer.

"Holy Mother of God!" Mrs Edwards cried, unfurling her legs from the chair and scrambling backwards towards the door. "He's awake!"

Signing the cross, she got up and recited a prayer as she rushed from the room and down the stairs. Voices rose up from below, then the sound of familiar, heavy footsteps pounded the staircase.

"Tarquin!" shouted Jeremiah, rounding the door and opening his arms to hug the boy. "Let's get you the language helper! Poor Mrs Edwards thinks you're pos-sessed!"

Tarquin was so happy to see his bear-sized friend that he hardly noticed the pain in his ribs from Jeremiah's embrace.

Working quickly, Jeremiah filled and plugged Tarquin's ears just before Mrs Edwards reappeared with the sergeant.

"Good morning, madam," said Tarquin, sitting up in bed.

Mrs Edwards shook her head and poked her ears with her fingers as the ser-geant cast a questioning eye over her.

"Oh," she said, eyeing Tarquin suspiciously before turning to her husband. "Best I prepare some lunch for you menfolk." She took another piercing look at Tarquin, who simply grinned and winked at her. Once again, she bustled from the room, the sergeant following her down the stairs.

Jeremiah closed the door and stood against it. "I am so proud of you, Seebee."

But Jeremiah's euphoria quickly evaporated when he saw the wrath in Tarquin's stare.

The boy crossed his arms and, tears stinging his eyes, shook his head in anger. "You left me to Blood!" Shaking uncontrollably, he wrung his pale hands. "I should be dead. I warned you it was dangerous but, oh no, Mr "Head Full of Muscle" Hay-Maker wanted to wrestle, to make history."

Jeremiah's face looked like a slow-motion car crash. Coming to the bed, he stood silently by Tarquin. His shoulders slowly sagged and he bowed his head. "I am so, so, sorry …"

Tarquin didn't answer, just let the apology hang unwanted in the air.

It was too much for Jeremiah. He collapsed onto the bed and hid his head in his hands, sobbing. "I knows I nearly got you killed, Seebee. It's all my fault. I don't blames you if you never speak to me again … I ruddy well deserves it."

Tarquin's adam's apple stuck in his throat. He looked at his broken, dispirited hulk of a friend and cried out, "Thank God you're alive, you old goat!"

He stretched out his arms, choking back tears. "Come here!"

Jeremiah's frame seemed to grow as Tarquin hugged him.

"Don't you ever, ever, leave me alone again."

"Never will, Seebee, never will."

They clung to each other like two delirious, disbelieving survivors of a terrible disaster. Jeremiah lifted Tarquin's head tenderly from his shoulder and looked into his dark eyes. "I have something for you. I found this on Blood."

He took a chain from his pocket and held up a small golden cricket bat.

At about six that evening, Jeremiah poked his head around the door of Tarquin's room. He was clutching a hairpiece.

"We've got to meet with the sergeant. Come down when you're able. Talbot's kindly given you one of his periwigs."

He threw the hairpiece on the bed and trundled down the stairs again.

With his flashbacks losing their intensity and frequency, Tarquin felt a lot better. Still unsteady on his feet, he dressed and went cautiously down the stairs, the small black periwig perched precariously on his head. He didn't get far before he was met by a barrage of cheers from the Tower guards and carried, gently, down the remaining stairs to a hero's welcome. After much back-slapping—thankfully not Tarquin's back—the Tower's sergeant-at-arms stepped forward.

"Master Clint, good news travels fast, especially around here." He smirked at his colleagues. "His Majesty the King commands that you and Dr Livingstone call on him at his London residence. The King wants to meet the heroes who saved the Crown Jewels."

Jeremiah's jaw dropped. "King … King Charles?" he mumbled. "He wants to meet us?"

"Yes, King Charles the Second," said the Sergeant, looking about the room before stepping forward and raising an eyebrow. "The first one lost his mind and then his head," he whispered with a wry smile.

Back on the planet Khufu, in a galaxy a billion light years from the Milky Way, Berbitedge Sludge bounced up and down on his shell, hollering and waving his six arms and forest of tendrils at the slow-motion replay of Jeremiah "siloing" Colonel Blood on his screen. Grappling humans had that effect on him.

CHAPTER 6

ALL THE KING'S MEN

Tarquin and Jeremiah set off with a military escort to the London residence of the King of England. After a pleasant walk, the escort stopped and shouldered arms. A burly man in his early forties, wearing the uniform of an officer, walked in their direction through an avenue of trees. The leader of the escort stepped forwards and greeted the officer, who smiled and turned to Tarquin and Jeremiah.

"Good morning, gentlemen. We've been expecting you." He offered his hand to Jeremiah and then to Tarquin. "Don't often get to meet real heroes. I'm Captain James T. Kirk of the Coldstream Regiment of Foot Guards. Please, follow me."

As they followed, Tarquin whispered to Jeremiah, "James T. Kirk! He's got to be kidding."

Jeremiah shot him a cold stare that said, Behave, Seebee.

On nearing the palace, Tarquin saw in the distance a group frolicking on the grass. "Ruddy hell, it's the King of Bling and his New WAG Model Army!" he exclaimed, recognizing Charles II sitting on a barrelhorse, cavorting with his courtiers in the sun on the rolling lawns of the Palace of Westminster.

"Begging your pardon, sir," interjected an officious and solemn voice from behind some bushes.

Captain Kirk halted the guard. Tarquin and Jeremiah could see a courtier with a face from a Hogarth cartoon staring at them from the foliage. The man raised a hand to his mouth and coughed gently before striding towards them.

"Alexander De Bosworth, at your service."

The man bowed elaborately, then, with the practised air of someone who relishes cutting people down to size, continued, "I know you are not from here"—he looked them up and down—"but the New Model Army were Parliamentarians, not Royalists. And those"—he pointed his cane in the direction of the king—"four-legged creatures"—his intonation rose along with his crevice-riddled nose until he craned so far back that he almost toppled over—"are most certainly spaniels. Not WAGs, or whatever you called them."

"Wives and girl friends," said Tarquin. "It's an acronym."

Alexander covered his mouth with a silk handkerchief.

"What me cousin meant is, that's the King of Swing," said Jeremiah, nodding toward the revellers, now wielding mallets, "See!"

They looked at the king, dressed in a silk jacket, breeches and a lace shirt and dripping with jewellery. He rode his barrelhorse as the mallet-waving courtiers danced around him, a drunken, bohemian circus troupe of preening men and plump women, wearing a smorgasbord of absurd European fashions.

They wouldn't look out of place in a nineteen-eighties pop video, thought Tarquin.

He turned to De Bosworth. "Sorry. It was spaniels I meant."

They watched the troupe clamour for the king's attention, throwing themselves in front of his barrelhorse and charging after each other like March hares.

"Anything to educate our country folk," said De Bosworth, clearing his throat and looking down his nose at Tarquin, before turning on the balls of his feet and striding towards the king in a cloud of French perfume.

Captain Kirk shook his head, said something under his breath, and signalled the escort away from the lawns towards a two-storey building, half a kilometre away, with a company of soldiers standing outside it. He marched briskly until he reached the structure, accepting several salutes along the way, then took Tarquin and Jeremiah inside and up the stairs to a main reception room on the first floor.

"This is where we plan our protection of the royal household. It's our command post," he said.

Tarquin pulled nervously at Talbot's ill-fitting periwig, trying to remember who England had been at war with in 1671.

Jeremiah was less circumspect. "Expecting trouble?" He was watching from the window as lines of marching soldiers did military drills in the yard below.

Kirk threw his hat on the table, signalled them to sit down and poured some wine. "Ever since the Royal Charles was taken we've been watching our borders and rivers."

"Charles kidnapped?" exclaimed Tarquin.

"Not really," said the officer, scratching his head. "The Dutch never asked for a ransom and, if truth be told, we weren't that bothered."

"Oh," was all that a stunned Tarquin could reply.

Kirk tapped his nose and winked. "Things are not what they seem, my lad."

"You can say that again," muttered Tarquin under his breath.

"Come, look at this." Kirk put his arm around Tarquin's shoulder as he walked the pair over to a large window. "Recognize him?"

Tarquin and Jeremiah shot each other a quizzical glance before looking across the lawn towards the revellers. The king whacked a wooden ball the size of a small football with his mallet and fell backwards off his horse. This was the cue for the menagerie of fawning women, men and dogs to join him in a fleshy mass of fuss, pander and fur.

"But that's King Charles the Second!" said Tarquin, pointing out the window, even more confused.

"He's a bloody menace, that's who he is," said Kirk.

Jeremiah's jaw dropped. "That's treason, isn't it?"

Kirk's tanned, weatherbeaten face creased like a worn leather sofa as he laughed. "Technically, yes," he replied.

Tarquin saw the glint in the man's eyes.

"But," Kirk continued, "technically that's not the King of England."

"Clearly not, if the Dutch have him," said Tarquin.

It was Kirk's turn to look bemused. "No, the Dutch don't have him. However, they do have the Royal Charles warship, stolen four years ago. Don't you know your history, lad?"

Finally realizing what he had seen, Tarquin looked out the window and sighed, "Of course. Body doubles." He turned to Jeremiah. "Like Kim Jong-un."

"Someone's a wrong'un?" said Kirk.

Tarquin felt the captain's steely eyes bore into him and his eureka moment evaporated. "No, I didn't mean—"

Kirk downed his wine and continued watching Tarquin closely. "Hm. We may have an opening for you. Out there, we have the best one we've found so far. But, frankly, the way he's behaving, he won't see tomorrow."

Tarquin's face turned white and he tugged hard at his periwig. "Really, I am not—"

"Only kidding," said Kirk, clapping his hands. Then with a grin he went on, "We have another one prepared. Besides, you don't look anything like the real king."

Tarquin tried to laugh but managed only an embarrassed squeak.

"I shouldn't be telling you this but, as you put your lives on the line for the king's interest, I think it's safe. We have word of a Dutch assassination plot against Charles. My regiment is tasked with special protection until we learn more." The captain moved to where a leather-bound book lay open on a writing desk by the window.

"Please, if you would be kind enough to sign your names in the—"

"Captain's log," said Tarquin, enjoying the puzzled look on Kirk's face.

"You're a strange one, Master Clint. You appear unaware that captains' logs are on ships. This is our regimental visitors' book."

"Of course. Sorry," said Tarquin. "Silly me."

He accepted the proffered quill and rolled it in his hand, not sure what to do.

"Allow me." Kirk took the quill back, dipped it in a nearby inkwell and recited their names as he wrote them in the book. "There, all done. Form and function, I'm afraid."

Tarquin was intrigued by the regimental crest and the Latin inscription on the front page of the visitors' book. "The regimental motto is not 'To boldly go where no man has gone before', by any chance?" he said, smiling inanely at the captain.

"Careful, Seebee. Enough's enough," whispered Jeremiah, trying not to move his lips.

"No," said Kirk, looking at Tarquin in puzzlement. "No, our motto is 'Second to none'. Are you feeling ill, Master Clint? Your eyes look very large."

"Couldn't be better!" said Tarquin.

Shrugging his shoulders, the captain continued, "Right, then, time we were off. You have an audience with the real king."

Kirk grabbed his coat, sword and hat and led the the two visitors to the court-yard, barking orders to his men. Eight soldiers hastily formed a double line outside the building and served as escort as Kirk led the way towards the main palace gates. Security was extremely tight, with armed men at every twist and turn.

The captain took at least another dozen salutes before they finally entered the royal palace. Once they were inside, a guard snapped to attention and saluted Kirk before guiding the party to a square anteroom where two soldiers guarded the French windows opposite.

"His Majesty will not be long," said Kirk.

Sure enough, the French windows soon opened to frame, in profile, a tall, elegant man dressed in blue silks and lace with piercing black eyes and an angular, hooked nose. The king paused for a second before striding into the room, followed by two private secretaries. He planted his cane in a slow, measured and authoritative manner. Kirk had taken off his hat and gone down on one knee as soon as the door opened. Seeing this, Tarquin and Jeremiah followed suit.

"Dr Livingstone, I presume." The deep timbre of Charles's voice resonated in the small room.

Jeremiah looked up and kissed the hand the king offered him.

"Arise, my grappling bear, you are no good to me or England down there."

The secretaries tittered politely. Jeremiah rose to his full, impressive height and bowed. Turning to Tarquin, the king once more offered his hand. "And you, Master Clint, a swimmer of some skill and a prolific drinker of my moat water, I am told."

This time the secretaries laughed more heartily.

"You can stand up, Master Clint. No one's going to hurt you here."

"Thank you, your Majesty," said Tarquin, getting to his feet with some difficulty. His broken ribs sent flares of agony through him, but he hid the pain as best he could.

The king's gaze flicked between Tarquin and Jeremiah before coming to rest on Kirk. "Perhaps, Captain, I should have my life guards swim it regularly."

Kirk nodded his approval of the king's suggestion. Before the secretaries could fawn any further, the king raised a hand to silence them. Turning to Tarquin again, he pointed at him with his cane. "And what do you think, Master Clint?"

"Of course, your Majesty, swimming is very healthy."

The king smiled and waved his cane in the general direction of one of the secretaries. The man stepped forward with an exquisite presentation box, opened it, and bowed.

Charles took something from the box and, turning to Tarquin, raised it above his head.

"To show my gratitude for saving my Crown Jewels, I present you with this greyhound medallion, once owned by my father."

Tarquin bowed and the king slipped the silver-chained decoration over the boy's neck.

Addressing Jeremiah, who was beaming with pride, the king said, "Now, Dr Livingstone, though I am indebted to you for fighting the Irish traitor, it would have been easier if you had simply shot the rogue." He looked at Jeremiah and smiled. "Come, man, do you not agree?"

Jeremiah gaped in awe. "Well, yes, yes, of course, your Majesty."

The king clicked his fingers and a secretary moved to his side with a second box, inlaid with ivory and jet and much larger than the other one.

"Trust me, don't sully your hands on the next brigand who attacks you. Just cut them down with these."

Charles opened the box and presented Jeremiah with a set of engraved duelling pistols. "Double-barrelled," the king noted. "Just in case."

"Thank you, your Majesty." Jeremiah bowed, face red.

"Gentlemen, your king and country salute you."

Realizing they were about to be knighted, Tarquin went down on bended knee and Jeremiah quickly did likewise.

The king removed his sword from its sheath and gently rested the blade on each of their shoulders in turn.

"Arise, Sir David and Sir Clint," said the king, smiling. "Good day, gentlemen, and enjoy your stay with my wretched, bawdy double." With a flourish, he replaced his sword. The French windows opened. Beyond them, a dozen soldiers lined the exit route. Charles strode from the room, followed by his kowtowing secretaries. In a moment they were gone, leaving the two time-travellers alone with Kirk once more.

Tarquin and Jeremiah were still trying to make sense of what had just happened to them when Kirk leaned forward. "Now, sirs, to continue the deception, I invite you to spend the afternoon with our other king!"

Escorted by Kirk and his guard, Tarquin and Jeremiah retraced their steps back out onto the lawn.

"Gentlemen, I must take my leave, but you will be well looked after. It was a pleasure meeting you both."

The captain saluted and was about to leave when Tarquin stopped him. "Captain, one last question if I may. Your middle name, it's not Tiberius, is it?"

Kirk laughed. "You are a strange lad indeed. No, it's Tremaine. James Tremaine Kirk."

With that he shook his head and marched the guard back to the command post.

"What the hell you doing, Seebee, asking that?" asked Jeremiah angrily.

"You weren't even a little bit curious?"

"Maybe, but that's not the point—" Jeremiah stopped abruptly. "What's wrong with your eyes?"

"Nothing. Everything's fine," Tarquin replied, shielding them from Jeremiah. "Must be the sun."

Jeremiah gave him a stern look. "Okay, but tell me if they starts troubling you. Remember, you were nearly killed yesterday!"

"How could I forget?"

"Anyways," said Jeremiah, remembering what he was trying to say, "these are dangerous times, what with the king's body snatchers and all."

"You mean 'body doubles'," said Tarquin, grinning broadly.

"You knows what I means. Come on, the idiot's waving at us."

A hundred metres away, the king's double had fallen off his barrelhorse and was waving at them. Reluctantly, the new knights of the realm waved back and went to join him.

After rearranging the fake king's wig and clothing, several footmen guided his boots into the stirrups and pushed him back onto the saddle of the toy horse. Digging his heels into the horse's wooden flanks, the king swung his mallet madly above his head and bellowed, "Tally ho!"

At this signal, six burly footmen picked up the horse and carried it at a canter towards Tarquin and Jeremiah. The fake king's entourage followed behind, skipping gaily, with a pack of spaniels snapping at their heels.

"Jolly good of you to make it!" roared the impersonator as he approached them, kicking the front two footmen into a gallop. "You'll stay for afternoon tea, won't you?"

Tarquin and Jeremiah bowed their acceptance. Tarquin suddenly thought of his father's description of a stuffy Buckingham Palace Garden Party with Queen Elizabeth II. The myriad of colourful images that flew around his head made him giggle. He felt Jeremiah's elbow in his side, and took a deep breath.

"I'm okay," he said quietly from the side of his mouth. "I can handle this, but stop hitting me in the ribs. It hurts so much I can hardly breathe!"

The fake king and his bearers stopped in front of them. The breathless footmen put down the wooden horse, with its supposedly royal jockey, and sank to their knees.

"Damn fine fillies, what!" said the impersonator, chortling as he ogled the female members of his camarilla. "I like a jolly good run of paille maille in the afternoon, builds an appetite for games."

Tarquin saw the man's eyes fix on one particular doe-eyed courtesan. "By gad, she's a goer!" said the pseudo-king, twirling his moustache and snorting like a stuck pig. "Rumpy, come and meet my new friends."

He turned and looked at Jeremiah through bleary eyes. With an extravagant shudder, he cried, "God, you're a brute, Doctor Big Bum!" Turning his gaze towards Tarquin, he continued, "And you must be the feisty accomplice I have heard about, Short Shanks."

Tarquin saw Jeremiah bristle at his nickname, and gently squeezed his arm. "Steady, Big Bum. Remember, he's a fake—and a poor one at that."

The last thing Tarquin wanted was Jeremiah to go down in history as the only Englishman knighted and beheaded on the same day.

Thankfully, the fake king's butterfly attention had already been drawn elsewhere. "Up and at 'em!" he cried, pointing his mallet at a gaggle of female courtiers.

With little enthusiasm, the weary footmen lifted the horse and shuffled off towards the giggling women. Embarrassed, Jeremiah and Tarquin stood watching, unsure what to do next.

A richly dressed woman strode up to them, laughing. "Oh, don't you be worrying about him. He gives everyone nicknames. We're his angels, he tells us— Charlie's Angels!" She curtsied. "I'm called Nell, Nell Gwyn, though I also answer to Rumpy as you'll have heard." She wiggled her bottom suggestively and pointed at the other women. "He's off playing with his latest favourites now. According to him, that's Squintabella, Pumpy, Mole, Rash and the twins Night and Day."

Jeremiah scratched his head under his periwig and shot Tarquin a look of horror. "You're not to listen to such drivel, cousin. That Nell be a very naughty girl."

In the distance the fake king yawned drunkenly and clicked his fingers. Taking a fresh glass of claret from a footman, he raised it high above his head and yelled, "Enough! To the palace! We do the medicine, then we paaaarty!"

The ensemble made its way to the building where Tarquin and Jeremiah had been knighted earlier, walking between the guards who flanked the path. Once inside, the group walked through gilded halls to the main billiards room, where the women dutifully lined up and stood before the stand-in king, hands outstretched. Last to arrive was the impersonator himself, who'd been carried through the building on his barrelhorse. He signalled to his bearers and they set it down. Smiling, he straightened his hat and dismounted. He took a leather pouch from one of the attending footman. "Afternoon, Angels!" he bellowed.

"Afternoon, Charlie!" chorused the ladies of his court.

Walking along the line, the royal stand-in poked and prodded the giggling women before pouring a small quantity of seeds into each pair of cupped hands.

Jeremiah persuaded one of the "angels" to give him some of the seeds. After a moment's examination, he turned to Tarquin. "Heath pea, Lathyrus linifolius. Taking it stops them from eating, keeps the weight down. Not very successful!" he whispered.

Tarquin grinned, "Charlie's Angels do Weight Watchers! That would make a good film!"

He winced as Jeremiah's elbow struck again.

With today's dose of peas dished out, and satisfied with the state of his harem, the fake Charles waved his hands in the air and yelled, "Party, party, paaaaarty!"

Musicians filled the room and began playing the latest melodies. The court descended into a hedonistic orgy of drink and carousing. Feeling very self-conscious, Tarquin moved quickly to the side of the room and, finding an empty chair, sat down. Jeremiah joined him, clutching his box of pistols.

"I am really not amused, even if he is a blithering idiot," said Tarquin, watching the impersonator drool over several women. "Surely they must know he's not the real thing?"

"Emperor's new sofa," said Jeremiah, nodding sagely.

"What do you mean?" asked Tarquin.

"What would you rather do, Seebee—go along with the deception or be thought a traitor and get your head chopped off for treason?"

Tarquin smiled, "It's the Emperor's new clothes."

A woman sat down next to Tarquin. "Want to play with me cuddlies?" she asked, in a heavy French accent. All too obviously, this was Squintabella.

Tarquin squirmed and stood up, trying to avert his eyes from her décolletage. Despite his best efforts, all he could see were two plates of his Aunt Mira's warm blancmange. He didn't know where to look.

"No, no, thank you, madam. Not now."

He turned his back and sat down again. The woman pouted and moved to sit next to Jeremiah, making the same offer and getting similar results. With a stamp of her foot, she cursed loudly in French and stormed off.

Nell, seeing the exchange, caught up with Squintabella and pulled her to a halt. A heated argument in French ensued. Their eyes blazed at each other. Their bosoms heaving in eloquent support, before Squintabella finally blinked, cursed loudly again and, with her nose in the air and a dramatic swirl of her dress, strode off.

Nell shook her head and turned to give Tarquin a warm smile. She walked over and sat in the place recently vacated by Squintabella. "I saw you watching me."

Tarquin looked at his feet.

"You're betrothed to someone, aren't you, Master Short Shanks?"

He turned and looked at her, red-faced. "Madam, I am only fifteen! How could I be betrothed?"

"Let's talk," she said.

Reluctantly, Tarquin nodded.

"You liking anyone in your town, Master Short Shanks?"

He gave a tortured sigh and looked away again. He felt a tap on his fingers and turned to look straight into Nell's kindly face.

"I'm not leaving until you speak to me," she said, gently covering his hand with hers.

"No," he said, frowning. "I haven't met anyone I like." He couldn't believe he was sharing his personal life with Nell Gwyn, surely the best-known of the king's mistresses. He had read about her colourful life in library books. To think she had once sold oranges and lemons for sixpence outside London theatres to survive, and now she lived at court with the King of England and could have anything she wanted!

"You're a fine catch, Master Short Shanks. There'll be someone for you someday, mark my words." She patted his knee, kissed him on the cheek and returned to the fray.

Tarquin finally looked up just as two girls smiled coyly at him from across the room. He turned despairingly to Jeremiah. "Please, can we go? I am so not into this sort of thing."

"Nor me, Seebee, nor me. Ingeborg would kill me if she knew I'd spent the evening with Nell Gwyn and all them other women!" Tarquin saw the look of stunned shock on Jeremiah's face. "I means, in a manner of speaking."

"Come on," said Tarquin. "Let's slip out the back while the idiot's occupied."

They stopped at the door to give the racy scene one last look. Just then a footman appeared beside them, bowing from the waist.

Am I ever going to get home? thought Tarquin.

The footman straightened up. "The Duke of Buckingham has requested you meet him in his quarters. He has a few questions for you." He showed them the way with a hand.

Tarquin looked at Jeremiah, who winced and nodded. "Best do as he says, Seebee. It gives us an excuse to leave."

"From the frying pan into the fire," mumbled Tarquin disconsolately.

The footman led them to a waiting carriage. They were helped on board and sat down. Alongside the carriage walked four soldiers. There was no escape. Tarquin thought of Wen Cheng, his Tibetan princess. Thankfully, the journey to Hampton Court was short.

The Duke of Buckingham, a nasty, cunning man but one with the ear of the king, sat languishing on the Coronation Throne as if he owned it. Around him were members of his and the king's cabal: Sir Thomas Clifford, Lord Arlington, Lord Ashley and Lord Lauderdale.

Seeing Tarquin and Jeremiah arrive, Buckingham rose regally from the throne and walked down the steps.

A footman belatedly announced their arrival.

"Dr David Livingstone." Jeremiah fell on one knee as Buckingham offered his hand for the big man to kiss. "And you must be Clint of Eastwood." Tarquin likewise knelt and bowed, resenting the pain it caused him.

"Arise, both of you."

Buckingham turned to Tarquin. "Well, young lad, the sergeant-at-arms tells me you were very brave in raising the alarm at the Tower."

"Thank you."

"I believe the king marked his gratitude with a gift?" continued the duke.

Tarquin removed the silver greyhound medallion from around his neck and showed it.

"Do you know what it is?" asked Buckingham.

Tarquin turned the greyhound over in his hand.

"It's a medallion shaped like a silver greyhound, probably given to a King's Messenger," said Tarquin, remembering his visit to the Foreign Office in London with his dad and the guided tour of the offices at King Charles Street.

Buckingham raised a quizzical eyebrow and a murmur passed around the room. "Pray continue, Master Clint. And what purpose does it serve?"

"The greyhound symbolizes that the owner is a trusted messenger of the king. Trusted, because the greyhounds, used as handles on a hunting bowl owned by the king, were broken off and given to the messengers."

The duke had been peering earnestly at Tarquin during this explanation. Now his face turned dark. "Only a few people know of what you speak, and they died in the Civil War."

Tarquin winced and swallowed hard. His knowledge and love of history had got him into trouble again, but this wasn't an irked college teacher. He blinked rapidly as an image of his head spiked and dripping blood on London Bridge rampaged through his mind.

"How do you know of such things, Master Clint?"

Thinking quickly, Tarquin replied, "My cousin from Hapsburg, Baron, ah, Baron Arnold von Schwarzenegger, he told me the tale of the greyhound!"

An awkward silence followed, as Buckingham and the rest of the cabal stared at Tarquin.

Then a smile broke across Buckingham's face, and he turned to Jeremiah. "And, as for you, the king's dancing bear," he said with a sickly grin. "A surgeon, I believe?"

Jeremiah nodded silently.

"The King's Ball takes place tomorrow evening. I have added you to my guest list. I expect to see you both there, you and Master Clint."

Buckingham's smile disappeared as quickly as it had arrived, and his eyes turned cold. Tarquin felt them drive into his very soul. "We will discuss this cousin of yours, this Baron Arnold von Schwarzenegger."

Tarquin and Jeremiah bowed their thanks and, given a dismissive wave by Buckingham, were ushered from the throne room and into the corridor.

Once they were on their own, Tarquin sighed, relieved the inquisition was over.

"What were that all about, Seebee?" said Jeremiah.

"A mistake." Tarquin shrugged. "A big mistake."

Jeremiah looked disappointed. "You've not been right since swimming in that moat. You told him something historical, that you couldn't possibly know, didn't you?"

Tarquin grimaced. "Yes. And now he probably thinks we're spies."

The pair quickly made for the open door.

"Master Clint, a moment please."

Tarquin froze. They hadn't heard or seen Lord Ashley striding towards them.

"Master Clint, I am intrigued to hear of your cousin, Baron Arnold von Schwarzenegger. I fear I don't know the man. Who is he?"

Tarquin, dumbstruck, stared at Jeremiah, his eyes pleading for help.

"Er … He's …" Tarquin's mind went blank. His heart rate soared. The blood pounded in his ears like kettledrums. "He's—" Visions from the Terminator movies and The Expendables coursed through his head.

"You haven't heard of Baron Arnie "I'll Be Back" Schwarzenegger?" said Jeremiah, coming to the rescue. "The greatest pugilist this side of the Thames?" As if to reinforce the point, Jeremiah shadowboxed in front of Ashley—two jabs, and a sweeping right uppercut.

Ashley looked surprised. "A baron's a bare-knuckle fighter? Comes to something when a bare-knuckle-fighting baron knows more about the affairs of state than the country's ministers!"

"He's a Hapsburg baron," offered Tarquin.

Ashley shook his head. "We'll talk tomorrow at the ball about your prizefighting relative."

The aristocrat turned and left them.

Tarquin watched Ashley walk away along the corridor. "We really must get out of London."

Jeremiah shook his head. "Can't. Wormhole's not opening for another day."

"What can we do?"

Jeremiah took Tarquin's arm and walked him along the corridor, scanning for the nearest exit. Once they were out of earshot of any guards or soldiers he spoke. "I've an idea. An old friend of mine lives here in London. He'll help us."

Persuading the sergeant-at-arms on the door that their lodgings were close by and that they didn't need an escort, Jeremiah and Tarquin set off for the streets of central London.

CHAPTER 7

AN EVENING WITH FRIENDS

Their night walk was cool, dry and quiet, a pleasant change after the fuss of the royal party and the sinister confrontations with Buckingham and Ashley. Jeremiah checked a small pocket compass and led Tarquin down several cobbled streets before finally finding his bearings and turning into a street called Seething Lane.

"Not far now. Just need to find the Admiralty offices," he said.

Two hundred metres later and he stopped to rap hard on a blue front door. The door opened and a servant looked up at the big man.

"I would like to speak with your master, Mr Pepys," said Jeremiah.

The servant bowed and disappeared. A minute later, a round, ebullient face, framed resplendently with a shoulder-length black periwig, appeared in the doorway.

The puzzled expression turned to a smile. "Well I never, Jeremiah Cavendish! What a wonderful surprise! How on God's earth are you?"

"Samuel, it's good to see you. This is me nephew, Tarquin Jenkins." Jeremiah pushed Tarquin forward.

"Welcome to my humble abode, Master Jenkins," said Samuel, shaking their hands. "Come in."

He ushered them down a corridor, explaining over his shoulder as he went, "I have a few guests around for a late supper and the wife's retired early. We have plenty to eat and drink, so why not join us?"

Jeremiah and Tarquin had not eaten all day and were grateful for the offer. They passed an open door and Tarquin saw a room full of books, all stacked up against a wall.

"Your coats, sirs," said the servant.

Their coats and Jeremiah's gun case safely stowed away, Samuel turned to Jeremiah. "And to what do I owe this unexpected pleasure?"

"We's up in London for a visit, and we's getting a bit late, so me thought I might impose on your kindness and see if you knows of lodgings nearby."

The wily lock-keeper got the reply he wanted.

"Lodgings? I'll hear nothing of it. You will stay the night with us. On one condition—that you regale my guests with one of your amazing stories." Samuel winked at Tarquin before continuing, "Also, my guests need a lesson in your peculiar fighting technique. You can stay as long as befits your purpose."

Tarquin looked at Jeremiah and raised an eyebrow. The big man merely followed Samuel into a smoke-filled back room where several guests sat around a table laden with food, flagons of cider and bottles of wine. The large hearth in the wall held a warming fire.

"Friends," said Samuel, "let me introduce Jeremiah Cavendish, an old friend from the south coast, and his nephew, Master Tarquin."

Jeremiah and Tarquin looked at the faces in the room and bowed.

"Jeremiah, may I introduce Mr Christopher Wren, Mr John Evelyn and Mr Isaac Newton, who I believe you met the last time you visited?"

Jeremiah nodded.

"We've just returned from a late sitting at the Royal Society and are about to eat," Samuel explained.

Tarquin looked quizzically at Jeremiah. As they took their seats, the big man whispered in Tarquin's ear, "It's a society of science and maths nerds who meet and bore each other silly."

"I know what the Royal Society is!" exclaimed Tarquin, looking at the people seated around the table.

Christopher Wren was the architect who designed St Paul's Cathedral, used for all manner of royal events, including weddings and Princess Diana's funeral.

Across from the famous architect, wearing a dour, hangdog expression, sat Isaac Newton, still decades away from his knighthood. Tarquin shuddered. By chance, he had watched a recent visiting lecturer at his college talk about Isaac Newton's personal life, and his vile temper. Knowing Tarquin had to write a paper on the man, Jeremiah had told him a very colourful story about "Neutron Bomb" Newton and Jeremiah's one meeting with him, stuck under a tree in an orchard, sheltering from a violent squall. As Jeremiah's version of the meeting went, he and Newton sat cowering as half a dozen apples bounced off Isaac's head, each one being met with a tirade of colourful expletives and, after the last apple had hit him, a rain dance that would have made a New York break dancer sit up and take notice. Tarquin wouldn't dare mention apples tonight!

Next to Newton sat John Evelyn. Tarquin knew little about Evelyn except that he studied trees, wrote many books and kept a diary, just as Pepys did.

Tarquin began blinking rapidly as a vision flooded his mind of their four heads—like the heads at the Mount Rushmore Memorial but cackling and laughing and pale not grey—leering at him from out of the white cliffs of Dover. He covered his eyes, hoping no one had seen his discomfort.

"Your visit is fortuitous," said Samuel to Jeremiah. "Isaac had a nasty run in with a footpad yesterday. The use of your Leaky Sump fighting technique would have done wonders."

"Ecky Thump … It's known as Ecky Thump," said Jeremiah.

Tarquin's ears pricked up. He had never heard Jeremiah mention any kind of fighting other than wrestling before.

"Well, we'll have a lesson in Ecky Thump after you've had some supper. We're all a bit hungry after tonight's debate."

The smells of food and the warmth from the fire were overwhelming Tarquin. He swallowed hard as a bead of sweat ran down his cheek.

Ever the mindful host, Pepys leaned forward. "Master Jenkins, is there something wrong? Perhaps a glass of medicinal claret would help?"

Jeremiah put his hand on the young lad's thigh. "Keep it together, Seebee."

"Thank you, Mr Pepys," replied Tarquin. "A glass might help settle my stomach. It has been a long and stressful journey."

Sipping his drink, he sat back in his chair and listened intently to the witty and high-level conversation. However, when Newton started talking about astronomy, Tarquin's least favourite subject at school, his empty stomach took over and he looked longingly at the food on the table. Pepys could see Tarquin wanting to eat, and signalled him to help himself.

Tarquin cut three doorstop-size slices out of a loaf of bread. A couple of slabs from a round of cheese joined them. He assaulted a joint of ham with similar ruthlessness, and added some pickles. He was so preoccupied with creating his favourite after-college meal, a triple-decker club sandwich, that he didn't notice the conversation petering out. With a surgeon's precision, he squared the bread, cut the sandwich in two, lifted one half to his mouth and stopped, suddenly aware that all eyes were on him.

"Master Jenkins, what is that?" asked Wren, pointing to the oblong wad of bread, meat and cheese in Tarquin's hand.

"It's a club sand—"

Tarquin hesitated, mouth agape, looking at the gathering. It dawned on him that to say "sandwich'" would mean he'd need to explain the link to a still-to-be-born earl or, worse still, find an elaborate correlation between the words "club", "sand" and "witches". Not a healthy predicament to find oneself in in the morbidly religious seventeenth century, surrounded by some of the cleverest men in London.

"It's a … a … Homer Simpson, named after the baker in my home village," he said quickly.

The next half-hour provided surreal viewing for Jeremiah and Tarquin. Newton, Evelyn and Wren competed to create their own elaborate Homer Simpsons on the dining table while Pepys sketched the extraordinary scene. Jeremiah sat shaking his head at Tarquin and tutting quietly. For his part, Tarquin devoured his own Homer Simpson and began crunching on assorted pickles.

Not satisfied with Tarquin's three slices, the guests built their Homers into towering columns of interlocking food until, with one slice of bread too many, Newton's overbalanced, collapsed into Evelyn's and felled them both, sending food everywhere. Seeing the demise of his colleagues' stacks, Wren rose triumphantly from his chair and, standing proudly next to his edible monolith, his tankard held on high, pontificated about his superior building technique. However, his crowing was short-lived. A well directed onion collapsed his structure, bringing hearty roars from around the table.

"You broke my St Paul's!" shouted Wren.

Newton shook a finger and laughed. "No, no, Christopher. If that foreign fellow, Gottfried Leibniz had his way, you'd believe the onion decided, through its infinite wisdom, to jump sideways and hit your Homer Simpson. Me, I say it was mere gravity that pulled it down!"

Roars of laughter filled the room, and the celebrated gathering tucked into the debris of their architectural masterpieces. After several jugs of mum, mead and wine, they finished the food (of which Jeremiah enjoyed the lion's share), and Pepys invited Jeremiah to explain his fighting technique.

For the next hour, Tarquin sat back and watched in awe and some merriment as Jeremiah led the Royal Society quartet in an Ecky Thump self-defence master class, hurling them, albeit gently, about the room. After being thrown to the floor for the umpteenth time, Wren grabbed a black pudding from the table and playfully whacked Jeremiah over the head. This was the catalyst for a jovial but fearsome food fight.

Pepys, wiping tears of laughter from his eyes, called for some order just as Tarquin was slapping John Evelyn forcefully about the face with a dried haddock.

"Please!" Pepys cried, raising his arms in the air. "I think it's time, gentlemen, for another round of drinks!"

Bludgeoned into submission with bread, fish, black pudding, meat and cheese, they all readily agreed.

The candles were growing inexorably shorter. Pepys busied himself filling his guests' tankards, then took the opportunity to remind Jeremiah that he owed them a story. The big man didn't disappoint, ending the evening with a tale about large metal objects travelling on thin lines of steel through tunnels between England and France.

That night Tarquin lay awake in yet another strange bed. Though he was exhausted, and still feeling the occasional agonizing twinge from his ribs, his mind was stuck in overdrive.

Something wasn't right. He rolled the cricket-bat pendant in his fingers. He was possessed by one thought.

What if our arrival in 1671 wasn't a coincidence? Could it be that visiting Samuel Pepys's house was something planned? If so, who planned it? Certainly not Jeremiah! Both Pepys and Jeremiah said they had met before …

Tarquin's thoughts turned to the vast piles of books he'd seen in Pepys's front room.

If over others you would leap, then in a book you must seek.

The words on his pendant inexplicably appeared on the bedroom wall. Even if he closed his eyes he could still see the inscription. When his father had given him the cricket bat, the words hadn't made much sense to Tarquin. Later, after talking with Jeremiah on the narrowboat about time travel, he thought they must be a reference to Mrs Beeton's works. Now, as he opened his eyes and imagined the piles of books from the room downstairs rising up through his bedroom floor, he wasn't so sure.

Then, as suddenly as they had appeared, the books were gone and he fell into a deep sleep.

The next morning, Jeremiah and Tarquin rose early. Not wanting to disturb their host and his wife, they sat reading in the front room. Jeremiah leafed through a collection of papers while Tarquin surveyed the piles of books he'd seen the previous evening, stacked against the wall. As he stood pondering what to do, a servant came into the room and prepared the fire. Not long afterwards Tarquin could hear the master of the house coming down the stairs.

Wandering into the room, Samuel Pepys saw Tarquin looking at the piles of books. "Are you a scholar, Master Jenkins?"

"No … I am at school, studying for my …" He looked to Jeremiah for support.

"Apprenticeship," said Jeremiah quickly. "Tarquin's going to be a master-carver. While we're up in London we're hoping to get him an apprenticeship at the naval dockyard."

"Excellent idea," said Pepys, going to the fire and stoking it. "If you need me to help, just let me know. And feel free to look through my collection while I talk with your uncle."

Tarquin turned back to the books and shook his head.

"Thank you, but you really need some bookcases, Mr Pepys."

Samuel looked at him quizzically.

"What are … bookcases?"

"Well, if you have a pen and paper I can draw you a picture." Tarquin ignored Jeremiah's signals that he should stop showing off.

Samuel passed a sheet of paper, an ink-pot and a quill to Tarquin, who carefully drew a rectangular box lined with six horizontal pieces of wood.

"You have enough books to fill several of these, and they'd each be as high as the ceiling."

Samuel gazed at the drawing, listening intently.

"You put the books on the shelves, in alphabetical order," said Tarquin, adding book-shapes to the shelves. "Some people even put doors here on the front to keep dust off."

"What an excellent idea, Master Tarquin! I'll have the navy carpenters look into it." Pepys folded the drawing and placed it in a drawer. "Now, Jeremiah, I am in the mood to be regaled with a story of derring-do over a breakfast of bloaters. Mrs Pepys has just started preparing them and wants to see you again. Would you care to join us, Master Jenkins? Or will looking through my book collection satisfy you for now?"

Tarquin could see his chance for an undisturbed investigation of Pepys's library. "No, thank you, Mr Pepys. I'll skip breakfast and look at your books—with your permission, of course."

Pepys nodded and led Jeremiah from the room.

Tarquin had worked his way down two piles of books and was at the foot of a third when he found a large leather pouch. He pulled it free. Though the pouch was badly charred, Tarquin managed to open it and take out a sheaf of handwritten papers, two books and a small journal bound in tooled leather. He put the papers, books and pouch on the table and scrutinized the journal.

Is this what I've been looking for?

He turned it over in his hands. Bound in purple and dark-green leather, it was covered in ornate diagrams on both front and back. A lead seal had once secured it, but this was broken and the book opened easily. He flicked through the pages of diagrams, and marvelled at the strange illustrations and elegant script in an alphabet he didn't recognize. He knew it wasn't cyrillic, as his father had owned dozens of Russian books. Tarquin thought it might be Georgian or Arabic, two other languages known to his father, but, as he examined it further, he came to doubt this.

He was so engrossed in the mysterious journal that he didn't hear Pepys return.

"Zut alors! I'd all but forgotten about my pouch!"

Tarquin jumped and dropped the journal.

"So sorry, Master Jenkins. I didn't mean to startle you." Pepys walked over to the table.

"I'm fine, Mr Pepys. I'd just found the pouch and was admiring this." Tarquin picked up the journal and handed it to his host.

Pepys saw the sheaf of papers on the desk. "What a charlatan that so-called literary agent Dunstable Slop was!" He picked up the papers and waved them like an incensed Member of Parliament trying to attract the Speaker's attention. "Promised to read my work and get back to me within a month. Never did hear from the wretched fellow again."

He rolled the papers into a tube and thrust them at Tarquin as if armed with a sword. "Though I often saw him imparting his wisdom to poor, gullible fellows in coffee shops around Spitalfields." The cutting and thrusting of Pepys's sword of papers made Tarquin take a step back. "When I confronted him, he had the bloody cheek to deny he'd received my work and, confound the man, he asked me to send it again!"

Tarquin moved to the safety of the other side of the desk as his host flicked and flourished the papers as if dismembering poor Mr Slop. Eventually, breathing heavily from his morning exertions, Pepys slowed to a stop. He sat down in what was evidently his favourite chair and started to thumb through the papers. Talking more to himself than to Tarquin, he slowly filled in the gaps regarding the unfortunate Mr Slop, finishing with the sad news that "Slop and his business were consumed in the Great Fire."

Tarquin saw that re-reading the papers had raised Samuel's mood. As the diarist leaned forward in the chair, seemingly ready to impart some nugget of wisdom, his black periwig swung back and forth like the ears of an aged bloodhound.

"You know, it seems only yesterday that your uncle and his friend Winston were here, the day before the Great Fire started."

"Winston?" Tarquin cried, looking hard at the man.

"Er, yes, that was his name. I remember the morning of the fire well. Your uncle, Winston and I set off through the London streets looking for Slop's office. I always thought it odd how Winston awoke that morning in a panic, as if he knew the whole of London was about to burn!" Pepys shook his head. "Anyway, we found Slop's house ablaze. Winston dashed inside. He found my pouch and those books and that journal on Slop's table, and rescued them. Never met the fellow Winston before, but damn' glad he visited with your uncle. He saved my diary!" Pepys looked heavenward again. "I never did find the owners of the books and journal. No one I showed it to understood the language or the meaning of the pictures. And then there's this …" Pepys took the journal and turned to the first page. "Strange, very strange …" His voice trailed off.

"What is it, Mr Pepys?" said Tarquin.

"Well, I have often wondered about these. They're the only things in it I can read!" Pepys laughed as he passed the journal back to Tarquin. In black ink, written on the reverse of the first page, were two letters and a series of numbers. T010300J

Tarquin's jaw dropped.

"Everything all right Master Jenkins? You look as though you've seen a ghost! If it's that charlatan Slop, give him a good roughing from me." Pepys sat back in his chair and guffawed loudly.

Those are my initials and my date of birth! This must be the book the inscription on my gold cricket bat refers to!

"I'm fine, thank you." Tarquin gathered himself together quickly. "It was just that I suddenly remembered something I should have done but didn't."

He smiled weakly at Pepys, who was pouring himself a large glass of claret.

Wine for breakfast? No wonder he had gout! thought Tarquin, grimacing. Turning back to the journal, he traced the numbers softly with his little finger, thinking about his father. He had to have this book!

"May I borrow the journal?" He found himself trembling for fear the reply would be negative.

"Well, Master Jenkins, though I like the cover, the insides do leave me feeling frustrated. Little use in my library if I can't read it!" Still laughing loudly, Pepys drained his glass. "Any chance your uncle might know someone who could decipher it?"

"Jeremiah's great friend… His great friend…" Tarquin's mind clawed desperately for a name to throw at Pepys. He was looking around the room for inspiration when Jeremiah walked in.

"Jeremiah," said Pepys, "remember that journal Winston found in the Great Fire last time you visited? Your nephew says you have a friend who might be able to read it?"

"Professor … Professor Pat … Pat Pending!" exclaimed Tarquin. "He'll be able to translate it!"

"Pat Pending?" stammered Jeremiah, picking the remains of a bloater from his moustache.

"You know, your great friend, the village scientist." Tarquin looked pleadingly at Jeremiah, wishing the big man would catch on and back him up. "Thin man, flash of red hair, white coat and drives a—" He stopped in mid-sentence. Cars didn't exist in the seventeenth century! He coughed loudly and continued, "Drives a horse and cart. Looks at the sky a lot."

Jeremiah gawped blankly, his knowledge of the cartoon series Wacky Races not as encyclopaedic as Tarquin's.

"Great, that's done then!" said Tarquin loudly, stretching out his hand for the journal.

Pepys turned it over in his hands, as if reconsidering the idea of lending it. "I haven't heard of this Professor Pending," he said, turning the pages, "but, if you say he might be able to decipher it, you can have it. It was never mine in the first place."

The deal done, Tarquin hurriedly pocketed the journal before Pepys could change his mind.

Jeremiah stood by the door, still looking bemused. "Well, nephew, if you're ready, we best be off. Got to see a man about a dog."

"Yes, the dog, of course, the dog. We must be off," agreed Tarquin.

Armed with two good-sized packed lunches, made by Mrs Pepys, Jeremiah and Tarquin bade their goodbyes and left the diarist slightly confused and one book down in his library.

As they walked in the early morning sunshine towards the end of Seething Lane, Tarquin turned to Jeremiah.

"My father was here, wasn't he?"

"Yes. Yes, he was."

"Why didn't you tell me?"

"I was going to, but things got out of hand."

"You came with him when he visited Pepys and the Fire of London. Why were you trying to get back here?"

Jeremiah stopped abruptly, removed his hat and wig and rubbed his scalp.

"It's complicated." He looked seriously at Tarquin. "You best explain that whole journal thing to me later. For now, we have to get home and I fears it won't be easy, what with all that's been going on this trip."

Tarquin's stomach flipped. In the excitement of finding the book, he'd forgotten about the Royal Ball, slimy Buckingham and the story of Baron Arnie.

They walked quickly through the early morning fog, trying not to attract the attention of the many people going about their daily business. Every now and then they'd hear a shout from a high window and have to avoid the contents of a chamber pot, splashing on the cobblestones. Taking care to hide what he was doing, Jeremiah turned on his time-travelling chair's homing beacon. Using the beacon as their guide, an hour later they found themselves on the rutted road near where Wythe Talbot had been injured. When they came to the abandoned house, they slipped silently inside and moved quickly upstairs.

Jeremiah opened the door to the upper bedroom.

And froze in the doorway.

Lounging on Jeremiah's ejector seat was Lord Buckingham.

The duke looked up and gave a cruel smile. "Dr Livingstone and the boy wonder! What a lovely morning!" He flourished his hands. "Meet my friends."

Soldiers of the king's bodyguard arrived on the landing behind Jeremiah and Tarquin, blocking their escape.

"So these are the spies!" said a tall man, coming out of the shadows to stand next to Buckingham.

"Bring them in!" the duke ordered.

Jeremiah and Tarquin were pushed into the room. Tarquin winced as he spotted the twisted remnants of his time-travelling dentist's chair scattered about the floor.

Buckingham smiled again. "Parlez-vous français, Monsieur Clint?"

Tarquin gulped.

"You don't speak French? Viscount Grandison here tells me you had quite a conversation with Louise de Keroualle at the King's party."

Buckingham didn't wait for Tarquin to answer but signalled to the soldiers. Three men took away Jeremiah's pistol box and dragged him in front of the duke. Another soldier grabbed Tarquin's arms and pulled him to the side.

"Now, Dr Livingstone, what do we have here?" Buckingham pointed to the big man's sleeve and nodded. A soldier pulled the coat fabric from Jeremiah's arm to reveal the tattoo of Elvis Presley jiving with his guitar.

"What does that say, Doctor?" sneered Buckingham.

"Elvis, the King," mumbled Jeremiah.

"Hah," shouted Buckingham, "Yet more evidence that you and your nephew are in the pay of the Netherlands!"

"You're talking double-Dutch. Elvis was a ruddy singer!" Jeremiah roared.

"Who ever heard of a troubadour being called Elvis?" shouted Buckingham. "No, it's code for William III of the Netherlands—that's your king!" He pointed his finger to the door and got up from the seat. "Take them to the Tower!"

"No! Wait," pleaded Jeremiah. "I need to speak." He stopped in his tracks despite the efforts of the soldiers to keep him moving.

"Unhand him," commanded Buckingham. "Let's hear what the Dutch rogue has to say."

He sat down once more in the ejector seat and adopted a mocking pose of patient interest.

Jeremiah pulled down his sleeve and, as he did so, deftly took something from his pocket.

Grandison saw the quick movement and instinctively grabbed the big man's hand, making him drop what he was holding.

Tarquin watched in horror as the ejector seat's remote control spun across the floor and stopped by his foot.

"You've got it all wrong," said Jeremiah, rubbing his wrist and glaring at Grandison.

"Enough!" cried Buckingham, sitting back on the seat. "You're just wasting my time. You'll not escape. Clap them in irons. The Tower awaits you both."

"Okay, okay," said Jeremiah unsteadily. "Me and the lad are spies." He bowed his head.

Tarquin couldn't believe what he'd just heard. He looked aghast at Jeremiah, whose eyes were fixed firmly on the remote.

"If you were just to push that red button," Jeremiah murmured in Tarquin's direction.

"What did he say?" asked Buckingham, rising in the seat.

Tarquin managed to surprise his captor and pull free. Diving for the remote, with musket butts raining down on his head and back, he pressed the red button home.

A rush of air blew everyone off their feet.

Buckingham was thrown upward from the ejector seat and caught in a vortex of air spinning around it. The chair itself began to rotate, faster and faster. Buckingham's face mushroomed, turned bright red and, as the spin rate increased yet further, appeared to smear, so that he looked like a tomato in a blender.

Echoing through the abandoned house, his terrified screams tailed off only when he and the ejector seat disappeared in a blast of steam.

Jeremiah was the first to gather his wits. He got to his feet and, seizing two pistols from the unconscious soldiers, levelled them at Grandison, who was just getting to his knees; at the sight of the two barrels the nobleman rolled his eyes and lost consciousness again.

Tarquin clambered to his feet and stood by Jeremiah's side as the lock-keeper turned his sights on the trembling soldiers, now struggling to wakefulness.

"What now?" Tarquin was terrified they might be stuck in 1671.

"Grab me box of pistols. I don't want to lose thems."

Tarquin saw the box lying close by, and picked it up.

"I always have me seat on standby, special-like for emergencies," said Jeremiah, his eyes scanning the fearful guards, looking for any sign of resistance. "Best cover your head, Seebee. That rotten duke's on his way back now."

A soft rustling sound, like a sheaf of papers caught in a breeze, filled the room.

"You best do likewise!" Jeremiah shouted at the bewildered soldiers. Still pointing the pistols at them, he knelt on the floor. Tarquin followed suit, as did the soldiers, their pale faces huddled together.

There was a loud bang and a hiss of escaping air. The guards covered their faces and a couple of them screamed. Poor sods. They must believe they're caught up in the middle of a maelstrom of necromancy! thought Tarquin.

Spinning wildly, the ejector seat materialized in the centre of the room. Buckingham, his head thrown back and his mouth wide open, was slumped unconscious on it.

The spinning slowed and finally the seat came to a standstill.

"Hold onto these." Jeremiah tossed the captured pistols to Tarquin and got to his feet. Clenching his giant fists and giving a low guttural growl, he appeared to grow in size as he walked to his ejector seat. He grabbed Buckingham by the lapels, lifted the limp duke off the seat like a rag doll, and laid him horizontally across his broad wrestler's shoulders.

"Nobody messes with me Elvis!" With a blood-curdling roar, Jeremiah put Buckingham into a wrestling move he had made famous, the Aeroplane Spin.

He body-slammed the duke into the huddle of soldiers.

"Now, Seebee, now's our chance!"

Jeremiah jumped onto the seat, opened the armrest cover and started to run his fingers over the instruments. "Everything looks okay, but you'll need to hang on real tight."

Tarquin looked at Jeremiah and felt queasy, like after eating far too much ice cream.

"You'll have to sit on my lap and carry me pistols."

As Tarquin hastily put the pistols into the box and sat on Jeremiah's lap, one of the soldiers rose unsteadily to his feet.

"Jeremiaho!" shouted Jeremiah, buckling up the harness straps on the seat, and grabbing hold of Tarquin. The chair lit up like a Christmas tree and hummed loudly, but then the lights flickered and dimmed. The sound from the seat stuttered and petered out.

Tarquin saw terror in Jeremiah's eyes and his heart sank.

The two time-travellers looked at each other in disbelieving silence. Around them, the soldiers were slowly getting to their feet. Buckingham was nowhere to be seen, and Grandison remained curled up in a ball, snoring.

A soldier summoned the courage to pick up his sword. "Okay, lads, let the foreigners taste some English steel."

Tentatively, the others collected their weapons and warily surrounded the seat, pointing their blades at its two occupants.

"What are we going to do?" yelled Tarquin.

The soldiers, growing in confidence, moved closer.

"I don't know, Seebee." Jeremiah was frantically pressing every combination of buttons on the remote. "I need me ruddy glasses!"

Without warning, Buckingham came careering bow-legged back into the room. His body was in a state of complete and utter flux, his face a mass of purple and pink blotches, his mouth drooling. The skin of his face hung in overlapping folds like chewed gum. He started running around the room like a bemused baboon, spouting gibberish and pointing in all directions.

Bang!

Jeremiah looked at Tarquin. The soldiers froze.

Bang, bang, wheeeeeeeeeeeee!

The chair began spinning.

Jeremiah grabbed Tarquin and laughed. "We're ruddy moving!"

The soldiers jumped backwards and, when the seat wobbled and rose into the air, dived for cover.

The lights of the seat came on and the spinning got faster.

When Buckingham lurched close enough, Jeremiah booted him hard in the rear, sending him straight out of the window.

Tarquin closed his eyes and thought of apple pie and custard.

CHAPTER 8

THE TOASTER

The ejector seat landed back in Ricketty Field as planned, but as it spun to a stop it pitched the unstrapped Tarquin headlong into a hedge a couple of metres away. Awakened by the landing, Tarquin pulled himself from the foliage and followed the rasping noise of Jeremiah's loud snoring. He found his friend still strapped to the ejector seat, which was sinking slowly sideways into a patch of mud mere centimetres from a steaming cowpat.

Tarquin rushed to help, but his legs crumpled and he blacked out momentarily, falling back into some bushes. When he came to, it was to an awful howling noise, followed by a barrage of choice words. Clambering groggily to his feet, he saw Jeremiah now lying face-down in the cowpat. Trying not to laugh, Tarquin scurried to push the seat onto its side and undo the buckle around Jeremiah's waist.

Jeremiah slid out of the chair and onto the sodden ground. "Pah, ughh! You might have told me about the country pizza, Seebee."

"I've only just come round myself." Tarquin winced at the strength of the afternoon sun. "I've a cracking headache to boot."

"Headache? Grrrrh! I've a ruddy tractor ploughing a morning's furrows through mine." Jeremiah massaged his crown and unwittingly smeared more dung across his head and face and into his moustache. As the big man got to his feet, Tarquin began gathering their scattered belongings. He was relieved to find Jeremiah's pistols, still in their presentation box, not far off.

"Okay," said Jeremiah, dragging branches toward the seat, "let's hide it and get us to the Silvery Moon. I'll collect the seat later. Ingeborg will be expecting us."

"Pity my own chair was destroyed by Buckingham's men. I was getting quite attached to it."

"No worries, I'll find you another." Jeremiah affectionately ruffled Tarquin's hair before the boy could step away. There was still dung on that big mitt …

Miss Amelia Hoploosley, a prim, tweed-suited, brogue-wearing spinster and Tarquin's overly inquisitive next-door neighbour, was enjoying the weather while taking her regular afternoon constitutional. She had reached the bottom of Ricketty

Field when movement on the edge of the copse caught her inquisitive eye. She watched, horrified, as that ghastly rapscallion Tarquin Jenkins, not to mention the even ghastlier Jeremiah Cavendish, each wearing a set of very peculiar clothes and a thick layer of muddy undergrowth—and worse, if her nose, sensitive even at this distance, was telling her no lies—broke from a line of trees and weaved drunkenly through the corn. Crouching out of sight close to the roadside hedge, Miss Hoploosley gazed dumbstruck as they slewed past her hiding place, laughing and wobbling unsteadily towards the canal. This was the second time she had witnessed Master Jenkins drunk in the afternoon—and wearing women's clothing. To cap it all, he was now under the unholy and inappropriate influence of that frightful, clearly demonic lock-keeper—the one who'd appeared on television wearing nothing but (she shuddered) his sequined underpants!

Reaching the safety of the Silvery Moon, Jeremiah and Tarquin boarded the boat, dumped their belongings in a pile at the bottom of the stairs and took off their filthy clothing. Steam seeped from under the two bathroom doors at the far end of the boat. Ingeborg had prepared them each a hot, welcoming bath. From the galley came the smell of warm, toasted bread and her soft, lilting voice as she sang.

"We're back!" shouted Jeremiah.

Inga's rosy-cheeked face popped out from around the galley door. Her blonde hair was piled high on her head and secured with a bright red comb. It looked like a children's spinning top.

"I found your message pinned to the door. Four o'clock, on the dot." Stepping into the gangway, she wiped her hands vigorously on her apron.

Tarquin grinned. Inga was a lively, interesting woman, full of information and bottomless pockets of sweets. She wasn't what you would call pretty—more like functional, as Jeremiah often said. A pious woman, devoted to her husband, she was half the size of Jeremiah, with a round, homely face that spoke of warm summer days, homemade lemonade and rhubarb crumbles.

"You look a little pale, Seebee. You okay?" She smoothed his cheek with the back of her hand.

"It's nothing." Tarquin leaned forward and kissed her on both cheeks. "Your husband saved the day."

Ingeborg gave a hearty laugh and shook her head. "I don't believe a word of it. Just happy you're back, safe and sound, if a little smelly." She took a deep breath, pecked her husband quickly on the cheek, and was about to squeeze his hand when she urgently changed her mind. "I'll keep your toasted sandwiches warm for when you're done. Take your teas with you and have your baths. You can eat after." She disappeared back into the galley.

It wasn't long before the two time-travellers were soaking in their respective bathtubs, drinking tea, singing and laughing about their adventure.

"Did you see Ashley's face when you mentioned the boxing?" called Jeremiah over the partition wall between the bathrooms. "He were not amused. And what possessed you to come up with Baron Arnie von Schwarzenegger?"

"No idea." Tarquin laughed. "It was the first thing that came into my head. Come to that, why on God's good earth did you teach Samuel and his friends a class in self-defence? I'd never heard of Leaky Pumps before."

"It's Ecky Thump!" groaned Jeremiah, "Ecky ruddy Thump. And I got it from the television."

"Whatever. Oh, yes, and let's not forget trains, planes and automobiles!"

"It were only trains. They'll never get it right, they be too taken with your Homer Simpson double-decker doubrie thingy to think about me lines of steel and tunnels."

Tarquin felt the small indentation above his heart. He checked it using the shaving mirror from the shelf.

"Did anyone stick a knife in me while I was unconscious?" he shouted. "I've got a hole in my chest that wasn't there before."

Silence.

"Jeremiah?"

"Jumpin' alley cats, you don't half ask a lot of questions! Yes, it were me. All part of me Dr Dolittle act to help you after your swim in the moat."

Tarquin smiled. "Thank you. It was Dr David Livingstone, actually."

"Anyways, time to be getting out and we needs to get you home. It'll be five-thirty soon." Jeremiah grabbed two large towels and started to dry himself off.

Tarquin threw a handful of soapsuds at an imaginary Buckingham before getting out of his bath. "Okay." He took a warm towel from the radiator just as the grandfather clock chimed five.

Feeling a lot better now that he was wearing his own clothes again, Tarquin sat next to Ingeborg at the table as he gobbled down a toastie and swigged another mug of tea. The artefacts taken from previous jumps lined the top shelf of the welsh dresser—all of them except Babe Ruth's baseball cap and Napoleon's coat, which he wore. He rested his gaze on them fondly. Washington's teeth, Manet's paintbrushes, Princess Wen Cheng's jade necklace, pirate Benjamin Hornigold's carved belaying pin … At the sight of the pin his heart missed a beat and his eyes glazed over.

It had been almost a year since his pirate adventure. He shook his head as he recalled what had happened afterwards. Returned from his trip to Jamaica and Hornigold, he'd gone to the Silvery Moon, revitalized himself with a refreshing mug of tea and some toasties, then left for home at around 11pm. He'd forgotten to mention the belaying pin to Jeremiah. He was walking along the canal path, admiring the full moon, when two purple, knee-high creatures stopped him, shouting in plummy English accents, "Stand and deliver!" His response was to run like hell, shrieking like a thwarted toddler, and dropping the pin in his haste. Thankfully the creatures hadn't chased him. The next morning, Jeremiah said he had found the wooden pin in the grass by the canal path and assured him that it was quite normal after a jump to experience strange and unexplainable things.

Tarquin turned back to the shelf. Standing next to the pin was a framed colour print of Napoleon Bonaparte, half naked and looking very surprised. Taking the medallion given to him by Charles II from his pocket, Tarquin placed it beside Napoleon.

"That's a pretty piece of silver," said Ingeborg, gazing at the greyhound.

"By royal appointment! Given to me by King Charles II, no less," said Tarquin proudly. "You should see what Jeremiah got!"

Ingeborg looked at her husband. "Come on, my darling. Let's see what you got."

"It be nothing, just a pair of pistols." Jeremiah pulled out the wooden box and lifted the lid.

"'Nothing', indeed! A beautiful pair of double-barrelled duelling pistols! Well, I never."

"Arise, Sir Big Bum," said Tarquin with a smile.

"'Big Bum'?" Ingeborg guffawed. "Tell me more!"

"I, I … it means we got knighted for saving the Crown Jewels, that's all," said Jeremiah.

"Hah! First of all the Big Bum and now the Crown Jewels! And my hubby's a knight of the realm! I don't believe it!"

Tarquin realized how much he'd missed her warmth.

"Joking aside, we were lucky," Jeremiah said, half to Tarquin. "Make no bones about it, Lady Luck shined down on us."

Tarquin nodded in agreement. He looked at the ruddy face of his friend. Ingeborg had stopped laughing.

"No more grappling contests, eh?" said Tarquin.

"Agreed." Jeremiah wrung his hands. "No more."

"I'm glad you're both safe," said Ingeborg. "I wouldn't know what to do if I lost you—either of you." She got up from the table. "I'll leave you to it. I have bread rising and a steak-and-ale pie to pop in the oven." She kissed Jeremiah and Tarquin on the cheek, ascended the companionway and headed back to the cottage.

Tarquin finished his second mug of tea and eyed Jeremiah.

"Do you think I'll have any side-effects from swimming in that moat?"

"Maybe best to see a doctor when you gets a chance. But be careful what you say this time," replied Jeremiah.

Tarquin nodded. "Why Winston?" he said.

An expression of surprise flickered across Jeremiah's face. "Winslow?"

"No, Winston," said Tarquin firmly.

Jeremiah looked at the ceiling.

"Malcolm Winston Jenkins—my father."

Jeremiah turned several shades of red and coughed loudly. "Yes, your father. We went to the Great Fire."

"You said it was complicated. Why?"

"It were nothing, just a figure of speech. I often travelled with your father, we were good friends. Sometimes he called himself Winston if there were things he were doing that he didn't necessarily want everyone to know about."

Tarquin knew Jeremiah was holding things from him. He felt sad. They'd just had the experience of their lives, and now Jeremiah wouldn't tell him the truth. He dropped the subject, at least for the moment, and stared morosely out of the window.

"What about the journal, then?" asked Jeremiah. "You've not mentioned it since we landed? I knows you found something in it. What you find?"

Tarquin shook his head. "Why don't you trust me?"

"Of course I trust you, Seebee. Now, let's see the journal."

Pulling the book from his pocket, Tarquin laid it on the table. Jeremiah took the leather volume and turned it over in his hands, caressing the binding with an artisan's care, then pulling a pair of spectacles from a drawer by the table. "I reckons this leather's not from around here. Not even from this planet."

Tarquin felt a surge of excitement course up his spine. "You mean it's—it's from an alien world?"

Jeremiah looked across at him. The ends of his moustache twitched. He rocked back in his chair and roared with laughter.

Tarquin stared at him with the bemused look of a small boy excluded from a grownup's joke. "I don't understand."

"Ah, not to worry, Seebee. It just made me chuckle when I seen your surprised expression, wide-eyed an' all."

Tarquin thought of the writing Samuel Pepys had shown him in the journal. If Jeremiah knew my father had left my date of birth and initials in the journal, he'd be on the floor having kittens!

Jeremiah wiped his eyes and opened the journal. "No, this is ancient, and I've never seen the like of this writing and illuminations before." He looked lost in thought for a few moments, then suddenly jumped up. "I have an idea." He went to a wooden bureau by the galley door, opened the lid and pulled out a tatty cardboard carton from which he started to remove handfuls of packing paper. Finally out of the carton came a steel Art Deco box with two book-size openings at the top and a pair of ebony handles on each side. He brought the mysterious object to the table, an electric lead unwinding itself from the back and a bakelite plug bouncing across the floor.

Just as Jeremiah placed the object on the table, the grandfather clock struck the half-hour.

"Jeepers," said Jeremiah. "You must be going, Seebee, before you're missed. Best take it with you." He pushed the metal cuboid at Tarquin.

"It's … it's a toaster!" Tarquin exclaimed. He'd thought he was being given something from another planet. Instead, what he was holding was an electrical appliance from, at a guess, the 1930s. It wouldn't have looked amiss on Antiques Roadshow.

"Of course it's a ruddy toaster!" Jeremiah glared at him. "I can't very well gives you something from the ruddy twenty-fourth century that looks like it comes from the ruddy twenty-fourth century, now can I? Here's how it works. You puts the journal in there"—he pointed to one of the book-sized openings—"and a blank notebook here"—pointing to the other opening—"and then you push down the handles just like it really was a toaster you was using. If it finds the language, it prints a translation onto the other book. Simple."

Tarquin suspected Jeremiah had not the slightest notion of how the device worked, but who cared so long as it did what he said it did.

"Oh, and you'll likely need to leave it running overnight. There are hundreds of thousands of languages it has to look through." Jeremiah looked seriously at Tarquin. "If you get problems, push this red button on the bottom." It always amazed Tarquin how many futuristic gadgets had important red buttons on their undersides. Jeremiah was saying: "It'll destroy the toaster and what's in it."

Tarquin leaned across the table. "Thanks, Jeremiah—thanks for taking me with you. I really enjoyed it, even the bad parts."

Jeremiah wiped his nose and swallowed. The big man was ever prey to sentimentality. "No, lad, it's me who be thanking you. I don't get to travel much these days," he added wistfully.

"Did you often get lost in time?" Tarquin took the toaster box from Jeremiah and started organizing himself for departure.

"Jeremiah Cavendish? Lost?" erupted the ex-wrestler. "Never! I knows where I am going every time I goes there. I just don't knows how we missed 1666!"

Tarquin smiled as he put on his jacket. So then, why did we arrive in 1671?

The pseudo-toaster held firmly under his arm, Tarquin climbed the companionway.

Jeremiah shouted after him, "Next jump in three weeks! Check the book I gave you for ideas! And, don't forget—any problems with the toaster, push the button."

Tarquin arrived home at exactly six o'clock. The gothic cuckoo clock in the hallway, a retirement present from his uncle's place of work, squawked loudly. He could hear his Aunt Mira and Uncle Harold in the loggia, potting plants and listening to the Archers weekly omnibus edition on BBC Radio Four. Tarquin poked his head round the outhouse door, announced his return, and headed straight to his bedroom.

He lifted the toaster/translator from its box and took a deep breath. Placing the journal in one opening and a blank exercise book in the other, just as Jeremiah had told him to do, he pushed down on the two side levers until they locked with a satisfying click. He covered the toaster with a jumper, shoved it under his bed, and plugged the device in.

For several minutes he lay on the floor, watching expectantly. Nothing happened.

Soon he got bored.

Sitting on the bed, he remembered Jeremiah saying that the toaster would likely need to work overnight. Tarquin stuffed several more jumpers on top of it and went downstairs to see his aunt and uncle.

He stood by the conservatory door listening to his aunt talk about herbaceous borders and his uncle reminiscing about his RAF (Rumbelow's Air-cushioned Footwear Ltd) days; two conversations, happily co-existing in the same room, but never meeting. It must be old-people love, thought Tarquin.

He awoke early the next morning and immediately peered under the bed. Hurriedly removing the jumpers, he pulled the toaster out and released the books.

But when he checked the exercise book he found it was blank. Nothing had changed.

Tarquin put the books back into the toaster, reset the wooden handles and hid the device under the bed again.

He puffed up his pillows and sat in bed, letting his mind run over recent events. His last adventure had been the most terrifying and exhausting thing he had ever experienced. He could have died in 1671, and very nearly had. Even so, it had been an enthralling, rollercoaster ride of a journey, and now he had a mystery to solve!

Invigorated, he got up, showered and dressed. Thursday was a good day at college.

Just before leaving, Tarquin took another look at the toaster under the bed. Still nothing. He replaced the jumpers and left for college.

On the way home a few hours later, Tarquin took out his small, leather-bound time-travelling planner. Jeremiah was right, the next date in the book was only three weeks away. Three wormholes would open at precisely 1:10pm over the Silvery Moon.

The first wormhole would allow a time jump to the Montmartre area of Paris in 1892. Tarquin loved art and the thought of visiting the Folies Bergère to see Toulouse-Lautrec and other Impressionist painters intrigued him. After all, didn't I help Manet with my photographs that time?

The second wormhole was to a music festival in 1969, at a farm called Woodstock. His father and mother had always claimed to have been at the festival, but Tarquin had his reservations. Too much mud and all that grandpa music, he thought. He'd seen pictures of the Glastonbury Festival and was unimpressed by the idea of roughing it.

The third wormhole was a three-day sojourn to 1829, where he could watch Robert Stephenson work on his locomotive. However, steam-powered machinery didn't interest him all that much—it wasn't exactly rocket science, was it?

As he chuckled at his own apology for a joke—well, someone has to—he thought again of the Folies Bergère. Yes, he'd visit Montmartre! At the weekend, he'd get some books from the library and begin researching his trip.

But when I get home, he said to himself, thinking about the toaster under his bed, I'll be reading all about alien worlds!

"Harold! Harold! I can't get this to open!" shouted Mira from the kitchen, her wooden spoon wedged in one of two openings of a metal box she had found hidden under Tarquin's bed while vacuuming.

"Coming, dear." The languid rustle of a newspaper was followed by the soft, steady padding of Harold's Garfield-shaped carpet slippers, a Christmas present from Tarquin. As he arrived in the kitchen doorway, he yawned, fed up to have been dragged from his midday slumbers.

"You fell asleep again, didn't you?" Mira shot him a look of bottled-up annoyance. "I found this old toaster hidden in Tarquin's bedroom." She pointed proudly at the box as if it were some hidden treasure. "It looks valuable to me. I'll bet the little rascal stole it."

Harold stared at the silver Art Deco box and nodded sagely. "Where do you think he stole it from?"

"Never mind that. Come and help me get it working."

Harold shuffled forward, unclipped his wire-rimmed NHS glasses from his cardigan and placed them on his nose. Carefully he turned the toaster several times in his hands before deftly pulling out the wooden spoon.

"Looks okay to me? Have you tried plugging it in?"

Mira rolled her eyes and looked skyward. "Of course I have."

Thoroughly unimpressed by her husband's grasp of the situation, she took hold of the flex and plugged it into the wall. "Listen."

They both craned their ears towards the appliance.

"There!" said Mira excitedly. "Did you hear that?"

Harold shook his head.

Mira sighed loudly, grabbed the wooden spoon from his hand and thumped the toaster. "There! You must have heard that, surely?"

Harold nodded, more to keep the peace than because he had actually heard anything.

"Okay, pass me two slices of bread," urged his wife.

Harold dutifully gave her the bread, and she dropped a slice into each of the slots.

"Now, if I push down the lever …"

Weeeeeeooooooweeeeeeeeee.

The sound, as of a passing police car's siren, made them both jump back from the toaster. Harold mopped his brow with a tea towel. Mira re-aligned her ill-fitting dentures and took a deep breath.

"You see, Harold, it makes a noise but nothing happens. It doesn't get hot. It must be broken. Tarquin put books inside the slots for some stupid reason—that boy! He's probably broken a perfectly decent toaster. Do you think you can fix it?"

She stood with her arms folded expectantly as Harold inspected the machine.

"There's a red button on the bottom …" He turned the toaster over and pointed. "Perhaps it's a master switch or something? Maybe this turns it on or resets it?"

"Well, push it, man!" commanded his wife.

Tarquin was taking his key out of the front door, when a loud noise and a flash like lightning came from the kitchen.

"Aunt Mira! Uncle Harold!"

Two pairs of startled eyes looked out from blackened visages as Mira and Harold slowly turned their gaze from the toaster to their nephew. The two faces, surrounded as they were by frazzled, silver hair, made him think of those bad old paintings you find in junk shops being sold only for their gilded frames.

Tarquin looked past them and saw the toaster, buckled and smoking, on the kitchen table. His heart sank. "You've broken my translator!"

Catching sight of her smouldering hair in the polished cooker hood, Aunt Mira shrieked. "Never mind the blooming toaster, what about my hair!" Waving her hands angrily, she was producing a laudable impression of the Bride of Frankenstein. "I've only just had it rinsed and set!"

Harold fawned wetly over his wife before turning on Tarquin with the ferocity of a disgruntled sheep. "Why on earth did you bring such a dangerous appliance into our home? Have you lost all your senses? You stole it, didn't you!"

Tarquin wasn't listening. "Where are the books!" He began searching the kitchen.

"In your bedroom, of course." His aunt was pulling clumps of singed silvery-blue hair from her head. "Why on earth you put books …"

Before she could finish her sentence, Tarquin leapt up and cried, "Oh, thank, you!"

He planted a kiss on Harold's bemused and sooty dome and another on his aunt's blackened cheek. "Thank you!"

Tarquin ran from the kitchen and charged up the stairs to his bedroom. The journal and the exercise book were on his desk, seemingly undamaged.

He opened the exercise book, hoping to find answers to the many questions rushing through his head. The first twenty pages were filled with writing, diagrams and drawings, but the rest were disappointingly blank. Tarquin looked despairingly at the journal, comparing the two, and realized, much to his dismay, that nothing had been translated—just copied.

The translator must have stopped when Aunt Mira found it!

Dropping onto the bed, Tarquin covered his head with his hands and closed his eyes.

Noooooooooooo!

After what seemed ages, he sat up.

I should go talk to Jeremiah. He knows far more than he's telling me. He'll know what to do.

He put on his frock coat and baseball cap. Just before he left he looked at the journal and exercise book on his desk. Not wanting his inquisitive aunt anywhere near them, he quickly hid them under his bedside cabinet.

CHAPTER 9

THE LEPRECHAUN STAKE-OUT

His aunt and uncle were in the bathroom cleaning up as Tarquin quietly slipped from the house. He reached the double lock at Steeple Snoring just as the sun disappeared behind the trees. The town-hall clock chimed seven.

He hastened down the path towards the Silvery Moon. Seeing lights on inside, he shouted for Jeremiah, keeping a wary eye on the bushes. Reaching the boat, he shouted again. Still getting no reply, he stepped aboard.

The top door was open and he cautiously peered inside. He'd expected to see Jeremiah in his rocking chair, smoking his pipe, with his massive army boots resting on the table and his head buried in the complete works of H.G. Wells or maybe an Isaac Asimov novel. Slowly, Tarquin descended the steps and looked around.

No sign of Jeremiah.

He called out yet again.

Nothing.

As he went deeper into the boat, he was struck by how preternaturally clean and tidy it was. Where mountains of magazines of practical electronics, woodworking and narrowboat building usually lay, there were eight chest-high stacks of magazines. He glanced through a stack and found it was even in date order! The boat's galley, normally festooned with laundry, was spick and span. The customarily cluttered table was loaded with clean clothes, all colour-coordinated and meticulously arranged in neat piles.

More than anything, Tarquin was worried by the neatness.

He moved quickly along the boat, hoping to hear Jeremiah's signature belly laugh or feel the familiar paw-like hand ruffle his hair, but all was quiet save the ticking of the grandfather clock.

Tarquin opened the steel door that led to the time portal. Once again, instead of chaos there was order. Jeremiah's workbench, so often strewn with half-finished wiring projects, lay empty. Stacked neatly on shelves were the big man's time-travel lotions and potions, each jar labelled with the language, dialect, mixing instructions and ingredients. Tarquin had never seen the jars on shelves, let alone labelled!

The only things out of place were two books lying on the floor behind the ejector seat. Tarquin went over and picked them up. One was a tatty copy of Dracula's Guest by Bram Stoker, the other Mrs Beeton's Book of Household Management, which was opened at Chapter 16.

He read part of the page:

General Observations on the Common Hog
765. THE HOG belongs to the order Mammalia, the genus Sus scrofa, and the species Pachydermata, or thick-skinned; and its generic characters are, a small head, with long flexible snout truncated; 42 teeth, divided into 4 upper incisors, converging, 6 lower incisors, projecting, 2 upper and 2 lower canine, or tusks, the former short, the latter projecting, formidable, and sharp, and 14 molars in each jaw; cloven feet furnished with 4 toes, and tail, small, short, and twisted; while, in some varieties, this appendage is altogether wanting.

Spidery annotations ran across the paragraph. Tarquin took from his pocket what looked like an unassuming pair of round, thick glasses and eyed the chapter again. The words "Ruddy Griddlebacks", done in glowing red handwriting, flew off the page. Several words in the text were also circled in the same red.

Thick-skinned—small head—tusks—short—formidable—sharp—twisted.

This was more than an animal description, Tarquin was sure. He scoured the bookcase until he saw what he was looking for: a thin, handwritten notebook with the word "Griddlebacks" in blue ink on the cover. Leafing quickly through the pages, he paused here and there to read about a race of highly intelligent, two-legged, leathery-skinned creatures with small, alligator-like heads. These were the Griddlebacks, who roamed galaxies and conquered planets.

The hairs on the back of Tarquin's neck stood up.

A noise on the upper deck made him cower against the bookcase.

What if there are Griddlebacks on board?

He waited, his ears straining for any sound. Trying to stop his fingers trembling, he pocketed the notebook as quietly as he could and put the two books back on the floor. He crept warily back through the boat until he reached the companion-way to the topside.

If Jeremiah's in danger, I should phone the police.

Peering over the hatch-door rim, Tarquin looked towards the lock-keeper's cottage. A reassuring plume of smoke wound its way skyward. He heaved a huge sigh of relief. Inga must be home.

He jumped off the Silvery Moon, jogged down the garden path and knocked loudly on the cottage door. He couldn't wait to see his favourite surrogate aunt again.

The door opened.

A small, elderly, white-haired woman, holding a ball of knitting and a skewer, looked up at him.

"Yes?" she said in a deep, baritone voice.

"I'm trying to find the lock-keeper." Tarquin attempted to peek past her into the cottage.

She looked him up and down. Her head movements were jerky and mechanical.

"There be no Jeremy Havendick living ere," she said.

"It's Jeremiah—"

"Not 'ere he not."

"Thank—" The heavy oak door slammed shut centimetres from his nose.

Bewildered, Tarquin walked back along the garden path. He had gone only a couple of metres before he saw a figure duck behind the Silvery Moon. Clenching his fists, he climbed the steps to the canal path, eyes fixed on the point where the figure had disappeared. Ready to run if the figure reappeared, his heart pounding in his chest, Tarquin reached the gate and ran toward the safety of a line of elm hedges near the road.

A hand trapped his ankle.

"Aaaaaagh!"

Thrown off balance, he flew into a clump of bushes.

The invisible somebody—or something—grabbed his legs and pulled him inside the clump.

"Don't kill me!" Tarquin screamed.

He slithered down a wet bank and looked up into the pinched face of—and this was the bit he couldn't believe—a very angry Hillary Clinton.

He sat up gawping.

"Yer eejit! Yer nearly ruined de stakeout!" Hillary Clinton's voice was, oddly, low and gruff with a distinct Celtic brogue. She threw Tarquin his baseball cap, which he'd lost during his pellmell descent.

Ronald Reagan and Jimmy Carter arrived at Hillary Clinton's side.

Tarquin desperately clawed the ground, pushing against the bank and looking for an exit.

"Naw movement in de house, boss," said Carter. His voice, too, had a Celtic twang. "Me t'inks da lad got away unheard."

"Tell me I'm dreaming!" moaned Tarquin.

Hillary Clinton's large hairy hand promptly covered his mouth. Reagan and Carter grabbed his ankles and dragged him further through the undergrowth into a dense thicket.

At the far end, set into a raised bank, was a small door with an even smaller window in it. Hillary Clinton opened the door and the three of them threw Tarquin inside.

He landed on his back on a mud floor in a room that was maybe three metres square and covered in roots.

Reagan closed the door and the three politicians stared through its aperture at the frightened boy.

"What the hell are you!" shouted Tarquin, scrabbling back into a corner.

"What yer think we are? We're bloody leprechauns!" retorted Hillary Clinton, crossing her mightily tattooed arms.

Tarquin looked at the three menacing faces. He was determined not to pee his pants, but it was becoming more and more difficult by the moment.

Then, unexpectedly, Jimmy Carter moved forward and offered his hand in greeting. "Good ta see yer, Seebee."

Tarquin stared open-mouthed as Reagan smiled and pointed a stubby finger at Mrs Clinton.

"Meet Calbhach O'Reilly. Da best Tuatha Dé Danann locksmith this side of Zwicky's Triplet."

Hillary Clinton's frown morphed into a smile. She pressed a thin circular ring near her throat and, within moments, her body wobbled and shrank in size until she was about a metre tall. Her face fizzed and faded from view, revealing in its place an elfish, weatherbeaten visage with thick pointy ears, a long red beard and a pork-pie hat that looked remarkably similar to the one worn by a bear in a beer advert Tarquin liked.

"But, but," stammered Tarquin, "you're an Irish myth!"

Calbhach closed one eye and glowered with the other. "I be da leprechaun, an me ancestors were leprechauns from the planet Prakachesioran, who found Ireland on our interplanetary travels and populated da Emerald Oisle with our cousins da filty clurichauns before yer 'umans did—and, should yer think ter ask, I have na crock of gold at da end of any bleedin' rainbow." With an expression full of gravitas, he continued, "Me brot'ers and me put all ta gold in savings accounts on Selmar Major with the Crustachione Federal Bank of Deposits and da Savings. We gets a healthy 8.75 percent per annum. And, if yer still t'inking I'm a myth …"

With an expression of grim determination, Calbhach began unbuckling his belt.

"No!" cried Tarquin, realizing the leprechaun's dire intent. "No! I said 'myth', not 'miss'!"

Calbhach squinted at him suspiciously but, mercifully, desisted from the unbucklement.

"Sorry," said Tarquin.

Reagan approached him. "Na worries. Me brot'ers and me were well impressed with yer adventures." He smiled and offered his hand.

Tarquin grinned wearily, trying to decipher the strong accent while feebly shaking Reagan's sausage-fingered mitt. "How do you know about my adventures?"

"Old Cavendish never stops yacking on about yer. Pinchin' da Babe Ruth's baseball cap and all—during a World Series game at dat! Wonderful stuff."

Tarquin started to relax. "Why the disguises?"

"People on dis planet t'ink we're a wee bit ugly and different, so we use ta disguises when we go out and ta bout," said Calbhach.

"It were me brot'er Finbar's turn to choose for da operation," said Reagan. He flicked his neck switch and a grinning, red-nosed, wart-encrusted face appeared. "I be Rhiordan Findus O'Mallerty."

Calbhach pointed towards Carter. "That dere be D'Arcy Ogrungion."

Carter nodded formally, and pressed his neck switch.

"Abraham Lincoln and George W. Bush are on ta ot'er side of da canal," Calbhach continued. "Barack Obama is back at ta command centre. And, before yer ask, da woman in ta house is an alien droid, like ta t'ing yer just saw movin' on ta boat."

Tarquin sat quietly, trying to take it all in.

The door opened and in walked John F. Kennedy. "Everyt'ing looks under control, boss." JFK started to open his knapsack. "I brought da doughnuts. Finbar went to da Tea Rooms ta fetch drinks ten minutes ago."

"There's one of you in the village?" said Tarquin.

"He be fine. He's got da good disguise," said Rhiordan.

"Which president is he?" Tarquin couldn't believe an ex-president of the United States could wander about Steeple Snoring without attracting attention.

"Bill Clinton," Rhiordan told him. "Calbhach's husband."

The leprechauns fell about with laughter. The doughnuts started to do the rounds.

The team of leprechauns resumed their surveillance of the Silvery Moon, the lock-keeper's cottage and the canal. Through small computers attached to their wrists and earpieces they passed messages to their hidden command centre.

Tarquin joined them in watching a procession of droids dressed as canal workers and dustmen systematically search the canal bank and the lock-keeper's garden. "What are they looking for?" he whispered.

"Nah sure, but as soon as Jeremiah disappeared wees were called in ta take a look," said Calbhach, drinking from a long green bottle. "I reckons poor Jeremiah found something da droids want."

Tarquin thought back to the journal he had found at Samuel Pepys's house. Have I put Jeremiah in danger?

He then remembered the books he'd seen lying by the ejector seat when he was on the boat. In his excitement he'd completely forgotten about the possible clues Jeremiah had left. He stood up and pulled the notebook from his pocket. "When I was on the Silvery Moon I found Jeremiah had left Mrs Beeton's Book of Household Management open at Chapter Sixteen." He handed the Griddleback book to Calbhach. "Jeremiah had hidden a message on the page. I think he was referring to the creatures in here."

Calbhach took the book and read a few lines. Then, hissing, he dropped it to the floor. He grabbed Tarquin by his frock-coat lapels and swung in midair, his squat, bunion-bedecked nose just centimetres from Tarquin's face.

"Ta Griddlebacks! I moight have known. They are ta evillest intelligent creatures in da universe. They'd split you in two and drinks yer blood rather than be looking at yer."

The weight of Calbhach was gradually pulling Tarquin to his knees. "I'm sorry, I was—"

Calbhach dropped to the ground and cut Tarquin off with a snap of his fingers. Dredging up a mouthful of phlegm, he spat venomously on the mud floor. "It's tem that be working ta droids. They're probably holdin' Jeremiah and Inga in another dimension. Tat's why we can't find 'em."

"There was something else," started Tarquin.

"Sorry, lad, ta seriousness of me mate's ploight is gettin' ta me." Calbhach patted the floor, suggesting Tarquin come sit beside him. "What else yer find?"

"There was a copy of Bram Stoker's Dracula's Guest beside the Beeton book."

Calbhach's shoulders sagged. "Leche," he said. "Jeremiah's telling us da nightmare's begun."

"'Leche'? 'Nightmare'?"

"'Tis just a figure of ta speech, I meant not'ing by it," said Calbhach.

For a few moments no one spoke.

Eventually the tension became too much for Tarquin. "Let me know what I can do to help. Jeremiah and Inga are my friends too, you know. If we work together we can get through this."

Getting to his feet, Calbhach playfully pulled the rim of Tarquin's baseball cap over his eyes. "Oi nu, lad, oi nu. Best leave it to us, da experts, all roight?"

Tarquin nodded.

"Friends?" asked Calbhach.

"Friends."

They shook hands to confirm it.

The leprechauns settled back into their surveillance routine. Some left the burrow to go back to the canal bank and double lock. On the big, portable screen in the burrow, Tarquin watched the live feeds from the leprechauns' eye monitors as they gathered intelligence on the droids using all manner of odd-looking instruments. To Tarquin, most of these gadgets bore an uncanny resemblance to kitchen implements his aunt used or tools from his uncle's garden shed. One in particular caught his eye, being operated by D'Arcy as he walked down the canal path. At one end was a mechanical egg whisk, all covered in wire and strips of tinfoil, at the other end a fork. Three small, translucent spheres of various sizes drifted slowly up and down the fork prongs as D'Arcy moved the device from side to side.

"Yer like that?" said Rhiordan.

"Yes," Tarquin replied, "but what does it do?"

"He's looking far ta breaks in ta fabric of time. Each sweep ta the left, it goes back a 'undred years, and to ta right …"

"Another hundred?"

"Nah, I have no idea," said Rhiordan with a smirk. "I'm messin' with yer head. Better ask D'Arcy when he gets back."

Periodically Finbar, still disguised as Bill Clinton, arrived back from the village carrying a welcome tray of teas, hot chocolate and a fresh supply of doughnuts. The leprechauns seemed a lot happier with a hot drink in their hands. Finbar sat down and told of a peculiar encounter he'd had in the village.

He explained that he was lighting his briar pipe outside the Tea Rooms when he collided with a tweed-suited old lady, sparking a tirade from her against the human male. After shouting several times, "Manners maketh the man!"—and despite Finbar wearing a hood—the woman recognized Bill Clinton's face and promptly fainted. Worried he would draw unwanted attention, Finbar quickly hid behind a wall.

A passer-by, seeing the comatose pensioner, called an ambulance. When the vehicle arrived, Finbar watched from his hiding place as the paramedics revived the woman and managed to get her to her feet. Then, without warning, she walloped the nearest paramedic with her handbag, saying she needed the police, not an ambulance. She'd met Bill Clinton, she told them, who had inexplicably touched her, and, as a tax-paying, law-abiding citizen with an MBE, she demanded action. It took several minutes for the pair of paramedics to disarm and sedate the woman and strap her onto a stretcher before they carried her to the ambulance.

Tarquin, happily munching on a custard-filled doughnut, listened intently, relishing Finbar's every word. Miss Amelia Hoploosley, without a doubt.

As the sound of a hooting owl echoed through the wood, the three remaining leprechauns out by the boat returned to the burrow and were introduced to Tarquin. There was Ardal, the trainee locksmith, and Brennan and Flaherty—the Brothers Grimm, as Calbhach delighted in calling them.

"Der bloody useless on da own, but terrific together," whispered Calbhach to Tarquin, before clapping his hands. As the hubbub died down he took up position on the only piece of raised ground in the room. "Okay me bro'ters, pack yer things and we'll be off."

Loaded with equipment, the leprechauns, Tarquin in tow, slipped quietly from their hiding place and followed the path down towards Tip Tree Farm. Arriving at a five-bar gate, Calbhach pointed at a tatty cream-coloured 1950s Willerby Vogue caravan, perched precariously on blocks in a field that backed onto the canal path. It looked like a large, rounded chicken coop. Tarquin smiled, wondering where the chickens were.

"Home," said the leprechaun enthusiastically as he lifted the latch and opened the gate.

Rhiordan reached the caravan first and, after checking no one was watching, pressed a button on a small metal contraption in his hand. The door opened and Tarquin and the seven leprechauns trooped inside.

"Wow! It's a time and relative dimension thingy, just like the Silvery Moon!" said Tarquin. "Bigger on the inside!"

Rhiordan gave him a quizzical sideways glance, "What were yer expectin', dat we lived in a box?"

The leprechauns removed their outer clothing and stacked up their knapsacks. Tarquin put his own knapsack with the others, and gazed around. He was standing on a Persian rug in the middle of a large, square hallway. Some fifteen metres from him, in each of the four walls, was a steel door.

As he looked at one of the doors it opened and a large, bustling silhouette appeared, accompanied by blaring music. He jumped backwards in startlement.

"Seebee, meet da Oleg," said Calbhach, chuckling.

The leprechauns backed away from the centre of the room, leaving Tarquin isolated. The shape, looming larger and larger, moved towards him, prancing sideways on its toes.

"He's all yours, lad!" shouted Calbhach above the music.

Oleg was a sturdily built man, getting on for two metres tall, with long brown hair, a bushy artisan beard, a tartan waistcoat, white trousers, boots and a necktie. He danced across the hall, humming and twirling a metal tube the size of a flute.

Tarquin tried to retreat, but leprechaun hands and arms firmly obstructed him, ensuring he couldn't leave the middle of the hall.

Oleg stopped less than a metre from Tarquin. His shining nose looked more like a pomegranate than a nose. His intense green-grey eyes fizzed. He examined Tarquin the way a psychiatrist examines a new patient.

"Aaargh!" shouted Tarquin. Not eloquent, but it was the best he could think of on the spur of the moment.

The music stopped and, with the anarchic expression of a lunatic who has just found the key to the asylum, Oleg moved even closer. "Da mihi sis bubulae frustrum assae, solana tuberosa in modo gallico fricta, ac quassum lactatum coagulatum crassum," he said directly into Tarquin's ear.

The leprechauns hooted with laughter. "Don't yer mess with da young'un, Oleg," said Calbhach.

Oleg stepped back and puffed out his sizeable chest. "I am Oleg! The greatest Russian troubadour!"

With an extravagant windmill bow, he spun like a whirling dervish and, handling the tube like a majorette's baton, thrust it at Tarquin.

"It good to meet you, Master Jenkins," he said with a sneer that was the opposite of his words. Then he turned and walked back to the room he had come from. A slam of the weighty door and he was gone.

"He be bonkers, but incredible with ta electronics and ta BRONCO," said D'Arcy in a soft, awed voice. D'Arcy was smaller than your average leprechaun, although no one had ever dared tell him this.

"Not bad with da fists and ta Bosun neither," added Ardal, demonstrating a powerful hook, a jab and a finger-blazing rat-at-tat-tat.

"Did he just point a gun at me?" squeaked Tarquin, still trembling.

"Der, sort of, but Oleg had tis Higgs Bosun phaser on da limiter. It wouldn't harm yer, merely rearrange yer for a while." D'Arcy rolled his eyes and did a weird belly-dance routine to show the effects of rearrangement.

"Higgs Bosun?" queried Tarquin. "Not Higgs Boson?"

"And what good would ta tiny Higgs Boson be at a toime like now?" said Calbhach peevishly.

Tarquin could think of no answer to that. Higgs Bosun it was, then.

"Standard issue on dis koind of mission," added Rhiordan, patting the smaller, pocket-sized tube he had in a holster hidden beneath his armpit.

"Let's get da supper and leave Oleg ta keep an eye on ta things." Calbhach opened the door nearest him and led the group into a kitchen and dining area.

The Brothers Grimm, with military precision, set about cooking. Blades flashed, vegetables got diced, meat was tenderized and several odd-looking cookers glowed. In a flurry of organized activity the other leprechauns set the table. Twenty minutes later, Tarquin and his new friends were tucking into a hot meal of Irish stew and dumplings.

Soon after, the door to the dining area opened and Oleg walked casually in. Ignoring Tarquin, he took a bowl of stew and some homemade bread and went to a corner of the room, where Calbhach and Ardal joined him. Tarquin watched nervously as the three sat hunched over their steaming bowls, deep in conversation. The word "Leche" was distinctly audible several times. Then, after refilling his bowl, Oleg went back to the control room and Calbhach and Ardal rejoined the others.

As second helpings of the stew were poured, Calbhach started to explain to Tarquin that Oleg's real name was Oleg Tremagenev. Trained as a computer scientist, Oleg had spent his working life hacking into American spy satellites and defence computers for the Soviet government. He was content in his job until, one fateful day in the 1970s, he was arrested by officials from the Soviet Interior Ministry. A vast collection of decadent western rock and pop music had been found in his apartment. Charged with "conduct incompatible with being a citizen of the USSR", he was sent to a Siberian gulag for five years. During this time, Oleg's alter ego had developed. He kept his mind alert by using his photographic memory to recall hundreds of rock and pop songs, and sang them to the guards at the slightest provocation. On release, he had fled to the West.

At the end of the meal, when Calbhach got up, Tarquin stayed him with a gesture. "You said earlier that the nightmare's begun. What did you mean?"

Calbhach didn't answer but, after a momentary pause, continued collecting dirty dinner plates and taking them over to the cleanse-o-matic in the kitchen area at the far end of the dining room.

Tarquin followed.

"Slip of da tongue," said Calbhach, shooting a furtive look from under his forest of eyebrows.

"Jeremiah left you a message on the boat, didn't he? Are he and Inga alive?" Tears welled in Tarquin's eyes.

"'Course he's aloive. He's just missin', t'at's all."

Tarquin saw the uncertainty in Calbhach's face. "He's my friend as much as yours. He's ... I really want to help ..."

Calbhach growled, threw the last plate forcefully into the machine and climbed onto the nearest chair. Tarquin took the chair next to him.

"You have naw idea what tis is about, have yer?" Calbhach crossed his arms and stared hard at Tarquin. "T'ink about it—time travel. We can see into da future, your future, everyt'ing's future."

Tarquin gulped.

"T'at's right," continued Calbhach, emphasizing the words by jabbing a finger at Tarquin. "Your future."

"But I'm just a fifteen-year-old boy—"

"Enough!" Calbhach said with an angry clap of his hands. He jumped off the chair. "I've said far ta much already. Yer Uncle Jules can tell yer more."

Muttering under his breath, Calbhach marched swiftly through the kitchen and out of the door. Tarquin composed himself and then headed back to the main group of leprechauns drinking at the kitchen table.

Suddenly Oleg's voice burst over the intercom. "Houston, we 'ave a problem."

Leaving their drinks, everyone rushed out of the dining room, down the corridor and through the door Tarquin had earlier seen Oleg emerge from. They gathered excitedly in the control room.

Tarquin could see, on one of a bank of monitor screens, a police car at the bottom of the track that led to the caravan. Everyone watched in silence as the passenger door opened and a policeman struggled to get out. Tarquin sighed, recognizing the unmistakable shape of Sergeant Sloth. There was a lot of shape to recognize.

Most of the local bobbies were fine, but even the stuffiest of Steeple Snoring's citizens —Miss Hoploosley excepted—referred to Sergeant Sloth as a plod. "A plod's plod," the more daring of them suggested.

Eventually the sergeant pulled himself free of the vehicle and began walking towards the caravan in that peculiarly slow pace that all police officers seem to develop.

"Ah, bejabers! Da fuzz!" moaned Rhiordan.

"We'll have ta kill 'im." Finbar ran a stubby finger across his throat.

Despite detesting Sergeant Sloth, Tarquin wanted no part of murder.

He had an idea. "Calbhach, quick, give me your identity thingy."

Calbhach handed him the thin metal neck loop, and Tarquin hurriedly placed it around his neck.

"Can you get news feeds on that thing?" He indicated the screens and looked pleadingly at Oleg.

"Of course! I am great Russian hacker!"

Oleg's fingers sped across the keys and onto the screens above him popped up news feeds from the BBC, Sky, Fox News, CBS, ITV, Reuters and the Associated Press.

Tarquin's eyes roved in desperation across the vast array until he saw what he was looking for.

Just then there was a loud rap on the caravan door.

"That one there!" Tarquin pointed at a face on the screen. "Grab his picture. Get me his voice."

Oleg's fingers worked faster even than before and the screens became one.

"Patch it into this neck thingy, quick!"

At last Oleg sat back with the exuberant flourish of a concert pianist. "Da!"

"What do I do to get this thing to work?" cried Tarquin, tugging at the neck loop.

"Press da ruddy button," yelled Finbar.

Tarquin found the button on the ring and pressed it. He felt a curious flowing and stretching sensation, as if he were an egg freshly cracked for poaching, and knew his face must be morphing into a replica of the one he'd seen on the screen. At the same time his body was growing vertiginously taller.

Oleg looked at Tarquin and, in a sombre voice, paraphrased the American actor John Wayne: "All battles are fought by scared men who'd rather be someplace else. And remember"—Oleg's eyes blazed—"if you've got 'em by the cherries their hearts and minds will follow."

Tarquin nodded, unsure what the Russian was getting at. Walking to the door, he took a deep breath and reached for the handle—

"Wait!" shouted Calbhach, running after him. "I'll best open ta top section, t'en da fuzz won't see anyone but yer in here."

Minutes earlier, Sergeant Sloth had turned to the young woman police constable sitting in the driving seat. "Stay here, Tomkins. I'll deal with this. This is no matter for a slip of a girl."

"But, Sarge!"

"No buts, Tomkins. You never know the type of people you'll find lurking in caravans. Travellers can be a strange and violent lot. Best we're careful." He nodded sagely. "I'll shout if I need you."

Straightening his clip-on tie, he tugged despairingly at his stab vest, which had long ago lost its battle to cover his expanding midriff. Patting the young WPC condescendingly on the thigh and ignoring her wince of revulsion, he struggled out of the car.

"I may be gone some time."

"Sarge, we're a team!" moaned WPC Tomkins.

Sloth smiled and shut the door. Covering his baldness with his cap, he left Tomkins sulking in the car.

If the owners of this caravan are illegals, they might be worth a bob or two. No point complicating things with sharing the spoils, thought Sloth, puffing loudly as he climbed the path towards the caravan.

He stopped and took a deep breath. This was his High Noon moment. He was Gary Cooper, striding down Hadleyville's main street on the hunt for criminals.

At the caravan door, he gave it his sternest knock.

The top of the door opened.

Despite his confident gait and his visions of Gary Cooper, Sloth managed just three words before his mouth froze.

"Excuse me, sir …"

Clunk! came the sound of a dropping penny, followed by another clunk, this time from Sloth's jaw. There would be no gunfight today.

"Sergeant Theodore Simon Sloth," said Tarquin, smiling. "How can I be of assistance?"

Sloth's eyes grew large. "You're …" was all he could manage before Tarquin continued, "That's right, I'm the Prime Minister."

Sloth stood to attention and tugged at his vest, trying to will himself into looking as if he were in full dress uniform.

"Begging your pardon, sir, but how do you know my name, and why are you in a caravan in a field in Northamptonshire?"

Tarquin gave him a grave and most serious look. "National Security, Sloth, need-to-know basis." The Prime Minister tapped the side of his nose. "However, during my time here, your name has come to my attention." He was beginning to enjoy himself. He folded his arms and looked down at Sloth. "Frankly, I'm not impressed by what your Chief Constable had to say about you."

Tarquin gloated. It was not every day that he had Sloth, the corpulent authoritarian bully, writhing on his string. This was cathartic. Payback for all the embarrassing moments Sloth had inflicted upon Tarquin at his college's police days. Payback on behalf of far too many of Steeple Snoring's population.

"Sloth, my presence here is pretty hush hush." Tarquin pressed a finger to his lips, and looked warily past the policeman's head before continuing. "I'd be grateful if you'd forget we ever met. You understand? I'll have a word with the Chief Constable and ensure your cooperation in this matter is recorded."

Sloth's eyes bulged like red-streaked kiwi fruit and sweat dripped from his double chin. He hurriedly wiped his slack mouth, nodded, saluted, turned on his heels, turned back again, gave another salute, and waddled off back down the path to the patrol car as fast as his pudgy legs would carry him—no mean feat since he had his tail stuck firmly between them.

"Who was that?" said WPC Tomkins, peering up towards the caravan as Sloth opened the door and squeezed himself into the passenger seat.

"Never you mind, Tomkins, need-to-know. Just forget we ever came here tonight, all right?" Sloth took out a grubby handkerchief and patted sweat from his brow. The WPC shrugged her shoulders and turned on the ignition.

"Anyone would think you saw royalty," she grumbled.

"No such luck," he said.

As the police car drove away, the leprechauns took turns to high-five Tarquin. It wasn't easy since, in his adopted form, he was nearly a metre taller than they were, but they proved able to jump like crickets.

"When you come slam bang up against trouble, it never looks half as bad if you face up to it," Oleg said, again in John Wayne mode. He slapped Tarquin hard on the back.

"Now I know why Jeremiah rates you so highly, Seebee. Dat was almost as good as a leprechaun could have done!" said Calbhach.

But then a piercing siren sounded in the caravan, and the euphoria instantly evaporated.

"Crikey! Dey's on ta move!" yelled Finbar.

Oleg turned, grabbed his Higgs Bosun tube from his seat and pointed it at Rhiordan. "Rhiordondo, fire up ze BRONCO!"

He ran from the control room into the corridor. Rhiordan hit a yellow button on the console and all the leprechauns headed for the door in pursuit of Oleg.

Calbhach grabbed Tarquin's arm. "Come on!"

As they raced along he explained. "Griddlebacks are jumping, we need to go a-fishing!"

The steel door on the far side of the hall from the control room was open now. Hot on the heels of Oleg and the other leprechauns, Tarquin and Calbhach ran through it and down a corridor until suddenly they arrived in a hangar the size of a football pitch. Some distance away was a transparent ball five or six metres across. Suspended within it, Oleg sat in a red bucket seat. This sphere itself floated in an outer, glowing sphere—a force field of some kind, was Tarquin's guess. Keeping the seat suspended at the centre of the inner sphere were twenty large silver springs that joined Oleg's seat to the inner sphere. On Oleg's head stood what looked like a hairdresser's drying hood, not too unlike those that Aunt Mira and Miss Hop-loosley spent most of their Tuesday afternoons under except much, much bigger. Instead of one thick cable at the back of the hood, a dozen cables disappeared down the rear of the bucket seat and into a knob-and-lever-encrusted console in front of Oleg.

Tarquin recognized the Look-Sees binoculars attached to Oleg's hood.

"Where's he going?" he asked.

"Ta catch a shipload of da trouble," replied the leprechaun.

"A shipload?" said Tarquin. "Surely you mean a—?"

"I tought we'd already had tis conversation about da Higgs Bosun, to be sure?"

Two rods the thickness of a man's arm extended either side of the bucket seat like the arms of a chair. On the end of each rod, at a comfortable height to be grasped, were red, baseball-sized glass orbs. Oleg finished strapping himself into the seat, took a gold mouthguard from a rack to his left, put it in his mouth, and gripped the orbs.

"What's he doing?" asked Tarquin.

"Waiting."

Oleg sat motionless, his eyes fixed on a line of numbers decreasing rapidly towards zero on the console screen in front of him, and on the huge wall screen. The leprechauns held their collective breath. The countdown reached 20, then 19, then 18, and Oleg began flicking switches, pressing buttons and pulling levers. The orbs under his hands gradually changed colour from red to yellow.

The suspense was too much for Tarquin. "What's he doing now?" he whispered, not daring to take his eyes off the Russian.

"Sorting out da music selection," Calbhach told him.

"Music selection?"

"Yep, yer got to be a-jigging when yer go do da time-fishing," said Rhiordan from Tarquin's other side.

Tarquin gazed blankly at him. "What the hell's time-fishing?"

"Griddlebacks invented it," said Calbhach. "Yer sit in da future, connected to da present. You cannot be seen in da present as yer in ta future, but when you've connected to ta present from ta future, yer can see into da now."

"Eh?" was all Tarquin could muster before he caught sight of a small plaque on the side of the sphere.

Brangleweed's Retrobuccled Occular Neutrocclusical Cementoblastoma Oligos MK VI (Supercharged) Manufactured on Earth by Sorayama Industries

"So, this is the BRONCO machine!" he said.

Calbhach pulled him by the arm. "Quick, everyone, out da room. He's about ta take off."

They rushed from the hangar. The last leprechaun out pulled a lever and a transparent door descended slowly behind them, closing off Oleg and the BRONCO machine.

8–7–6–5 …

"Ta lad's on his own now." Calbhach peered through the transparent doorway.

4–3–2–1 …

Under Oleg's whitening knuckles, the yellow orbs turned green. Classical music filled the air. The chair's springs began extending and contracting, building momentum, until Oleg and the seat became a blur, oscillating inside the sphere at incredible speed. The outer skin of the sphere started rolling, although Oleg, bouncing up and down inside the inner sphere, didn't turn with it.

Building momentum, the BRONCO raced along the floor and suddenly took off, soaring into the air towards the hangar's side-wall—which now seemed a lot further away than just the length of a football field. Distances could be deceptive, Tarquin knew, but the hangar appeared now to be at least a couple of kilometres across, and maybe many times more than that.

He watched horrified, expecting an almighty crash, but the BRONCO merely bounced off the hangar's rubbery wall, hit the floor and ricocheted up and off another wall, rather like a pinball but in three dimensions.

"Let's go, BRONCO!" yelled the leprechauns as the music changed to a fast, electronic, four-four rhythm.

Tarquin gripped Calbhach's shoulder. "Where's he going?"

"You see da numbers on ta screen over t'ere?" Calbhach pointed to a large electronic counter floating in the air, similar to those you see at football grounds. "It shows to da nearest millisecond when da Griddleback ship Oleg's chasin' will enter and disappear down da wormhole. He has to follow da ship and position himself behind it, then—"

Calbhach stopped abruptly. His mouth dropped open as the sphere flew to the top of the hangar and disappeared. After a moment he shook his head. "He's on der Everest climb. He won't be back for da while."

"What's going on?" Tarquin looked around the empty hangar.

"Oleg must follow da Griddleback ship down da same hole at precisely da same toime, to keep with it. Space is full of da wormholes, just like da barrel of Swiss cheese, so a wrong move could send da BRONCO off into da wrong dimension. By hookin' into the Griddlebacks' ship's alcubierre drive and surfing along its proteon wave, da skilled BRONCO rider can follow ta ship unnoticed. It's ruddy dangerous, though. One wrong movement and da connection's lost, along with ta Griddleback ship and our Oleg."

"Where is the other ship?" asked Tarquin, looking around the hangar's interior as if a spaceship might suddenly appear from nowhere.

"Yer can't see it. Ta Griddleback ship's not here, precisely. It sits in da parallel dimension with Oleg. Roight now, if we opened ta hangar door, we'd be sucked into da void and blown to pieces."

A loud popping noise inside the hangar startled them both.

The sphere reappeared and they watched it descend to the floor and bounce several times before rolling towards the door. Inside it, Oleg's biceps bulged under the strain of the constant oscillation as he clung to the orbs. The skin of his face looked as if it had been spread across his skull like warm margarine. His bloodshot eyes bobbed like marker buoys on a turbulent sea.

Even though protected by the transparent barrier, everyone automatically ducked as the sphere got closer. Just before it reached the door it rolled to the left and banked, then accelerated and shot across the hangar. Each twist and turn was met with gasps, claps and roars from the leprechauns. Muffled by the intervening barrier, the music segued seamlessly from rock-and-roll to classical and back again.

"Da pilot of da Griddleback ship must be a veteran," explained Calbhach. "He's picked up dat we're following him and is doing da crazy things ta get loose of Oleg."

During one pass, the sphere somersaulted and corkscrewed in an arc. Without warning, Oleg lost his grip on the left orb and the sphere wobbled viciously.

"Oh no, da Crankivodi death wobble!" shouted D'Arcy. He rushed forward and began to paw at the door.

"No, yer could kill us all!" Calbhach grabbed him and yanked him back. "What happens, happens."

The vibration broke Oleg's harness and threw him from the chair. He was hanging from the console by his fingertips. His left leg, entangled in a broken hydraulic spring, poured blood. A mixture of hydraulic fluid from the broken spring and Oleg's blood splattered the inside of the sphere's walls like a Jackson Pollock painting, and the Russian slowly disappeared from view.

The sphere flew around the hangar a few more times, bouncing off the walls and floor, before it climbed and disappeared again into the darkness above.

Except for the sound of the watchers' strained breathing, there was an eery silence. Tarquin looked to Calbhach for reassurance but saw only fear. The others weren't in any better shape, chewing their fingers or tugging their beards.

Then, in the darkness, there came a sound like a fast-approaching steam train. From the gloom overhead a bright spot descended until they could see it was the BRONCO, locked in a terrifyingly steep dive. They could just see, through the wall of the blood-splattered sphere, Oleg holding onto the console with one hand, the other pulling at a red lever, his feet swinging like twigs in a gale.

The sphere soared again, levelled out, and once more climbed until it disappeared from view.

Silence.

Then again the steam-train noise.

They craned their necks and stared towards the hangar's distant roof.

"Can't see anything," said D'Arcy.

"Over t'ere!" Rhiordan pointed to the far side of the hangar. For the moment the BRONCO was just a bright dot, and then it was racing horizontally towards them, a metre or so above the hangar floor.

The leprechauns panicked falling over each other as they tried to get away from the door.

"What now?" cried Tarquin.

"If he hits da door he'll kill us all. Run!" Calbhach hared away along the corridor as fast as he could go, Tarquin and the rest right behind him.

D'Arcy stumbled and would have fallen had not Tarquin managed to grab his collar and wrench him upright.

"Wait!" roared a voice above the panic.

They looked back.

Rhiordan was still at the door, jabbing his finger excitedly towards the sphere.

Two hundred metres away it had started to slow and the wild lurches, wobbles and rotations were becoming less violent.

"It's … it's stopping," said Rhiordan.

Tarquin and the leprechauns stared at each other, then crept back towards the door.

"I got 'em!" cried Oleg over the ship's loudspeakers.

The sphere drifted more and more slowly towards the door until finally coming to a stop just a few centimetres from it. The piercing express-train shriek ebbed to become a noise more like that of a deflating balloon.

Minutes passed, and then the transparent door opened.

Pulling his leg clear from the springs, Oleg threw off the hairdryer helmet. He was plainly at the outer limits of exhaustion. He climbed from the sphere, tripped, and fell flat on his face.

The leprechauns rushed to his side. The tall Russian rolled onto his back, grinned, and looked up at the screen on the wall.

"Three days, four hours, three minutes and seconds, thirty-six!" he said through his pain and gritted teeth.

As the leprechauns cheered, Oleg's signature anarchic expression returned. He dragged himself to his feet and hopped on one leg, punching the air, before anti-climactically collapsing again.

Tarquin had half-expected the Russian to emerge from under the hair-drying hood with a blue-rinsed perm, the preference of his aunt and Miss Hoploosley. Thankfully, Oleg's hair remained the way it had been—brown and unkempt.

The leprechauns picked up their stricken friend and carried him on their shoulders in triumph from the hangar.

D'Arcy stayed behind, pulling Tarquin to one side. "Do yer fish?"

Tarquin was bemused by the question.

"Do yer like ta fishing?" the leprechaun repeated.

"Yes. I've even been sea-fishing. But what's that got to do with anything?" They walked down the corridor together.

"Well, time-fishing is a bit da same. Yer throw a loine into the future. Yer can't see the end of the loine from ta present, but yer know it's there because yer holdin' ta end of it. Oleg hooked onto what yer and me can't see. On ta end of the loine he grabbed, sittin' in the future, is da Griddleback ship."

Tarquin looked thoughtfully at his small companion. Calbhach had said something like this a bit earlier, but it hadn't seemed to make a whole lot of sense. Now it did. Well, sort of.

He smiled. "That's why we couldn't see the Griddleback ship near the canal. They're here, but in the future. They're using a line to see back to the present!"

"You got it," said D'Arcy. "When ta Griddlebacks decided to leave wherever they are in ta future, Oleg grabbed their loine as it began leaving and followed them down da hole."

"But I didn't feel the caravan move. We're still standing in the field, aren't we?" Tarquin suddenly thought of his own time-travels. "Did we follow the ship or are we still here in the now?"

"Good question. We're still here. Ta BRONCO hooked da Griddleback ship and followed it to da canal bank but at another point in ta time. Think of da BRONCO being attached to da fishing line that's then attached to da rod. Ta caravan's ta rod and it stays in the same place while the BRONCO, attached to da line, follows the Griddleback ship through the water—through time—to wherever it stops."

"Thanks," said Tarquin. "I almost feel as if I understand it now. Thanks."

In the kitchen, Calbhach called everyone together. He jumped up onto a chair to address the gathering.

"What we've just witnessed is da greatest BRONCO rider this side of da Zwicky's Triplet in action!" he proclaimed. Meanwhile, Ardal sprayed the wound on Oleg's leg with what D'Arcy told Tarquin were quick-healing cellulose particles. Once more the leprechauns applauded.

Oleg's face donned a look of smug satisfaction and, his leg already scabbing nicely, he strutted—insofar as it's possible to strut with a limp—towards the door.

"Way yer go!" shouted D'Arcy, launching himself at Oleg in an attempt to high-five him as he passed. Smaller than your average leprechaun, D'Arcy often forgot his physical limitations. He missed and fell in a heap.

"Follow me," said Oleg. "I show you something."

Everyone obediently went with him to the control room and watched as he took his chair by the flight console. They crowded around him.

"See." Oleg pressed buttons and turned knobs.

A strange alien-looking spaceship materialized on the screens above them. Grinning inanely, Oleg turned and looked at his friends, his eyes burning wild with rage.

"And see now!"

He lifted a flap on the console and pressed a red button underneath.

The hull of the Griddleback ship, which had been a smooth, steely bluish green, was suddenly covered in thick, lumpy yellow and brown goo that bubbled and spat like toasted cheese left under the grill too long.

Oleg roared with laughter and, seeing Tarquin next to him, thumped him hard on the shoulder. "You see, English boy, good fun, eh?"

Tarquin rubbed his shoulder and grinned. Toasted cheese be damned. The Griddleback ship was now entombed in Aunt Mira's speciality: cold Sunday lunch in a sea of congealed onion gravy.

"They won't be going nowhere for long time! It take age to clean glup from sensors!" cackled Oleg.

After a while someone mentioned hot chocolate. The leprechauns, whose attention spans seemed to be somewhere south of that of a three-year-old, trooped off to the kitchen for refreshments.

Passing Tarquin a mug, Calbhach sat down and explained what Oleg had just unleashed on the Griddleback ship. Hundreds of races travelled through space and time using wormholes. As a result, the holes regularly became clogged with anti-matter's flotsam and jetsam, the nature of which was far too complicated to describe right at the moment beyond that it was stinky and corrosive—a gelatinous glue that could stick to ships like used bubblegum to the sole of your shoe. Oleg delighted in collecting the stuff. He'd just emptied a full tank of it onto the Griddleback ship.

And then Oleg, the leprechauns and Tarquin—declared an honorary leprechaun by Calbhach and the others—set themselves to celebrating in earnest.

Hours later, Tarquin looked at his phone. "Cripes, is that the time!"

It was nearly midnight. He'd have some explaining to do when he got home.

"I have to go!" he told Calbhach urgently.

As they stood in the cool night air outside the caravan a few minutes later, Calbhach pulled a small tube from his pocket. "With Griddlebacks about, you'll need protecting. Take my Higgs Bosun. No one will know you've got it. There'd be trouble, were it found. Yer needs a half day's course to learn it, but it's real simple. Point with this end and think nasty thoughts. The Bosun will do the rest. Limiter's set on it, so you can't do permanent damage. Things could get tricky here. Best not visit again. I spoke with Jules. He told me to give yer this, too." Calbhach handed Tarquin a small metal disc. "It's a communicator. If it makes a sound and you see your Uncle Jules's ugly mug here"—he pointed at the centre of the disc—"it'll be important."

Pocketing the items, Tarquin had another question. "What will happen to Jeremiah and Ingeborg?"

"These are early stages. Griddlebacks go by their own timing. We have orders just to watch." Calbhach's eyes narrowed. "Don't worry. I'll not sit idly by and see my friends harmed."

The leprechaun coughed and gave a furtive look back over his shoulder, as if afraid there might be an eavesdropper. "I'd not be taking afternoon tea in the Tea Rooms with yer relatives," he said in a low voice. "Nor congregating with any wrinklies, neither. Just sayin'."

"What do …?" began Tarquin.

"I've said too much. It's a habit with me. Look after yerself, young'un. When we meet again, tonight never happened, okay?"

"Okay. Er, one more thing."

"Yes?"

"When I first met you guys, I could hardly understand you the brogue was so thick. And now …"

"Yes?"

"Well, you still have an accent, but …"

"But it's not ta same, begorrah, to be sure?"

"That's right. Were you just putting it on?"

"Loike for tourists?"

"That sort of thing, yes."

"Nah. It's just that you're getting used to our way of speaking an' so you don't notice it so much. Accloimatization, it is. Either that or"—Calbhach winked—"it's magic. And who would believe in magic in this day and age?"

Still not entirely convinced, Tarquin set off down the hill towards Winchester Close. He glanced up at the clear night sky and shivered. Somewhere out there were Jeremiah and Inga.

When he got home, only the porch light was on. His aunt and uncle must be in bed. He sneaked into the house and quickly up the stairs. Creeping past his aunt and uncle's bedroom door, he could hear them snoring like a pair of cement mixers with severe indigestion.

Once in his room he checked that the journal and exercise book were untouched, put the Higgs Bosun phaser and the communicator disc under his pillow, changed into his pyjamas, dived into bed, and fell at once into a deep sleep.

The next morning Tarquin woke very early, fished out the communicator disc, and lay in bed rolling it between his fingers, hoping it would spark into life.

It didn't.

Outside his window the dawn chorus began as the sun rose through the trees.

Tarquin stretched, climbed from under the covers and padded over to get the journal and exercise book. Back in bed, he opened both books hoping for an epiphany.

Except for a murmuration of starlings passing noisily overhead, nothing happened.

He looked at the Hitchhiker's Guide to the Galaxy poster on his wall and closed the books. Marvin the Paranoid Android stared down at him, showing no sympathy at all.

Tarquin shook his head. His friends were missing, he had lost the translator and, worse still, he had a full day at college to get through.

"Tarquin!" shouted Aunt Mira from the kitchen. He'd forgotten what was truly the worst thing of all: the inevitable inquisition about why he'd got home so late last night.

He pocketed the disc and, squaring his shoulders like a Spartan hero, went downstairs.

It was an uneventful day at college, and Tarquin arrived home just before four. After making himself a cheese-and-ham toastie and a cup of tea, he looked at the communicator disc. Just like the fifteen other times he had looked at it that day, nothing happened.

His aunt opened the door. "Tarquin?"

"Yes, Auntie." He quickly put the disc back in his pocket.

"We're off to the Darby and Joan Club's bingo night, at the scout hut, so you'll have to look after yourself this evening. I've left supper in the fridge. Your uncle would like you to clean the conservatory windows while we're away. The Steeple Snoring Garden Committee comes tomorrow, and Harold wants it looking its best."

Clearly she'd forgotten the frosty discussion at the breakfast table as to Tarquin's whereabouts last night.

"Will do," said Tarquin, remembering last year's invasion of the anorak-wearing, clipboard-touting fogies with a shudder. He watched his aunt and uncle through the kitchen window as they drove off. Taking out the disc again, he rolled it in his fingers.

Nothing.

He trudged upstairs to change out of his college clothes.

He looked at the communicator once more.

Still nothing.

Resignedly, he got out his homework and began a history essay.

Two hours later he closed his laptop, looked once more at the communicator—nothing, yet again—and lay down on his bed. He wondered if cleaning the conservatory windows would brighten up his evening.

He woke with a jump to the shrill of the doorbell ringing and the boom of someone thumping the front door.

Tarquin quickly got off the bed and went downstairs. He opened the door to be confronted by an uncompromising and aged face, bedecked in mud-splattered flying goggles. Then there was the smell: a heady mixture of stale sherry, rough shag pipe tobacco, mothballs and camphor.

"Great-Aunt Polidori!" said Tarquin, still half-asleep.

"George Gordon Byron!" she barked. "Stop cowering behind the door and let me in."

Pushing him forcefully aside with her regimental swagger stick, Great-Aunt Polidori strode with a swish of her kilt into the house, her polished ghillie brogues scrunching loudly on the acrylic carpet. She stopped in the hallway and sniffed the air.

"Have they gone?" she asked.

Stunned speechless by her unexpected arrival, Tarquin nodded.

Great-Aunt Polidori dropped her Gladstone bag on the floor and removed her Lenin cap, revealing a cropped, spiky, black-and-white mane—an aged zebra having a bad-hair day.

Tarquin looked at her clothing: masculine, brutish and strikingly out of place—nothing unusual there. Shrouded from neck to knee in a hound's-tooth tweed cape, Argyle jacket and heavy kilt, Great-Aunt Polidori looked like an overdressed bouncer at a Scottish working men's club. On her legs she wore the horizontally striped rugby socks that had caused so much angst the last time she visited. Woollen and grossly oversized, they hung around her ankles like hoops on a hoopla stall. She claimed they came from a famous Barbarian she had met, though Tarquin had a hard time believing Genghis Khan or Attila the Hun had conquered half the world wearing socks like those.

No one dared question the spinster's unique and uncompromising dress sense—no one who valued their continued physical well-being, anyway.

"Well, George, don't just stand there." She moved towards the living room. "I've travelled a long way and I need to sit down." She arrived at the sofa, threw off her cape and irritably puffed up a cushion; once satisfied she'd beaten it into submission, she threw it into the middle of the settee and sat on top of it, crushing any last shred of resistance.

She pulled off her goggles and gauntlets. "Tea."

Tarquin fled to the kitchen and opened the cabinet above the sink. His aunt and uncle always kept a packet of chrysanthemum and Chinese wolfberry tea bags in the house, just in case Great-Aunt Polidori dropped in. Tarquin put the kettle on, found her Keep Calm & Carry On mug, and popped the bag into it. The instructions for making the tea were yellowing on the inside of the cabinet—they hadn't been used for two years.

Waiting for the kettle to boil, Tarquin spied on his great-aunt through the open kitchen door. He remembered Jeremiah calling her Churchill's Backbone. More often she was called the Bulldog. The knowledge that his great-aunt was another time-traveller scared him half to death.

From one of her numerous jacket pockets Great-Aunt Polidori produced a tarnished silver tin with the name "Audley Bowder Williamson" printed on it in faded gold letters. She scooped a wad of emerald-green slime from the canister and rubbed it into her hands. Tarquin had never had the courage to ask why her handcream was green, not white like his aunt's.

Satisfied with her work, Great-Aunt Polidori pocketed the tin and took from her waistcoat a cut-glass atomizer. He recognized it immediately. It was her Pocket Rocket throat spray, made by the Rocket Chemical Company.

First used when dinosaurs ruled the Earth, thought Tarquin.

Great-Aunt Polidori sprayed some atomized liquid into her mouth and smacked her rubbery, lipstick-encrusted lips several times before returning the Rocket to her Pocket.

Behind him, the kettle came to a boil. Tarquin prepared his great-aunt's chrysanthemum and Chinese wolfberry tea according to the instructions, checked the colour against the colour chart she'd supplied and, satisfied he wouldn't get a rollicking—well, maybe not—took the tea in to Great-Aunt Polidori.

She eyed it carefully and set it on the table beside her.

Tarquin heaved a deep sigh of relief. The tea had seemingly passed muster.

Great-Aunt Polidori took a leathery, hook-shaped object from her waistcoat. Tarquin felt sick. What she held was an emaciated finger with a curving ivory claw. It had been cut from its unfortunate owner just above the second knucklebone and neatly capped with a silver end-plate. She prised open this lid, emptied a small amount of dull black powder onto the back of her hand, and snorted it hard.

Tarquin recalled the first time he had seen her take snuff—or, rather, "snort the Prime Minister", as she called it. At eight years of age, he'd been convinced the powdered remains of the "odious Mr Wilson"—Polidori's term for the ex-Prime Minister—were what she was honking up her nose.

After wiping the snuff residue from her nostrils with a flourish, Great-Aunt Polidori returned the macabre snuffbox to her waistcoat and sat glaring at Tarquin. An oiled kiss curl, an emblem of long-vanished femininity, lay flaccidly on her forehead.

"What did you find at Samuel Pepys's?" she asked, taking a mouthful of tea and gargling it with the sound of an overflowing storm drain.

Tarquin's felt his eyes grow like balloons. "How—?"

Great-Aunt Polidori cut his question short. "Never mind how. I asked what."

He felt uneasy. Conversation with his great-aunt was like biting into a fistful of lemons and then getting a sharp tap on the back of the head. You knew it was going to be bitter and painful, but it still surprised you how much of both it was.

"I found a book," he said, bowing to the inevitable.

She thrust out a wizened hand, expecting immediate delivery.

"I'll get it." He rushed upstairs, mind alive with questions. How did she know about the journal? He picked up the journal and reached for the exercise book, but hesitated.

No, she's not getting that.

The idea of defying Great-Aunt Polidori was terrifying, but at the same time exciting.

Leaving the exercise book, he rushed back downstairs.

For the next fifteen minutes, Tarquin squirmed under his Great-Aunt's inquisition, describing his visit, the Tower of London, the meeting with Charles II and the evening with Samuel Pepys and friends.

"Well, at least your tea's palatable," said Polidori at last, putting down her mug and sitting forward. "You've been busy. Frankly, I didn't think Cavendish was the right choice to instruct you, but it appears I was mistaken, irremediable oaf that he is." She opened the Audley Bowder Williamson tin, scooped out another handful of cream, and mounted a fresh assault on her hands. Her piercing eyes, red like glowing coals, stared straight into Tarquin's.

He felt his neck tightening.

"What I am about to tell you, George," she said, "will change your world."

His adam's apple seemed to grow uncomfortably large.

"Forever," Polidori added. She paused, letting the thought sink in. "That bumbling Cavendish and his dowdy wife Inga were abducted by aliens, looking for this." She waved the journal at him. "Both primates were returned to their hovel after mind-cleansing …"

"'Cleansing'!" exclaimed Tarquin.

A derisive grin broke across Great-Aunt Polidori's face, and she shook her head. "I'm told the cleansing didn't take too long. It didn't need to. There wasn't much there to cleanse."

Tarquin's skin crawled.

"Frightens you, doesn't it, boy?"

"Yes," he said, "yes, it does. They're my friends."

Great-Aunt Polidori sniffed and continued. "Calbhach and his ne'er-do-well cousins found them in time. They've lost only three months of memory."

Tarquin looked at his great-aunt. "My father left the journal for me, didn't he?"

Polidori inhaled deeply and her plucked, pencil-thin eyebrows melded to form one continuous horizontal line. "As an old friend of mine once said, 'Vision is not enough, it must be combined with venture.' It's not enough to stare up the steps, you must step up the stairs."

"Oh," said Tarquin, wondering if his great-aunt shouldn't opt for a better quality of inspirational self-help books.

"Right. Now I must go." Polidori swept up her cape, grabbed the journal and stood. "You are not to visit that atavistic monstrosity Cavendish until the day of your next trip."

Her gaze combed him again, analyzing his intentions. Tarquin looked shiftily away.

"And don't expect that reprobate Jules Rigsworth to contact you any time soon," she added. "Concentrate your energies on school."

"It's a coll—"

"Don't interrupt!" snapped Great-Aunt Polidori.

"Sorry."

"Right." She took a compact from her pocket and, staring into the mirror, contorted and stretched her mouth in some sort of weird oral yoga until her dark-red lipstick cracked around her lips.

"Did you understand what I said?"

"But—"

"Good. That's settled, then. And, whatever you do, George"—Great-Aunt Polidori pointed her swagger stick at him—"don't ever admit to meeting those uncouth, inbred little people with the warts and no manners. I can protect you from many things, but not a bad reputation."

With something approaching military precision Great-Aunt Polidori placed her goggles over her eyes, clamped her stick tightly under her arm and pulled on her leather gloves.

"On arrival at the Silvery Moon for your next trip through time, you will act as if nothing unusual has happened." She slanted her cap over her right eye. "Choose wisely one of the places on that blessed wish list you have. Jeremiah won't remember your journey to 1671, nor the journal, so don't mention it." She checked her kilt and glanced at her pocket watch. "Time's pressing."

Her cape flung over one shoulder, she marched to the door, her shoes squeaking like frightened rats.

She put the journal in her Gladstone bag and snapped the latter shut. Tarquin felt as if she'd stolen his heart from his chest.

Like an obedient lapdog he opened the door for her.

Still she wasn't done with him. Turning at the top of the path, she thrust her swagger stick under his nose.

"I have my eye on you," she growled. "And one more thing. Stop stealing stuff!"

Off she strode resolutely down the path. The epitome of a person possessed of an indefatigable and unbreakable belief in her own superiority, she walked briskly to the bottom of the road. At the corner, she disappeared behind a line of trees.

Tarquin leaned on the closed front door and breathed a sigh of relief. She didn't know about the exercise book.

With his next time-jump a couple of weeks away, Tarquin spent his spare hours searching libraries and the Internet for the language of the translation and speculating on the reasons his father might have had to leave the journal in the seventeenth century for him to find. With Jeremiah's memories cleansed, Tarquin's only option was to speak to Jules. He checked the communicator regularly each day, but there was never anything there.

One morning, in frustration, he dropped it into his bedside drawer and left it there.

On the day of his next jump, Tarquin awoke to a frosty November morning. He sat on the edge of his bed and opened the exercise book.

What if Great-Aunt Polidori comes back looking for it, or if Aunt Mira fnds it? Best keep it with me.

He put the exercise book into his knapsack, dressed and went downstairs. As it was a Saturday, his aunt and uncle had gone shopping. Taking the last tablespoon of his foul-tasting time-travel elixir, Tarquin sat at the kitchen table and quickly polished off three bananas. His next adventure could be an interesting one—or more than that. The past few weeks he'd been wondering if, during this jump, he might find something else left by his father.

Looking out across the front lawn towards the iron bird table—a hideous present done in the Gothique style and given to his uncle by Great-Aunt Polidori—a sudden movement caught his eye. At the end of the road, standing by the letterbox, was a tall thin figure in a long black coat and a wide-brimmed hat. The man—if it was a man—had dropped into a crouch and was peering through the fence into the next-door neighbours' garden at No. 33.

What happened next made Tarquin rub his eyes in disbelief. From a squatting position, the figure leapt the two-metre fence into next-door's garden with ease and, seconds later, leapt out again with Puggles, No. 33's fat cat. The figure landed gracefully but the cat was gone.

Tarquin gaped. The figure was now gliding with unnatural speed down the road. Puggles' tail protruded from between its lips.

For a while Tarquin just stood there trying to make sense of what he'd seen.

His train of thought was disturbed by the cuckoo clock in the hallway squawking ten-thirty. Time to leave for the canal. Putting his plate in the sink and the memory of the mysterious cat-eating figure out of his mind, he grabbed his frock coat, pulled on his baseball cap, checked his pocket watch and ran from the house.

Minutes later he was turning down the canal path. After all the dire warnings his great-aunt had given him, he was relieved to see Jeremiah kneeling in front of the Silvery Moon's brass nameplate with a can of polish and an old rag in his hand, polishing and singing.

Waving and shouting, Tarquin ran along the towpath, happy to see his old friend wave back.

Without warning, a loud bang erupted from within the narrowboat, followed by a blue flash and an eruption of smoke from the topside door.

An old man's wizened face, eyes boggling, mouth open wide, a nest of grey matted hair on his head, appeared at a port-side window.

"Oi! What you think you're doing?" Jeremiah leaped onto the deck as the face disappeared.

Tarquin followed his friend down into the boat's innards. At the bottom he found Jeremiah staring at an old man who sat in a sedan chair, naked but for Jeremiah's old fireman's helmet on his head and a book clutched to his chest.

The man's eyes met Tarquin's.

"Beatus!" the ancient shouted, thrusting out a bony hand and sitting upright in the chair. "Beatus!" he cried again, shaking wildly, repeatedly jabbed a finger at Tarquin.

"Come here, you," said Jeremiah, moving toward the chair.

The old man cowered down in the chair. He made the sign of the cross and mumbled the words "Deus misereatur" before reaching under the seat.

"No! Don't hit the button—!" cried Jeremiah, but it was too late. The sedan chair began spinning. "Come back, you hairy goat!" he shouted, grabbing at the side of the sedan.

"Die dulci fruere," hollered the man as a blast of scalding steam forced Jeremiah and Tarquin to find cover.

When they turned back, the chair was gone. Only Jeremiah's fireman's helmet remained, spinning on the ground. Jeremiah kicked a pile of dog-eared old Narrowboat magazines hard across the floorboards, and roared, "Have a nice day, indeed!"

He looked at the magazines, books and furniture scattered around the boat. "I must have missed a bulletin. To top it all, Loopy Nostrils has half-inched me copies of Rigsworth's Guide to Time Travel and Scouting for Boys!"

Baffled, Tarquin surveyed the chaos. "Do you know him? And why was he shouting and pointing at me like that?"

"Heavens to Betsies, Seebee!" shouted Jeremiah. "Know him!"

The big man waved his hands in the air like a demented traffic policeman in a Milan rush hour. "Know him!"

Dropping to his knees, he rummaged through the mess on the floor. Finding an unopened Narrowboat magazine, he waved it at Tarquin.

"He's ruddy well been here looking for something, and I've missed him again!" Ripping open the plastic covering, Jeremiah flicked through the classified advertisements at the back of the magazine. "There, you see? I knew it." He poked a page so venomously that Tarquin could hardly read the small box advert.

Old Friend returning to the Union Canal in November. Please organize a surprise welcoming party. Contact Jules Rigsworth PO Box 121212.

More confused than ever, Tarquin handed the magazine back to Jeremiah, who hurled it to the floor and massaged his head like a stung bear.

After several minutes of awkward silence, Tarquin said, "I was a Scout … once … but I was never very good at making fires, well not in the places they wanted me to make them. I remember …"

"'Scout'? What you talking about, Seebee?" Jeremiah sounded accusatory. "It's not the book that's important, it's what's inside the blooming book. I'd ruddy well tucked the blueprints for a time-travelling chair inside it!"

Shaken to see his friend so upset, Tarquin suggested he make them both a nice cup of tea.

The big man's shoulders dropped. "Nay, nay, lad, this is my boat." With a sigh he headed for the galley. "You're me guest. I'll clear this up later."

Jeremiah's grumbling rumbled through the boat like distant thunder. Occasionally, the opening lines of an aria seared the air like a fireball. The welcome whistle of the boiling kettle arrived not a moment too soon.

"Tea's up," said Jeremiah.

Tarquin put the fireman's helmet on his head and peered into the galley.

Jeremiah laughed. The ice was broken.

"Ah, it be all right, lad. Your old pal Jeremiah isn't going to do anything silly."

Tarquin relaxed, happy to hear his friend's voice warming. He put the helmet on the shelf next to Washington's teeth.

"How's Inga?" asked Tarquin.

"Fine. She's in town shopping. She wanted to be back to see you before you left. Probably got caught in traffic."

Jeremiah came out of the galley and placed a mug of steaming tea on the table in front of Tarquin. "This is the second time I've missed the old goat. He's lost his marbles, what with all his travelling. Yer know, after this second time, Jules will stick two fingers up me nose, his thumb in me mouth, and ruddy well use me head as a bowling ball!"

They both chuckled.

"Who was he?" said Tarquin, sipping the tea.

"A right royal pain in the wedding tackle is Monsieur Nostradamus."

Tarquin's jaw dropped. "The Nostradamus? You're kidding me!"

"I wish I was, young'un. Plain fact is, I'm not. Jules has been after the rascal ever since he stole a sedan chair during a tourist jump two years ago. Moreover, with me blueprints, Loopy Nostrils has everything he needs to time-travel properly. Who knows what damage he could do!"

Jeremiah took a large gulp of his freshly made brew. Tea dripped from his moustache like water off a walrus. "Methinks the Time Guardians are messing with Loopy's head. He's always naked when he's spotted."

"Time Guardians"? Will I ever learn what's going on? Thought Tarquin.

Jeremiah got up and went to his bookshelf, returning with a book. The cover read: The Book of Nostradamus.

The big man flicked through the pages. "Goobledegook to me," he said, passing the book to Tarquin. Then he stiffened. "Riddle me giblets! Is that the time? Quick, we must get you ready for your journey. Where you wanting to be going today?"

"On my wish list, you put 1892 Montmartre as a possibility." Tarquin unfolded a poster he'd pulled from his pocket. "I'm studying Toulouse-Lautrec at college, and would love to visit the Folies Bergère."

"Right then," said Jeremiah, admiring the artwork. "Monsignor Lootwreck it is. Clothing's in the back. I'll sort your equipment."

Tarquin went to the large cupboard beyond the steel door, rummaged through the clothing he found there, and returned dressed in a top hat, tails and spats.

"Okay, get on the chair," said Jeremiah.

Tarquin opened the steel door to the time portal. "You've got me a new time machine!"

It was a handsome device, too: an antique barber's chair upholstered in dark red leather. He climbed into it and rubbed the armrests. "Nice."

Jeremiah came into the room. "I picked it up in Yorkshire and done the modifications meself." He grinned. "Should give you a smoother ride." He loomed over Tarquin, fumbling with the gloop syringe. "I have a request. Ingeborg and me have an anniversary soon and I reckons a little something done by Mr Lootwreck would not go amiss in Her Majesty's cottage."

Tarquin nodded, keeping a wary eye on the syringe. "Of course. I'll see what I can find."

"Thanks, young'un. You're just like your father." Jeremiah thrust the syringe into Tarquin's right ear and pushed the plunger.

"Aaaaargh! That's unfair! I wasn't ready!"

Unmoved, Jeremiah emptied the syringe, plugged Tarquin's ear, then spun him around. Grabbing a fresh syringe from the table, he plunged it into the boy's other ear.

"Done," he said at last. "There, Seebee. Parlez-vous français?"

Tarquin was about to treat Jeremiah to a few choice words in français when the grandfather clock struck eleven-thirty.

"Jeepers! Time is pressing. You hear me right?" said Jeremiah.

Tarquin nodded.

"Okay, time you was off." Jeremiah threw Tarquin his hat, cane and backpack, then stepped away from the chair. The machinery began to vibrate. Coloured lights flashed all around it.

Tarquin shouted above the noise, "I didn't see you use the Look-Sees! What about the Look-Sees?"

Through the enveloping steam Tarquin saw Jeremiah's guilt-ridden face.

"Wait!" Tarquin yelled. "Where the hell am I gooooooiiiiinnnnnggggggg–?"

The chair started spinning, and very soon it disappeared from the Silvery Moon.

Chapter 10

Uncle Jules Reappears

Tarquin opened his eyes and looked up into a quartet of smiling faces.

"Uncle Jules!" he exclaimed, recognizing the ruddy, jovial face of the man he had last met two years ago wearing a bear suit in the Enchanted Teapot. Today, Jules Rigsworth wore a curly black wig streaked with yellow highlights. It swayed precariously, reminding Tarquin of a hive of angry bees. Perched on the wig's top was a very small plumed hat. At Jules's throat was the largest Elizabethan ruff Tarquin had ever seen, and his uncle's signature goatee was dyed bright orange. Wrapped tightly around Jules's shoulders was a crimson cloak—Dracula gone Shakespearian. With him, wearing jeans and shirts, sans ruffs or hats—in fact, looking decidedly normal—were a bunch of people and several silvery metal humanoid figures.

Dazed from the journey, Tarquin clutched his backpack to his chest and warily sat up. His hat and cane fell to the floor.

Dramatically spreading his cloak, Jules cleared his throat and, in the manner of an American TV evangelist, raised both arms skyward. "Tarquin Seebohm Jenkins! Welcome to the twenty-fourth century!"

The audience smiled and applauded politely.

Tarquin leaned forward to speak into the ear of the man nearest him. "Why are we on a stage in an empty theatre?"

Before the man could reply, Jules's beady eyes locked onto Tarquin. As he approached, the welcoming committee stepped smartly back. Silence reigned. Enwrapped in the plush velvet cloak like some weird human chrysalis, Jules stared at his nephew.

Tarquin pushed back into his chair and returned the stare.

Only Jules's hat and wig moved, slowly back and forth.

A minute passed and then, with a flourish, Jules threw open his cloak again, pirouetted on the balls of his feet, and gambolled to the front of the stage, his wig now looking like a lemming ready to leap. He stopped at the edge of the stage and turned, flung his cape theatrically over a shoulder, and stood stock-still, again drilling Tarquin's gaze with that intent stare.

Tarquin felt for the red button under his ejector seat. He tried removing the cover, but it wouldn't budge—someone had stuck tape all over it.

Another minute passed, and then …

"Yes!" shouted Jules.

"Arghh!" cried Tarquin in shock. His heart pounded inside his chest as if trying to escape.

"All worlds are a stage," cried Jules, "and all the men, women, droids and aliens merely players. They have their exits and their entrances …" He jumped high into the air and thrust a finger like a fencer's rapier at Tarquin. "And one boy travelling through time plays many parts."

Jules smiled, saluted and, nodding to Tarquin, signalled one of his colleagues. Out of the corner of his eye Tarquin saw the man press a button on a small box in his hand. Laughter, applause and cries of "Bravo!" filled the theatre.

Jules spun around to the empty auditorium and bowed lavishly, his wig and hat finally giving in to the pull of gravity and falling off. Ignoring his wardrobe malfunction, he continued smiling and nodding to the empty boxes on the left and right. Then, with a casual swish of his own silver hair and a tug on his cape, he swivelled and, acknowledging his colleagues' deferential applause with a brief nod, strutted across to Tarquin in the barber's chair.

"Miss Collins," he said, catching his breath, "please be so kind as to help Mr Jenkins remove his language facilitator. French is not required here." He winked at Tarquin. "Glad to have you aboard." He grabbed Tarquin's hand and pumped it vigorously. "Hope you liked your welcome. It was all my own idea."

Before Tarquin could respond, Jules was striding off the stage towards an open door at the back, his colleagues and the silver humanoids trailing in his wake. He was nearly through the door when he paused. "Miss Collins, help him adjust. I'll catch up with you all at breakfast tomorrow."

"Uncle, I need to talk with you!" shouted Tarquin, but too late. Uncle Jules had made his exit.

Miss Collins was a tall girl with green, almond-shaped eyes, a button nose and red hair pulled into a shoulder-length ponytail; she looked to be about Tarquin's age. She stepped up to him and smiled.

"Hi. I'm Rhiannon, but my friends call me Rhia." She reached out to take the pack from Tarquin's lap.

"No, I mustn't lose this!" He clutched the pack to his midriff.

Rhia backed away. "It's all very confusing isn't it?"

Tarquin nodded. "Sorry, I need to keep this with me."

"I understand."

"My real name's Tarquin but my friends often call me Seebee." Cautiously, he looked towards the exit at the rear of the stage. "Why on Earth was Jules misquoting Shakespeare?"

"Oh, that." Rhia rolled her eyes. She picked up his hat and cane and placed them on a table. "He was planning to organize a grand tour of the original Globe Theatre in London, and claims he lodged with the Bard for a couple of weeks. Apparently they got along like a house on fire. Jules has been quoting and dressing like Shakespeare ever since."

Her infectious grin made Tarquin smile back. "Who told him he could act?"

Rhia chuckled. "Who's going to argue with him! He thinks it's fun for new arrivals to materialize on a theatre stage. A captive audience. I suppose."

"He's loopy," muttered Tarquin.

"Jules is just a harmless, bohemian eccentric." Rhia put a bowl under one of his ears, gently unplugged the wax seal and emptied out the gloop.

Tarquin winced.

"You did very well not to overreact to him," said Rhia, wiping around his ear. "Last week he performed the finale from Romeo and Juliet to some poor girl from the Liverpool Canal. She was so confused she hit the red button on her office chair straight away and reappeared in the home dressing room of Liverpool Football Club—and on a match day! We know she's safe, but she's not been back."

They both laughed as Rhia moved around to empty Tarquin's other ear.

Tarquin put his top hat back on. "And what were those silver things?"

"Droids. We have thousands of them here. They help us."

Just then a droid walked onto the stage and came over to them.

Tarquin looked warily at it. "Artificial intelligence," he mumbled.

The droid heard him, turned and smiled. "Hello, Dave. How may I help you?" It put its silvery hand out.

Tarquin looked nervously at Rhia before shaking the proffered hand.

"My name's Tarquin. I don't know who Dave is, unless you're trying to be funny?"

"I am sorry, I don't understand?" replied the droid.

"2001, A Space Odyssey, where the computer takes over?"

The droid stood motionless.

"You can get out of the chair now," said Rhia, breaking the uncomfortable silence. "The droid will assist you if you're feeling weak."

The droid took the boy's arm and helped him to his feet. Tarquin leaned unsteadily against the chair.

"Take your time," said Rhia. "It's always horrible after a jump, isn't it?"

He nodded and took several deep breaths. His barber chair wasn't the only time-travelling vehicle on the stage, just the latest in a line that included a beige sofa, a gilded chaise longue, a shiny black leather office chair, and an ornate eighteenth-century commode.

Rhia saw that his eyes had settled incredulously on the commode. She laughed. "Can't imagine travelling very far in that!"

Tarquin grinned, feeling the colour return to his face.

"I like the outfit," she continued, handing him his pack and cane. Where did you think you were going?"

"Paris, 1892."

She sighed. "I've not done the Paris tour."

With the droid's help they walked across the stage.

Movement made Tarquin queasy. "I'm very sorry, but where and when am I?" he mumbled groggily, loosening his cravat. "Is this really the twenty-fourth century?"

"Yes, welcome to 2340. Come on, let's get you a drink and we can sit and talk. We don't have to go far."

Her quiet tone and soft Welsh accent reassured him. He was a long way from home, but in some ways not so far.

A few minutes later they were in a brightly lit glass atrium decked with tables, potted trees and plants. Above their heads a blue sign flashed:

RIGSWORTH'S AMERICAN DINER—WE TAKE YOU TO THE STARS!

Tarquin gawped at the garish décor. Hanging in a line along the atrium wall to his right were a dozen framed and signed American football shirts worn at various Superbowls. On the wall to his left were over a hundred baseball caps. Rhia and the droid guided him through the array of sporting memorabilia and into the diner before heading toward a dimly lit, crescent-shaped booth in the corner.

Rhia turned to the droid. "Thank you. You may go now."

The droid bowed its head and walked off.

"Fancy a custard doughnut and a cup of tea?"

Tarquin nodded, yawned and dropped like a sack of potatoes into the plush red-leather booth. He looked around at all the stainless steel and raucously coloured plastic and felt awkward, dressed as he was in a starched shirt, tails and spats. Thankfully, the diner was half-empty. No one was showing much interest in him.

"Good evening. What music would you like?" The female voice emanated from the small 1950s Rockola jukebox on the booth table. Startled, Tarquin peered at the fascia's myriad coloured-glass buttons.

"Good evening. What music would you like?" repeated the voice in its sickly US Midwest accent.

Tarquin looked around for help from Rhia, but she was at the other end of the diner ordering food and drinks.

"Nice music?" replied Tarquin, just before spotting a button entitled "Modes". He pushed it and five hand-sized holographic figures jumped from the box and gyrated on plinths on the booth counter in front of him. Each plinth was labelled with a musical genre.

"May I suggest, based on your style of dress, musicals, baroque or classical?" said the voice.

"No thanks," said Tarquin. He pointed at the little figure at the back playing guitar.

"An excellent choice," trumpeted the voice.

A syncopated four-four rhythm pounded throughout the diner as a three-metre-tall 3D projection of a gyrating Tarquin appeared on the back wall. He watched in horror as his doppelganger dropped to its knees and laid down a chugging, heavy metal riff on an imaginary guitar.

Diners turned to watch.

They turned to giggle.

Quite a few seemed to be making videos to ensure Tarquin went viral on whatever was the 24th-century equivalent of YouTube.

"Karaoke, air guitar!" announced the jukebox's voice excitedly over the diner's speakers.

Tarquin's panic-stricken face stared down from the wall. He'd noticed that the figure on the plinth had a guitar. What he'd not noticed was the plinth's label: "Karaoke with Everyone!"

Prodding wildly at the holographic figure cavorting on the table in front of him, he eventually hit it a glancing blow. It disappeared from the table. In the same instant the wall projection also disappeared.

Tarquin's relief was short-lived. Five three-metre Tarquins replaced the original projection. Worse, they were wearing miniskirts and gaudy make-up and holding microphones.

"Oh, nooooooooo!" he wailed. He had morphed into a girl band!

He poked, prodded and despairingly slapped the holographic figures on the plinths. To his immense relief, the Five Tarquinettes fizzed and disappeared.

Diners turned to gaze at him, laughter all over their faces. He could only respond with a banal grin.

Rhia arrived at the booth carrying a plateful of doughnuts and two mugs of tea. "Oh dear, that's a shame," she said, biting her lip. "I was looking forward to hearing you sing!"

Tarquin wished the floor would swallow him up.

Rhia sat down and passed him a mug of tea. "I'm from the Llangollen Canal in Wales," she said, tactfully changing the subject. "What about you?"

"Grand Union, near Pottersbury, Northants." He grabbed the nearest doughnut. Moments later a large blob of custard dripped from his chin to his waistcoat. His attempts to look real cool in front of this wonderfully attractive girl really weren't working out too well. "Sorry, time-jumping makes me very hungry," he added sheepishly.

Rhia giggled, biting daintily into her own doughnut. Swallowing, she said, "May I change the programming? I don't think you're into 1990s Muzak."

She deftly interacted with the holograms until melodic electronic pop filled the booth.

"Who are they?" murmured Tarquin, nodding in the direction of a camera-wielding group who had just sat down at a large, food-laden table in the centre of the diner.

"Japanese jumpers, probably back from the Fall of the Holy Roman Empire tour," Rhia said nonchalantly, as if time travel were like taking a trip to Brighton for a long weekend.

"Jeremiah said there were others, but—"

"'Jeremiah'? Jeremiah Cavendish?" Rhia's eyes lit up. "He's a legend. He trained you?"

Tarquin nodded. "Yes, I've been travelling two years with his help."

"You must tell me all about your adventures!" She inched closer to Tarquin.

For the next hour the young couple ate doughnuts, drank tea and compared notes on wormholes, follies and the waterways of the British Isles.

"Oh, I nearly forgot," said Rhia at last, taking a tablet from her coat pocket. "As luck would have it, I borrowed this from the library today." She flicked through the electronic pages to the end and pointed to a map. "You see that line?"

Tarquin looked at the map and nodded. Dozens of intersecting coloured lines and hundreds of station names swam before his eyes. It looked like the London Underground map on steroids.

"There," she said, pointing to a dogleg bend on a line of green coming out of Milton Keynes. "The lock-keeper's cottage on the Grand Union Canal at Steeple Snoring. 'Travel Manager, Jeremiah Pharaoh Cavendish.'"

Tarquin laughed. He'd always wondered what the "P" stood for.

"I see you're getting to know our new traveller." A stocky young man with short blonde hair and striking blue eyes moved into the booth to sit next to Tarquin.

"Hello," the newcomer said, his accent crisply Scottish. "I'm Archie, Archie Campbell, from the Union Canal near Edinburgh."

Tarquin shook Archie's hand.

"Archie's a dab hand at time-travel guiding," said Rhia. "He qualified last year and has been guiding time-tourists ever since."

Archie smiled, feigning modesty. "Don't believe a word this lass tells you."

Though tired, Tarquin felt a great weight lift from his shoulders. Since his first jump, he had wanted to share his incredible experiences with others. He'd tried it once, but none of his college friends believed him. Now, in an American-style diner somewhere in the twenty-fourth century, he was with people who understood.

The sound of a familiar voice made Tarquin sit up.

"You're the lad that snaffled Napoleon's frockcoat."

Tarquin looked at the jukebox, then at Archie, then Rhia.

A rasping cough came from under the booth table and they all looked down. Standing with his arms crossed was a short, elfish, weatherbeaten fellow with thick pointy ears and a long red beard. On his head was a pork-pie hat.

He looked up and smiled. "Good to meet yer, Mr Jenkins."

Calbhach! Tarquin was just about to greet him like an old friend when he remembered their agreement on the canal to keep their first meeting a secret.

"Tarquin, meet Calbhach O'Reilly," said Archie, helping Calbhach climb onto the seat next to him.

The leprechaun extended a stubby hand and Tarquin shook it. It occurred to him that he'd been doing a lot of hand-shaking since he'd arrived here.

"Me and me brothers were well impressed with yer nicking things," said Calbhach.

Rhia looked crossly at him. "Time travel is not about stealing things!"

Tarquin cringed. He was about to speak when Archie changed the subject by suggesting another round of doughnuts and drinks.

Time passed. As the friends sat eating and talking, Tarquin's eyelids drooped and his head began bobbing up and down like the head of a plastic dog on the back shelf of a car.

Rhia noticed he was fading. "Time you went to bed. Let's get you to your room."

"I best be going too, got ta see a leprechaun about a t'ree-legged trundogan racing whippet. Sleep tight, Seebee." Calbhach jumped from the seat and trundled off.

Tarquin had been allocated Room 101, just along the corridor from Rhia's room, which was opposite Archie's. They stopped outside Tarquin's door and Archie opened it.

Rhia smiled. "Sleep well. Breakfast is at nine. I'll collect you. You'll find some more suitable clothes in the dresser." She kissed him on his cheek and Tarquin blushed.

"Thanks," he mumbled, feeling both embarrassed and excited as he closed the door.

His mind was on fire. Ideas, questions for his uncle, thoughts and images whizzed inside his head, exploding into even more images, thoughts, questions and notions but, when he found the bed, he was asleep before his head hit the pillow.

He woke to the soft, dulcet tones of classical music being played by a holographic quintet sitting in the corner of his room. Rays from the rising sun streamed through a large round window above his bed. He stretched, feeling rested and refreshed. The previous day had been one of the weirdest he had ever known.

He looked around his apartment. He'd barely noticed it last night. Cream walls and stainless-steel fittings gave the impression of clean, fresh modernity. His bed had pleasant light-blue sheets and was pill-shaped, with lots of dials on the head-board. Beside the bed was his knapsack, just where he'd dropped it.

A shadow passed the window, blocking the light. Intrigued, Tarquin stood on his bed to have a look.

He wasn't sure what he'd expected, but what he saw astounded him. Outside his window was a boundless glass and metal metropolis shrouded in morning mist. The flying object that had cast the shadow was sausage-shaped, metallic bronze in colour, and the size of three jumbo jets. It hovered silently, one of a group of five, above a cluster of triangular smoked-glass skyscrapers. Each building was linked to the next by dozens of translucent tubes. Small red-and-green craft with bulbous headlamps and topped by large glass domes flew in all directions, weaving and diving between buildings and vast 3D advertising projections. He recognized a few product names—Coca Cola, Honda, McDonald's—but there were plenty of unfamiliar ones, too, like Macrohard, Nanobot and Sorayama. It was like Blade Runner, but more so.

Amidst the flashing signs and spinning 3D projections, one video advertisement caught his eye. It began with a balding man with wisps of silvery ginger hair, wearing black-rimmed glasses and a bright red tie, smiling from inside one of the red-and-green flying bubble cars. The car flew into the air with the man giving the thumbs-up before it darted between buildings and swooped low across huge tracts of desert. Close-ups of the car showed the man inside the glass dome grinning. The advert ended with the man and his family standing by the car in front of a large silver pyramid with opaque, oblong windows and a white picket fence. A tagline appeared below the fence:

GO TO WORK IN AN EGG!
(ECOLOGICAL, AND GOVERNMENT-GUARANTEED)

He seemed to have seen the man's face many times before.

Tarquin turned back into the room, jumped from the bed, and searched for his clothes. He found them in the dresser, as Rhia had promised. Everything was there: leather jeans, jumper, boots, frock coat and even his prized New York Yankees baseball cap. Jeremiah must have sent them on.

Seeing what looked like a shower cubicle in the corner of his room, he walked into it. The cubicle door slid efficiently shut behind him.

A seductive female voice asked him to remove his underwear.

Embarrassed, Tarquin tried to open the door but it had no handle. Pushing it achieved nothing. He examined the cream ceramic walls for a button to open it, but all he saw were hundreds of tiny nozzles flush with the ceramic. It had to be a shower.

A drawer opened in the wall. The female voice returned, asking him, a little more testily now, to place all clothing "in the drawer provided". Cowed into obedience, he stripped off the jockey shorts and socks he'd slept in and followed instructions.

Swoosh!

He was buffeted by a 360-degree blast of warm water, followed by hot, scented air. The whole process took about five seconds, and then the door opened. The voice, friendly again, told him to "Have a nice day."

Grinning, Tarquin stepped back into the cubicle and showered another five times. He was beginning to like the twenty-fourth century.

He was pulling on his motorcycle boots when there was a knock at the door. He opened it expecting to see Rhia or Archie. To his surprise, a tall, metallic, curvaceously female droid stood in front of him.

"Good morning, Dave. I come with the compliments of Jules. I am here to help. May I come in?" she said, with the same amiable but by now more than mildly irritating US midwest accent he had heard in the shower and the diner.

"My name's Tarquin, not Dave."

"Sorry, Tarquin." The metallic female sashayed into the room and turned on her spiked heels to face him. In place of eyes she had a blue horizontal slit running across the front of her face. For ears she had two vertical antennae about ten centimetres tall. Her skin, for want of a better word, was iridescent and bluish silver chrome. Despite having lumps, bumps and curves in all the right places, she was definitely a machine.

"If Mr Tarquin would care to sit down, I will run through today's programme of events."

Tarquin sat on the end of his bed and listened attentively. The more she spoke, the more the droid's voice—a turgid, sibilating whine—hammered inside his head like a woodpecker learning to box. When he thought he could take it no longer, he stopped her in mid-flow, rushed to his knapsack, rummaged through its contents, and pulled out his iPod.

"Can you sample voices?"

"Of course! I am a Sorayama 27200," she said proudly.

"If I give you this, can you sample one of the singers on it and put it into whatever your voice thingy is?"

"My history database recognizes this ancient device, but I already have a catalogue of different voices you can choose from?"

She gave him a remote control. He looked at the smooth egg-shaped metal device, full of silver pins.

"Thanks for the offer," said Tarquin, handing back the remote, "but the woman's voice on these music videos will be fine."

"Would you like me to download all her music videos and interviews from our extensive historical library here in the centre? I can then replicate her movements as well."

Tarquin thought for a moment and smiled. "Great idea, copy everything!"

To his amazement, the Sorayama 27200 opened her mouth, swallowed the iPod, and sat down on the edge of the bed, crossing her legs. Several minutes passed, then a flap opened in her stomach and she passed the iPod back to Tarquin.

"Do you wish me to start speaking with this voice?" she said.

"Oh, yes, absolutely!"

"I will adjust my persona to match her movements and speech."

"Wow! How do you do that?" asked Tarquin.

"I analyzed her songs, performances and interviews from the historical data. With this information, I can become her."

"Cool!"

"And," said the Sorayama, "how would you describe her?"

For the next fifteen minutes, a heavy twang flowed from the droid as Tarquin listed words to best describe the pop diva. There was a sharp rap on the door. Tarquin jumped up and opened it to Rhia and Archie.

"Ready for breakfast?" asked Rhia, her face aglow with the strong sunlight streaming into the room.

Before Tarquin could reply, Archie spotted the droid. "Wow, a Sorayama 27200! Who gave you this?" He pushed clumsily past Rhia.

The droid walked over and extended a metal hand. "Hi. I come with Jules's compliments."

Archie shook her hand. "I love the voice. She sounds very familiar."

"Oh, yes, this is one you'll know," said Tarquin.

Tarquin and Archie huddled with the Sorayama 27200, deep in conversation, leaving Rhia by the door.

"She needs a name, not too obvious, but one that represents her new persona," said Tarquin.

Archie looked deep in thought, and then he slowly smiled, saying, "I've got it. Let's name her Maddy!"

"Come on you two," Rhia interrupted. "Bring your toy and let's get breakfast." As she turned to lead the way, she gave Maddy a suspicious, squinty look.

The diner was packed full of aliens, droids and humans. As they walked to their reserved table, Tarquin's head turned back and forth like a one-eyed dog's in a butcher's shop as all manner of creatures sat in groups, lumbered, oozed, strutted, crawled, jerked and jumped inside the diner. He stopped, open-mouthed, to watch a droid escort to its table a lolloping orange stick-like creature with one eye, its three arms carrying what looked like an accordion and a grin on each of its six rubbery lips.

"I must be in a science fiction film," Tarquin said to Archie.

"Where do you think Lucas did his research for the bar scene in Star Wars? Come on, let's sit down. I'll get the menus."

Archie slid into the booth, followed by Rhia. Hexed by an undulating female alien and her five preening children walking towards them, Tarquin had to be pulled to his seat. Maddy sat down beside him.

"You have no idea the embarrassment those Gerash Miijala's cause, with their uncontrollable kids," said Archie, nodding towards the female as she passed their booth with her leering brood. Archie turned back and pressed a green button on the jukebox. Hologram menus appeared and floated in front of all of them, except Maddy. Rhia chose quickly and spoke her order into the jukebox. Tarquin was less sure and filtered suggestions through Archie. Each of Tarquin's suggestion was met with either a tortured expression or a "not before you have been here a while" comment. His fifth choice, the Big Bang Breakfast, received a shrug and a look of "maybe", so Tarquin settled for that.

Tarquin was talking with Rhia when the food arrived. He was eager for his breakfast.

The waitress put his plate down in front of him.

"Oh." he said.

He looked up into the waitress's smiling, leathery rainbow-painted face.

"Um," he said.

He pointed to the tiny orange pill placed in the exact centre of his large dinner plate.

"Is that it?" he said.

He'd been expecting much, much more.

The waitress's smile froze. She shook as if struck by lightning.

"Oh, no," said Archie, turning and ducking behind Maddy.

Rhia hastily dived into her backpack, looking for nothing in particular.

The waitress growled. Her false eyelashes flittered up and down like a stuck venetian blind in a storm. Her lipstick-encrusted cave of a mouth puckered as she hauled air like a jet engine between her broken yellow teeth. Wrapping her pencil in her slavering tongue, she rolled it to the corner of her mouth and directed towards Tarquin an expression of vindictive malevolence and a string of curses so vile that he wondered momentarily if he'd strayed into a Quentin Tarantino movie.

She was insulted. Magonoid Shagganats do not like to be insulted.

"Eeeez puurfect. Look clossly!" she grunted, her low, rumbling voice reverberating painfully inside Tarquin's chest. Feeling as if a train had passed through him, he leaned over the plate and peered closely at the pill.

"Tarquin! Don't look at the—" shouted Rhia, peeking out from behind her backpack. It was too late.

Baaaaaaang!

Tarquin sat up sharply, breakfast running down his face.

"Iz Big Banga Breakfast no? Ha, ha, ha," cackled the waitress.

She turned and waddled off towards the doors to the kitchen, her vast rump gyrating like a sack full of amorous rabbits.

Maddy, who had sat silently, let out a terrifying howl and leapt after her, beating the waitress to the kitchen doors. She grabbed a pencil from the Magonoid Shagganat's diner uniform and pointed it menacingly.

"Strike the pose!" commanded Maddy, lunging forward and sinking the pencil tip into the waitress's bulbous, purple nose. The waitress cried out, and with flailing arms lumbered after Maddy, but the Sorayama 27200 was quicker.

"Like a Shagganat ..." sang Maddy, ducking artfully under a bearlike swat. In a blur of speed she slipped behind the waitress and shrieked into her shell of an ear, "Tweaked!" She rammed a fork into the Magonoid Shagganat's expansive rear. "For the very first time!"

The waitress howled more from embarrassment than pain, then spun round, trying to catch Maddy. No such luck. Maddy danced, sang and circled around her, poking, prodding and sticking her at will with the fork, accompanied by cheers and olés from diner customers.

The exhausted Magonoid Shagganat waitress finally gave up and, with roars from customers ringing in her ears, stumbled towards the safety of the kitchen doors, knocking over several kitchen droids as she disappeared inside.

"I don't think I'll have the Big Bang Breakfast again," said Tarquin, still removing wads of breakfast sludge, hash browns and egg yolk from his curly hair.

"The Big Bang Breakfast needs room to expand," replied Rhia sympathetically, helping him mop up the remaining food. "That nasty creature made you put your head close to the bang so you became part of the expanding breakfast." Rhia pointed at the small print warning under the breakfast's description on the holo-gram menu. "The devil is in the detail. It could have happened to anyone. Go on, try another."

With the waitress refusing to come out of a store cupboard, Maddy took over making things happen in the kitchen. Tarquin swallowed his pride and tucked into a fresh Big Bang Breakfast. Creatures passing the booth made gesticulations with various appendages that Tarquin understood to signify a thumbs-up. Some stopped, shook Tarquin's hand and told him how they had wanted to give the grumpy waitress a lesson for years, but were too afraid.

The three youngsters had polished off their meals and were enjoying a cup of tea when Jules appeared. He was dressed in a sharp dogtooth-check zoot suit, a black, pencil-thin tie and a wide-brimmed felt hat.

"A killer-diller coat with a drape shape, reet pleats and shoulders padded like a lunatic's cell," he said in a strange quasi-American drawl, before his jovial demean-our disappeared and he jabbed a gloved finger at Tarquin.

"We need to talk. Now!" he barked.

"Of course, Uncle Jules. Sorry, Mr Rigsworth," stumbled Tarquin. He had so many things he wanted to ask! Leaving the booth, he turned back to look at Rhia and Archie with a silent plea for guidance, but they shrugged their shoulders.

Tarquin followed Jules down a wide corridor, through a reception area and into a large oval office.

"Take a seat," said Jules, pointing to two leather armchairs facing each other. He threw his felt hat onto a coat rack and sat down. Tarquin took the seat opposite.

Jules stared at him, occasionally drumming his fingers on the chair arm, then suddenly leaned forward. "What I am about to offer you will change your life for-ever."

Tarquin gulped.

"Time to make a decision, nephew. Your progress is passable, so I'd like to offer you a new life, here in 2340. You will of course be on probation for a while, and will have a lot to learn quickly, but Jeremiah is confident you'd make a good agent."

At the mention of the word "agent" Tarquin mouthed, "Wow!"

"You'll remember," Jules was saying, "that I told you your father and mother worked for an organization that monitors Earth's space and time. I am one of four British Earth directors of that organization. Along with my colleagues, we protect humanity's interests, have a place at the Interplanetary Confederation and negotiate with aliens throughout the universe, and beyond." He sat back in his chair and smiled. "Agent Jenkins Junior, welcome to the British Intergalactic Foreign Service. We affectionately call it the BIFS."

"Thank you, Uncle Jules!"

"But," said Jules, "before we return you to 2015, I want you to use the remain-ing four days you have here to think it over."

"Going back?" said Tarquin. "I need to ask you some questions. I can't go back!" He stared at the zoot-suited man behind the desk. "Please. I need your help."

Jules's eyebrows meshed together. "Tea, we need tea," he said, pressing a button on his desk and placing an order for a pot with biscuits. "Now, Tarquin, what's troubling you?"

Tarquin had rehearsed this meeting a hundred times in his bedroom, but now, with his crazy uncle in person sitting opposite him, his mind went blank.

"Well …" he said, thinking of the journal and the half-translation.

Maybe Jules would know what to do? He looked at his uncle. Perhaps better not to involve him yet. My father didn't take this to him, and who knows what Jules would do with my exercise book.

"Why did you throw that silly party at the Enchanted Teapot for Donald McCauly's shed when I was thirteen?" asked Tarquin.

Before Jules could speak, a droid arrived with a tray of tea and two packets of custard creams (sell-by date 2008). Pouring the tea, Jules placed several custard creams on a plate for Tarquin.

"Drink and eat, while I tell you a story."

Taking his mug, Uncle Jules sat back in his chair.

"Calbhach said you'd read about Griddlebacks, and that he'd mentioned the Leche to you. We knew that Leche were lurking around the farm, so we decided to hold a party using droids and leprechauns disguised as bears, and check out the area. We also took the opportunity to talk with you."

"Is Mr McCauly okay?" asked Tarquin.

Jules nodded. "Whatever the Leche were up to, they disappeared soon after we arrived." He smiled. "You must have a hundred and one other questions for me, Tarquin."

Jules was right. Tarquin asked a plethora of questions about his parents, Jeremiah, the universe, time travel, and the human race's part within the scheme of it all. However, as he rattled off the questions, he was careful not to mention the journal.

His final question brought a smile to Jules's face. Tarquin had noticed that a vast number of twentieth- and twenty-first-century cultural influences moulded many aspects of twenty-fourth-century life. Why?

"Simple," said Jules with a grin. "The century you lived in and its predecessor were the most creative in world history. It's normal now to quote from or describe things according to those centuries."

Jules wrapped up the meeting by explaining that, regardless of his decision, Tarquin would have to return to 2015 in four days' time and resume his normal life. If he accepted the offer of a new life in 2340, Jules would work up a story for his disappearance and, sometime soon, Tarquin would return to the future. If, however, Tarquin decided 2340 wasn't for him, he would wake up with a sore head in a corner of a field or on a park bench somewhere and remember nothing about his time-travel adventures. Jeremiah Cavendish would be just another eccentric aria-singing lock-keeper, raising worms and tending his garden.

"Take this and put it into the Edubed." Jules passed Tarquin a sliver of metal. "It's the Tour Guide School's Prospectus. The school is used as a cover; you need to learn about tour-guiding to maintain that cover. First you become a tour guide, then you become an agent."

"What's an Edubed?"

"Okay, Edubed, crash course coming up." Jules moved his hand over his desk and the back wall turned into a screen filled with a picture of a blue, pill-shaped oblong bed.

"The Edubed …"

For the next ten minutes, Jules explained how the Education Bed (Edubed) worked. Knowledge was loaded into the contraption and, while the bed's occupant slept, parts of his or her brain talked to the Edubed and learned.

"The bed in your room is an Edubed," said Jules, telling Tarquin what he'd already deduced. The zoot-suited man closed the screen with another wave of his hand.

"Did my parents go to the Tour Guide School?" asked Tarquin.

"Yes. Your father specialized in seventeenth-century European history, your mother in ancient Egypt."

Tarquin smiled. "That explains a lot!"

"For your remaining four days in 2340 CE," said Jules, standing up, "you will accompany Rhia Collins to school. I'll see you out." He walked Tarquin to the door. "One more thing," he continued, tapping his nose. "Most of the recently arrived students to the school aren't told it's a cover for our agents. We have a stringent selection process and, as I've told you, those who aren't suitable are returned to their prior lives with all their memories of 2340 harmlessly expunged. Do you remember we told you in the teashop about being a spy, because of your parents? Miss Collins has recently arrived and doesn't know anything about the spy aspect of the school. Please don't mention it to her. She's not ready yet. Archie Campbell, whom you met last evening, does know, and is already undergoing training to be a BIFS agent."

"Understood," said Tarquin.

"Oh, and take this," said Jules passing Tarquin an envelope-sized metal tablet. "We use these devices here in the twenty-fourth century to keep track of our thoughts and ideas."

"Thanks Uncle," said Tarquin getting up to leave.

During the day, Tarquin and Rhia attended Rigsworth's Tour Guide School, taking part in practical lessons. At night, while he slept, the Edubed fed into his brain the theory and knowledge to go along with the daily practical lessons. Books were loaded onto small slivers of metal and placed in a slot on the side of his bed. It was like placing a memory card into a computer. This was how twenty-fourth-century humans studied.

On the second morning of school, while taking a shortcut through Rigsworth's Library of Antique Lexicography & Linguistic Books, Tarquin stopped and slapped his forehead. He looked around, thought of the exercise book and groaned. He was passing through a vast repository of ancient and modern languages in their original form, and on computer! He laughed loudly—a bit too loud, in fact. A tall, blue, gangly humanoid alien, wearing a white laboratory coat and bow tie, ran out of a side room and stared at him with bright yellow eyes.

Tarquin raised his hand. "Sorry."

The alien made a sharp, tut-tutting noise, pointed a webbed finger at him and then disappeared back into his room. Even in the twenty-fourth century, libraries were places of silent contemplation.

Tarquin hurried through the vaulted chamber, trying to think up an excuse to stay in the library and research the language he'd seen in his exercise book rather than go to school.

He'd arranged to meet Rhia at the far side of the library. She was waiting at the door. He hurried to meet her.

"I need to spend some time looking for something in here. I won't be going to school today."

Rhia looked disappointed, but her face soon brightened up and she gave a mischievous smile. "That's okay." Her green eyes glinted. "We'll only miss a session on How to Blag Your Way into a Victorian Séance. We have a couple of hours—"

"'We'?" said Tarquin.

"'We'," Rhia confirmed. "What exactly are we looking for?"

Tarquin glanced around the area near the library entrance in case someone or something was within earshot. Satisfied they were alone, he delved into his knapsack.

"I want to know what language this is." He passed the exercise book to her. "I found it on a trip to seventeenth-century England."

"Oh, goody." Rhia's face lit up with interest. She flicked through the pages. "I like a mystery."

"Trust me," said Tarquin, warming to her enthusiasm, "this is one hell of a mystery!"

"It's beautiful," she said, looking at the script.

Tarquin nodded, taking back the book.

"Come over here." Rhia led Tarquin to a bank of machinery at the centre of the library. "I remember listening to a lecture by one of the librarian droids on how this works. You just have to place the original book in here." she pointed to a silver-coloured machine on top of a carved wooden pedestal table.

Tarquin recognized it immediately. "It's another ruddy toaster!" he exclaimed, rather too loudly.

The tall alien reappeared, this time darting out from behind a table. His saucer-sized ears moved back and forth as he stood glaring at the two humans.

"It never ceases to amaze me," said the alien in a plummy, affected English accent as he swept a webbed hand through his mane of white hair and walked towards them, "that you humans ever thought you were one of the universe's intelligent species." He stopped in front of Tarquin and crossed his arms. "Please keep your noise down. A cartload of students is exploring the 'infinite human' theorem in my laboratory, and we need total silence to concentrate."

"Sorry …Emily. Emile. I meant Emile!" said Tarquin, reading the badge on the alien's laboratory coat.

Emile shook his head and raised himself to his full height of two metres, pushed out his round chest and looked at them proudly. "We are almost, surely, about to succeed."

He turned and disappeared behind a wall of bookshelves. Rhia shook her head. "Ignore Emile. He and his colleague, Darwin, have been using newbie time-travelling guides as guinea pigs to plonk on typewriters in his so called lab ever since Archie first arrived."

"He said the 'infinite human' theorem. Shouldn't that be monkey theorem?" said Tarquin, remembering his school's maths master, dressed as a monkey and thumping a typewriter during a school open day.

Rhia nodded. "Sadly, yes. Emile, being the chief librarian, likes to investigate old mathematical theories. He found a book by a mathematician called Emile Borel in here. His own real name is unpronounceable to humans, so everyone calls him Emile. Not having any monkeys, he set up his lab using human students. The pay's small, but it's a useful allowance for sitting and thumping a typewriter all day." Rhia took Tarquin by the arm, "Come on, let's put your book into the machine before he returns."

They walked to the pedestal and Tarquin dropped the book into one side of the toaster. Rhia pointed to a small screen below the device. "Hopefully the machine will be able to identify the language."

Tarquin peered. "It says here it takes at least forty-eight hours."

Rhia shot him a look of amusement. "Only if you want to actually translate the book. We'll find the language first, which shouldn't take any more than a matter of minutes, then we'll find books on the language in the library. You can put them all into your Edubed, learn the language overnight, and tomorrow morning you'll be able to read the book!"

"Oh," said Tarquin. "I hadn't thought of it like that."

He looked at Rhia and they both laughed.

"You have soooooo much to learn," she said, squeezing his hand.

They waited. After a few minutes had passed, they were still waiting. A few minutes grew to be quite a lot of minutes.

Rhia looked at the console. "Very strange." She pushed a few buttons, then thumped the side of the machine. "It must be out of order."

Tarquin moved closer and peered inside the two chambers. "Aaaarghhhoooooooh!"

A shaft of light shot out from the side of the toaster and wrapped him in a deathly blue glow.

"Tarquin!" screamed Rhia.

A dozen heads turned to look. Someone started to say "Shhh …" but stopped.

"Ooooohflayooooh—" Tarquin observed.

The light disappeared, leaving him shaking uncontrollably, like a child who's come out of the sea on a cold day. Losing his balance, he staggered a metre or two backwards and fell to the floor.

"Whazzzzz te—?"

"You have been categorized," said Emile, standing at the head of a group of concerned onlookers, as Rhia rushed to stop Tarquin crabbing around the floor in small circles.

"Waaaz tat?" asked Tarquin.

"Wait here." Emile turned and started to disperse the people who'd gathered round.

Rhia heard a noise from the toaster. "You feeling okay, Seebee?" she said. "I need to go and check the machine."

Tarquin nodded and propped himself up against a bookcase. Rhia ran to look at the toaster. A button was flashing, so she pressed it. The machine pinged and the exercise book popped out of a small tray. The screen flickered into life and a short paragraph described the language.

Emile reappeared and went straight to Tarquin.

"You're Malcolm's son. I heard you'd arrived. Sorry, I didn't recognize you." Emile smiled and extended a blue hand. Tarquin took it and got to his feet. "We need to talk," said the librarian.

"Right." Rhia joined them, bearing the exercise book. "It's in the ancient language of the Nerydire. I'll get some language books and we can both learn Nerydire overnight. Tomorrow we'll be fluent in it!"

Emile looked sceptical. "No, you won't be fluent. There's something you don't know. The Nerydire language doesn't exist. Hide whatever it is you took from the tray in your pocket, and follow me."

"But your language thingy?" said Rhia, nodding towards the toaster.

"Shhhh!" Emile glared at her.

"But—"

Emile hissed at her a withering "Not here!"

Swivelling his neck from side to side, Emile beckoned them to follow him. With his long, galloping gait, he set off across the floor at speed. Tarquin and Rhia hurried after him through the library, up and down flights of metal stairs and across walkways until he stopped in front of a large painting of a face, its cavernous purple and crimson mouth wide open.

"That's totally weird," said Rhia, looking at the artwork.

Emile put a finger to his lips and craned his neck, listening. "Okay. I don't think anyone tailed us." With a wave of his hand, he jumped inside the painting, ran across the foreground and disappeared inside the wide-open mouth.

"That's, that's impossible!" said Tarquin.

Emile's head popped out from behind the uvula at the back of the mouth. "I said, follow me!"

Tarquin held Rhia's hand. "In for a penny."

They jumped together into the painting.

"Wow! It's three-dimensional," cried Rhia, running with Tarquin along the tongue and into the back of the mouth. When they reached the uvula they fell half a metre or so, landing heavily in semi-darkness on a stone floor.

Emile, hands on hips—assuming he had hips—looked down at them. "Never, ever mention the Nerydire outside of here again." He wiped the smooth, hairless ridge above his eyes with a monogrammed handkerchief.

Tarquin, bruised from his fall, sat up and gestured with his thumb towards the painting on the wall. "Did we come through there?"

"Clever, eh? It's one of Jules's better ideas," said Emile. "If you see a painting that's square and looks like a music CD cover, it probably hides a portal."

Tarquin and Rhia got to their feet and looked closely at the painting. It was identical to the one they'd come through.

"What is it?" asked Rhia.

"One of Jules's obscure musical interests. King Crimson. The painting's the cover of their 1969 album In the Court of the Crimson King. But," Emile continued, "be careful. Only paintings with doors, alleyways or openings like a mouth are portals. It could be painful trying to get into a two-dimensional painting if it's not a portal. Now, follow me."

Tarquin and Rhia in tow, Emile set off along a stone corridor towards a warm yellow light. At the end of the corridor Emile stopped before a steel door. "This is where we keep our collection of Nerydire artefacts, hidden from spies and prying eyes."

At a wave of his hand the door opened.

"It responds to my DNA. Now, in you go."

As Tarquin walked into a room the size of his small bedroom, Rhia shot him a look of incredulity and mouthed silently, "What the hell's going on?"

"This is the repository for every book and relic Jules and his agents, including your father, have found belonging to the Nerydire people." Emile turned on a wall light.

"That's not very many." Tarquin looked at the paltry collection of leather-bound books on a shelf above an unrecognizable stuffed animal the size of a large dog, standing next to a big, well used leather armchair.

"For much of their history the Nerydire kept their information in the oral tradition, only committing knowledge to books in their last few decades," explained Emile.

"Why?" asked Rhia, poking the stuffed animal with a cricket stump she'd found on the floor.

"They realized too late that their time was running out and their civilization was crumbling. Ironic, when you recall that they were the original Time Guardians." Emile put on a pince-nez and took down a tome from the shelf. "That was when time-guarding was an honourable profession." He climbed into the leather armchair and opened the book. "Sadly, things have changed. They let anyone in as Time Guardians these days."

"These are just old books from a lost civilization. Why not put them in the library?" Rhia was trying to pull the cricket stump from the stuffed animal's jaws.

"There's far more to the Nerydire civilization than meets the eye, and we don't want to share what we already know. It's too dangerous." Emile closed the book sharply and covered himself in dust. "The Nerydire had great powers before their civilization imploded. Some say they traded their powers to survive, others that they simply lost them. It's a mystery Tarquin's father was trying to solve."

"You keep mentioning my father. How well did you know him?"

"He never spoke of me?" said Emile in an incredulous tone.

The thought of Dad telling his son that he was the friend of a talking, intelligent, bow-tie-and-pince-nez-wearing, blue alien humanoid made Tarquin giggle. "Funnily enough, he didn't."

Emile looked back at him, bemused. "Well, your father had a great sense of humour. He was very dedicated. And he loved his tea."

"Yuk!" cried Rhia. Tarquin and Emile turned round. Rhia was gingerly waving the stump in the air with the dead animal's jaws and part of its skull attached.

Emile shook his head in annoyance. "Why do you humans have to fiddle and break everything!"

"Sorry," mumbled Rhia. She began an attempt to push the jaws back into the remains of the animal's mangy head.

Emile tutted histrionically, then: "Yes," he continued, turning back to Tarquin, "the Nerydire lost everything, not just the ability to travel in time like us by using wormholes, but the ability to manipulate it at will."

"Time travel without using wormholes and books? Surely that's impossible," said Tarquin.

Emile shrugged. "Maybe, but everything we've found points to an amulet of immense power. Jules and your father believed that the powers were not lost, but hidden—"

"The amulet! To be found and used again," said Tarquin, thinking of the book his father had left with Pepys.

"No!" shouted Emile, jumping out of the chair. "That's not it at all! The amulet is to be destroyed!" He reopened the book he'd consulted earlier and started walking in small circles, reading and gesticulating angrily. "You know yourselves how travelling in time is governed by wormholes. Well, imagine not needing them. Imagine going anywhere, anytime and with anyone and rewriting history whenever you wanted to. No civilization or race should have that power!" Emile stopped abruptly and his shoulders sagged. "But we've hit an impasse. We've had people looking everywhere for a missing book, the Nerydire Book of Dreams."

"What's that?" asked Rhia, realizing she had reinserted the jaws upside-down.

"There are many theories," said Emile, "but all of them agree that the Book of Dreams is the key to the amulet. It's the missing link."

"Do you believe the book and amulet can be found?" asked Tarquin.

"There's an ancient belief, passed down in legends, that the Nerydire's power was manifested in the amulet and that the Book of Dreams is the amulet's instruction manual."

"How did you know I was Malcolm's son?" asked Tarquin out of the blue. The question had only just occurred to him.

Emile grinned. "We put a limiter on the translator. Only your father and mother, Jules and I can work with the Nerydire language. The screening light checked your DNA and saw a match with your father. A bit of a lad, your dad was." He walked over to a large rectangular shape covered with an old Soviet trade union banner. "Just look at these!" he said, pulling off the banner to reveal a metre-high glass case containing shelves filled with a crowd of grinning bobbleheads.

"These bobbleheads are all of Jules!" said Tarquin.

"Ah, yes, fame can be so transient."

"Tell us more." Rhia knelt down beside Tarquin to look at the dozens of smiling Jules Rigsworth bobbleheads. They were all about twenty centimetres tall, dressed in Montréal Canadien hockey jerseys, plus-fours and Breton caps.

"Your father had them made for Jules's fiftieth birthday," said Emile, "but we simply couldn't sell them. After a while we couldn't even give them away." He shook his head ruefully. "Your father was too kind-hearted to tell Jules the truth and so he stored the unsold ones here. Jules thinks there are just a few here, the rest being treasured ornaments aboard spaceships and in homes, offices and art galleries throughout the galaxies."

Emile slid open a door in the case and took out a bobblehead. "All your dad's work. I spent a lot of time in here with him. You're practically family." He put the bobblehead back on the shelf. "So, where's this book you want to translate?"

Rhia looked at Tarquin, who nodded. She took the exercise book from her pocket and gave it to Emile.

Flicking through the book, Emile looked startled. "Where did you get this?"

"I found it," Tarquin told him.

"Where?" Emile insisted.

Tarquin shuffled his feet, avoiding Emile's eyes.

"I can only help you if I know the truth."

"How can I trust you? I've only just met you."

"True, but I worked with your father and he trusted me."

Tarquin made up his mind. "Okay, I'll explain. My father left the original for me in seventeenth-century England; I found it. This is a partial copy."

Emile opened the exercise book again and studied the first page.

"'The Journal of Metapheesis Olgiblat Screet'," he said. He turned quickly through the twenty or so pages of writing. "We've seen mention of Screet in some of the books here, but never seen his journal! What happened to the original?"

"Not good news, I'm afraid."

Emile raised a bushy blue-and-white eyebrow.

"My Great-Aunt Polidori paid me a visit … I managed to make a part-copy before she took the original journal."

"Mad Polly!" said Emile, sounding exasperated, "This is bad." He ran his hand through his hair in a curiously human gesture. "She knew you had it? I need to tell Jules immediately!"

He turned to go, but Tarquin stopped him. "I could have told my uncle the day I arrived, but I didn't. Is it wise to involve him?"

"We need every friend we can get. It also wouldn't do any harm for you two to learn the Nerydire language tonight," Emile added. He went to the bookcase and picked out two small slivers of metal, giving one each to Tarquin and Rhia. "Usual Edubed procedure. By tomorrow, you'll be able to read the books in here—not to mention Screet's journal, or at least as much of it as you managed to copy."

"Thank you," said Tarquin.

"Just give me the nod when you've read it and want to discuss it. This room is off-limits to everyone except me and Jules but, as you're Malcolm's son, just let me know when you want to get in."

"Please don't tell my uncle I have the part-copy," said Tarquin.

As Emile regarded the boy curiously, the smooth ridges above his eyes seemed to swell and bind together. "I don't understand why, but for now I won't mention it, agreed?"

"Agreed," said Tarquin.

Rhia nodded. "Agreed."

Emile took a breath. "Now, I suggest you both wait a few minutes before you follow me out. I'll go and find Jules."

He strode off down the corridor towards the painting.

"Wow! You're an exciting person to be around," said Rhia, grinning from ear to ear. "I haven't a clue what that was all about! Agents, aunts and amulets—sounds like a wacky film title!"

Tarquin winced. "It's fast becoming the story of my life!"

Rhia went to the diner counter to fetch food and drinks while Tarquin slipped past her and made for a booth, keeping a cautious eye open for the Shagganat waitress. Rhia soon joined him with a couple of doughnuts and a pot of tea.

"Explain," said Rhia, taking her first sip of tea and helping herself to a doughnut. "Please explain what the hell just happened!"

Tarquin saw the passion in her eyes and looked away. He thought of the solemn promises he'd made to his uncle about the school and the BIFS. He looked at her again and sighed. For far too long he'd had to hide his adventures from his friends at college. This had made him miserable and a loner. Until he met Rhia, Jeremiah had been his only real friend.

Not again. If I can't trust Rhia to keep promises, who can I trust?

He smiled at her and took a deep breath. For the next fifteen minutes Tarquin explained everything. From the teddy bears in Steeple Snoring to his swimming the Tower of London's moat and saving the Crown Jewels. From meeting Charles II and being knighted to having dinner with members of the Royal Society and finding the journal his father had hidden in Pepys's library.

"And there's one more thing," he concluded. "I'm not supposed to tell you this either, but there's more to the school than meets the eye. It's a cover for an organization that monitors aliens and Earth's borders."

"I knew the school wasn't just about guiding!" said Rhia. "So, what do we do now?"

"If you don't want to be involved, I'll understand," said Tarquin.

Rhia looked at him incredulously and threw her ponytail over her shoulder. "And let you have all the fun? No chance!"

Tarquin went pale.

"What's the matter?"

"Over there!" Tarquin nodded toward the kitchen. The Magonoid Shagganat waitress was on duty!

Seeing Tarquin, she crashed through the doors and made a beeline in their direction.

"I think it better if we continue this in my room, don't you?" said Tarquin, gulping down his tea, pocketing a doughnut and hurriedly getting up.

Rhia nodded. "We don't want you getting egg on your face again, do we?"

He caught the wicked glint in her eye and tried to stifle a smile, but couldn't. Laughing, he chased her towards the diner's exit just as the waitress reached their booth.

Back in his room, fortified by the custard-filled doughnut he'd snatched, Tarquin sat Rhia down and continued his story, ending with the meeting with the leprechauns on the canal stakeout.

"I wondered why Calbhach smiled when he met you in the diner," said Rhia. "Who is that woman you mentioned, the one with your journal?"

"My Great-Aunt Polidori. She arrived unexpectedly and took it. She knew I had it."

"Why didn't you stop her?"

"You haven't met my great-aunt!" He took a deep breath. "Think sweaty bulldog with shark's teeth all wrapped in a perfumed kilt."

"That's very scary." Rhia wrinkled her nose.

"Very! I don't understand how or why she wanted the book, but she knew all about my travels."

"Ever since I've been here, I've wondered if there was more to Jules and this place," said Rhia.

Tarquin looked at her. "That's everything I know. Like I said, I couldn't lie to you, even though I was supposed to keep these things secret."

"I told you I already suspected the school wasn't quite what it seemed. Don't worry, I won't say anything." She stood up and pecked him on the cheek. "Now, let's get an early night and learn that language. I'll see you in the morning and you can tell me all about the book."

"Another tea?" asked Tarquin, hoping their day together wouldn't end.

"No, I really must be going," said Rhia, "I have to catch up on my studies." She looked him in the eyes and laughed. "Silly me, training to be a sham time-traveller's guide and here I am bothered about getting my homework done!"

Tarquin waited until she had gone before slowly opening the door and watching her walk down the corridor. She was truly captivating.

After showering for the fifth time, Tarquin finally settled down in bed. He placed the Nerydire sliver of metal in the Edubed and readied himself for sleep.

Waking early, Tarquin nervously picked up the exercise book. He closed his eyes, took a deep breath, opened the book, and …

THE JOURNAL OF METAPHEESIS OLGIBLAT SCREET, ALSO KNOWN AS OLGIT THE WISE

"Ruddy hell," he gasped, punching the air. "I can read it!" With an hour before breakfast at the diner he hastily made a mug of tea, puffed up the pillows on his bed, and jumped back in with the book.

Dear Reader,

I pray that whosoever finds my journal is of sound mind and body, as what lies within will, and has, tormented the strongest of souls.

While searching for enlightenment on Saramontel in the galaxy of Orrn, I came across the decaying body of a mature female Grissal Thrape. Using my blessed bandana, I protected my face and nose from the stench of decay and slashed my way through the Thrape's armoured underbelly. Fashioning a hole in her stomach wall, I squeezed between broken ribs and waded shoulder-deep within its lower gut toward my holy goal. Cutting a path through her entrails, I released their contents until the fluid level dropped below my knees and exposed her sacred yellow gallbladder. I cut it out and felt the many stones of wisdom held within.

To my surprise, next to the gallbladder, trapped inside the Thrape's lower third stomach, I saw through the thin membrane the desiccated body of a humanoid. I slit open the flesh and the putrid contents gushed forth and slopped around my thighs. By the nature of the undigested armour, sword and helmet, I believed the body to be that of a warrior. Around the remains of the humanoid's neck was an amulet. I pulled the amulet from the foul soup and, tying the holy gallbladder to my back, I cut my way out of the Thrape's gut.

As is the vocation of a High Seer, I faced the twin northern moons and dug a circular pit in the wet forest floor. Taking armfuls of the Thrape's entrails, I filled the pit. After blessing the bladder, I slit open the thick walls and emptied the contents over my head and body, smearing the pungent liquid into my face and hair. I counted the stones: 32, a holy number. Fashioning a Cap of Solitude from the bladder, I placed it tightly over my head. With a stone under my tongue and seven in my left hand, and eight in my right, I signed the symbol of Krea and placed sixteen stones in a circle amongst the gore. Satisfied the pit was blessed according to the ancient traditions, I waded into the sticky offal, easing myself slowly into its clutches, sinking into the pit's middle. With my head just above the pit's rim, I took up the contemplative position of Krea, recited the Five Mantras of Divinity, and drifted into the Sleep of a Thousand Sensations.

"Eeeoy yuck," said Tarquin, looking at a picture of the bladder-wearing alien wallowing neck-deep in bloody entrails. "He looks like a zit!"

Scanning ahead through the pages, he searched for anything describing the amulet. On the last page he found a drawing of what looked like an amulet and a map. The chapter was called "Passageway to a Hundred Corridors". He started reading:

> Before their great migration, the peoples of the Nerydire worshipped a group called The Draugurs of Sheol. The group's origin was unknown and it wielded immense power.
>
> In the oral tradition, ancient stories were passed down through generations by Nerydire soldiers returning from war, with tales of hopeless battles being won by The Draugurs of Sheol, a terrifying, marauding army that appeared and disappeared at will, commanded by a group of long-dead Nerydire warriors, wielding axes of fire and wearing long crimson cloaks. It was believed their power came from an amulet worn around the neck by their leader, Gn'Gorean Crashreen, the warrior whose remains I found in the Grissal Thrape.
>
> Jealousy and rage took control of the Draugurs, and the amulet was lost. Unprotected, the Nerydire dynasty died out. It was rumoured that in the Nerydire's darkest hour The Draugurs of Sheol would once again appear and save them from their enemies.
>
> I, High Seer Metapheesis Olgiblat Screet, found the amulet and have harnessed its powers for many years. I have seen and witnessed events that no other being has seen. Now the amulet's power has turned upon me, and I must rid myself of it or die. The Illuminati are closing in and they will use it for their own purpose and kill me if they find it. I do not have the strength of will to destroy it. Therefore, I have hidden it far, far away from here. Only the Nerydire Book of Dreams can give you the knowledge to understand, use or destroy the amulet. Be warned—only the bravest of the brave will be able to resist its power. Destroying it is no easy task, as it is protected by sorcery and bedevilment. Only learning the truths in the book can protect you. If, dear reader, you decide to go on this quest, you will need—

The sentence stopped, unfinished. Tarquin flicked hurriedly through the blank pages hoping to find more. There was nothing. His meddlesome Aunt Mira had seen to that.

I have one day left in 2340, he thought. If my father left me this, he may have left me other clues to the whereabouts of the Book of Dreams. I have to go to the library and read more of the Nerydire volumes there.

He dressed quickly and picked up the exercise book.

If only I could get this copied to the tablet Jules gave me, he thought.

Opening the door of his room, he saw a silver droid in the corridor. Maddy!

He called her and she came obediently

"I need you to do something," he told the droid as she entered his room. He quickly explained.

"Of course, Tarquin," said the droid. She took the book, placed it on the bed, and scanned each page with her eye slit. Then she picked up the computer tablet and, after a couple of seconds, handed it to Tarquin. The whole process was over in a matter of moments.

"Is there anything else you would like, big boy?"

"No, that's great, thanks!" He ushered the droid out the door, hid the book under a pile of clothing, grabbed his knapsack and headed off to Rhia's room. He knocked on the door and Rhia opened it immediately.

"Tarquin?" she looked sad and confused. "It's only eight-fifteen. Breakfast is at nine."

"I think I've found something." Tarquin took out his tablet. "Can I come in?"

"I'm not dressed."

Tarquin opened his tablet and, standing in the doorway, showed her the last page. "We need to go back to the library, today."

"I … I can't. I have to go to school."

"Oh." Tarquin was puzzled by her dour expression, "I thought—"

"I have to," she said sharply, avoiding his eyes.

"Is there something wrong?"

"No. I just can't make it today."

Rhia was lying, but he didn't know why. He tried his most persuasive tone. "You know I leave tomorrow, this is my last—"

"Best if you go. I can't help you."

Rhia closed the door.

Bemused, he walked slowly down the hallway, occasionally looking back, hoping to see her grinning face as she told him she'd just been pulling his leg.

No grinning face.

"Master Jenkins?" said a mechanical voice.

"Ouch!" exclaimed Tarquin, bumping into the metal shoulder of a droid. "What?"

"I tried your room but you had gone. You must have this."

The droid held out a small communication key. Tarquin read the message on the screen:

The Bulldog, that aunt of yours, knows you have been to the Nerydire library. Be careful. Please do not come to my room.
Rhia x

Tarquin thanked the droid and hastened to the library to find Emile. He discovered him in his laboratory fixing new ribbons to a line of Underwood typewriters.

"Emile, I need to access the Nerydire books. Now. It's very important," said Tarquin, catching his breath.

"Problem?"

Tarquin nodded.

"Okay," whispered Emile, looking around the room. "Jules was in a right state last night. He said something about stopping Polly from finding our collection."

"Mad Polly?"

It was Emile's turn to nod.

The pair rushed through the library, heading for the portal that led to the Nerydire repository.

Once they were there, Emile checked to make sure no one was about. "Go inside, find what you need and leave quickly. Best you don't stay long if Mad Polly's on the warpath."

Tarquin stepped into the painting and hurried along the tongue. He fell out of the painting on the other side and and ran to the repository. Going straight to the bookshelf, he began scanning the books, looking for anything that might refer to the High Seer Metapheesis Olgiblat Screet. He found nothing.

Taking out his tablet, Tarquin brought up the map.

"Okay," he said aloud, sitting down in the leather armchair beside the stuffed animal. Maybe Dad didn't get any further?

Frustrated, he looked towards the door, hoping impossibly that Rhia would appear. Seeing the cricket stump poking from the animal's head. he smiled, remembering her futile attempts to reinsert the jaw. The dead beast looked at him with large doe eyes, like one of those badly made fake unicorns the Victorians loved.

He stood up to go back to the bookcase for one last look. As he did so, he brushed against the stump, sending it and bits of the skull and jaw flying. The headless animal rocked and fell over. Sawdust stuffing scattered across the floor.

"Blast!"

He dropped to his knees to start clearing up the mess. Emile would have a fit if he saw this.

As Tarquin scooped up a handful of sawdust, a small bronze ball the size of a marble dropped between his fingers and rolled away from him a metre or so.

Vrrrrrumph!

Tarquin fell sideways, knocked over by a wave of pressure that sent a cloud of sawdust into the air.

He scrambled to the safety of the armchair.

"Tarquin Seebohm Jenkins?" A disembodied voice filled the room.

He spun round to see that a large rectangle of blackness had appeared in the middle of the room, its edges undulating and fuzzy.

"Who's there?"

An angular, purple holographic face with a squashed and blackened nose began to form from the darkness. The owner of the face peered furtively over its shoulder into the gloom behind it, then stared straight at Tarquin.

"Only your DNA can open this communication ball."

Tarquin could see beads of viscous yellow sweat drip from the face's ridged and furrowed brow.

"I pray you found the journal hidden by your father in Pepys's library and know of its significance," said that spectral voice.

Again, the owner of the purple face looked around.

"Your father gave me a message to pass on to you. He found the Nerydire Book of Dreams, and had to hide it." The creature raised two furry claw-like hands and pointed them at Tarquin. "You must find the Book of Dreams, complete your father's work, and destroy the amulet. You haven't long. There are others seeking it, and they will do anything to possess the amulet."

The creature glanced back over its shoulder a third time, took a pocket watch from a waistcoat that Tarquin hadn't noticed there before, and continued: "Do you remember where your father took you on your tenth birthday?"

A spotlight suddenly seared across the creature's face and it staggered back, covering its eyes and dropping the watch.

As Tarquin looked on aghast, several shadowy shapes appeared from the sides of the black portal and started wrestling the creature to the ground.

A deep, mournful cry came from the darkness, then a ghastly silence.

The transmission ended and the blackness disappeared.

Tarquin found himself shaking uncontrollably.

Taking a deep breath, he climbed off the chair and picked up the ball, then slid to the floor. Head in hands, he sat cross-legged, trying to remember any details of his tenth birthday. Was that the year he was in Canada? He wasn't sure. He remembered one birthday watching a hockey game with his parents in Montréal. He got out Jules's tablet and searched for details of the Montréal Canadiens 2010 season. He'd seen them play against the New Jersey Devils, but the only thing he could clearly remember were the Devils' shirts. What was the significance? He looked at the ceiling for inspiration and then at the strange, headless animal lying on its side on the floor.

"Canadien bobbleheads!" Tarquin cried, snapping his fingers as he leapt up and dived for the cabinet. Pulling away the banner, he gazed at all the copies of Uncle Jules's caricatured face.

Which one?

He took a bobblehead at random from the cabinet and examined it. Nothing unusual. He looked at another. The same.

Twenty minutes of frustrated searching later, having examined most of the bobbleheads in the cabinet, all that Tarquin had found was that one of them had the words "Remember, remember" etched crudely into the wooden base.

He turned the bobblehead over and over in his hands. Aside from the etching, it looked like every other bobblehead in the collection. The inane, smiling face and bouncing head seemed to be taunting him to solve the puzzle.

He needed time to think. Putting the bobblehead into his knapsack, he shuffled the remaining dolls a little to disguise the fact that one was missing and replaced the banner.

"Tarquin?" It was Rhia's voice.

Tarquin jerked around towards the door. "Jeez! You scared me. I thought—"

And then his mouth went slack. Striding through the doorway and into the repository, her hand firmly under Rhia's arm, came Great-Aunt Polidori.

"The Bulldog," he whispered, feeling his throat tighten.

"Well, well, well," said his great-aunt, her voice loud and condescending. "It seems you and your father have more secrets to share."

Great-Aunt Polly released Rhia's arm and the frightened girl cowered against the wall.

Cornering Tarquin, her hawkish eyes boring into him, Great-Aunt Polly pushed him down into the chair with her swagger stick. Tarquin thought he was going to vomit.

"Well, what did we steal this time?" The Bulldog lifted his chin with the tip of her stick, "And what's all this sawdust doing on the floor?"

Tarquin gulped and stared up the length of the stick. The seething, perspiring bundle of dogtooth-check-clad woman glared back.

"I'm sure Tarquin will tell us all when he's ready," came another voice.

Great-Aunt Polidori swung round, closely followed by her dervish-like kilt.

Just inside the doorway stood Jules, alongside Emile and several more blue aliens.

Tarquin closed his eyes and exhaled with relief, pushing the stick from his face. The cavalry had arrived in the nick of time.

"Shouldn't you be elsewhere, Polly?" said Jules quietly.

Tarquin watched his great-aunt's face go a dozen shades of purple and wobble like a jelly in a Tokyo earthquake. She drew a breath as if it were her last and strode toward Jules, stopping only when their noses almost touched.

"We'll speak of this again," she growled. She was squeezing the bulb of her swagger stick so tightly that her bony knuckles had turned a ghostly white. "This is not over, not by a long chalk."

Tugging her cap firmly down on her head, Great-Aunt Polly regained her composure, thrust her nose in the air and made for the door. Jules, Emile and the others parted like the Red Sea to let her go by, and a moment later all that remained in the room of Great-Aunt Polly was the aroma of her sickly-sweet perfume.

Before Tarquin could speak, Jules raised a hand. "Please, not a word. Emile told me everything. Paraphrasing a dear friend of mine, 'There are more things in heaven and earth, Tarquin, than are dreamt of in your great-aunt's philosophy."

"You really did know Shakespeare?" said Tarquin.

Jules nodded smugly. "Now, both you two young people go and get something to eat. Whatever Polly is up to will have to wait for another day."

Elated that Jules had dismissed his bullying great-aunt, Tarquin rose from the chair and picked up his knapsack.

Rhia was grinning from ear to ear.

"My lecture begins sharp at two o'clock this afternoon, so don't be late," said Jules.

Tarquin and Rhia nodded.

"And, Tarquin"—Jules's expression changed from gleeful satisfaction to a stern and foreboding look—"come to my office after the lecture and we'll discuss what happened just now. I also want to know if you're still keen to come back."

Tarquin nodded, and hurried from the room with Rhia.

As they left, Tarquin overheard Jules say to Emile, "Move the collection to Teurpicon, where the Illuminati can't get at it."

The moment they were out of earshot, Rhia grabbed Tarquin's arm. "I'm sorry, I tried to warn you."

"No problem."

"You found something, didn't you?"

Tarquin slowed as they neared the painting. "Yes, a puzzle—but not here, Let's get breakfast."

They climbed into the painting, scurried through the mouth and jumped out the other side, then headed for the diner. Finding an empty booth, they dived in and caught their breath.

"Tea or coffee?" asked Tarquin, putting on a show of casualness.

"Never mind that, what did you find?"

"Tea or coffee?" Tarquin insisted, folding his arms and closing his eyes.

"Woz yer want?"

At the sound of the dreaded voice, his haughty demeanour turned to fear and his eyes shot open …

To see, not the dreaded diner waitress, but Rhia giggling at him.

"Fooled you!" She applauded herself quietly. "That'll teach you to try to keep things from me!"

She giggled again as Tarquin clutched his chest in mock agony. "That's not nice—" he said.

"So, what did you find?"

Tarquin held out his hand and showed her the ball. "This is some sort of communication device. An alien thingy told me to remember what I did with my dad on my tenth birthday."

"Well?"

"I remembered what it was and found a clue." Tarquin pressed a finger to his lips. "Not here. Who knows who might be listening."

"You left it in the repository, didn't you?"

Tarquin quickly checked the tables near them and then, as afterthought, looked under their own table. "No, I put it in my bag just before we left."

"Clever boy!"

"The Bulldog's not going to give up just like that, so we need to hide it somewhere safe until we can work on it." He looked into Rhia's green eyes. "I want you to look after it."

"Me?"

"I told you, I trust you."

She leaned across the table and kissed his cheek. "I'm so glad we met. What do you fancy for breakfast?"

"You decide."

Rather than risk another incident with the waitress, Rhia went to the counter and took two breakfast pills. For the next hour they discussed the Bulldog and what Tuerpicon might be.

"There's a reference to the Illumanati in the exercise book," Tarquin said as he finished his tea, "but they don't appear to be the good guys."

Rhia looked at her watch, wiped crumbs from her mouth and pushed her cup of tea aside. "I need to get off to my morning lectures."

Tarquin passed her the bobblehead under the table. "Don't forget this."

"Okay, I'll hide it in my room and meet you at the lecture theatre at two," she said, slipping the bobblehead into a bag she took from her pocket.

After Uncle Jules's two o'clock lecture, Tarquin went to meet him in his office. He felt as if he'd been sent to see the headmaster—which was in a way, he thought, exactly the reality of the situation.

"Come in," said Jules, now wigless and dressed in a Roman toga and a crown of laurel leaves. "Tell me what you've decided."

He sat back in an insanely large bat-winged hoverchair and looked down at Tarquin, twiddling his thumbs.

Tarquin sat in a smaller, lower hoverchair across from Jules's desk.

"I'd like to come back and work for you," he said.

A smile flashed across his uncle's face.

"But," Tarquin continued, shifting in his chair, "I have a few questions."

"Go on."

"Emile told me about my father and your search for the Nerydire Book of Dreams and the amulet."

"I know," said Jules. His chair rose further above the table and turned sideways. He peered down over the edge of it at his nephew. Tarquin recognized his uncle's look: part inquisitor, part madman, part Kilroy Was Here.

"Finding the Book of Dreams," Uncle Jules said, leaning yet further over the chair arm, "was the last thing your father was working on before he disappeared."

"I thought he died with my mother in a plane crash?"

"Sorry—I meant 'before he died'," said Jules hastily.

"And why is my crazy great-aunt following me!"

Jules rubbed his cheek. "Polly's well intentioned, I think. She just wants the best for you, and us, but she can be a bit of a loose cannon. She likes things ordered, set out, constant. Religious. She's a bit old-fashioned is our Polly."

Tarquin nodded, but he knew there was far more to Polly than his uncle was telling him. "And," he continued, "where's Tuerpicon and who are the Illuminati?"

Jules's eyebrows went north and he stared wide-eyed at Tarquin. For a split second all traces of manic exuberance disappeared.

"Gosh, is that the time?" Uncle Jules said with a forced smile. "Best you be getting along. I'll be in contact when we have a story prepared for your disappearance, but it may take some time. And don't forget to keep the communicator disc that Calbhach gave you beside you wherever you are."

He pointed to the door. "Till we meet again, Master Jenkins."

Tarquin found Rhia in the library, sitting at a round table surrounded by dozens of small metal strips.

"Done and dusted," he said.

Rhia looked up, but she didn't smile.

"I leave tomorrow," he added.

"Yeah, I know, you have to go home." She closed the book she was reading, stretched and stood up. "Let's go to my room and take a look at what you found."

Tarquin helped put the metal strips back into their appropriate slots in the library.

In Rhia's room, Tarquin made them a pot of tea while she retrieved the bobblehead from its hiding place. They sat opposite each other and stared in silence at the grinning face of Jules. After a minute or two Tarquin flicked the bobblehead and watched it lurch from side to side.

"Why would my father leave this as a clue?"

Rhia picked it up. "Perhaps there's something inside it ?"

She examined it carefully, pulling its feet and head, looking for an opening.

"Try twisting the middle," suggested Tarquin.

Rhia gripped the doll's legs and chest and twisted. "It's moving, but it's very stiff. You have a go."

Tarquin took the toy in both hands and imagined he was trying to open a recalcitrant jamjar.

The bobblehead broke into two pieces. A large iron key and a scrap of paper fell out onto the table.

Rhia picked up the paper and carefully unfolded it. There were just two handwritten words on it. "Remember, remember," she read

Tarquin took the note and examined it. "I've no idea what that means."

Rhia picked up the key. "Don't suppose this means anything to you either?"

Tarquin shook his head. "We have an iron key and a cryptic clue. Nothing is ever easy in my life."

After a few moments he looked at his watch and downed his tea. "I've an early start tomorrow and need to eat some more bananas and take the elixir. I'll take a quick picture of the key and, if it's okay with you, leave it and the bobblehead hidden here in your care—no point me taking them back to 2015. In fact," he added, taking out the exercise book, "if you want you can read the journal while I'm gone. I copied it to my tablet."

"Wow, thanks!" Rhia took the exercise book from him. "When will you be back?"

"Jules said they need to work up a story to explain my disappearance. Not long, I expect."

Rhia looked down at the key and bobblehead. "No real idea, then?"

Tarquin sensed her disappointment. "I am coming back. I promise."

"I know," said Rhia, getting up from the table and walking into her room's small kitchenette. "Let yourself out."

Next morning, after showering for the sixth time, Tarquin was ready for his jump back to 2015. He had followed Rigsworth's Diet and had just downed the last glass of the vile elixir when there was a knock on his door.

He opened it to find Rhia looking at him with sad eyes. Instead of her swishing ponytail she was wearing her hair loose. She peered out from behind her fringe.

"This is it, then," she said quietly, entering his room.

Tarquin nodded and shuffled his feet.

"It's only for a while," she said. "Still, it's hard to say goodbye."

"Parting is such sweet sorrow," said Tarquin, reverting to cliché to cover up his feelings.

"Jules even has you quoting Shakespeare!"

"I'll be back," he said in his best Arnold Schwarzenegger accent.

Rhia bit her lip and turned on her heels. Head bowed, she opened the door and walked quickly off down the corridor.

"Wait!" Tarquin grabbed his backpack and baseball cap and ran after her. He caught her as she reached her door. "I really enjoyed the time we spent together."

A smile flickered across her face.

"I really will be back, trust me."

She wrinkled her nose in the manner that she seemed to have patented. "Promise me we'll find out more about the Nerydire together?"

"I promise."

Rhia took a carved bloodstone pendant from her pocket and gave it to him. "Till we meet again?"

Tarquin nodded, rolling the pendant in his hand. "Yeah, till we meet again."

She kissed him softy on his lips and he was lost for words.

The door closed and she was gone.

"Okay," roared Jules above the clattering and whirling noise of the machinery gyrating on the floor in front of him, "you're going home in this reconditioned bathtub!"

He thumped the wheezing machinery with a length of metal piping, and followed this up with a hefty kick. "The barber's chair went back to Jeremiah earlier in the week."

Tarquin looked at the rusting, Victorian scroll-top tub in front of him, and gingerly stepped in. He clutched his knapsack to his chest, pulled his baseball cap firmly onto his head, put the tails of his frock coat into his lap, and settled down.

He peered over the rim of the bath like a nervous bobsleigh rider on his first Cresta run.

"I've entered the coordinates for Cretins' Copse." Jules put a pair of Look-Sees over his eyes. "Jump arrival area clear!"

He gave an exaggerated thumbs-up and pushed several levers back and forth, apparently at random. "You'll arrive back a few seconds after you left."

Jules came across to the tub and gave it another good kick. Feeling like the clapper in a church bell, Tarquin gripped the sides.

"Not to worry," said Jules, patting the iron bath affectionately. "This tub's one of our reconditioned environmentally sensitive models. It'll fall apart soon after you arrive."

Tarquin wondered whether it'd last that long, and if kicking it was a good idea.

Jules turned and went back to the levers. "Bon voyage," he shouted, pulling and pushing.

When the room began to spin and melt, Tarquin closed his eyes and thought of Rhia.

"Urrghhh!" remarked Tarquin, waking to the feel of a dozen wet tongues roving lasciviously across his head and face.

"Mooo," came the chorusing reply.

Disorientated, groggy and feeling very sick, Tarquin tried opening his eyes. Everything was a blur, so he felt for the edge of the bath to lever himself out. He managed to stand, but then a wet, rough tongue ran across his cheek and he lost his balance, falling forward out of the tub and into a puddle of mud.

Soaked, dirty and still feeling sick, he sat disgruntled on the ground.

"I hate cows!" he growled, as another inquisitive bovine stuck its tongue down the back his neck.

He pushed the cattle away and picked himself up. Slowly his vision cleared.

Grabbing his knapsack, he staggered into Ricketty Field and headed for the nearest gate.

Miss Amelia Hoploosley was taking her daily constitutional when she spotted Tarquin break from a line of trees and weave unsteadily through a cornfield, clutching a bag. This time he was alone. She made a mental note to raise the matter of his drunken behaviour with his Aunt Mira once more, and at the earliest opportunity. Male drunkenness at two in the afternoon was a sin. It was her calling to administer judgement as a crusader for sobriety enforcement, and as a past doyen of the Steeple Snoring Temperance League (disbanded due to a palpable lack of interest and an unfortunate incident when a double-booking at the scout hut pitched the Temperance League up against the burly stalwarts of the Steeple Snoring Home-Brewing Society).

This was the third time she had caught Master Jenkins inebriated, unclean and unkempt. He needed to be taught a lesson. Besides, he had probably had something to do with her enforced stay at Northampton General Hospital.

As Tarquin stumbled down the field towards the gate, he saw Miss Hoploosley staring at him. A courteous lad, he was about to exchange pleasantries when, shrieking like a wild turkey, she launched herself at him, raining blows on his head with her paisley-patterned umbrella and her heavy-duty leather handbag. He cringed under the assault, choosing his moment to take flight when her onslaught flagged.

Lumbering groggily up the road toward the village, he occasionally glanced back at the small rotund figure in the Tyrolean hat, still waving her umbrella at him.

Tarquin climbed Copse Hill and, after passing the village post office, cut across Latimer Street towards the duck pond and the Nag's Head pub. He kept thinking about Miss Hoploosley and her unexpected, almost barbaric assault on him. He knew she had his aunt's ear, and wondered at the sort of reprimand he would have to endure. Whatever it was, it would be All His Fault.

He walked through the pub parking lot, kicking leaves as he went, turned left into Wilson Avenue and then entered Winchester Close.

Some while later he was relaxing in the bath, thinking about Rhia, the book and his trip to 2340, when his solitude was shattered by his aunt's shrill voice.

"Tarquin? Tarquin! Miss Hoploosley said she saw you drunk. Again!"

He threw suds at the tiled wall. He had had enough of Miss Hoploosley for a lifetime.

"I'm speaking to you!"

His aunt's voice was closer now and threatening. Suddenly the bathroom door shook with the pounding of his aunt's fist. "I'm speaking to you!" she repeated.

"I'm not drunk!"

"She says you are!" His aunt's voice climbed an octave and several decibels.

"Oh, well, the daft old bat must be right, then." Tarquin threw some more soapsuds at an imaginary picture of Miss Hoploosley on the bathroom wall.

"Have some respect for your elders!" His aunt was now in full crow mode and circling her pound of flesh. "She saw you staggering out from Creature's Copse carrying a sack full of drink. What do you have to say!"

"It's Cretins' Copse."

"I don't care what it's called, you were seen staggering out of it, drunk!"

"Mea culpa," sighed Tarquin. "Mea culpa, mea culpa! I am now a fifteen-year-old alcoholic!" he shouted, before sinking beneath the water, holding his breath for as long as he could.

He resurfaced, gasping for air, to the sound of his aunt's slippers growing distant as she shuffled down the stairs. Tarquin heard his uncle taking the brunt of Mira's next assault.

I bet Hoppy didn't mention her crazed attack on me.

He yanked out the bath plug, grabbed a towel and went to his room, where he dressed in front of his Hitchhiker's Guide to the Galaxy poster. When the noise downstairs stopped, he left his room to craft himself a peanut-butter-and-jam sandwich. He had nearly made it to the kitchen when his uncle cornered him, next to the rubber plant.

"Your aunt's a bit under the weather, Tarquin. If you could go a little easy on her." His uncle's eyes were bulbous and unnerving, two watery eggs alarmingly distorted by chunky glasses. He reminded Tarquin of Mira's prized goldfish, Lancelot, magnified by his bowl as he gawped bemusedly at the world passing by.

"Of course. But I do wish she wouldn't always believe that old battle-axe Hoploosley before listening to me," said Tarquin. "Do I look drunk?"

Uncle Harold tilted his head sideways, leaned forward and sniffed Tarquin's breath. His balding pate glistened under the yellowing 40-watt bulb. A pained, weasel-like expression slunk across Harold's face before, wordlessly, he crept back to the refuge of his television chair and a pile of library books.

Tarquin shrugged and went into the kitchen. He'd made himself a sandwich and retreated to his room by the time his aunt reappeared from the garden.

He loved his aunt and uncle, but he could never be whatever they wanted him to be. In many ways, he was both sad and glad to be leaving 2015.

Back in 2340, Rhia was feeling tired after a long day of lectures and just wanted to wallow in her room and listen to music. She pressed a button on her leisure module and ten holographic folk singers appeared, standing on pedestals playing guitars. Selecting a diminutive young girl with a battered twelve-string, Rhia positioned her at the end of the bed. The other holograms fizzed and disappeared.

From her bed, she looked at the cosmos through the vast glass ceiling of her room. She relaxed, closed her eyes and, as the music washed over her, allowed the soothing, softly stroked guitar and angelic voice to wash around her. Three weeks had passed since she'd first met Tarquin, and now she was missing him. There was something captivating about his dark, soulful eyes and mop of curly hair. She giggled, remembering his attempt at karaoke air guitar, his first Big Bang Breakfast and his fight with his great-aunt, the bullying Bulldog. He'd floundered beautifully in the twenty-fourth century, and that endeared him to her.

Memories of her own life took over. She relived her first meeting with her mentor Eunice, a lock-keeper on the Llangollen Canal. Eunice Merryweather Temple-

Smith had been the nearest she had to family but, when asked if she'd be willing to leave twenty-first century Wales, Rhia had had few qualms. After living in orphanages most of her life, she yearned for adventure and meaning in her life. It hadn't been a difficult decision to take.

Rolling thunder rumbled in the distance. It started softly but increased steadily in volume until Rhia couldn't hear the singer. Irritated, she sat up, turned off the hologram and looked at the wall. As the noise became deafening she covered her ears.

With a burst of light and a clap of thunder, a wicker bath chair materialized in the centre of her room.

She sat up, gaping.

Hanging precariously over the side of the chair was Jules, his body covered in an assortment of weird, flashing gadgets. When he saw Rhia he beamed, the grin turning into a scowl when he realised his wig was on fire.

As if concluding some masochistic ritual, he jumped up, whacking his head furiously to quel the flames.

His head still puffing smoke like a dozen blown-out candles, he yelled, "Tarquin's in trouble, and I can't warn him! No time to lose! This is all a cover, we don't exist, you don't exist, time is an illusion, we guard it, and the Griddlebacks and Leche abuse it!"

He took a deep breath, looked at a large band on his wrist, and pointed at the door. "Sofa arriving any second—hurry!"

Jules dropped into the chair and pulled a pair of smoking Look-Sees over his eyes. He grabbed the bath chair's steering handle firmly in his hands. As the chair bounced up and down he rode it as if it were a bucking bronco. With a loud screech, the chair stopped, wobbled right, wobbled left, and then soared upward, dematerializing just before it hit the ceiling.

Hearing a racket from the corridor, Rhia leapt up and ran to the open door. Outside, Archie sat on a cherry-red leather Chesterfield, his hair and jacket smouldering. Like Jules, he was covered in gadgets.

"Grab your coat!" He slapped his smoking head. "We have to go! I'll fill you in when we get there."

Her heart pumping, Rhia grabbed a duffelcoat from behind the door, and jumped onto the Chesterfield.

"Drink this! Eat that!" Archie shoved a mug of thick green liquid and a large banana into Rhia's hands. Gulping down the vomit-worthy liquid, she chomped on the banana and then hastily struggled into her coat.

Archie pulled on his Look-Sees. "Okay, hold on tight—we're off!"

Rhia clung to his arm, closed her eyes, and wondered where Tarquin was now.

Chapter 11

Terror at the Tea Shop

Three weeks had passed since Tarquin's return to 2015 and, although he kept the communication disc with him wherever he went, there was never a message from Jules. Despite this lack of contact, Tarquin had been busy. After a bit of research, he felt he understood the rest of the cryptic clue. The words "Remember, remember" were part of a verse referring to an attempt by Catholics in 1605 to blow up the Houses of Parliament with the English king, James I and all his noblemen inside. It was known as the Gunpowder Plot.

Remember, remember, the fifth of November,
Gunpowder, treason and plot.
We see no reason
Why Gunpowder treason
Should ever be forgot.

How the clue or the key could be related to the Nerydire Book of Dreams was anyone's guess but, after showing a picture of the iron key to one of his teachers, Tarquin believed it was very old and would likely fit the lock of a very heavy door. It wasn't too big a jump for him to imagine that it might open a storage cellar under the Houses of Parliament—the very storage cellar that housed the gunpowder used in the plot!

Well, okay, maybe it was too big a jump. But the prospect tantalized him anyway.

One afternoon, after Tarquin had finished college for the day, he wandered along the bottom of Ricketty Field, close to where the leprechauns' caravan had stood. For the last three days he'd taken this same route, and each time he'd looked into the field hoping to see the lopsided and battered Willerby Vogue caravan balancing precariously on its pile of house bricks.

No such luck.

He looked across the field and sighed. Scratching at the ground where the caravan had stood were several chickens. Seeing a windfall apple on the gravel path, he gave it a hearty kick then dribbled it all the way to the top of Steeple Snoring's high street. Spotting a pillar box within range, he belted the apple with his left foot. The fruit splattered satisfyingly against the box. Hands high, he wheeled away from the parked cars and into the centre of the road, celebrating his cup-winning goal at Wembley.

Feeling better, and pleased with his moment of football fame, he jogged back onto the pavement. Putting his earphones in his ears, he hitched his pack higher on his back and ambled down the high street towards the line of shops that formed the parade.

As he reached the village bookstore he saw Sarah, the owner's teenage daughter, arranging a window display for a recent series of books. Tarquin smiled at the display of wands, pointy hats and strange metal brooms.

I would have made a good wizard, he thought.

He was nearing the Enchanted Teapot when the communicator disc began to vibrate in his pocket and Beethoven's "Ode to Joy" burst through the blare of his MP3 player. Hastily pulling the disc from his pocket, he took out his earphones and hit the disc's green button. "Hello, Uncle Jules?"

All he got in return was a sudden burst of static and a shrill voice yelling something he couldn't understand.

"Hello!" he shouted again.

Another burst of static, followed by a few indistinguishable words, then silence.

He tapped the disc on his leg and pressed the green button again and again, but it wouldn't light up.

I'll go to the tea rooms and sort it out. If it's Jules he's bound to call back.

Tarquin ran down the road to the tea shop, coming to an abrupt halt at its doorway.

The OPEN sign, shaped of course like a teapot, was turned around, and the faded sunflower-patterned curtains were closed so he couldn't see in.

He tried the door, but it was locked. Most unusual at this time of day.

Curious, he walked to the front bay window and peered through a crack in the curtains. To his surprise, the tea room was full of elderly couples, sitting and standing, all staring stony-faced towards the food counter. He briefly thought it might be a coach party from Northampton, but it was the closed season for tourists, and anyway the only historical monument of interest—the thirteenth-century church—was closed for steeple repairs.

He tried the door again and this time it opened, just as "Ode to Joy" burst loudly once more from the disc in his hand.

Fifty shades of grey turned as one to look at him.

Tarquin smiled sheepishly, took a couple of steps into the tea shop, closed the door, and quickly pressed the green button on the flashing and buzzing communicator disc.

To his dismay, it went dead.

No static, no voice.

"Tabbycats!" he cursed.

It was an oath that Archie had taught him, looking furtively around in case anyone overheard him. Apparently it meant something quite extraordinarily obscene on the planet Qqrrg.

Movement within the shop caught his eye and he looked up.

The pensioners were out of their seats and creeping slowly towards him, their arms raised and their fingers pointing, like wrinkled monsters from a budget horror film.

Unnerved, he backed toward the door.

The doorknob wouldn't budge.

He pulled back the curtain on the door and there was Uncle Harold standing outside, holding the doorknob and leering at him. Tarquin tried to force the door, but his uncle held it tight.

"Tarquin, would you like a cup of tea?" asked Aunt Mira, standing at the front of the waddling wall of grey, her movements oddly mechanical.

Tarquin just gawped at her and clutched the disc.

Assisted by several other pensioners, she poked, prodded and pulled Tarquin away from the door towards a chair and table in the middle of the room. With one particularly spiteful dig, she forced him to sit.

A pensioner carrying a tray with cups, saucers and a large teapot walked over to Tarquin and threw the contents of her tray on the table, covering him in lukewarm tea and bits of pottery.

"Milk and sugar?" oozed his aunt, turning her head in a strangely robotic manner.

"You should know, you adopted me," mumbled Tarquin, brushing pottery shards from his clothing.

The cloak of grey closed in around him. It was then that he remembered Calbhach's words in the caravan at the stake-out: "I'd not be taking afternoon tea in the Tea Rooms with your relatives. Nor congregating with any wrinklies, neither. Just sayin'."

Bit late now, Tarquin thought.

Suddenly he recognized the thin man in black standing behind the serving counter.

"You swallowed Puggles!" he shouted, jabbing a finger at the man.

"Curiosity killed the Tarquin, just like his parents," said Aunt Mira with a sneer, clamping her hand with surprising strength over Tarquin's throat and squeezing hard.

Taking the sugar bowl from a colleague, she spilled the contents over Tarquin's head. Next, she poured the milk, cascading it slowly across his face and forcing him down against the chair back.

The thin man appeared behind the chair, took Tarquin's milk-soaked face in his pale, bony hands, and squashed it until Tarquin cried in pain.

"Your family's always in the wrong place at the wrong time. First your parents, now you," the man said, still holding Tarquin's face firmly in his grip.

Aunt Mira released the boy's throat and took a few paces back.

"What about my parents?" cried Tarquin, trying to squirm free of the thin man's unwavering hold.

"No one's told you?" said the thin man. With a sneering gloat, he pushed his sharp fingernails into Tarquin's flesh, drawing blood. "That's such a pity."

Uncle Harold stood in front of the chair and pointed a crooked finger at Tarquin. "Where's the book?"

His eyes lit up as he noticed Tarquin's knapsack, still on his back.

Several pensioners pulled the pack from his shoulders, spilling the contents on the floor. Several more scrambled amongst the contents, like pigs in a trough.

"Where's the book?" shouted the thin man.

"My great-aunt's got it," said Tarquin, squirming and kicking. He struggled to loosen the thin man's iron grip, but he wasn't strong enough.

A pensioner grabbed Tarquin's flailing arms and held them firmly. Another encircled the chair and Tarquin's chest with a rope, pulling it tight.

"Without the book, you're worthless," said the thin man. He slowly tightened his grip, suffocating the boy. "Goodbye, Tarquin."

The room darkened. Tarquin felt his body float towards the ceiling. There was no pain, just a sense of utter bewilderment.

Then, way off in the distance, he heard a voice calling his name, again and again, echoing, reverberating, slowly getting louder and louder …

It was next to him now: strong, powerful, commanding.

"Strike the pose!"

Tarquin opened his eyes. He found himself flying across the tea shop.

Landing amongst a group of pensioners, he knocked them in all directions, as if he were a well-aimed bowling ball. He gasped for air and looked up, groaning.

In the centre of the room, hands on hips, caught in the only shaft of sunlight that had sneaked between the closed curtains, was the silhouette of a shapely silver female.

"Maddy!"

He scrambled over the disorientated pensioners and hid under a table at the side of the room.

From the safety of the table legs he watched Maddy scythe her way through the horde of grey droids like a tornado through a trailer park. Metal limbs flew, heads spun, fountains of green fluid and goo erupted from severed necks, limbs and spinning heads. High-pitched squeals of metal on metal and the whirling and churning of disembodied machinery rent the air. Wall plaster, wooden mouldings and faded prints of Constable and Turner, hit by fragments of broken droid, fell from the walls. Hundreds of ornamental teapots, brought by visitors and placed lovingly on the shelves running around the walls, danced and imploded, flinging lethally sharp fragments of pottery across the room like shrapnel.

Tarquin screamed wildly with delight as he watched the cold, mechanical efficiency of Maddy's orgy of droid destruction. The metal pensioners didn't stand a chance.

Ten minutes later and the only droid left standing aside from Maddy herself was the old woman he'd met in the lock-keeper's cottage. The sole sound was the descending whine of dying machines. And the smell! Hot metal, burning oil, the sickly sweet essence of old people's cologne …

A thick cloud of dust filled the room. Torn curtains fluttered, caught by the breeze coming in through the shattered bay window.

Her hands once more on her hips, Maddy stood silently in the centre of the tea room.

Pushing aside metal debris, Tarquin crawled from his refuge. Shaking uncontrollably, he thrust a bloodied finger at the old-lady droid.

"Destroy it! Destroy it!" he screamed at Maddy.

Maddy remained standing, her head bowed.

Tarquin got up from his knees and, in a state of adrenalin-fuelled excitement, cursed loudly at Maddy and launched himself at the confused and damaged old-lady droid, rugby-tackling her to the floor. Before the droid could so much as raise a knitting needle he had it pinned to the floor. Sitting astride its chest, he clawed at the artificial flesh. He gouged out its eyes and threw them against the wall, where they burst like two ripe tomatoes. Still enslaved by his rage, he ripped open the side of its mouth, he pulled out its metal teeth and covered himself in green droid fluid.

In the corner of the tea room, a small pocket of steam vapour appeared and grew. When it reached the ceiling, a spinning red Chesterfield sofa materialized inside the cloud, descended to the floor, and spun to a stop. Rhia and Archie were clinging to the armrests.

"Oh, my God!" cried Rhia. Tarquin was bouncing the old-lady droid's head like a basketball on the floor. "Tarquin's lost it!"

"Tarquin!" yelled Archie. "Leave her alone!"

Tarquin was too engrossed in obliterating the droid to hear them.

Bounce, bounce, bounce.

Unknown to him, a second weather front appeared outside the shop. Moments later, Jules crashed through the front door in a bath chair with the OPEN sign around his neck. Bits of the door, its surround and the bath chair flew across the tearoom.

Bounce, bounce, bounce.

Seeing Tarquin, Jules picked himself up and staggered groggily towards him.

"Stop, Seebee! We need to keep one!"

Tarquin turned to face Jules, his bloodshot eyes wide and unblinking, the droid's skull gripped tightly in his hands.

"It's over, lad," said Jules, putting his hand on Tarquin's shoulder. "They can't hurt you now."

Archie and Rhia unbuckled themselves from the sofa and, their heads clearing, climbed over piles of metal debris towards Tarquin.

Wuuuuumppphhhh!

The explosion blew them all off their feet.

Lances of white light fragmented the room.

Maddy lay crumpled on the floor, spewing viscous orange liquid, with Rhia and Archie motionless nearby.

Only Jules and Tarquin were still mobile.

"Go!" yelled Jules. With a great effort he pulled himself to his feet and pushed Tarquin forcefully towards the Chesterfield.

Turning back for the others, Jules slapped Archie into consciousness.

"Get Rhia!" Jules shouted, pointing to where her body lay spreadeagled near the counter. "We have to leave, now!"

Jules stumbled towards the sofa and Tarquin.

Just as Archie was about to reach Rhia, the kitchen door behind the service counter opened and a wet brown leathery face appeared.

"Griddlebacks!" cried Jules. Flipping open the sofa arm, he pulled out a small console and worked the controls.

Seeing Rhia's unconscious body on the floor, the creature walked towards her, slathering mucus and bile across its face and tusks. A long slimy yellow tongue darted from its lipless mouth and smeared spittle over its cold, reptilian eyes.

It stared at Archie, then down at Rhia, and snorted steam from its scarred and bloated snout. A putrid odour of death and decay filled the room.

Archie tried to block its progress, but the heavily built creature swatted him across the room like a troublesome fly.

The Griddleback wrapped a clawed foot around Rhia's leg and ululated triumphantly as it dragged her across the floor in the direction of the kitchen door.

"No!" cried Tarquin. "Leave her alone!"

He half-fell off the sofa and began crawling towards the creature, blood pouring from his nose. Scrambling among the broken metal pieces littering the floor, he slowly closed on the retreating Griddleback. He grabbed a broken droid leg up from the floor and somehow managed to get to his feet, swaying in the wake of the departing alien.

The Griddleback turned, just in time to feel the full force of Tarquin smashing the leg into its armoured midriff. Thrown off balance, it took a swipe at Tarquin as it fell, knocking him to the floor.

There in front of him lay Calbhach's Bosun. He'd put it into a pocket of his backpack at the caravan and forgotten about it. It must have fallen out when the droids rifled his pack. His mind filled with pure hatred, he picked it up, pointed it at the Griddleback, and pulled the trigger.

A fizzing orb of violet light crashed into the back of the creature's head.

The Griddleback lurched sideways and staggered a couple of paces before collapsing on top of Rhia.

"Come on, we have to go!" yelled Jules, dragging the semi-conscious Archie towards the sofa.

Tarquin tried to pull the creature off Rhia, but it wouldn't move. He kicked it hard in its belly and cursed.

Moaning pitifully, the Griddleback clutched its head and rolled off Rhia.

Tarquin seized her arm and lifted her like a fireman onto his back just as four more Griddlebacks erupted through the kitchen door.

Tarquin staggered in the direction of the sofa, trying to place his feet as carefully as he could among the slippery debris on the floor.

He was less than a metre from the safety of the sofa when, in the tea-room mirror, he saw the thin man behind him stretch out an emaciated arm and point at him.

Cold filled his bones and he froze.

"Leche!" screamed Jules.

Three bolts of light thudded into Tarquin. Spun around by the force of the blasts, he dropped Rhia and fell to his knees, open-mouthed, gazing dumbfoundedly at the laughing thin man.

A fourth blast hit Tarquin in the chest and threw him a metre backwards through the air.

He was unconscious by the time he landed on the already-disappearing sofa.

Belching smoke and flames, the Chesterfield materialized in the hospital emergency port at BIFS headquarters. Spinning wildly, it crashed into one wall and caromed off to hit another before skidding to a halt. Jules, Tarquin and Archie lay on the sofa like limp, discarded toys on a child's bed. Rescue personnel pulled them off just as the sofa erupted in a ball of fire.

Jules and Archie coughed and hacked on all fours, but Tarquin lay motionless, face-up … and terrifyingly silent.

Professor Tommy Cramdunkle, an eminent surgeon as well as a professor of alien biology, had received an automated emergency message from the sofa. He arrived on the scene with a team of doctors and paramedics just as the Chesterfield came to a halt at the emergency port. Several of the team rushed to assist Archie and Jules, while Tommy and the others carefully lifted Tarquin onto an emergency hover trolley.

Tommy ran diagnostics and checked the boy's vital signs. There was a pulse, but it was faint and irregular.

"Let's get him to isolation," said Tommy.

After Tarquin had been rapidly hooked up to an array of instruments, the trolley, with Tommy and the resuscitation team riding the footplates, flew on autopilot down the hospital corridor towards the isolation area.

Tommy looked at Tarquin's pale face and put a couple of fingers on the boy's carotid artery. "I'm losing the pulse."

"He's flat-lining. Let's go team!" said a paramedic.

Tommy pressed buttons on the CPR machine covering his patient's chest.

Tarquin's head lolled to one side, his eyes bulged and his tongue, now blue, fell from his mouth.

"Cardiac arrest!" the paramedic shouted.

"Injecting 30 milligrams neo-epinephrine," said another.

"Still flat-lining."

"Not on my watch," said Tommy grimly, slowing the trolley's speed to a gentle cruise and quickly removing the CPR machine. Using his hands, the instruments and years of experience, he calmly worked over Tarquin's chest.

Each member of the resuscitation team, like a Formula One pit crew, moved up the gears and worked their area of recovery expertise.

Nobody spoke. They didn't need to.

After several minutes, Tommy looked up and smiled.

"Good work, everyone. The lad's back with us."

The team members smiled and nodded.

Tommy took the trolley off cruise control and it sped up.

"He's damn strong," said one of the doctors as they rounded the corridor and arrived at the isolation docking station.

Confederation police officers arrived and gave first aid to Archie and Jules before arresting them. Archie was allowed to leave after questioning and giving a statement, but Jules was cuffed and charged with manipulating Earth history to save a cognitive lifeform. Saving a life in the past had unpredictable and possibly disastrous consequences for the future. It was a very serious offence.

Jules was put immediately before a Confederation judge, and denied bail. Within five hours of arriving back in 2340, he was booked onto a prison ship to Antriconian, the Confederation's penal colony, to await trial. Allowed one call before leaving and another on arrival, he contacted Archie with a list of instructions. Archie was to pick up Alice Cooper, a young time-travelling apprentice, and travel to the planet Tharg to find Smodius D. Munchfumble, a Zargothian advocate. Smodius was an old friend as well as a brilliant lawyer, and would take Jules's case.

"Don't use wormholes," said Jules. "They'll be monitoring them. Use your wits and dangle."

Archie duly contacted Alice and, after he'd explained the situation, she agreed to meet him at the isolation wing of Tommy's hospital.

Later that day, Archie stood before a plate-glass cubicle and watched Tarquin in silence. The awful realization that Rhia was dead and Tarquin barely alive hit him hard. He rolled Rhia's trainee time-traveller's guide disc in his fingers. He'd found the disc at the back of the burning couch and remembered how proud she had been to receive it. She had had no idea about the BIFS and their battles against Griddlebacks, aliens, Leche and other despotic civilizations.

A tear ran down Archie's cheek and he let go of the disc. Wiping his face, he stood on the disc and cracked it under his boot. Rhia's fairytale was over and the same might be true of Tarquin's, even though it had barely begun.

He looked again at Tarquin's unconscious body, lying inside a silver mesh tunnel, indistinctly visible through a translucent grey metallic shroud. Flying at incredible speeds across Tarquin's chest were a score of thin metal droid arms.

Above the arms, a plethora of colours flashed and throbbed in a dervish dance of light.

Tarquin's head, covered by a transparent sphere and held in place by a metal collar, was surrounded by bubbling blue liquid. His eyes were closed and his long, curly hair was gone. His pale, expressionless face was gaunt and drawn.

A nurse-droid monitored computer screens full of graphs, coloured bars and screeds of text that moved at breakneck speed above the tunnel.

Archie shivered. His new friend's shaved head seemed to be boiling like an egg inside a cold blue lightbulb full of effervescing chemicals.

"Would Archie Campbell please come to the Medical Reception Centre?" boomed a voice from a speaker. "Archie Campbell to the Medical Reception Centre."

Tommy Cramdunkle sat on his hoverstool inside the command centre of the isolation unit, high above the patient pods. He was staring at one particular screen.

There was a knock at the open door. Archie Campbell stood in the doorway.

"Come in, Archie. I've a couple of questions for you." Tommy pointed to a hoverstool beside him.

Archie sat down.

"Do you know this Jenkins boy well?" asked Tommy. He pursed his lips as he watched the screen.

"Not well, not really," said Archie. "But everyone said he had potential."

The professor pressed buttons on a console in front of him. "Look at this."

The image rapidly magnified and soon the screen was filled with silver roundels eating red and yellow starfish-like creatures.

"Ughh! What are those?"

"Dr Phillius Santander's nanobots. Millions of them," said Tommy. "They shouldn't be there, but I am damned pleased to see them."

Archie scratched his head. "They're …" He looked queasy. "They're … inside Tarquin, aren't they?"

"Yep. Santa's little helpers are rounding up the Leche poison spores and murdering them."

"Spores, like in hay fever?"

Tommy turned and looked at Archie. "Far, far worse. Leche pulse lances are laced with spores that latch onto healthy cells, multiply inside their host at terrifying speed, and corrupt their DNA."

Archie's shoulders sagged. "He's going to die, isn't he?"

The professor didn't answer. He was watching a vast wave of silver roundels herd the starfish-shaped spores through Tarquin's aorta and away from his heart.

"Professor?"

"Sorry. Those bots are amazing! Any idea who put them there?"

"Put them there?"

"Yes. I found a puncture scar over his heart. They were injected within the last three months."

"How can you be so sure?" asked Archie.

The professor smiled and took from his pocket a silver pen-like instrument with a dozen coloured pins.

"You programme them through this injection device. You push the pins in a given sequence and then dial in a number here." He pointed to the base. "This controls the quantity of bots released and how they act." He stabbed the needle end into a rubber heart on the desk next to the console. "Press, and the bots start pumping through the body."

Tommy pulled the syringe from the rubber heart and passed it to Archie, then turned back to the screen. "But," he said, shaking his head, "this is different."

"Why?"

"Shooting this combination and quantity was a death sentence. It's ludicrously strong for any disease or virus known on Earth."

"You still haven't answered my question."

"No," said Tommy, suddenly grinning. "He's not going to die—far from it! The bots have a timing mechanism, and were about to start eating him from the inside when the Leche spores arrived." He pointed to the screen. "Look, the Leche spores would normally sweep through a host body and kill in minutes, but when they entered Tarquin they were met by the ravenous bots."

"That's incredible," said Archie, watching the carnage on screen.

"Brilliant," replied Tommy, shaking his head. "Bloody brilliant. Someone made a huge mistake."

"And it just happened to save Tarquin's life?"

"Or," said Tommy, shaking his head, "someone tampered with the medical kit, hoping to kill the boy, not expecting him to be shot by a Leche soon after."

For several minutes they watched the screen like two young children playing a video game, applauding enthusiastically every time the bots gobbled a group of their foes.

"How long before we can talk to him?" said Archie.

The professor looked at the figures pouring across the screen. "Four days if all goes well. Maybe five. Once the bots have finished eating the spores we have to carefully remove them from his body. They can be crafty so-and-sos, but we know what we're doing. However," he added, "the side-effects of the hallucinogens the spores carry could be more problematic …"

Feeling much better, Archie left the professor and, with a smile on his face, went back to look at Tarquin through the glass.

"Come, we should visit Smodius," said a voice behind him. He turned to see Alice Cooper. They had started at guide school together several years ago. She was from the Shropshire Canal region.

"I've got everything you suggested," she said, swinging a pack onto her shoulder. "It'll be like old times."

"Cool." Archie smiled.

She looked through the glass. "Is that Tarquin Jenkins?"

"Yes."

"Will he make it?"

"Yes. Tommy Cramdunkle says he's a fighter," said Archie. "And a very, very lucky guy."

Jules's rescue of Tarquin provoked a political tsunami. The Griddleback and Leche ambassadors demanded that the Confederation Security Council act on the rescue. They helpfully provided a long list of time-travel ordinances that Jules had broken, and evidence to go with it, even suggesting it was an act of war by Earth against the glorious Griddleback and Leche civilizations, though no one knew exactly how. The Confederation Security Council had little choice but to meet in emergency session.

Four hours later and Jules's fate had been decided. Thankfully the Council didn't view the episode as an act of war, despite the Griddleback and Leche protestations. But Jules would be put on trial and, in the words of Toeschoos Macingraude, the Griddleback Ambassador, he would be made an example of and left to rot in prison.

Archie took Alice to the hospital tower carport. Heeding Jules's advice, he had hired a silver Sinclair 5000 for the trip to Tharg. Silver Sinclairs were the most prolific form and colour of transport on Earth, and thousands made the journey to Tharg each day.

Despite Calbhach and the leprechauns wanting to help, it was decided that Archie and Alice would have a better chance of making the journey undetected if they were on their own. Calbhach provided a couple of persona rings.

Archie located the Sinclair and loaded it with their luggage. They took their seats and he set the destination for the Zargothian colony on Tharg, then put the controls on autopilot.

The Sinclair climbed into the night sky to join the interstellar freeway, heading for the hyperdrive portal.

As a precaution the two young people had programmed their persona rings to show the faces of a couple of New London residents.

On reaching the portal they had a thirty-minute wait while clearing customs. Luckily it was midweek and interstellar traffic was heavy, so that customs and the other agencies were kept busy. Once they were through the red tape, Archie put the Sinclair into hyperdrive and sat back.

Thirty minutes into their four-hour journey, he felt peckish. He took a bag of sweets from his knapsack and offered them to Alice.

"Fancy a jelly?" he said. "They're a brand new style."

Alice looked at the colourful contents of the bag and wrinkled her snub nose. "Yuck! They're—"

"Eyeballs, I know, but they're delicious. Go on, try one." Archie opened the paper packet wider. "They come in sixteen different flavours."

Alice peered apprehensive at the six or seven gooey life-size eyeballs looking up at her. "Okay, then."

Each time Peaches Technology introduced a new gadget they brought out a complementary line of sweets, designer clothing, space-car tool kits and lingerie. The eyeball sweets accompanied their iBall Personal Management System (iPMS).

Alice selected an apple-coloured one. She looked at it warily, rolling it across her palm.

"It won't bite you. Go on, try it," said Archie, tucking into a black one with a loud slurping noise.

"Everything's peachy with an iBall," he sang, waving his arms like a tic-tac man on Derby Day, lampooning the actor in the iBall commercial.

The slogan that accompanied the iBall had become the most irritating advertising tagline on Earth. The competing product from Macrohard, a cheap knockoff called "The Pear", had been greeted with derision. Macrohard's slogan, "Everything's Gone Pear-Shaped", became an embarrassing millstone around their corporate neck. The advertising company neglected to check the slogan against historical context.

Archie concluded his lampoon with, "Ooh, my favourite! A slippery wet Shagganat eyeball!"

"Very funny." Alice grimaced. Closing her eyes, she popped the eyeball into her mouth. To her surprise, it tasted sweet and fruity. She bit into it and honey nectar filled her mouth.

"That's delicious," she said, eyeing the bag.

Archie passed it to her and smiled. "Knock yourself out. You always did like sweets."

It was getting late, so after her third eyeball Alice puffed up a pillow and curled up in her seat. Several questions preyed on her mind.

"Why did the Griddlebacks kidnap the Canal Guardian at Steeple Snoring?"

"You're well informed," said Archie.

"I had a quick briefing before I met you at the hospital."

"Don't know, though Calbhach reckons it has something to do with Tarquin's parents and a book he found."

"Back at the hospital you said Tarquin was a very lucky boy. What did you mean?"

"He's either very, very lucky or 'others' have an interest in his survival."

"Jules keeps things very close, doesn't he," said Alice, nestling into the pillow.

"Worryingly so. He told me to use my wits and dangle. What's that supposed to mean?"

Alice didn't answer. Her soft, regular breathing was all he could hear. Outside was the cold darkness of hyperspace.

While Alice slept, Archie arranged an appointment with Senator Smodius D. Munchfumble to discuss the case against Jules Rigsworth. Smodius was a brilliant barrister, but he was aged, cantankerous and a Zargothian to boot. His race suffered fools badly, human fools even worse.

Archie recalled Rigsworth's hurried conversation.

"Archie, you've heard of a warrior race? Well, find Senator Smodius D. Munchfumble. He's a Zargothian advocate, and a member of the lawyer race. He throws words instead of spears. He'll know what do. He owes me big time. He will help us. Just be very careful and read everything you can on Zargothian etiquette. Whatever you and Alice do, don't upset him!"

Archie was apprehensive. What he had learnt about Zargothians was not encouraging. They lived to argue, to debate, and to lord it over courtrooms when in session. It was no surprise they were known as the judiciary race. Within the Galactic Confederation, it was commercial suicide for multinationals and multiplanetary companies not to employ a phalanx of permanent Zargothian legal teams. Planets had their Rule of Law created by them, and their Judiciary run by them. Zargothians lived and worked in a colony on Tharg, similar to the twenty-first century colony on Earth called Hong Kong. The Tharg economy relied solely on the Zargothian ability to conduct legislative work around the universe and charge a hefty premium for doing so.

Archie got out his voice-activated iBall and set it in the cup holder on the dashboard. He spoke into it, selecting paperback mode for presentation. A 3D paperback appeared in front of him. His second command brought up a list of books, some humorous, some serious. He read the list:

> 1001 Uses for a Dead Zargothian Advocate.
> Zen and the Art of Zargothian Etiquette Maintenance.
> The Zargothian Eunuch.
> Far From the Maddening Zargoth.
> War & Peace—Zargothian Advocacy in the 22nd to 24th Centuries.
> Zargothian Etiquette for Dummies, Volumes 1-6.
> Everything You Wanted to Know About Zargothians, but Are Too Terrified to Ask.
> Zargothian Drinking Songs (also known as Zargothian Dirges & Death Chants).
> Tess of the Zargothians—A Case Study in Relationship Law.
> Hard Times—Bankruptcy Law.
> Three Zargothians Arguing in a Boat—Maritime Law.
> The Merchant of Vorlokia—Trade and Retail Law.
> One Zargothian Flew Over the Cuckoo's Nest—Mental Health Law.

He needed something basic to read during the journey that would give him a chance to communicate and not look stupid. He chose Zargothian Etiquette for Dummies and went straight to the two-page summary of Dos and Don'ts at the back.

Do ...
i) Take a gift. A piece of legislation from your own country/planet/solar system would do nicely.
ii) Always appear deferential.
iii) On introduction, immediately wave your hands above your head. In ancient times, it was common practice to shoot Zargothians on first introduction because they were so extremely rude—rather than stand and receive a berating, people simply shot them. This was a cultural misunderstanding. It is imperative that any introduction is accompanied by waving your hands above your head and clucking like a small animal. On Earth, the animal best suited to the Zargothian's voice is called a hen. You do this so a Zargothian can see you don't have a gun, are as important as a small animal, and won't run away.

Don't ...
i) Raise your head above theirs.
ii) React adversely to sounds of flatulence. Zargothians show their tacit acceptance of someone by flatulating (otherwise known as passing wind loudly from one's buttocks) at regular intervals. To the uninitiated, the wheezing and ripping noise can be unnerving, but it is a sign of acceptance, whereas a high-pitched whine and a wobbling of their gizzard-like neck shows immense displeasure. If you are unlucky enough to witness this behaviour, you should make your excuses and leave immediately.

He read on, but his eyes were heavy and he was soon asleep. The Sinclair sped through the night on autopilot, unnoticed among the thousands of identical Sinclairs and other vehicles on their way to Tharg, and beyond.

The law firm of Munchfumble, Scrumble & Twee sat at the top of a glistening silver tower. The offices were palatial, and no expense was spared to make the partners look vastly superior to every client—alien and Zargothian—who entered.

Soothing music, soft lighting and tinkling fountains greeted Archie and Alice as they walked along an avenue of small trees into a vestibule. As they stood waiting they looked at the enormous oil paintings of the three partners surrounding them. A hologram reporting on the partners' many successes filtered into visibility. The lion's share of the information it showed was about Smodius. The presentation lasted several minutes and Archie and Alice had little choice but to watch.

As the hologram eventually fizzed and disappeared, a door opened in the painting of Twee. A droid dressed as a human in a black suit and tie walked forward.

"Please, follow me," said the droid in perfect English. It led them through the door into a reception area manned by three similarly dressed droids. They gave automated smiles.

"How may we help you?" asked the middle droid in a soft metallic voice.

"I'm Archie Campbell and this is Alice Cooper. We have an appointment to see Advocate Smodius D. Munchfumble III."

"You are expected," said its colleague.

A side door opened and the droid pointed into a vast open-plan office. "Please go through the office, enter the middle door and await his eminence."

"Have a good meeting," enthused the third droid.

Inside the office, secretarial droids rushed around like bargain hunters at Selfridges during the January sales.

In the distance, high above the melee hovered Smodius. Dressed in his advocate's representational robes of purple grillion fur, he barked orders and pointed prodigiously with his ring-encrusted fingers from a customized Sorayama Hover-throne. Strengthened for his weight, and with added Alerion drives, his throne was fast, silent and the ultimate in hover stealth. Edged in white fur and gold-leaf fili-gree, it befitted his messianic status in the judicial world. As junior partners, Scrumble and Twee had only the basic, ungilded, furless, moderately fast upright Hover Chair model.

Archie clutched tightly, to his chest, copies of The Basic Law of Hong Kong, Negotiating with the Chinese and a first edition of a book initially published in 1997 called The Last Governor. These were to be his gifts to the famed lawyer.

With Alice by his side, he walked resolutely towards Smodius.

"No, you must not disturb his eminence. Follow me," said a droid, guiding them away from Smodius towards three doors. The middle door, Smodius's, was double the size of the other two. His name was emblazoned on it in large gold lettering followed by a litany of letters and symbols. Underneath, in slightly smaller lettering, appeared a brief biography and a long list of court cases that he'd won. A successful Zargothian wore his superiority on his sleeve, chair and office door.

They reached the door and it opened automatically. The droid ushered them in and showed them to two basic, hoverless seats.

At exactly nine, Smodius swooped in and hovered regally above them. Archie dropped from the chair to his knees and averted his eyes. Alice, wondering what Archie was doing, followed suit.

Edging toward Smodius, Archie offered up his gifts.

Smodius wheezed.

Archie crawled over to Smodius's large wooden desk and placed the books in a pile on it, then moved back into a crouching position by his chair.

"High Counsellor, " he said, clucking like a hen and waving his hands above his head in a spiralling dance, "Jules Rigsworth is in desperate need of your services."

Alice looked on in astonishment. A period of silence followed.

"Sit," commanded Smodius, lowering his throne to hover a metre off the ground.

Relieved, Archie shuffled back onto his chair. He took a deep breath and looked up.

Though approximately humanoid, Smodius's Zargothian visage was bestial. His ears were almond-shaped and, donkey-like, filled with curly tufts of silvery hair. The head was long, ending in a flat, wide nose with round nostrils the size of golf balls. Red piggy eyes protruded from the side of his face like two cherries that had slipped down the side of a birthday cake. In human terms, Smodius was 150 years old. Grossly overweight, even for a Zargothian, he had pale parchment skin that draped in folds like wallpaper ready to be hung. The flesh beneath his small chin was like a turkey's gizzard; it swayed alarmingly when he moved and spoke. Apart from the tufts in his ears, he had no facial hair. A shar-pei/moose mix, minus the antlers but with a hint of turkey.

"I have seen the charges," said Smodius, waving his chubby hands. "They are grave indeed." His ears pricked up and his lips curled into a smile, followed by a loud ripping noise. "But far from impossible for me to counter."

Hearing the ripping noise, Alice sat bolt upright, looked wide-eyed at Archie and tried hopelessly to stifle a giggle. Archie's stomach churned—he's forgotten to warn her about the flatulence!

"What can we do to help?" he asked, trying to draw attention away from Alice.

"Well, young human, let's see, shall we?" Smodius spun his hoverthrone around and moved swiftly to the back of the room.

As soon as Smodius turned his back, Archie signalled to Alice to calm down.

Returning to his desk with a tablet in his hands, Smodius produced a noise like a slowly deflating balloon.

Alice bowed her head, snorted and clutched her sides.

Archie, panicking, dug her hard in the ribs, making her cry out.

A soft, high-pitched whine came from Smodius.

Archie thought quickly. He jumped up (ensuring his head stayed below Smodius's, of course) and pointed at Alice. "Your eminence! My colleague is suffering from interplanetary travel sickness."

Alice glared at him, rubbing her side.

"The journey was long," Archie continued, "and she hasn't had time to recover. Is there anywhere she could go to rest?" Smodius stopped whining and looked at them down his long nose. With a dismissive waft of his arm and a sway of his gizzard, he pointed through the doorway to the open-plan office. "There is a Dome of Contemplation on the left."

Archie pulled Alice to her feet and pushed her towards the door.

"I hope you feel better soon," said Smodius, flapping an ear.

Alice turned, bit her lip and bowed stiffly, then left.

The moment she was outside the room she broke into more giggles.

Unfazed by the laughter, Smodius handed the tablet to Archie, who read it. "Crikey!"

"Quite. Now you see what we are up against."

"Does Jules know about this? It looks bad," said Archie.

"Bad?" barked Smodius, his ears going north. "Dear child, it could not be much worse."

Archie read the document again.

UK EYES ONLY

Steeple Snoring, Earth
Message timed at 13:30
Willerby to Green House
Griddleback ship on fishing line. Believe intending to jump. Steeple Snoring and Jenkins in grave danger. Permission to act.

Director
Message timed at 13:32
Green House to Willerby
Hold fast. Only observation permitted. Await further instructions.

Steeple Snoring, Earth
Message timed at 14:00
Willerby to Green House
Situation critical. Ship landed. Griddleback droids in village. Permission to act.

Director
Message timed at 14:02
Green House to Willerby
Stand down. Repeat, stand down. History must take its course.

Steeple Snoring, Earth
Message timed at 14:10
Willerby to Green House
Standing down.

Smodius moved his throne to the picture window so that he could look out over Tharg. "That company of Griddleback troopers went on a secret mission to Earth, though of course their president has already denied it. They landed in Steeple Snoring and were about to replace the villagers with droids when Jenkins arrived. As you can see from the messages, Jules knew what was happening."

"He told us Tarquin was in danger but he never mentioned Griddlebacks!" said Archie, blowing out his cheeks.

"You were very lucky to escape," said Smodius. "I have no idea why he risked you all to save the boy, but as a consequence a young girl has died and Jules himself has fallen into a bigger trap." Leaning forwards, the Zargoth picked up a yellowing newspaper from his desk.

"No wonder their ambassador was bleating to the Security Council. The Griddlebacks and Leche will ask for a life sentence of banishment for committing the cardinal sin of saving a life. God knows what the Time Guardians will do! It will mean the end of Jules and severely dent the operational abilities of the BIFS."

"But how did he know?"

Smodius handed him the paper. "It's a copy of a newspaper from three hundred years ago."

Archie looked at what was obviously a national tabloid newspaper. The headline read:

FEMALE ARSONIST STRIKES AT TEA SHOP

On the front page, seven columns wide, was a picture of the smouldering tea shop. The charred body of a 16-year-old orphaned girl named Rhia Collins had been found at the centre of the fire. The paper speculated that she was a troubled individual and that this had led her to firebomb the tea shop.

"Rhia!"

"Yes, history has changed. It should have been the Jenkins boy who died in the fire."

"Why was Jules arrested and not me?"

"I don't know. I expect he's the only one they wanted."

Archie looked thoughtful. "Who are 'they'?"

"I'm surprised you don't know. Our good friends, the meddlesome Griddlebacks and Leche."

Archie bowed his head. "They killed a good friend of mine."

Before Smodius could respond, a communicator flashed and buzzed on the wall.

"Ah, this will be Jules. I managed to persuade the detention counsellor to get me a link. We don't have long."

They looked at the wall. Jules's pale face filled the screen.

"Good to see you, Archie. I am so, so sorry about Rhia. How's Seebee?"

"He's in isolation, but he should be okay," said Archie. No need to complicate the issue right now by talking about the nanobots.

"And Alice! Did she get the message? Is she with you?"

Before Archie could respond, Smodius interjected. "Getting to grips with Zargothian etiquette, I hope." He looked at Archie and waggled a knowing ear.

"Yes," Archie confirmed, "but she's confused as to what we're doing here."

Jules sighed. "Tell her I'll explain everything when I get the chance. Now, down to business."

Smodius pointed a box at the screen. It flickered and went black briefly, then Jules's tired face reappeared.

"You have perhaps two minutes before they realize I'm encrypting this transmission," cautioned Smodius.

"Archie, I've had time to think. We must get evidence of Griddleback involvement at Steeple Snoring for my trial. A Griddleback clean-up crew will have cleansed what remains of the tea rooms, and wiped the memories of any villagers who got in their way. I suspect they'll leave a team in the village until my trial is over. At least the village and its people are safe for now. Jeremiah Cavendish's lock-keeper's cottage is the best place to find evidence. Let's hope they got lazy when they were kidnapping Jeremiah and left some clues."

"Thirty seconds," said Smodius, watching the atomic clock on the wall.

Jules leaned forward, "We need to play dirty. Find Georgia Blade and explain the situation to her. She'll understand what to do. She owes me a favour and she hates Griddlebacks. Smodius knows her reputation and hopefully he can tell you her whereabouts. Good luck."

The screen dissolved and a stern-looking face appeared. "High Counsellor, the transmission is closed."

The image disappeared.

"Who is—?" Archie began.

"Not here. Even my walls may have ears. I'll take you to the Dome of Contemplation."

Hovering on his luxury chair, Smodius led Archie to the dome.

Alice looked up, startled, and got to her feet. "I am so sorr—"

Smodius waved his hand dismissively. "We have no time for human egos and apologies." He beckoned them closer to his throne. "Listen carefully. La Rousse Fatale—Georgia Blade—is a renegade, a space pirate and a talented one at that. But she was also once a Time Guardian, and is always interested in new cases of Griddlebacks meddling with other people's planets. If you can find her, and between the three of you, get me evidence of Griddlebacks in Steeple Snoring, we may have a chance to save Jules."

Alice began to speak, but Smodius raised his hand to silence her.

"You must go quickly. Blade never stays long in one place. I've put a droid at your disposal. He'll take you shopping for clothing and equipment, and then to her last known position in Sleazeeze. If she's no longer there you'll have to find her yourselves."

"What's Sleazeeze?" said Alice.

"A lawless zone on the far side of Tharg." Smodius gazed at her, his face softening. He made a faint ripping noise. "Take care, humans."

The throne rose in the air and headed for the door, but was intercepted by a droid carrying a message. The droid gave it to Smodius, who read it, turned around and looked down once more at Archie and Alice.

"The Confederation's Security Council has invoked emergency trial procedures. No doubt under pressure from the Griddlebacks and Leche representatives. You have five days to get me evidence before Jules goes to trial."

Alice and Archie bowed, said goodbye and hurried from the offices of Munchfumble, Scrumble & Twee. Standing by Archie's Sinclair in the auto park outside the offices was a droid dressed in a sharp black suit, tie and sunglasses. He saw them coming and walked towards them, offering his hand. "Good morning. I'm Therius."

Archie looked at him and then at Alice. "I'm sure you are. Personally, I prefer a bit of humour."

"You misunderstand. I'm Therius."

"I do understand, but not now, okay?"

Alice pulled Archie to one side. "I think his name is Therius."

The droid overheard and beamed. "Ha, ha, ha, ha, ha," His high-pitched metronomic laugh was loud and painful to hear. "Yes, that's my name. Therius. I am Mr Munchfumble's personal assistant, and here to help you."

They exchanged pleasantries and Therius suggested he be the one to drive. "If you have any questions," he said, slipping into the driver's seat, "just ask."

Archie jumped in the back and Alice sat alongside Therius. They set off.

Archie was the first to speak. "Tell us about Sleazeeze."

"It has the highest concentration of brigands, fly-by-nights and ne'er-do-wells in the galaxy," said Therius gleefully.

"Shouldn't we have some protection?" said Alice.

"Yes, miss." Therius's head spun around and he grinned at her. "I am taking you shopping." His head spun back and he laughed that rebarbative laugh.

Archie leaned forwards and whispered in Alice's ear, "I think his happy circuit has got wrapped around his pleasure board."

The journey to Sleazeeze was short and uneventful.

"We are coming in to land," said Therius, flashing a toothy, metallic smile. His gleeful demeanour was beginning to grate. They landed in a large carport full of broken Sinclairs, rusting military vehicles and space junk. Before them was a huge yellow 3D sign that pulsed to the sound of heavy metal music. It read:

BURT DANGLE'S SLEAZEEZE EMPORIUM
EVERYTHING YOU NEED, PLUS A WHOLE WORLD MORE!

Archie grinned. "Use your wits and dangle," he said to Alice. "Now I understand what Jules meant."

Therius jumped from the car. "Let's shop till you bop," he shouted. He rushed around the car, opened the door for Alice, and helped her from the Sinclair.

"It's 'drop'," said Alice, irritated by Therius's inane grin. "You shop till you drop."

Therius's head rocked from side to side to the music and he sang repeatedly, "You shop, till you drop, oh yeah, you shop, till you drop, oh yeah!"

Archie looked around the port. "It's a breaker's yard for space junk. Why bring us here?"

"We can't arrive in the centre of Sleazeeze all shiny and new," said Therius. "We'd get noticed."

Archie frowned. "Well, whatever we get better work," he said quietly to Alice as they followed the still-singing Therius to the emporium's rooftop entrance.

"Wait!" said Alice, after Therius bellowed too close to her ear just once too often. She pulled a small oblong instrument from her knapsack. "Therius," she said in a commanding tone.

"Yes, Miss."

"Please sample the singer's voice on these songs and the language he uses. Research him and replace your voice and persona with his. Do you understand?"

"Yes, Miss."

Therius took the oblong and swallowed it. After several minutes, the iPod popped out of a flap in his stomach and his expression changed from glee to a tortured frown.

"I suppose," said Therius, his voice now a melancholic drawl, "you want me to speak to you?"

Archie's jaw dropped.

"That is so, so much better!" Alice cried. "Now, please call me Alice. This is my friend Archie. Archie, Therius is now to be known as Liam."

Liam walked ahead of them toward the door, scratching his temple. "That's a bloody depressing name."

"Liam!"

"Yes, Archie."

"Absolutely no swearing."

"Okay, no swearing." No more happy tone. Just incredibly cool grumbling boredom.

"Why have you stopped dancing, Liam?" said Alice with a grin.

"Dance? I don't do dance. I'm not here for that."

"Excellent!"

"Hey there, pretty laaaady." The booming voice came from a two-metre-tall hologram of a man in a tight-fitting, all-in-one camouflage suit and a red bandana standing by the entrance. "Going to the dark side?"

Without warning, the hologram, brandishing a large tube on its shoulder, jumped out in front of Alice.

She squealed.

"Need a little insurance, a little firepower?" said the hologram, emphasizing the word "firepower" by gyrating its hips and lewdly caressing the large metallic tube on its shoulder. "Well, today is your lucky day." Winking, it threw back its mane of black, curly, greased hair. "It's 50 percent off with any ex-demonstration, pre-owned, fully repaired and limited-use camouflage uniform."

"Guns, guns, guns. The galaxies' problems solved with guns? No, thank you. We already have one." Liam took Alice's hand and pulled her straight through the hologram, making it crackle and disappear. "We need clothing, not guns."

"Looks like an old-fashioned military surplus store," said Archie, following Liam past aisles full of one-piece camouflage suits, silver space helmets and backpacks. Liam led them toward a sign:

DOUBLE DISCOUNTED, PRE-OWNED, BLADE RUNNER-STYLE CLOTHING

"Now, that's what I call clothing!" exclaimed Alice, seeing a burgundy-red leather catsuit.

Archie was too busy pulling down a leather trench coat to hear her.

"This all looks very twenty-first century," he said, eyeing also a pair of leather trousers and motorcycle boots.

"It's the current rage," explained Liam. "Everything is so retro on Sleazeeze these days. No originality." He picked out a black leather jacket for himself.

It didn't take long for them each to select several items of clothing. Archie had chosen a silver teeshirt to accompany the trench coat, leather trousers and motorcycle boots. Alice wore the burgundy catsuit, a large black belt and a black bomber jacket. Liam was all in black: leather jacket, roll-neck jumper, scarf, jeans. He told them it matched his persona.

They moved on to the gadget section.

"Okay, we need communicators," Liam informed them. "And what you call satnav, so we can find each other if we get lost. Oh, and these." He took down a pair of what looked like opaque sunglasses and passed them to Archie, who put them on and started laughing.

"What's so funny?" asked Alice.

Liam smirked and passed her a pair. She put them on and looked at Archie.

"You have got to be joking, Archie Campbell! Stop looking at me!"

"Alice Cooper!" he said, waving his hands in the air and mimicking the tone of her voice. Open-mouthed he parodied her expression and scanned her with the glasses.

"Enough, game over," said Alice, frowning.

"They're actually a cool tool," said Liam, stifling a yawn. "They strip away the outer layer of clothing to show concealed weapons and explosives. They work up to a thirty-metre radius. Very useful in Sleazeeze." He pointed to the side of her pair of glasses. "They come with several settings of intensity. I'm sure I'd enjoy them more if I weren't a droid. Droids never get to enjoy the good things."

"Well, Archie isn't a droid. And if he doesn't take those things off right now he's not even going to be a male." She brandished an expressive fist.

Liam paid for the shopping and bought himself a slab of Enforcer chewing gum. Not that droids chewed gum, but he had seen humans chewing and felt he'd be less obtrusive if he was doing the same.

The purchases made, he said, "Next, we need a vehicle that blends in."

He led them back to the rooftop. "Burt will know what we need."

They stepped onto the roof just as Burt Dangle's heavyweight frame jumped from a hover slab and jogged—or, rather, wobbled like a jelly—towards them. An overabundance of gold chains of various sizes danced and jigged around his thick, bronzed neck. He pulled up in front of them, wheezing and puffing. Running one ring-encrusted hand through his platinum blonde buzzcut, he pointed at Archie with the other.

"Burt Theodore Dangle, at your service." He flashed a gold-plated smile.

Archie put out his hand and Burt grabbed it, then pulled Archie tight to his side, wrapped his other arm around the boy's shoulder and walked him over to a line of hovercars.

Alice followed, waving her hand in front of her nose as Burt's sickly cologne gripped her throat.

"Panther Regis XL67, twin thrusters, with"—Burt paused for effect and looked deep into Archie's eyes—"cloaking!" He winked.

"It says here, 'One Careful Lady Owner'," Alice observed.

Burt quickly moved in front of a huge dent in the side of the car.

Alice shook her head and pointed past him at the dent. "What was she, blind?"

Burt gave a high-pitched laugh and, with Archie still held tight, walked briskly to another car. "Low-mileage Jetson Interceptor, MK45, single thruster with modified tracerion overdrive."

"What about this one?" said Alice, standing beside a car at the back of the lot.

Burt shook his head. "You're joking, right?"

"It would blend in nicely," said Alice, looking significantly at Liam. Absently she tried to straighten a curling piece of plastic trim.

"It's a mass-produced rust bucket," said Burt, letting Archie go. "It's done more space kilometres than a Kartoleon hyperfreighter." He waved his arms expressively. "And it's been in more accidents than a Shagganat taxi driver! Why on Rambo's earth would you want that!"

"Because we're not on Rambo's earth," retorted Alice.

Archie, freed of Burt's grip, walked over to the car. "I agree. This is what we need."

Liam nodded and pulled out a gold card. "We'll take it."

After filling in the paperwork with Burt, Liam took the pulse key and returned to the carport. "Time to rock and roll."

Burt brought the maroon hovercar to the front of the lot. "As agreed, I'll have the Sinclair stored here safely for your return." He was trying unobtrusively to re-attach the two furry dice that had fallen from the car's mirror.

"No problem," said Liam.

"Could you also remove the banner from the windshield?" asked Alice, "I'm not riding in 'Randy and Stella's Smoochicoach'!"

"Of course." Burt peeled the translucent banner off.

Liam opened the driver's door and popped a piece of gum into his metal mouth. "Time to find the Blade."

"Yeah, time to lock and load," said Archie enthusiastically. He opened the boot and loaded it with their purchases.

Alice looked skywards and shook her head. Boys.

CHAPTER 12

MICHEL DE NOSTREDAME MEETS LEONARDO DA VINCI

The room shook to the sound of thunder. Painters standing on wooden platforms high above the floor fell to their knees, grabbing anything to keep themselves from falling. Closer to the floor, an ornate Chinese sedan chair materialized, spinning violently. Held within a vortex of steam, it scattered the wooden platforms like twigs in a breeze, sending the painters crashing to the floor, before tearing a metre-long section of plaster from the wall.

Buried beneath plaster, rubble and wooden planks, the chair spun slowly to a stop. Half a dozen artisans lay groaning amid the wreckage.

From within the chair came a scrabbling noise, then a hand poked through the pile of debris.

A naked, hairy man, blinking fitfully, emerged from the sedan chair's doorway. His wide beady eyes scanned the bewildered faces looking at him. Recognizing one of the watchers, he let out a tortuous wail and forced the chair's door completely open before scrambling over the mess and stumbling open-armed, towards the familiar face.

"Leonardo, Leonardo! I need to speak with you!" he shouted in faltering Latin.

Two men barred his way and he fell to the floor, babbling.

Surprised he could understand the crazed-seeming stranger, the master painter said, "I am Leonardo, yes. Who are you?"

The man grasped the ankles of the nearest artisan and gawped at Leonardo through the stalwart's legs, like a prisoner through cell bars. "Your humble servant, Michel de Nostredame." He fell forward and spread-eagled himself in supplication.

Leonardo looked down on the prostrated caveman and then at the large hole in the painting where Judas Iscariot had once stood next to Jesus, and pointed angrily at the open sky visible through it.

"I don't care if you're the Devil himself, you've just destroyed my Last Supper!" he roared. "Do you know how much it costs to hire a good model in Milan these days?" He pointed at the flaxen-haired woman sitting dumbstruck, covered in dust but thankfully unharmed, on a wooden chair.

Nostradamus raised himself to his knees, shook himself down like a dog, and pointed to the rubble. "Please, inside my chair I have books, many books you should see!"

Leonardo angrily picked up a length of wood and walked toward the uninvited visitor. Several students hurried to restrain him.

"Let me alone," he shouted, glaring at the naked man cowering on the floor.

"No, master, not until you have calmed down." One of the workers returned with a blanket for the intruder.

"Enough!" said Leonardo, pushing the students from him. "Let us listen to the wretch's story. Then I'll beat him." He took a deep breath. "Where are you from, old man?" asked Leonardo.

"The year of our Lord 1550."

Leonardo seethed. He grabbed the wretch by his hair and, before anyone could stop him, threw him against the wall.

"You're mad," he shouted. "The year is 1497! How could you have come from 1550?"

Turning to his colleagues, he pointed to the street. "Put him out there where he belongs with his imagination … and get a mason in here—we need to rebuild the wall."

Michel de Nostredame was dragged away, screaming about his books and his chair.

A student close to the rubble saw a piece of paper half-hidden under a section of plaster with a strange-looking object drawn on it. Pulling it from the mess, he stood gaping at the picture.

Leonardo noticed what he was doing and walked over, snatching the paper from his hand. He looked at it and frowned. "Bring the cur back and dig out his chair!" He stared at the weird drawing of a winged, sausage-shaped object, with the words "British Airways" written on its silver tail.

Some while later Michel de Nostredame, his sedan chair and his books were taken to Leonardo's quarters.

The master ordered that he and his guest were not to be disturbed and that food should be left at the doorstep.

The door was locked.

CHAPTER 13

GEORGIA BLADE, SPACE PIRATE

Georgia Blade lounged at the end of the bar, nursing a rye whiskey, casually rolling a cheroot between her rouged lips. In the smoky yellow gloom of the bar a Magonoid Shagganat plonked heavily on a battered, steam-powered pianoforte in the corner, soulfully crooning the final verse of a Crinoleon love song.

With an exaggerated flourish, the Shagganat pianist, Samanuel, ran triplets down the ivories and ended by repeatedly thumping the C key. He looked expectantly at his audience of one.

Georgia didn't look back.

Muttering something under his breath, the Shagganat shrugged his shoulders and sidled off the stool to an unlit snug for a break. There, three litres of Bender Ale slipped easily down his twin gullets, complimentary, on the house.

The silence was deafening.

Georgia lived for noise.

"Play it again, Samanuel," she said, flicking a Kartoleon dragmat into the snug.

A grumbling noise came back.

Georgia smiled and downed her drink, then clicked her fingers at the bar droid for a refill.

Inside the snug, the Shagganat emptied another tankard down his throats, belched and rubbed spillage into the ruffles on his purple dress shirt. After cracking his twenty-two fingers—the sound was like that of splintering wood—he took out a white handkerchief and carefully wiped his glistening brow. Picking up the dragmat from the bottom of his glass with a curse, he lumbered from the snug. Positioning the stool under his folds of heavy flesh, he hunched over the piano and crashed his way through a poorly segued homage to the legendary Kartoleon blues singer Blind Crusty Fudwad. Crusty would have spun in his grave if he'd been dead.

Liam, Alice and Archie hovered at the top of the wooden staircase. A chance meeting with a freighter pilot had given them Blade's location, along with a mouth full of obscenities and a death threat. As they stood watching the leather-clad redhead, cloaked as she was in the gloom of the bar, the smell of sweat, perfume and caustic smoke raked fingernails down the backs of their throats.

"Come on down and join the party," said Georgia, spotting them.

Nervously they descended the frayed, heavily soiled red carpet and walked towards her.

"Jules Rigsworth sent us," said Liam, chewing conscientiously.

Georgia pulled on her cheroot and sized them up with her solitary blue eye.

Archie looked at the studded black-leather patch where her other eye should have been, and shivered.

She saw his reaction and smiled. "I lost it in a duel, my human friend," she said nonchalantly.

Archie dropped his gaze. The Shagganat, watching from the safety of its piano, belched, as Shagganats do.

"He's in trouble," said Liam, a little louder. "Jules is."

Georgia shook her head. "And I should care?"

Draining her glass, she stubbed the glowing cheroot hard into her palm. The pirate slipped from her stool and, taking a long, speculative look at Archie, sashayed past them to climb the stairs. Framed in the doorway like a gunslinger against the sun, Georgia Blade was shown to best advantage: nearly two metres of bad, curvaceous space pirate, dressed in her signature leather thigh boots, tight britches and silk blouse. Her .44 Magnum revolver was slung in a shoulder holster.

She shook her hair and the street lighting haloed around it.

"Is he in big trouble?" she asked with a coy smile, her eyes fixed on Archie.

"Big trouble," replied Liam, looking bored.

"Wants me to help, does he?" Her gaze did not waver.

Archie looked as if he was about to catch fire.

Alice shrugged. "Yours was the only name he mentioned."

Georgia smiled again and ran her tongue across her glossy upper lip. "The only one he asked for, eh?" she said to Liam. "I guess, droid, we'd better talk."

She turned and glided out into the brightly lit street. Like the children of Hamelin village, Archie, Alice and Liam ran up the stairs in pursuit of her.

Just as they emerged, a shadow descended from out of the night sky.

Liam, Alice and Archie saw it and ran for cover.

The shadow grew ever larger until a scaly bird the size of a vulture, with blood-red claws and orange feathers, swooped over their heads and landed deftly on Georgia's shoulder.

"What's that?" cried Alice, getting up from the wet cobblestones.

"Lucretia. She guards my back." Georgia stroked the bird's bare yellow neck. "She has a penchant for eyes."

The pirate offered her pet a ball of flesh from a small bag on her belt. Lucretia snaffled it and launched herself back into the sky.

"Hostel owners don't like me taking her inside," Georgia explained. "They say she intimidates their customers."

The newcomers trotting along anxiously behind her, she turned down a sidewalk, crossed a narrow street and stepped into another dank and dingy cellar bar. At the top of the bar's steps she told Liam, "I drink whiskey rye, on the rocks, with a twist of lime. Two shots should start a conversation. Three often finishes one. Four …" She looked at Archie and leered, then laughed and pointed into the darkness below. "We'll be over in the corner, droid."

"My name's Liam," he grumbled, but he headed obediently for the bar to get the drinks.

At a greasy-looking table by the wall, Georgia waited for Archie to take his seat and then sat next to him.

"How do you know Jules?" asked Alice.

Georgia took a pack of silver cheroots from her silk blouse pocket. "We go way, way back." The pirate lit up and exhaled a plume of acrid smoke. Archie got a faceful of it and began hacking loudly.

Alice, not amused, glared at Georgia, who simply raised an eyebrow.

Liam arrived at their table with the drinks.

Taking a gulp of his orange juice, Archie started explaining to Georgia the predicament Jules and the leprechauns were in. The case against them was strong. For Smodius, their lawyer, to be able to cast doubt on their guilt, they had to find evidence that Jules was not the only one violating the galactic code. Ideally, they needed hard evidence of Griddleback involvement in kidnapping humans from another time zone.

Georgia listened carefully, shaking her head as the story unfolded. Occasionally, she would draw on her cheroot and look at the ceiling, or pump up her red hair and laugh.

Once Archie had concluded the story, Georgia was silent for a few moments.

When she finally spoke it was in a thoughtful voice. "Jules Rigsworth is a prize catch for the Griddlebacks. They've wanted him out of their scales for a long time now." She pushed her glass towards Liam. "I need more think-juice, droid."

Liam shook his head and went off again to the bar.

Georgia looked as if she were weighing up a multitude of unspoken considerations. She said nothing more until Liam had returned with another whiskey. Downing it in one, she muttered under her breath, "Damn you, Jules."

She looked at her companions around the table, as if to assess their capabilities. "I'll help you. I owe him this, but remember: I'm in charge, you do as I say, and we'll use my wrecking crew."

"We have our car parked close by. Should we follow you in it?" said Archie.

Georgia grinned. "You left it unattended?"

"Yes. Is that a problem?"

"No. Not for me it isn't. But don't bother looking for it. It'll be in a back-street chop shop by now."

She rose from her chair, spun round and, with the speed of a Major League pitcher, hurled her empty glass into the fireplace. "Time to rock and roll."

Two more glasses smashed against the hearth. A third, thrown by Alice, bounced off the rear of the chimney and rolled back out onto the floor. "I meant for it to do that," said Alice.

They followed Georgia into the street, wary of Lucretia circling invisibly above them.

The pirate set off down a long narrow street, glancing warily into shadows. Fearful of losing her in the labyrinth of downtown Sleazeeze streets, the others walked close behind her as she found her way into a closed yard.

At the back of the yard, she turned. "This is Pandora, my transport."

She pressed a button in her hand and there appeared in front of them a large pink truck, with furry dice, dark glass and a green sunscreen emblazoned with the name "Pandora".

"I liberated her when I did your tiny planet during my Milky Way Galaxy tour in 2000," said Georgia, walking to the driver's cab.

"Wow! She's beautiful!" Archie gazed at his reflection in the door.

Alice was more practical. "Isn't it a little bit loud? I mean, how do you blend in, wandering the galaxy in a bright pink—?"

"Elephant," said Liam, his irritation at the mysterious, egoistical pirate showing through. "It's a pink elephant, an albatross around our feet. They'll see us coming a galaxy away."

"You're mixing metaphors. It's a white elephant," said Alice. "And it's an albatross around our necks, not our feet."

"Whatever," Liam said through a yawn.

Georgia turned to Archie. "It's a Peterbilt custom big rig with a few twenty-fourth century modifications." She pressed the button again and the rig disappeared.

Liam walked forward with his hand outstretched. "Interesting party trick, but it's still there." He kept walking. His hangdog expression turned to one of surprise when his outstretched hand touched the yard's back wall.

"Displacement technology. Not even the Griddlebacks have perfected this," said Georgia, bringing Pandora back with a touch of the button. Liam jumped nervously out of the way. "I liberated the blueprints for converting a ship after a dalliance with a Sarcothian fighter pilot in the twenty-fifth century. My wrecking crew did the modifications."

She laughed and walked over to Liam. "Don't be so judgmental, tin man. As an old friend often said, there is more in heaven and Earth than in your dozen or so processors." She tapped his head hard.

"Isn't taking technology from other eras illegal?" said Alice, looking worried.

Georgia lit yet another cheroot. "Totally. That's why I have a bounty of twenty thousand Confederation tokens on my head. Didn't Jules tell you anything?"

No one answered her.

"Get inside. We have a lot of work to do," said Georgia after a moment

The truck doors opened. Liam, Alice and Archie climbed into the cab and dropped to the floor, followed by Georgia.

"Wow! It's just like my narrowboat on the Shropshire Canal, so much bigger on the inside than it is on the outside!" cried Alice. They were standing in a large, well-lit circular room with a vaulted ceiling. There were doors along the walls and an instrument panel and couch in the centre of the area.

A blood-curdling caw rent the air as Lucretia dived in through the open cab door. Archie yelped and cowered as the bird swooped low over their heads and landed on a custom-made perch next to the instrument panel.

"Sit down," said Georgia, pointing at a long, leather couch.

As they took their seats, Lucretia watched them closely, flexing her claws. She eventually settled her stare on Archie's blue eyes.

"Lucretia wants you to give her a gift," said Georgia.

Archie gulped. Reaching slowly into his coat pocket, his every movement followed intently by Lucretia's cold and beady gaze, he took out a packet and opened it before her.

"Eyeball?" he asked, trembling.

Lucretia looked at him, then at the bag as he gently wiggled it in front of her. Swaying left, then right, Lucretia stretched her neck to look into the bag. Deftly plucking out an eyeball, she swallowed it whole.

Relieved, Archie placed the bag carefully on the instrument panel next to her and watched as she pecked and chomped loudly on the sweets.

Georgia took the middle seat, and fastened her harness. "You've made a friend there. Now, buckle up, everyone, and be prepared to meet my wrecking crew."

Pandora rose into the air and soon left the squalid downtown area behind. Her passengers followed their progress on a large screen on the wall above the instrument panel as she flew high above broken signs, half-lit skydomes and wrecked, burning vehicles.

"Hold tight," said Georgia, changing gear.

There was a loud hissing noise as the ship went into Alterian drive and they were pushed back into their seats. It was a short burst. The feeling of being squeezed and then pushed forcibly through the eye of a needle was, thankfully, momentary.

They slowed. Far below, they could see the tops of buildings and advertising lights.

Georgia brought Pandora in to land. The pirate's space portal sat undetected atop a large block of abandoned apartments in the centre of Sleazeeze. Using technology liberated from the future, Georgia had constructed a fourth-dimensional holding and repair bay for her ship and that of her wrecking crew. From outside, the bay didn't exist. Only with the appropriate dimensional key could the bay doors be unlocked and access gained to the inside. It was like a pocket on a pair of jeans. From the outside, you couldn't see the size or depth of the pocket. If you disguised the pocket's opening you wouldn't see it at all, but it would still be there.

Getting duplicate portal keys for her wrecking crew had been a nightmare. The keysmiths on Rigalnus Minor, where Georgia had stolen the technology, were an officious bunch. But she'd managed to "persuade" them, and some still had the scars to show for it.

Screwball sneered and spat a wad of masticated tobacco into a priceless Ming Dynasty vase by his feet. Hugh Willard threw down another marker and pointed at the board.

"That's rooked yer," he said, venomously. They all looked at the Raggedy Rook board.

"Yeah, you've been well rooked, Paddy. Hand over the loot," said Seamus De-Woods Kelly.

Paddy snarled and threw a handful of pearl chokers, jewellery and precious stones on Willard's pile.

"Another game anyone?" asked Willard, clawing the loot back to his pile. Seamus looked away, Merv Mulligan and Dave Moriarty shook their heads, and Big Joe Damanski got up and wandered to the back of the room to light his pipe.

"What's wrong with yers all? Can't take a good rooking?" said Willard with a grin as he straightened his pile.

"What's the point of playing Raggedy Rook if we already owns more stuff than we know what ter do with?" said Paddy, waving his hands in the direction of the piles of boxes, trunks and cabinets overflowing with priceless artefacts, gold bullion and gems that covered the floor of their lair.

"Cause I like ta beats yers all, and ta take yer money, dat's ter reason why," Hugh roared, mimicking a low-brow leprechaun accent. They all laughed, and got out their briar pipes. Paddy picked up a squeezebox and, before you could have said "Val Doonican's riding Paddy McGintie's goat in the Irish Stakes at Leopard-stown", there were fiddles, pipes and crates of beer on display as seven clurichauns sang their lungs out.

"What's that awful noise?" asked Alice, covering her ears. She'd just climbed down from Pandora and was beginning to wish she hadn't

"Have you met clurichauns before?" asked Georgia above the din, helping Archie out of the cab.

"No," said Alice anxiously. "But I've heard about them."

"What's the matter, my human?" said Georgia to Archie. Lucretia hopped from the cab onto Georgia's shoulder, and likewise looked at Archie, who shuddered. The last thing he wanted was a possessive harpy and her jealous carnivore picking over him, even if the thought of being picked over by Georgia did make his mouth go suddenly dry.

"Well, we do have leprechaun friends," he replied.

Georgia pressed Pandora's cloaking button and laughed. "Best not to mention that … if you want to keep those," she whispered in his ear, pointing south and winking.

The night was gloomy. Tharg's three moons were hidden behind clouds. It also didn't help that most of the lights on the high-rise were broken and a pall of smog clung to its top.

Georgia walked them closer to the ventilation shaft from which the cacophony was coming and set off down a long flight of steel steps below it. The others followed, gathering in front of a steel door. Through it they could hear, even louder than before, the sound of raucous laughter and singing.

The pirate tapped in a code, flung open the door and turned to her guests.

"Meet my wrecking crew," she bawled, barely audible over the din.

They peered inside the smoke-filled room. Seven soused clurichauns were rolling on the floor, fighting amidst priceless furniture, paintings, boxes of jewels, and piles of gold bars, drinking beer and singing bawdy folk songs. Sometimes they managed to do all of these things simultaneously.

Georgia pulled out her .44 Magnum revolver and pumped a couple of bullets into the ceiling, focusing attention.

"Okay, boys, we've just been selected for a job." She holstered her gun under her arm. "An old friend of mine is in trouble and I owe him. Plus, and this is the important part, it's to do with Griddlebacks."

The gaggle of bodies on the floor unfurled, dusted themselves off, and stood in a line. They were an ugly, unshaven, disparate bunch of rogues, dressed in an assortment of leather trousers, waistcoats, hats, woollen overcoats and hobnailed boots. Willard spat on the floor and walked up to Archie.

"I smell leprechauns," he growled, sniffing the air close to Archie.

Wallop!

Merv Mulligan had belted Willard on the end of his snout with a brass candlestick.

"You and your turdy leprechauns, can't you give it a rest? Anyone can see these people are human!" Merv turned to Archie. "Begging yer pardon. He's an obsessive compulsive paranoid schizophrenic with psychotic tendencies."

"Not any more," grumbled Willard, gingerly rubbing his throbbing nose. "I got a certificate proving I'm as sane as you."

Over a hearty meal of stew, the clurichauns introduced themselves, then settled down to play music and drink long into the night.

"We'd best all sleep in Pandora," said Georgia, looking around at the mess.

After a quick tour of Pandora's amenities and sleeping quarters, Archie and Alice went to bed. Liam lay on the floor in the corridor between their rooms. Lucretia had her own cage and was soon asleep.

Archie spent a restless night, worrying about their mission, Georgia Blade and her clurichaun wrecking crew. He was still tired when he woke, and it was a struggle to get out of bed. He found the shower, bathed and dressed.

Feeling better, he went to the galley to make breakfast.

There he found Alice hunched over the table with her head in her hands, looking glum. Liam was outside on the roof with Georgia.

"What's the matter?" asked Archie, pulling up a stool.

"This whole thing's getting out of control," she said in a hushed voice, glancing at the doorway. "Do you trust this crazy woman?"

"Do we have a choice? We have to believe Jules knows what he's doing." Archie took her hands and looked into her green eyes. "Hang in there. I'll look after you."

Alice crossed those same green eyes expressively. "Thanks, Archie."

He chose to ignore the sarcasm. "Not a problem. Let's make breakfast. I'm starving!"

Outside, the space-parking bay was a hive of activity. Georgia, with Liam's help, was preparing Pandora and the clurichauns' spaceship, Prometheus, for the journey back to 2015 and the tea rooms in Steeple Snoring.

After a porridge-and-oatcake breakfast, Big Joe took Archie and Alice to see what Prometheus looked like.

"Holy cow! It's a Russian Zil," said Archie loudly.

"Yep, it's a Zil, all right," said Joe. "A Zil 41047." He tapped the bonnet and his small eyes glinted. The hairs on his facial warts quivered with excitement as he enthused about the car. "Peripheral welded, with stiffening sections and a closed box section. It was originally built with four doors, three rows of seats, a partition and an air-conditioning system, two drive shafts with a pillow block, and three couplings on needle-bearings with a 7.7 litre V8 engine. It's a Politburo muscle car. We just added the smoked-glass windows and modified it a wee bit."

"Where did you find it?" Alice asked, intrigued by Big Joe's knowledge of the car.

"Merv and I found it in a parking lot in Washington DC in 1985 and liberated it."

Paddy, passing by with a keg of beer, overheard Joe talking and chuckled, calling to the others. "Hey, everyone, Big Joe's going to tell us a story!"

The clurichauns crowded around Joe, who looked flustered, his private Zil eulogy gatecrashed.

"Where was the parking lot again, Joe?" said Paddy, laughing and pretending to look quizzical.

"Er, well, at da time, it was just inside da Russian Embassy," mumbled Joe, playing with his odd-shaped fingers.

"And the three Russians inside the Zil, what happened to them?"

Big Joe raised his hands defensively. "They shouldn't have been in the car."

Screwball turned to Alice and Archie, and in a loud voice said, "Let me explain what really happened."

Big Joe's shoulders sagged.

Screwball patted him on the back and smiled. "Big Joe and Merv decided to go pilfering on their own in Washington DC, and they saw this car at the Russian Embassy. Thinking it would make the ideal shell for a spacecraft, they nicked it, along with three very surprised Russians sleeping inside."

There was a chorus of sniggers from the clurichauns.

Screwball nodded at his companions. "I came to the rescue and smoothed everything out."

"What?" said Big Joe. "You sorted it out?" His eyes blazed and he thrust his red nose at Screwball. "Yes, you sorted it out. You dropped the Russians butt naked in New York's Central Park with a story about alien abduction planted in their heads!"

Screwball pushed Big Joe into Paddy who tripped and fell over Seamus. "And who was the wise guy who thought it would be fun to plant outrageous thoughts in their memories about a hose pipe, funnel and fruit!" he cried.

Big Joe was about to punch him when Georgia stepped between them. "Now, now, boys," she said, pushing them apart. "Let's keep the fighting for the Griddle-backs."

Big Joe sneered, pumped out his chest like a rooster and strutted past Screwball, who gave him a one-fingered salute.

"Anyway," said Seamus quietly to Archie, "it's a grand ship and we love it."

"What happened to the Russians you abducted?" whispered Archie.

"That's another story," said Seamus. "The Russians at the embassy closed ranks over the incident, and Boris, Havel and Giorgi—the three Russians we abducted—ended up in Siberia. We rescued them, and they now run a specialized Ikebana firm out of Gamma Major called GBH. We hear from them every now and then."

"What! They're flower arrangers?" said Archie.

"History re-arrangers," said Seamus with a wink. "Totally illegal, so they use flower-arranging as a cover."

"Okay, boys, let's lock and load." Georgia opened Pandora's cab.

Soon Archie, Alice and Liam were buckled up on the leather couch.

"What's that!" asked Alice, leaning over and pointing at the dashboard.

"It's a Jules Rigsworth bobblehead. I thought it appropriate to dig it out. He would be touched if he knew."

Georgia tapped Jules's grinning head and it bounced up and down.

Lucretia, who was now sitting on her perch next to it, opened one eye and, squawking loudly, launched a devastating attack on it, gouging out chunks of plastic and sending it into a crazed dance routine.

Georgia laughed. "I'd forgotten what he did to you." She quickly moved the bobblehead out of the bird's range.

"What did he do?" asked Alice.

Georgia just smirked.

"Why—?"

"Why a bobblehead?" queried Archie, before Alice could finish her question.

"They were made for Jules's birthday," said Georgia, adjusting her seat and signalling to the clurichauns to fire up Prometheus. Turning on Pandora's flight console, she entered a ten-digit number. A row of figures filled the console screen and started what looked like a countdown.

"Locked," she said into a small microphone as the changing figures began to slow down. Pandora and Prometheus were now joined together and locked into the decreasing cycle of numbers.

Georgia moved along the console, as if seeking something. The numbers continued to drop.

2,098,761…
She looked edgy.
150,345…
"Anything your side?" she barked into the microphone to Screwball, gazing along to the end of the console and back again.
98,002 …
"Nothing yet," replied Screwball.
34,006 …
"You must have something?" she cried, looking worried.
1,256 …
"If it's there I can't see it." The tension in Screwball's voice was almost tangible.
56 …
"Corner pocket, corner pocket! Green ball, green ball!" screamed Screwball.

With three numbers remaining on the sequence, Georgia yelled, "Got it!"

She slammed her foot hard on a floor pedal and thrust forward what looked like a gear stick by her side. Pandora shot upwards, the sound of Dixieland horns blaring through the ship. Prometheus followed in a stream of water vapour and Alterian drive particles.

"Yes!" said Georgia punching the air. "I've caught the travel bug!"

As Pandora climbed, the skin on the faces of her occupants rippled like canvas in a gale, stretching across their skulls.

Their ascent into the wormhole was brief. Soon the ship slowed and levelled off.

Georgia settled back in her chair, and looked very smug. Archie and Alice looked bewildered and very ill. Lucretia looked very carnivorous. Liam, for his part, just looked very bored.

"What?" said Georgia, seeing the two humans' ashen faces. "You've never hitched a wormhole ride behind a freighter before?"

They shook their heads.

"Sick bags are under your seats."

After Georgia had set Pandora on autopilot to follow the freighter along the wormhole, she explained what had just happened. It was illegal to enter a highway wormhole without an identification beacon. This was similar to having a number plate on a car back in their own time. Space vehicles without identification could cause chaos and, most likely, catastrophes if, for instance, two hyperfreighters wanted to use the same hole at the same time and couldn't see each other. Every ship had, by Intergalactic Ordinance, an identifying designation code beacon. But it was not in Georgia's nature to fly with identity beacons. She cruised the galaxies on her terms: illegally, for the highest bidder, and with a custom-built ship packed with stolen technology. She had taken Pandora and Prometheus close to where a highway wormhole was about to open and waited, cloaked and unnoticed. When the next space freighter came along to use the wormhole, Georgia had tucked Pandora in behind it and ridden the other craft's slipstream—or, rather, its Alterian particles—into the hole.

"If you're skilled," she concluded, "you hitch a ride and hide within the freighter's particle stream. Get it wrong, though"—she chuckled—"and you're worm kill."

Archie had questions. "Why the corner pocket? And what's a green ball?"

"Space-trucker speak." Georgia pointed to a screen on her console. "Look."

On the screen was a simulation of a three-dimensional pool table, complete with balls.

"It's a pool table?" said Archie.

"Yep. We followed the green ball down the corner pocket. In this case, the space freighter was the green ball, using the wormhole to swing past Earth in 2015 to get to the outer galaxies. The pocket in the corner was the opening to the wormhole he went down. We find it easier to use a pool table as a reference."

"Why does Earth influence so many things in the universe?" asked Alice, perplexed by the myriad of references to Earth culture she kept hearing.

"You're a quirky race, I guess. Despite your limited advancement, everyone either loves you or hates you. Most races in the galaxies have visited the third rock from the sun that you call Earth, even the Griddlebacks. They've been after your piece of real estate for centuries."

"It's difficult to think of you as not being a human," said Archie. She certainly seemed to have human … attributes.

"Well, I'm certainly not! I'm descended from an ancient bloodline of warriors."

Archie would have questioned her further but, just then, the ship shuddered and flipped upside-down, sending pieces of furniture past their heads and Lucretia flying upwards from her perch. He and Alice hung from their seatbelts, groaning.

"That's not good!" shouted Georgia. She leaned down to grab the microphone. "Are you with us, boys?" she yelled into it.

Nothing came back from Prometheus.

"We started coming out too early," she said, watching numbers flash on the screen. "Prometheus, do you copy?"

There was only static.

"Oh, don't give me grief!"

Georgia stared at the screen. The numbers had stopped at 1773. "We've arrived on Earth, but in 1773!"

Then the power failed, leaving the ship with just a solitary light on the console.

When Prometheus turned upside-down Screwball's seat belt snapped and he dropped through the air to land heavily on the ceiling. As he scrabbled about and Prometheus began spiralling out of control, the craft's gravity stabilizers started to malfunction, so that he went tumbling back and forth from ceiling to floor, yelling and swearing. At last he managed to hang onto a cross-beam on the ship's ceiling.

In front of Big Joe, the flight console lit up like a Christmas tree.

"Hold on, we're coming in for a rough landing!" he shouted, reaching over and taking the controls in place of the absent Screwball.

Prometheus lurched and dipped, prising Screwball's grip loose of the cross-beam. He fell into the arms of Merv.

With a series of shudders and cartwheels, Prometheus slowed and came to rest the right way up.

"Where are we?" said Merv, shoving the disorientated Screwball back into his seat.

"I've no idea. Most of the instruments have gone arse-over-tip." Seamus tapped the console with his fist.

"Give me a visual," rasped Big Joe.

"Can't, not responding."

Screwball reached up and pulled a lever. "Going to manual."

He ducked as a periscope dropped from the ceiling and swung mere centimetres from his head. Big Joe grabbed it and looked into the eyepiece. The crew watched the periscope's view on the console screen. It looked as if they were inside a wooden building. Large blackened oak beams ran in all directions. The wooden floor was covered with water. Something moved and Big Joe zoomed quickly onto it.

"Rats," he said, focusing on a group of black furry animals that huddled on a beam corner just above the water level.

Screwball placed a small round ball on the console and watched it move from left to right. "Look at the ball. I think we're aboard a ship."

Feeling slightly less groggy, he turned to Seamus. "We need to know our where-abouts and a date. How long to fix the console and get us back online?"

Seamus looked thoughtfully at the smouldering control panel. "If we got the spares, three or four hours. Maybe."

"Okay, as fast as you can." Screwball got up from his chair. "Who wants to come with me for some air?"

When Screwball opened the outer hatch of Prometheus (the boot or trunk, in car terminology), the smell of rotting garbage and cold salty air filled his lungs, making him dry-retch loudly. He covered his mouth with a scarf, put on his goggles, zipped up his spacesuit, checked no one was around, and climbed onto the roof of the Zil. Merv, Seamus, Paddy and Willard, likewise wearing spacesuits and goggles that could look through structures up to a distance of thirty metres, joined him. They soon realized that the Zil was floating in a water-logged cabin.

"Okay, let's see what we can find," said Screwball.

He dropped into the waist-deep bilge, followed by his friends. The cold, murky water slowed their progress, as did the need to climb over submerged wooden beams and rubbish to move forward. In front of them was a near-vertical set of steps leading up to another deck.

As they gathered around the foot of the ladder, Screwball signalled to the others to wait, and began climbing.

He heard the sound of voices. Using his goggles, he saw a group of men playing cards on the next deck, with an upturned barrel for a table. Slowly he climbed to the top of the ladder. Turning his goggles to camera mode, he filmed the men for several minutes before descending to join his friends.

"Let's go the other way. This way's blocked by humans."

They went back past Prometheus and on towards another ladder. Their goggles showed them that this time there was no one on the deck above. In single file, they ascended the ladder until they saw blue sky and white clouds, and heard the flapping of canvas.

Screwball started his camera again and filmed everything he could see. He zoomed in on a large brass bell at the rear of the vessel. On its side was the name of the ship, HMS Beaver.

There was a shout and they froze.

The shout came again. "Land ahoy!"

In a sudden rush of activity, humans ran about, pulled down canvas and tied ropes.

Screwball signalled the clurichauns back to Prometheus. He had enough information for now.

Back inside the spaceship, he pored over the footage and photos. Without working instruments and the advice of a specialist in human history, researching the vessel was impossible. Merv remembered a pillaging spree he had been on back in the eighteenth century, and thought the wooden planks looked familiar. He reckoned this was a similar ship to the ones he'd been on, and that they'd probably landed in a part of it called the bilges. Everyone noticed how his eyes lit up when he spoke about "the best pillaging job I've ever been a part of". He told of boxes of gold, hundreds of valuable paintings, and rows upon rows of chests full of precious stones.

"Do you think it's the same t'ing?" asked Big Joe excitedly.

"I don't see why not. It would make sense," replied Paddy, already thinking of the mountain of gold he might find.

"Shame not to help ourselves, would it not be?" said Seamus, rubbing his hands.

Only Screwball raised a voice of caution. "I'd prefer to know more about this ship before we start in on any pillaging of it."

The rest looked at him suspiciously.

"I reckon you already knows there's gold aboard and you want it all for yourself," said Big Joe. He shook his fist at Screwball. "Let's take a vote on it. We either leave a ship full of booty or we take it fer ourselves!"

Screwball knew when he was outnumbered. "Okay, but we wait until the ship reaches land. You lot can go and find the gold. I'll stay and look after Prometheus."

The clurichauns roared their approval, and out came a dozen crates of beer, a squeezebox and a fiddle. Four hours later, having repaired the console, Seamus joined them in their sleeping quarters, dreaming of their hoard of gold.

Georgia sat in her chair feeling perplexed, as ever drawing on a cheroot to help her think. Lucretia flew down and landed on her shoulder. Georgia couldn't understand how they'd lost that freighter. It had never happened before. She looked at the motionless numbers on the instrument panel and then at the screen in front of her. Leaning down to the side of her chair, she grabbed a lever and pulled it forcefully upwards.

Pandora shuddered. The ship's power and lighting came back on, and the flight console flashed into life.

She pressed a button on the console and the inside of a dimly lit building filled the screen in front of her.

"We need to find our location quickly." She jumped from her chair, sending Lucretia flying off into the bowels of the ship. "Liam and Archie, come with me. Alice, you stay here in Pandora."

Georgia took the boy and the droid to the cargo bay, where they put on thermal jumpsuits. She handed each of them a belt loaded with all manner of gadgets. She quickly briefed them as to how these worked, beginning with a short tube—a Bosun—and finishing with night sights that looked like swimming goggles.

"Ready?" she asked finally.

"Shouldn't we be wearing eighteenth-century clothes?" Archie asked her, feeling more Ghostbuster than Georgian gentleman.

"No time. We need to find out where we are, swiftly, then get out of here."

Georgia walked rapidly to the hatch. "Okay, stick with me."

She lowered her goggles, raised her Bosun and opened the cab door. Outside, the temperature was below freezing, but their thermal suits regulated their temperature. After they'd jumped down, Georgia pressed a button on her hand-held device and Pandora disappeared, cloaked.

The pirate looked around. They had landed in a barn. Moving quickly to the barn's side, they worked their way towards a window, feet rustling through thick straw.

At the window, Georgia looked out onto a bustling street. Ahead of them, a brightly lit building overflowed with crowds of excited people.

"Look," she whispered to Liam and Archie, "I'm worried about how we got here. It doesn't make sense that we're lost. I have to assume we're here for a reason." Again she squinted at the people crowding around the building. "Something's happening in there and we need to know what."

Liam tapped Georgia on the shoulder. "Anything to alleviate the tedium. Get me some clothes and I'll go mingle with the proles."

Georgia smiled at him. "Just what I was thinking."

A search of the barn revealed some old overcoats in a store cupboard, and Liam put one of them on. He didn't look great in it but, as the others pointed out, he wouldn't have looked great in anything else, either. Moments later he was gloomily mingling among the scrum at the front of the building.

"Tap your communicator if you can hear me," said Georgia.

Liam tapped twice, then struggled through the throng towards the crowded building, Once inside, he found himself squashed among a multitude of local people, listening to speaker after speaker, all complaining about a problem in the docks. They had weird accents and dialect, as if they'd just jumped out of a Shakespeare play and were trying to swallow a budgie.

No one knew what to do. They wanted to protest, but they couldn't agree how.

A new speaker had just taken the stage to rapturous applause from the crowd when a man pushed his way into the building shouting that he had important news. The crowd parted, letting him rush onto the stage. He pointed excitedly towards the quayside. A ship rumoured to be the HMS Beaver was coming into port on the high tide, to join HMS Eleanor and HMS Dartmouth. If the ship was indeed the Beaver, it would be carrying a cargo of tea like the other two.

Back in the barn, Georgia nudged Archie and gave him a perturbed look. She pointed to a small screen in her hand. "Liam isn't the only tin man out there. There are two Griddleback droids somewhere in the crowd."

She relayed this information directly into Liam's computer brain, and told him to ask someone the date and place and then get back to the barn.

"Boston, 15 December 1773," said Liam on his return a couple of minutes later. He closed the barn door behind him.

"Back to Pandora," said Georgia, de-cloaking the ship and opening the cab doors.

Once inside, she gathered everyone in the kitchen area. Liam prepared a meal while the rest sat around the table.

"Well, my human friends, does 1773, Boston Harbor, mean anything to you?"

Archie glanced at Alice, and they both shook their heads.

"Jeez, don't they teach you kids any history these days?" Georgia rolled her eye. "I think we've arrived at the Boston Tea Party, the catalyst for the American War of Independence. I said we're here for a reason," she added, "and finding Griddleback droids was no coincidence. We've been deliberately crashed here to find them. I suspect the Time Guardians are playing more of a part in all this than they're publicly admitting."

"Weren't we going to Steeple Snoring to find Griddlebacks there?" said Alice.

Georgia's face lit up. "Yes, so let's take advantage of the situation and find out what they're doing here instead." She turned to Liam. "First, I need to work on the ship while you try and find Prometheus. We won't be going anywhere without a repaired ship and my wrecking crew."

"Nothing's supposed to happen until all three ships are in Boston Harbor. That won't be until tomorrow morning," said Liam, whose databanks were better equipped on Earth's history than were the humans' brains.

"We meet back here for breakfast, six sharp." Georgia grabbed a plate of food and headed for the door. "Tin man, follow me!"

In the control room, Georgia sat Liam down and produced several silvery balls.

"Stingers," she said, rolling three of them in a circular pattern in her palm. "I've programmed them to lock onto a Griddleback droid and incapacitate it. They move too fast for the human eye to see." Liam's habitual expression of boredom disappeared as Georgia handed him the spheres. "Now, get to work on the ship and meet back here tomorrow at six after you've recharged your cells, or whatever it is you droids do for breakfast."

Next morning Liam was despatched to find out what was happening dockside and locate the Griddleback droids. He soon reported back via his communicator that a crowd of several thousand people had gathered on the docks, and that he'd located the two droids among them.

With Georgia's permission, he followed the droids to the front of the crowd, where they stood before the captains of the Eleanor, the Beaver and the Dartmouth and a small number of British sailors. Heavily outnumbered, the captains were negotiating the well-being of their ships and crew. The two Griddleback droids left the main group and moved towards the quay, where HMS Beaver had docked that morning. Liam followed and, reaching the Beaver, saw something he wasn't expecting.

"You're not going to believe this!" he whispered to Georgia.

"What?"

"Can you use my eyes to see on deck?"

Georgia punched a couple of buttons on the console and, through Liam's eyes, scanned HMS Beaver's superstructure.

Dozens of boxes were raining down into the harbour, thrown over the ship's side by several pairs of stubby little arms.

"How the...? How the hell did they get here? And what the hell do they think they're doing?" She thought fast. "Quick, Liam. You've got to stop the droids before they get on board the ship."

Liam ducked in behind a pile of barrels on the quayside some ten metres from where the droids were standing before the Beaver. Pulling two marble-size electronic stingers from his belt, he hurled them towards the Griddleback machines.

The stingers took off like incensed wasps and milliseconds later thudded into the backs of the droids' heads, felling them both.

He watched to see if anyone was concerned by the droids' sudden collapse. No one seemed to have noticed.

"Sanitized," he whispered into his microphone.

Leaving his hiding place, he walked over to the droids and quickly dragged them behind the barrels.

He was just in time. A large crowd arrived and started to congregate before the Beaver.

Georgia and Archie hurried to the quayside from Pandora and found Liam with the droids. They dumped the droids into two empty barrels and carried them away just as the party on the dockside began. Boxes were now flying from all three ships into the water, spewing out tea bricks like sparks from a Roman candle.

Archie looked at the scene and chuckled. "Your wrecking crew's just a bunch of tea ladies!"

Georgia gave him a withering look. "If we get out of this, I'm sending them all to a penal colony."

They dumped the droids in a nearby warehouse. Leaving Liam to guard them, she and Archie went back to the quayside and HMS Beaver.

They pushed through the crowd and strode up the gangway to the deck. The first person they saw was Big Joe.

Georgia walked menacingly towards him. "What do you think you're doing?" She pointed her Bosun at his head. "I should shoot the lot of you and string your rotten carcases up in the rigging."

Six startled clurichauns stared at her. "Georgia Blade! Are we glad to see you!" Seamus cried. The six friends dropped the boxes they'd been just about to hurl overboard and ran to join her.

"Where the hell's Prometheus?" she asked.

"In the bowels of this ship," replied Paddy.

Georgia grabbed hold of Big Joe's wart-encrusted ear and pulled him to the side of the boat.

'What do you see?" she asked, pointing at the Eleanor and the Dartmouth.

"Damn and fidgety bit it!" Big Joe cried, slapping his forehead and looking at the boxes flying from the ships into the sea. "Come on, lads, we got us the wrong ship! The gold must be on the others!"

She grabbed his nose and pulled him back, plonking him unceremoniously on his backside. He looked up at her, face full of puzzlement.

"No, you lumpy clot! Have you any idea what you've started?" Her patience had been exhausted some while ago, and his vacuous expression made the idea of mindless, bloody violence very tempting indeed. She beat back the urge with some difficulty.

"Ahhh, you bunch of half-witted Shagganats!" she yelled. "You've bloody well kick-started the American War of Independence!"

Picking up Big Joe by his ears, she thrust him head-first into a half-empty tea chest. His legs twitched in the air, his knees knocking together.

The other clurichauns backed away.

"It was all Screwball's fault," said Paddy, sounding as convincing as someone claiming the dog had eaten their homework.

"He said the ship was full of gold," whimpered Big Joe from inside the chest.

His fellow clurichauns nodded, fearful of Georgia's simmering rage.

"And just where is your captain?" she asked, hands on hips, looking around for Screwball.

"He's back repairing Prometheus," said Merv, surreptitiously checking the chest beside him in case he'd missed something.

Georgia saw the movement and exploded. "These are tea chests, you fools! There's no gold, no precious gems, no furniture, just tea, bloody tea." She emphasized the point by kicking a pile of tea bricks. "You've just started the biggest bloody tea party in history!" she fumed. "And where's the ship's crew?"

"There weren't many of them, so we tied them up and left them on the lower deck," said Seamus.

"Okay, let's sort this out quickly," Georgia said, taking a deep breath. "Paddy, Merv, get down to Liam on the quayside. He's got two Griddleback droids stashed. They're incapacitated—don't worry. You and him get the droids back to Pandora as fast as you can." She turned to Archie. "Somewhere here in Boston is a Griddleback controlling the droids. Sooner or later he'll realize something's gone wrong. We need to move Prometheus into the barn with Pandora."

Georgia looked over the side of the boat. The crowd was cheering and waving, chanting, "More, more, more."

"Okay Seamus," said Georgia, "here are the coordinates for Pandora. She's cloaked in a barn not more than a kilometre from here. Get back to your ship fast, before this lot come aboard, and tell Screwball to hop Prometheus over to join us as soon as he can."

Seamus nodded and, with the other clurichauns in tow, disappeared below.

"We need to leave. Now!" said Georgia.

Once back on Pandora, Georgia had the droids taken to the ship laboratory. She was sure that finding the droids in Boston was something that had been planned—the reason behind their detour to 1773 Boston.

Inside the laboratory, the two droids lay on examination tables. Georgia had Archie and Liam examine one droid, while she and Alice examined the other. They emptied the droids' pockets and put everything they found into a tray. Georgia pored over a pile of letters, identity documents and personal items.

After a few moments she stopped. "Griddlebacks, huh!" she said in a derisory tone

She passed a couple of letters of identity to Alice and Archie. "Thomas Jefferson. George Washington," she said.

"Future presidents of the United States!" cried Alice, who knew some history after all.

"Looks like the Griddlebacks planted these two in expectation." Georgia shook her mane of red hair.

"How do you know Griddlebacks are involved?" said Archie, prodding the podgy, lifeless face of Thomas Jefferson.

"Only Griddlebacks create droids using human flesh on titanium skeletons." She lifted Jefferson's head and pressed the skin at the base of his neck. Peeling back the skin from the titanium skull, she used a screwdriver-like instrument to remove the top of his skull. "The brain," she said, pointing to a glowing sphere held inside a ball of gel.

"Won't the Griddleback controller know we have their droids?" said Alice. She looked as if she was about to puke. Archie already had.

"With luck, not yet. The last thing the Griddleback controller saw was a view of tea chests flying over the side of HMS Beaver. The stingers scrambled the droids' brains and left no trace of forced entry. I doubt a Griddleback would be wise to stingers. The controller—or controllers, more likely—will think the droids malfunctioned, so they'll be on their way to locate and repair them."

She collected a handful of tools and turned to George Washington. "If I can isolate the droids' visual memory, we may get a chance to see the controllers. Controllers are typically only lightly armed, and if these ones aren't suspicious we can try to lay a trap for them." She prised a small red rectangular block out from behind Washington's eyes.

"We need to get history back on course," said Archie.

"Yep, and that gives us even more reason to remove the controller, find the real Jefferson and Washington, and release them." Georgia took the cube to a workbench. "Get yourselves some food. Leave me to carry on here. Liam," she added, "can you go find Screwball and check the power situation."

The droid nodded depressedly and followed the others out of the room.

Once she'd removed the second droid's visual-memory unit, Georgia placed the two small blocks carefully on a wired platter in a tank full of slimy blue liquid. At the press of a button, a pair of date-logs came onscreen. She picked 1 July 1770, it being the earliest available date.

A sequence of events, seen through the eyes of the droid, ran in reverse until the face of an aged Griddleback appeared. She immediately stopped the process and leaned back in her chair, looking at the leathery face filling the screen.

"Well, well, Granwold Burbart, we meet again," she said quietly, looking into his cold, reptilian eyes. "I think the Time Guardians want you and me to dance, Granwold."

Screwball's repairs of Prometheus had been successful, finally. Soon after he'd finished he was parking the clurichaun spaceship alongside Pandora in the barn. Archie met him and explained the situation with the Griddleback droids. Georgia had activated one of the droids' distress beacons inside the barn, and was preparing for the Griddleback controllers to arrive.

"Okay, lads, time ter redeem yerselves," said Big Joe as the clurichauns jumped from Prometheus. With Liam's help they carried the droids from Pandora to place them near the barn doors. Dressed in impressive body armour, the clurichauns fanned out, taking up positions behind bales of hay close to the droids.

Maybe half an hour later, a small grey ship, about the size of a van, materialized in a cloud of water vapour in front of them.

"Griddlebacks," murmured Georgia. She, Alice and Archie were watching the scene on Pandora's flight console.

An oval hole opened in the side of the ship and steps unfolded to the floor. A small white furry creature—a mixture of a rabbit with long floppy ears and a wallaby, with the face of an aardvark—hopped down the steps and onto the barn floor. Its big brown eyes blinked rapidly and its long, furry nose twitched from side to side.

"Oh, isn't it cute!" cried Alice, looking at the nervous bundle of fur.

Following behind the animal was a Griddleback, clawing its way down the steps.

"Yuck, not so cute," she added.

The furry animal hopped towards a pile of hay and sniffed it.

"Wait for it, lads. There should be two of them," said Screwball excitedly over his communicator.

The Griddleback dredged up a mouthful of bile and spat it on the floor, where it bubbled and fizzed. The creature was elderly and, according to Georgia, suffering from oxygen contamination. It peered around warily before shuffling towards the droids by the barn door. It looked them up and down, then turned back to the ship and ululated a high-pitched squeal.

Another, younger Griddleback emerged from the ship and walked down the steps.

"Slam the door, slam the door!" shouted Screwball.

Merv broke cover and fired a Bosun shot at the ship's hatch, melting its surrounds and blocking the Griddlebacks' escape. At the same time, Paddy and Seamus stood up and sent a withering blast of Bosun fire into both Griddlebacks. Jumping and jerking, the aliens collapsed to the floor, squealing.

The furry animal hopped around in the straw, looking very distressed.

"Good job, lads. Now, secure da filt'." Screwball's voice was as calm and professional as a clurichaun's could be.

Soon the people from Pandora had joined the clurichauns on the barn floor. Georgia and Archie walked over to the unconscious Griddlebacks, already trussed up like Christmas turkeys by Big Joe and Merv.

"We call them Griddlebacks, but what exactly are they?" said Archie, squatting down next to the older one and wincing. The odour made his eyes water.

"They're a warrior race called the Putriryosomatidarectem, originally from the planet Putrios. Everyone calls them Griddlebacks as it's easier to say, and because of these." Georgia used her foot to roll the younger one on its front and pointed to a series of bony ridges on its back. "These platelets denote rank and age. He's probably only a hundred, whereas this one"—Georgia moved to the older Griddleback and rolled him over—"is a veteran. Just look at all those battle scars." She squatted down and pointed to swathes of deep cuts all along his body. She counted his ridges. "At least three hundred Earth years. He's a good catch. If we can get him back to 2340, Smodius can use him as a bargaining tool."

Alice was more interested in the distressed furry animal, and tried to catch it as it hopped about the barn. With Paddy's help, she finally captured the animal. It had a rough leather collar tight about its neck, and appeared to be choking.

Paddy used his screwdriver to prise off the collar and the animal wheezed out a sigh, its soulful, bushbaby eyes looking longingly at Alice.

Smitten, she lifted it into her arms and rocked it like a baby. It nuzzled its cold, wet snout into her face. It was soon purring happily, its oversized paws hanging loosely over her arm and its long tail coiled about her wrist.

"Look, everyone! It's turning pink!" cried Alice.

"That's because the Wopplefop is content," said Georgia. "The Wopplefops communicate by appearance and their language has just three words. Roughly translated, these are white for 'worry', pink for 'contentment', and blue for … well, if you see two blue Wopplefops staring at each other as if they'd like to get better acquainted, it's best not to get between 'em."

"What did you call it?" asked Alice.

"It's a Wopplefop, a type of …" At an unusual loss for words, Georgia shrugged. "Well, it's a Wopplefop."

"Why was it on their ship?" asked Alice, stroking the fine fur.

"The Griddlebacks keep them as pets."

Georgia's face belied her words. Alice was too busy cuddling the bright pink Wopplefop to notice. "Can we keep it?" she pleaded.

"They don't do anything except change colour and hang upside-down. Except in the, er, blue season."

Alice was about to ask how they hung upside-down when her fingers touched the underside of a paw.

"Suction cups!" she cried, lifting a paw to see rows of tiny, leathery pink cups. "Way cool!"

"I guess if you want it you can keep it," said Georgia, puzzled by the attention Alice was lavishing on the edible ball of fur.

"Great! I'm going to call it Flopsy Wopsy after my childhood rabbit at home in Shropshire." Alice stroked a long floppy ear.

"Georgia, Seamus has found something interesting," said Big Joe, examining the younger of the Griddlebacks. Georgia left Alice and went over to Seamus.

"Under his body armour he's got gold flashes on his tunic," said the clurichaun, pointing at the uniform.

Georgia knelt down to scrutinize the embellishments and winced, annoyed that she'd missed them earlier.

Standing up, she addressed the company. "We're all in grave danger. The younger Griddleback is royalty. By now every Griddleback ship in the vicinity will know he's in danger. We have to move fast."

She turned to Screwball, and pointed at the Griddleback vessel. "Find the real Washington and Jefferson in there, disable the ship, and remove anything useful you can find. Seamus, Dave, Big Joe, help Liam and Archie get the Griddlebacks and their droids onto Pandora, and move like your lives depended on it! Alice, with me."

Alice followed the pirate into Pandora's control room. Georgia rootled through a drawer on the flight console and came up with a palm-sized silver block indented with hundreds of tiny jewels. She pressed a button and a thin pipe of glass rose from the console. Georgia placed the block on the pipe and ran a sequence of keystrokes on a three-dimensional keyboard floating in front of her.

"This is beyond weird," said Alice, as she watched Georgia work.

"You humans would regard this as like a type of satnav for a twenty-first century car. I won it in a game of shuck poker on Sleazeeze. I've never been desperate enough to use it until now." Georgia looked at the assortment of coloured buttons on the keyboard, and hovered a finger over a blue one entitled EXPAND. "Let's see what we have."

Taking a deep breath, she pushed the blue button. Ships and planets flew out of the cube, filling the control room and enveloping the two women in a colourful high-resolution 3D universe.

"Wow!" exclaimed Alice as she became part of this new cosmos, surrounded by thousands of miniature spaceships of various sizes and complexities. She watched gobsmacked as a tiny silver-grey, sausage-shaped ship drifted from right to left just a couple of centimetres from her nose.

"Am I safe?" she whispered, terrified that the slightest movement on her part might cause the sausage to crash. The Wopplefop in her arms looked equally unsettled, snapping at the ships that floated around it.

Georgia smiled. "No problem. It's purely visual, and not a threat." She pressed a sequence of buttons and most of the ships disappeared. "We should be left with just the Griddlebacks and us," she said, pointing to a schematic representation of the Earth. There were three lights on the planet's surface, and four more nearby that indicated Griddleback battlecruisers closing in.

"I feared as much," she said, checking the details. "The nearest ship is at most two hundred years away and will be here in thirty minutes."

Something caught Georgia's eye and she took a closer look at the schematic Earth. "Interesting," she murmured to herself.

"Can we outrun them?" said Alice, stroking her new pet.

Georgia didn't reply. She sat hunched, deep in thought. Beads of sweat ran down her cheeks as she wrestled with their limited options. At last she stood up, emitted a loud sigh and faced Alice.

"No option but to stand and fight. We're damned if we don't, and damned if we do."

She broke into a smile and looked as if a vast weight had been lifted from her shoulders.

Fighting was good. Fighting she could understand. And she had a plan, sort of…

The clurichauns found Washington and Jefferson aboard the Griddleback ship in a form of suspended animation. Big Joe led a team of clurichauns in carrying the two future presidents over to the barn doors, where they were left slumbering. Washington and Jefferson would have to deal with any nightmarish residual memories of the Griddlebacks when they woke up. The clurichauns collected the droids and took them back to Pandora.

With time running out, everyone gathered in front of Georgia on Pandora's steps.

She smiled. "Boys, we've been to many places and done many things. When called upon, you have served without question. Today I ask you, once again, to follow me. I believe in you all. I expect no less in return. There are four Griddleback battlecruisers converging on us. In less than fifteen Earth minutes, the first will arrive. We have no option but to make a dash for our base in Sleazeeze. Yet, before we do, I have a plan. Pray we are better pilots than they are."

Archie looked at Pandora and Prometheus, and then back at Georgia. "How are you going to outfox four battlecruisers in these?"

"Size isn't everything, my human friend," she said with a wry smile. "In this case, small is beautiful. I have a few tricks left in Pandora."

Turning to the clurichauns, she signalled to Screwball. "I want a quick briefing with you and Big Joe."

Georgia, Big Joe and Screwball huddled together, the seriousness of the situation etched on their faces. A few minutes later, they laughed, made strange hand movements and the conversation ended with the clurichauns wiggling their bottoms. Georgia grinned, dropped her cheroot and crushed it underfoot.

"Okay, boys, lock and load."

She turned back towards Pandora and smiled again. "Where's Lucretia?"

Screwball's restraining belt had been torn in two during Prometheus's crash-landing in the Beaver, so the clurichauns decided to tape him to his chair, hoping that this time he'd stay put. Despite their camaraderie, Big Joe took the opportunity to swaddle Screwball's head in sticky tape.

Inside Pandora, Archie, Liam and Alice sat in silence as they watched Georgia take a battered copy of Mrs Beeton's Book of Household Management and place it on the console. Flicking through the pages, the pirate scribbled a few notes in various margins. She glanced at the clock on the console screen, then returned to her reading. With an expression of triumph, she closed the book and explained to her comrades what was about to happen.

In five minutes a special type of wormhole—a branch wormhole—would open over Boston Harbor. This wormhole was only just wide enough for a Griddleback battlecruiser to pass along. The next highway wormhole, a much wider wormhole, wouldn't open up over the town until tomorrow at 15:00. Georgia was gambling that the four battlecruisers wouldn't wait until then to mount their rescue of the royal prince but would risk flying in single file through the branch wormhole. Georgia's plan was to draw freighter vessels along the branch wormhole and pack them all into a single section, thus creating the largest intergalactic traffic jam in recorded history.

Turning back to the 3D console, Georgia hit the blue button again. The holographic representation of the universe reset itself, and every ship in their vicinity reappeared. She looked at the numerous ships surrounding Earth, then tapped quickly on the keyboard, removing unwanted ships until there were just seventeen freighters left in Earth orbit. She found all four Kartoleon freighters and listed them onscreen, including the arrival time for each one. The nearest was just five minutes away, the farthest over six hours. On the monitor, she scrolled through examples of Confederation document headers until she saw the one she wanted.

Grinning mischievously, she loaded the header and started typing:

Dear Kartoleon Freighter Captains,

Intergalactic ordinance number 249/216/1773 empowers me to command you to attend a sanitizing sweep immediately, at the following co-ordinates: 09/352/1773-Segment B5.

Your cargoes will be checked for and vaccinated against a plague of Angreallus Weavil Drads, which are virulent in this segment.

The Intergalactic and Interplanetary Department for Trade and Commerce (IIDTC) apologizes for this inconvenience.

Please confirm your attendance by return cipher.

Have a nice day.

Relaying the encrypted message with a stolen authentication key, Georgia sat back in her chair and watched the confirmations come in. The freighters began joining the branch wormhole through the nearest entry points and stacked up in a line. Her plan was working.

Stuck in the middle of the queue of freighters sat the four Griddleback battlecruisers.

"Now for the coup de grâce," said Georgia, typing a message to the Kartoleon freighter captains directly in front of and behind the four Griddleback cruisers:

Dear Captains of the Kartoleon Freighters Rumplardy and Balladosh

We have been informed that the wormhole is displaying unusual behaviour, and we ask you not to move or exit until we can confirm your safe arrival.

Please confirm receipt by cipher.

Have a nice day.

Confirmation came back immediately. Georgia watched the Rumplardy, at the front of the queue, slow down and stop. The remaining ships, including the Griddleback battlecruisers, slowed and stacked up behind the Rumplardy. The Balladosh, sitting at the back, also stopped. The Griddlebacks were trapped like potato crisps in a cardboard tube. Each ship was stacked one behind the other, with no room to manoeuvre. Georgia had picked Kartoleon freighters, knowing their captains were the most pedantic form-filling sticklers for rules, and the most prolific cargo haulers working the galaxies. Armed with a piece of paper, the captain of the Rumplardy wouldn't leave or move along the wormhole until ordered to, or by, another piece of paper, even if a black hole or a white dwarf appeared right before him, or the Devil himself put in a personal appearance.

With the Griddleback ships nicely contained, Georgia started Pandora's engines and, with Prometheus close behind, they cloaked, moved to the opening of the nearest wormhole, and waited. When it opened, they moved slowly inside. Both Pandora and Prometheus were small compared to the other ships, and Georgia had calculated they had enough room to fly comfortably past the freighters and Griddleback ships along the hole and away to freedom.

They soon had gone past the Kartoleon freighter Rumplardy, two more freighters and the first of the four Griddleback battlecruisers.

"Ready, boys?" said Georgia to the clurichauns aboard Prometheus as the two small ships scooted past another pair of battlecruisers and a couple of freighters. Up ahead was the last Griddleback battlecruiser.

Guiding Pandora and Prometheus towards the giant cruiser's bridge, Georgia grinned.

Charged with the overall protection of Prince Solace Ruttfarter, sixth in line to the Griddleback throne, Gruilash Vandergaard was desperate to rescue him. The one time he took his eye off the ball, the prince disappeared.

Gruilash smashed his fist into the console and ululated. He did not like sitting impotently behind a line of Kartoleon freighters. He snarled at the Griddleback officers around him. He was fed up wet-nursing Solace and his long-time servant, Granwold Burbart.

A Kartoleon captain's face filled the screen.

"This is Captain Gruilash Vandergaard of the battlecruiser Tarakan III. I politely request you to leave this wormhole immediately." It was Gruilash's sixth such request, and for the sixth time it was met with the same look of officious piety.

"This is Captain Rogbodle of the Kartoleon hyperfreighter Rumplardy. I understand your request, but Intergalactic ordinance 34/98/tr/-23-34 states—"

Gruilash put his snout in his hands and banged the back of his head hard against his seat. He had had enough of ordinance-quoting Kartoleons. An ear-piercing burst of Irish jig music filled his bridge, and Kartoleon Captain Rogbodle disappeared from the screen.

The Griddleback officers on the battlecruiser's bridge looked at the screen. Seven step-dancing clurichauns appeared, singing their lungs out. They turned and dropped their trousers, thrusting their warty bottoms at Gruilash and filling the screen with quivering hairy pink flesh.

Mystified, Gruilash scowled at his communications officer.

Then Big Joe came onscreen, wearing a tricorner hat that was emblazoned with a skull-and-crossbones. He had a patch over one eye. Lucretia sat quietly on his shoulder.

He waved an egg whisk at Gruilash. "This is Cap'n Jolly Roger," he said in an affected Kartoleon voice laced with an Irish accent. Gesturing rudely at Gruilash, he blew him an enormous raspberry.

On cue, Lucretia leant forward and squawked loudly, "Have a nice day," before the screen flickered and the pietistic face of Captain Rogbodle reappeared, still quoting ordinances.

Gruilash exploded the only way an insulted Griddleback could—in an apoplectic rage of splattered phlegm, steam and fizzing bile.

"Get your ship out of my way!" he screamed, jumping to his feet and shaking his fists violently at the Kartoleon. Unmoved, Captain Rogbodle looked disdainfully down his nose, and began reciting Chapter One of the sixty-volume Intergalactic Code of Space Etiquette.

Archie fell about laughing and pointed at the console. "They bloody well mooned the leathery bastards!" he spluttered.

Alice gawped at the screen.

"Yeah, they crack me up sometimes with their bare-faced cheek," said Georgia. She guided Pandora past the remaining freighter and down the hole away from the jam. Prometheus followed easily in Pandora's hyperspatial wake.

Frequently consulting Mrs Beeton's books, Georgia planned a series of hole-hopping manoeuvres to disguise their return to Sleazeeze. Their Grand Tour began on 13 September 1759, on the Plains of Abraham. At Quebec, they picked up a hole to the third quarter of 1985's SuperBowl XIX, where they floated alongside the TV blimp. Patching the live TV feed into their control screens, they watched the game as they waited for the next wormhole to open. They then arrived in England sometime in 1977, and hovered precariously above a busy section of the A22 near Croydon while waiting for another connecting wormhole to open. Next they flew on to 2200, and the Raging Fires of Hrotso, before swinging past the planet Arterius and flying low across the Plains of Trim. Their final leg took them to Tharg and Sleazeeze, where they arrived thirty seconds after their journey had begun.

On the planet Arterius, in a galaxy far, far away, an army of terrified knuckledog riders looked up as fiery trails streaked across the purple night sky.

"It's a sign!" shrieked Termalan the Wise, a toothless soothsayer riding with the Royal Prince at the head of the Troglagit Army. Startled, his knuckledog reared up and sent him crashing to the ground, denting his jewel-encrusted mitre.

Panic spread like a tsunami through the massed ranks of knuckledogs, unseating their Troglagit warriors, sending them flailing to the icy floor.

"We must not go on! It is a sign!" screamed Termalan, his shrill voice echoing across the mountain ranges of ice-blue silica. Hurriedly, he threw runes on the ground and thumbed through a large leather tome. "The Gods have spoken. We must flee the Whispering Planes of Trim!"

So the Troglagits' month-long sojourn across the immeasurable Icelands of Arterius to lay siege to the Murag capital was halted. In centuries to come, Muragothian balladeers would sing of the golden rain in the sky that turned away the Troglagit invaders and saved the Murag dynasty from extinction.

Georgia carefully manoeuvred Pandora into her cloaked space portal, followed by Screwball in Prometheus. They took their belongings and, carrying the two unconscious Griddlebacks and their droids, descended from the roof to Georgia's lair.

"We're being followed!" whispered Georgia, coming to a sudden halt. "Take them inside, Screwball. You know what to do."

The party continued on towards the lair's large metal door, leaving Georgia on the stairs. Pulling out her .44 Magnum revolver, she hugged the wall and slowly climbed the stairs.

When she reached the door to the roof she looked cautiously out.

Then:

"Bloody typical!" she said, shaking her head. Holstering the revolver, she stepped out onto the roof. Expensive French perfume filled her lungs.

Two blue skeletal creatures, about thirty centimetres tall and with puppy-dog eyes, stood before her. They were dressed in brightly coloured silk, powdered wigs, pink hose and weird platform shoes, and each held a walking cane in one of its four hands.

"Well, Redhair, we meet again." The creature who spoke had a high, lisping voice. Georgia knew of old that the other did too.

She shook her head.

"You've followed us ever since we left Sleazeeze, and you crashed us in 1773. What the hell do the infamous Time Guardian twins, Castor and Pollux, want with us?"

Pollux sidled forward. "The Griddlebacks have influence. Give them back the prince and all charges against Rigsworth will be dropped."

"Why don't you stop them? You see what they do!" said Georgia firmly.

Castor huffed. "There was nothing left in that village for you to find. The Griddleback clean-up crew saw to that. You needed to find something to bargain with, so we diverted you to 1773 Boston."

Georgia stood with her hands on her hips and shook her head. "So, Time Guardians interfere with history!"

"We sometimes manipulate events to correct history, not to change or create it!" Pollux stamped his foot.

"You of all people should know we have no enforcement role," said Castor. "We can only guard and protect time. We can't interfere in history," he added piously.

"You were one of us, until you—" added Pollux.

"Don't go there, Pollux," rasped Georgia, wagging a finger. "If I give them to you, I want insurance."

"Going to mind-map them, are we?" said Castor haughtily.

Pollux fluttered a lace handkerchief in agreement.

Georgia ignored the goading. "They can have them in twenty-four hours, but we play to the rules of love poetry."

Castor sighed and gave a delicate little cough. "They won't like it."

"It complicates things," said Pollux, shaking his head.

"In twenty-four hours we hand them over in the Bloated Shagganat in Sleazeeze, according to poetry rules. Or"—Georgia paused and glared at the twins—"I simply kill them."

Pollux tutted. Castor tried to, but his lisp got in the way.

Georgia continued, "Their commander must recite Shakespeare's sonnet number 18 to me, and look as if he means it."

"Okay, okay, but if it goes wrong we know who to blame," said Pollux, pointing three handfuls of fingers at Georgia.

She laughed disdainfully. "Go find another piece of history to insult, boys."

"Bah, humbug!" they retorted as one, sticking their luminous noses in the air before turning and disappearing into the darkness of the roof.

They had not the first idea that what they'd just said was a literary quotation.

The steel door opened and Georgia entered her lair. The clurichauns were in the kitchen preparing stew when she walked in. "I need to talk with all of you in the dining room in ten minutes. First, though, I need to make a call."

Alice, Archie and Liam joined the clurichauns in the dining room, waiting for Georgia.

"Right," the pirate said without any introduction when finally she walked into the room. "Castor and Pollux, the Time Guardian twins, followed us when we left Sleazeeze. They were the ones who crashed us in Boston. They've done a deal with the Griddlebacks to drop all charges against Jules if we return their people." Georgia chewed on her omnipresent cheroot. "However," she said, blowing a ring of smoke and smiling wickedly, "I have a few ideas ..."

Alice turned to Archie. "I've heard of the Time Guardian twins, but who are they, and what do they do?"

"Jules told me about them once," said Archie. "Castor and Pollux are eccentric little twerps but, as Time Guardians, they're very powerful."

Georgia overheard their conversation. "They could seriously harm the Griddle-backs at any time but they don't, believing this would be contrary to their warped interpretation of the Intergalactic Code and whatever game they're playing. If they didn't follow orders they'd be peer-marshalled."

"What's 'peer-marshalled'?" asked Alice.

"Hung out to dry by your Time Guardian peers," said Georgia. "Kicked out and left to rot."

"Oh," said Alice. "That could sting."

Georgia threw her cheroot on the floor, stamped on it, and left the room.

Alice pulled Liam to one side. "What's this about love poetry?"

"When the Griddlebacks invaded Georgia's planet, they forced her president and royal family to recite love poetry to the battleship commander. Then the Grid-dlebacks shot them all and blew their planet to smithereens so they could mine the debris for minerals."

Alice swallowed hard.

Her stomach churned.

"Oh," she said.

CHAPTER 14

SURVIVAL

Professor Tommy Cramdunkle was content. Known for its excellence, his research laboratory and training hospice had today surpassed all previous achievements. Being a bald, wiry Liverpudlian with silver muttonchops and a dyed-ginger handlebar moustache, Tommy was used to defying the odds. Though trite and offensive to many, the sign on his desk said it all:

MIRACLES WE DO TODAY.
THE IMPOSSIBLE WILL COST AN ARM, A LEG AND YOUR LIVER
AND WILL TAKE MUCH LONGER

The impossible had taken four days. At 12:00 noon, Tarquin Seebohm Jenkins would be wakened from his coma and begin his life again.

Medical interns crowded excitedly around the glass sphere watching the Coma Team's every move. They were witnessing history being made.

"Tarquin, Tarquin Seebohm Jenkins?" A soothing voice seemed to come from above.

"Seebee, can you hear me?"

Tarquin stretched and squinted into the light, trying to see the owner of the voice.

"Tarquin Jenkins, can you hear me?"

Tarquin opened his eyes more fully and looked around, hoping it was Princess Wen Cheng. Or Rhia. But there was no one.

Instead, he felt uncomfortably dizzy.

"Tarquin, wake up. It's time to wake up."

The godlike voice was calm and reassuring.

A round face appeared in front of him. At first it was just a blob, but as it grew the features became clearer. A bald-headed man with a long ginger moustache looked down on him with a smile. Tarquin reckoned the moustache was dyed.

"Tarquin, you're safe." The man grinned and squeezed Tarquin's hand. "I'm Tommy. Professor Tommy Cramdunkle."

"Whia?" rasped Tarquin, unable to speak properly. Definitely dyed.

A dozen people in silver suits gathered around the bed, clapping. Tarquin raised a hand and managed a short, bemused wave. The suits cheered.

With help from Tommy, Tarquin sat up in bed. He looked at the smiling faces and then around the room. He was inside a transparent glass cubicle, full of machinery and doctors. Outside the cubicle, onlookers continued to clap, shake their fists in triumph and punch the air.

"It's a pleasure to meet you at last, Tarquin," said Tommy.

"Am I in Heaven?" stuttered Tarquin. Maybe everyone in Heaven had a dyed moustache. Sort of like a halo, but lower down.

"Good Lord, no." Tommy's smile grew even broader. "You've just been asleep for a while."

"How long?"

"Four days, twenty minutes and thirty-six seconds."

"Holy s—" Tarquin's frail voice gave way.

Tommy took his hand. "You're back among friends."

"Where's Rhia?"

Tommy's smile disappeared as if switched off, leaving Tarquin's question hanging in the air. The professor nodded towards a large shape hovering by the door.

"Five minutes only," he said to the man as he got up from the bed and ushered everyone else from the room.

"Jewimiah?"

"Ay, lad, it be me." Jeremiah walked to the bed clutching a brown bag and a bunch of flowers. "Seebee—"

"She's dead, isn't she?" Tarquin's eyes filled.

"Yes, lad." Jeremiah put the bag and the flowers at the bottom of the bed and sat down. "That she be." Leaning forward, the big man put his arms protectively around Tarquin. "I knows as you liked her. Jules told me."

Tarquin looked up at his friend. "Why? Why couldn't I have died instead?"

"I don't know, young'un. I just don't know."

They held each other tight. Tarquin let out an anguished wail and sobbed, his tears raining down on his friend's shoulder.

"It's not fair." said Tarquin. "Not fair!"

"Easy, Seebee. We'll get through this, mark my words. We'll get through this together."

"I hate Jules and his infernal time travel. I hate them all!"

Jeremiah said nothing in response. Tears of his own flowed down his cheeks.

Eventually Tarquin's breathing slowed and he slipped gently off to sleep.

The professor returned to the bedside. "Thanks for being with him, Jeremiah. We need to get him up and into rehab this afternoon, so best if you leave him to us now. We'll let him sleep a while."

Jeremiah nodded and gently laid Tarquin's head back on the pillow. "You rest, young'un. I'll be back."

He turned to Tommy. "Appreciate it, Doc. I thought it best if the news came from me."

Tommy nodded. "I can mend the physical, but he needs his friends."

"I knows, Doc, I knows." Jeremiah slowly made for the door.

"I need to ask you a question," said Tommy.

"Okay, Doc."

"Tarquin has a puncture wound in his chest. Would you know anything about that?"

"Weird," said Jeremiah scratching his head. "I want to say yes, but in truth I can't remember." He looked at Tommy with a bewildered expression. "My mind's gone a complete blank."

"Okay. No problem."

"You sure, Doc?"

Tommy nodded. Seeing the paper bag and flowers on Tarquin's bed, he picked them up. "You left these."

"They're for Seebee. We take grapes and flowers when visiting people in hospitals back in the twenty-first century."

"Oh," said Tommy, looking at the peculiar mix of daffodils, rhubarb, dahlias, barley wheat and wild roses held together with a frayed shoelace. He opened the brown paper bag to find it full of pips and grape stalks.

"I thought you said there were grapes?"

He looked up, but Jeremiah had already beaten a retreat.

Several hours later, Tarquin was awake again. He had just got the news from Tommy that Jules was on trial for saving his life. His thoughts turned to Rhia, the journal, the bobblehead, and the finding of the amulet and book. With the amulet, he could go back in time to Steeple Snoring and save Rhia. Maybe things weren't so grim after all …

"Rise and shine. You have a lot to learn about yourself this afternoon," said Tommy, walking in alongside a droid nurse who was carrying a plate full of lunch.

"Hi, Doc. What do you mean, 'learn about myself'?"

The droid put the food on a hover tray and positioned it midway down the bed.

"While you were in a coma, I took the opportunity to tune your DNA," said Tommy enthusiastically. "Sit up. I need you to eat."

He pushed a button and the bedhead rose until Tarquin was sitting comfortably before the food.

"My DNA?" said Tarquin, puzzled.

"It's all the rage nowadays. Take out this, add a little bit of that. Think of it as an oil change and tune-up."

"Is tuning me up safe?" Tarquin worriedly pressed the yellow mass on his plate.

"Well," said Tommy, twirling one end of his handlebar moustache, "I can think of some Booger Burros on Gripnal Minor who wouldn't want to eat you now!" A smile flashed across his face. "But they're fussy eaters." He grinned. "You're probably safe."

As Tarquin prodded and tasted his way around the plate of food, Tommy explained the rehabilitation process and ended by asking about the puncture wound on his chest. All Tarquin could recall was swimming in the Tower of London's moat and nearly drowning. He had felt a sharp pain in his chest before waking up to find Jeremiah sitting on top of him.

At the mention of Jeremiah, Tommy burst out laughing. "Trust Jeremiah to be at the bottom of this, even though he says he can't remember a thing about it!"

"What's he done now?" asked Tarquin.

Still laughing, Tommy sat on the bed and took one of Tarquin's hands. "He's saving the world, as he sees it."

After an afternoon of tests and games of intellect, Tarquin went from the glass chamber to a private room in the hospice. It was early evening when he arrived. His new quarters were spacious, with cream-coloured walls and large picture windows. One side of the living room looked out onto the bright lights of the Metropolis, the other onto an oasis with a pool of sparkling water, complete with palm trees and a citrus grove. He went into the bedroom and saw his frock coat and his cap on the bed with the rest of his clothing, folded neatly. Feeling hungry, he went into the open-plan kitchen area and found a familiar drink-and-food-generating machine. He programmed in a hot chocolate and a round of peanut-butter-and-jam toasties. It was hard to get them the way he liked them. Science still couldn't produce the required amount of toasty crispness he liked in his bread.

Settling into a reclining chair to eat, he thought of Rhia and the amulet. The debilitating effect of having been so seriously ill sapped his physical energy but, though his body was weak, his mind was racing. The first task was to get hold of the bobblehead he'd given Rhia.

With his stomach full, his thoughts finally slowed and his eyelids drooped. Minutes later he was fast asleep.

He awoke to see the sun rising across the citrus grove as the sweet aroma of oranges and lemons flooded the living room through the open window. He had slept in the chair all night. Sleep had eased his mind. Today he would simply search Rhia's room for the bobblehead.

He got out of the chair and found the shower in his bedroom. It was identical to the one he had used on his first visit to 2340.

Buffeted and washed, he reluctantly left the shower and dressed in the sports fatigues Tommy had provided. He opened the bottle of hair-growth lotion and rubbed a dollop of the stuff onto his bald head.

Next he went over to the communication screen that took up the majority of one wall. His daily routine, set by Tommy, dictated that he tune in to a fitness programme for ten minutes a day. He turned to the programme and imitated the shapely droids as they went through the exercises.

When the programme had ended, he limped to the motorized massage recliner parked next to the opposite wall. Tommy had explained that the recliner was for him to move about his quarters when he felt tired, and especially after his daily exercise. The chair's therapeutic massaging abilities would help him relax and increase the blood flow to his arms and legs.

Tarquin flopped into the chair and it straightened out, moulding to his body and gently massaging him. A 3D console popped up in front of his face, and a small steering column rose up alongside his hip.

Without warning, the recliner shot across the room towards the open picture window, halting just centimetres from the frame.

Shaken, he gripped the chair's armrests.

What was that all about?

He climbed stiffly from the chair and looked at it suspiciously. He hadn't touched the controls, so why had it acted so strangely?

Then the answer hit him.

"Up," he commanded.

The recliner lifted off the floor.

"Down."

It dropped obediently.

The next time he didn't say anything, just thought it.

Up.

Once again the recliner hovered above the carpet.

Down.

It descended with a bump.

Tarquin was very impressed. In the twenty-fourth century, advances in technology had given him a thought-controlled chair! He was surprised Tommy hadn't mentioned the feature. Probably too busy dying his moustache.

His interest piqued, Tarquin climbed into the chair, took a deep breath and closed his eyes. Up, he thought, and then opened his eyes. The chair was hovering a metre from the floor. He closed them again and returned the chair to the floor. The moment he thought of the citrus grove, the recliner set off for the window.

Just then the door spoke in the customary mildly irritating midwestern accent. "Jeremiah P. Cavendish to see you."

Tarquin quickly lowered the chair, eased himself out of it and opened the door.

"Come in. What a lovely surprise."

The big man's moustache twitched and his round, ebullient face broke into a smile. "Seebee! What happened to you?"

"Sorry?"

"Your hair—you're covered in it!"

Tarquin went to check in the bathroom mirror, and cursed loudly. "I've put too much growth cream on my head!"

"I'll be getting you a hairdresser droid," said Jeremiah, laughing. "Anyways, it's good to see you up and about. I've brought you something from the canal, as a reminder of good times. Two somethings, in fact, but I've ate the one Inga cooked for you. Powerful long journey it is, from Steeple Snoring to here." He headed for a table close to the wall, and carefully put down a silver-covered package he'd brought with him. "That be heavy, even for a wrestler," he said, flexing his arms.

Tarquin looked at the package and then at Jeremiah.

"It's great to see you again, you old goat! Do you want some tea?"

"Let me be doing it. You needs to rest. The Duck tells me you need lots of recuperatings."

"You mean quack."

"That's what I said."

Tarquin nodded, and began slowly circling the silver oblong. Jeremiah went into the kitchen and started programming the machine for tea. "Toasties?" he shouted.

Getting no reply, he came back into the main room. Tarquin was standing over the package.

"Okay, you can open it." Jeremiah chuckled. "And do you want toasties with your tea?"

"Yes. Yes, please," said Tarquin absentmindedly, pulling at the silver-foil wrapping.

Soon the salty smell of toasted bread and cheese wafted from the kitchen, intwined with the sound of an aria.

Tarquin gasped. "It's, it's the—"

"Silvery Moon," said Jeremiah, breaking off from song and coming back in with a tray. "I been making it for ages."

Tarquin was looking at a beautifully crafted scale model of Jeremiah's canal boat.

"I wants you to remember our times together."

"Jeremiah, it's beautiful."

"I knows, I knows." Jeremiah blushed.

Tarquin lifted the model carefully from the table and carried it reverentially over to a shelf above the communication screen.

"'Drink your tea, young'un." Jeremiah sat down at the table and passed Tarquin a mug of tea and a plate of toasties.

"I heard that Jules is in prison awaiting trial," said Tarquin.

Jeremiah nodded. "He saved your life."

"I know."

Jeremiah smiled. "Not for you to worry about, Jules has everything under control."

Tarquin saw the glint in the big man's eye. "Really?"

"Oh, yes." Jeremiah chortled. "He's got the best lawyer in town and a red-haired devil woman to sort it out!"

"Tell me more," said Tarquin, leaning forward excitedly.

"Nah. I've said enough! Let me get you a hairdressing droid."

As they sat eating and drinking, waiting for the droid to arrive, Tarquin looked at his old friend and wondered how much he should trust him.

"Jeremiah," he said abruptly, "if I told you about a puzzle, would you help me solve it?"

Tarquin had seen the look on Jeremiah's face a hundred times. It was of a man about to jump into a wrestling ring. Fear and excitement rolled into one.

"I reckons I help if I can, but me maths and biologicals is a problem."

Tarquin stifled a smile. "It's not that sort of a problem."

For the next thirty minutes, Tarquin told Jeremiah everything he knew, from finding the translation to Rhia's hiding of the bobblehead.

"We need to collect the bobblehead," he concluded.

After they'd finished their tea and toasties the hairdresser arrived, and soon Tarquin's hair was back to its usual mop. Next they went to Rhia's room in hopes of finding the bobblehead. Jeremiah stood on guard as Tarquin went inside.

The room had been ransacked. He looked in every drawer and possible hiding place he could think of, but found nothing. Standing in the centre of the room he thought back to his last day with Rhia.

"Emile!" he exclaimed, rushing from the room and grabbing Jeremiah by the arm. "The library, quick!"

He pulled Jeremiah down the corridor, through the Rigsworth Library of Antique Lexicography & Linguistics, and straight into Emile's office.

Emile sat at a work-bench plying a screwdriver among the innards of an Underwood typewriter.

"Emile, did Rhia give you anything when I was last here? A bobblehead and a book?"

"Well, hello, Tarquin," said Emile, slowly getting up from his chair. "So glad you're looking better, although a little hairy for my taste. And, yes, I'm feeling not too bad either, thank you for asking."

"Sorry, I'm in a bit of a rush."

"Yes, she left me a bobblehead and an exercise book," said Emile. "I'd forgotten about the book until you mentioned it. The bobblehead's on my desk. I'll go get you the book."

He pointed to a pile of papers as he went over to a cupboard. "I think the bobblehead's under those."

Tarquin found it there almost immediately.

"And here's the book," said Emile, returning. "What's going on?"

"Life, the world, tea breaks, everything. Many thanks!" Tarquin grabbed the bobblehead and book and ran from his office, Jeremiah lumbering behind him.

"What be it now, Seebee?" gasped Jeremiah.

"I'll tell you in the restaurant."

They walked in silence, trying to look normal. Finding an empty booth in the diner, they sat down. Tarquin tried not to think too hard about the times he'd been here with Rhia.

"Did anyone suggest you should give me the boat as a present?" he asked, pretending to look at the menu.

"Yes, your great-aunt did. She said it would be a nice gesture, seeing as you'd had a real nasty shock. She sees me working on it when she were visiting Steeple Snoring last week."

"The ruddy Bulldog!"

"Bulldog?"

"She's not what she seems," said Tarquin.

"Your Great-Aunt Polly?"

Tarquin nodded sourly. "Yeah, everybody's favourite apple-pie auntie."

"What's got into you, Seebee?" asked Jeremiah.

"Did you leave her alone with the model at any point?"

"Only to make some toasties. And, well, I had a bit of the tummy collywobles while she was on the Silvery Moon, so I had to spend another few minutes … ah … elsewhere."

"Had she given you anything to eat?"

Jeremiah's eyebrows meshed in concentration. "Only a couple o' they nice little pastries she'd brought with her. Sennapod cookies, she called them."

"That settles it!" cried Tarquin, then remembered to lower his voice. "It's as I thought. She got you out of the way and then planted a bug in the model. Your boat has been listening to us!"

Jeremiah looked aghast. "If I'd only known …"

"It's not your fault, old friend." Tarquin put a hand over one of Jeremiah's. "Could have happened to anyone. But we'll need to be careful of what we say in my room from now on. She could be listening to our every word."

"Well, I—"

"Nothing's lost—I hope. Now, let's see what we have here."

Tarquin took out the bobblehead from his bag and, without ceremony, pulled it apart. "Yes, the key's still here!"

He quickly pocketed the key and re-assembled the bobblehead, then turned to Jeremiah once more. "I think Great-Aunt Polly is trying to find the clues my dad left me, just like I am. She wants the Book of Dreams and the amulet."

"Perhaps we should just give 'em to her?"

Tarquin looked incredulously at Jeremiah. "My dad wants me to find the Book of Dreams, no one else. Don't you see, I'm the only one my dad trusted."

Jeremiah nodded and took out his pocket watch. "I have an idea. The Yelts Inn's open."

"What's the Yelts Inn?" asked Tarquin, following Jeremiah from the restaurant.

"Where good people go to drink and talk, and the bad people go to play Raggedy Rook and act like silly buggers."

Jeremiah stabbed the call-button for the lift nearest to the restaurant. The door opened and they stepped inside. The big man made a palaver of finding a small brass square called "Bugbrook" at the bottom of the panel beside the lift door, and pressed it.

"Hold tight and close your eyes. Interdimensional transport starting up," said the standard midwestern voice.

The lift began to spin. Tarquin felt his lips peel back, his hair stand on end and his teeth go cold. Terrified, unable to open his eyes, he held onto the brass rail that ran around the lift's walls.

Soon, mercifully, the lift slowed and spun to a stop.

Tarquin pulled back his eyelids. His stomach—or most of its contents, at any rate—was in his mouth, and his head felt like a melting ice cube. He needed to focus on something.

The door opened and he felt a warm, summer's breeze on his face, heard birds chirping, and breathed in sweet honeysuckle. Silhouetted against the blue, hazy sky about a kilometre away stood a coaching inn at the side of a deeply rutted mud road.

"Come on. The walk will do you good. You need fresh air." Jeremiah started ambling along the road towards the inn. Tarquin followed.

As they came closer to it, Tarquin saw that the inn looked abandoned, its doors and windows boarded up and the cobblestoned courtyard overgrown with vines and weeds. A faded sign painted with the words YELTS INN creaked soulfully on its one remaining hinge in the breeze.

They turned into the courtyard. Stuck between the cobblestones at various heights and angles were a forest of white signboards, each one with a different grinning leprechaun face. It looked as if a hundred different estate agents were vying to sell the inn.

Tarquin examined the sign nearest to him. Nailed to the metre-tall upright beneath the sign was a small wooden plaque bearing words like "spacious saloon", "snug", "toilets", "cellar" and "space-park".

He was still looking at the sign when a small, burly man in a green tweed suit and a pointy hat came swan-diving out of it, narrowly missing Tarquin before rolling nimbly on the ground and getting to his feet.

"Beyasus! I'll be telling yer!" he shouted, turning to the sign. Brushing himself down, he tugged at his hat, oblivious to Tarquin standing next to him. "It was nah time for—"

Before he could finish, a weatherbeaten face with a bunion-encrusted nose, thickset eyebrows and a curling sneer popped out from the same sign, champing hard on a briar pipe.

The small man stepped toward the disembodied face and angrily squared up to it.

"Yer were cheating," said the face. "I caught yer. Now come back and play the Rook right this time!"

Before the tweed-suited man could reply, two brawny arms extended from the sign, grabbed him by his jacket lapels and hauled him back in.

Tarquin stared, open-mouthed, not sure if he could believe his eyes.

Jeremiah laughed and headed for a sign with the word SALOON in large letters on it. He ducked down, stepped into the sign and disappeared.

Tarquin went after him as quickly as he could, worried that, if he stopped to think too much about this, he'd realize it was all impossible and find himself walking into solid wood.

Next thing he knew, he was falling out of a painting that hung above a roaring fire. Somehow he landed on his feet, narrowly avoided two amorous Cullark monks in ceremonial kaftans who were flailing wildly in a tortured, six-tongued embrace as they writhed on the floor.

Overwhelmed by the noise and the warmth, and not wanting to dwell too long on what the monks were doing, Tarquin stared wide-eyed at the decor. It reminded him of the Saracen's Head, an old seventeenth-century English coaching inn Uncle Harold had taken him to in Towcester, England—but with a difference. Hung on the Towcester saloon's wood-panelled walls were paintings and portraits from a bygone age: austere-looking, moustached and bearded military dignitaries, weighed down with orders and medals and all looking down their noses at him. Here it was the same, but the subjects of the portraits weren't human: most were leprechauns, while a few were clearly aliens of one kind or another.

Opposite the roaring fire, three rows of horse-racing paintings covered the entire wall. Long-bodied racehorses with six stumpy legs and grossly oversized teeth—a sight to make orthodontists gleefully rub their hands—were all being ridden by the same intense-looking dwarf, decked in coloured silks and long trailing scarves.

As Jeremiah and Tarquin moved through the room, Tarquin read a couple of the plaques beneath the equine oddities: "Transient Mumblarch III, Winner of the Ankatrurian Derby 2234, ridden by Droby Dortal"; "Davies Trenchard Merryfowl II, Winner of the Fusaliane 500 Cup 2236, ridden by Droby Dortal."

Squeezing past long oak tables, they watched a smorgasbord of humans, dwarfs, leprechauns and aliens singing, drinking and laughing together. Shagganat barmaids in risqué costumes bumbled uneasily amidst the raucous menagerie carrying armfuls of frothing tankards; they slopped ale across the masses like waves breaking on a beach, but no one seemed to mind.

Weaving their way, Jeremiah and Tarquin moved through the crowd, colliding with punters and igniting the occasional punch-up.

"Give us yer coat," came a menacing voice from close to the floor where Tarquin was walking.

"It's mine, get off!" responded Tarquin, his shout barely audible above the noise coming from the bar.

A wizened dwarf, with a face in which warts fought for recognition among numerous yellow boils, dug him painfully in the ribs with a large Dublin pipe.

"I sees it, I wants it," snarled the dwarf, tugging hard at Tarquin's coat-tails.

"Get off!" shouted Tarquin again.

But the little man was having none of it. Clenching his pipe between his broken, gold-filled teeth, he hauled himself up Tarquin until they were face-to-face.

"Oi!" bellowed Jeremiah, turning around and grabbing the dwarf by the throat. "I don't agrees with dwarf-throwing no more'n I do with bear-baiting and cock-fighting, but you're an exception." Jeremiah grabbed the struggling dwarf's collar and waistband and heaved him through the nearest oil painting.

"How did you know that painting was a portal?" said Tarquin.

"I didn't."

Tarquin laughed nervously. "What was that all about?"

"A pint-sized idiot. He recognized the coat and thought he'd got himself a quick souvenir."

Jeremiah pushed Tarquin ahead of him towards the snug, then tensed.

"Watch yourself in here," he said, glancing furtively around the room. "It's full of oddballs, lunatics and"— he scratched his head—"even more lunatics."

"Who are we looking for?" Tarquin shouted above the noise.

Ahead, a rolling maul of shoulders, arms and legs swerved around a pillar and cut a swathe through the crowded saloon, narrowly missing Tarquin and Jeremiah on its way to the bar. It crashed into the solid oak frontage and a head popped out from the middle wearing a green trilby hat and wire glasses. The little man pulled himself free, climbed on top of the pack, crossed his arms and stood facing the bar.

"T'ree Brocca Bogglers, t'ree Bender Ales, and one fer yerself, darlin'," said the man in green, winking at the nearest Shagganat barmaid before extending a stubby little hand full of coins.

Her face creased and she gave him a toothy, Stonehenge-like smile before plumping up her sagging chest, fluttering her greasy eyelids and taking the money.

"We've found them," said Jeremiah with a grin.

"Flippin' heck, it's Rhiordan!" said Tarquin, recognizing the leprechaun order-ing the drinks.

They shoved their way towards the huddle by the bar.

"Master Tarquin and Jeremiah!" roared Rhiordan. The scrum of leprechauns broke up as the others came to greet the newcomers, leaving Rhiordan cursing as he hung from the bar by his fingertips, his hobnailed boots sliding frantically up and down the panelling. His grip gave way and he collapsed to the floor in a heap.

"We heard you were dead!" said Calbhach, thumping Tarquin on the thigh as if to check he wasn't a ghost.

"Calbhach, Finbar, everyone! It's good to see you again," said Tarquin, shaking each stubby hand thrust toward him. D'Arcy attempted a high-five, but missed.

"How?" begun Finbar. "How are you alive?"

"Long story," said Tarquin, "a very long story…Where's Oleg?" he asked, look-ing around for the crazed Russian.

"Tinkling on the ivories." Calbhach pointed to the corner of the room where the bear-sized Russian sat hunched over an upright piano, plonking merrily away on the keys. In front of the piano, three pale-blue egg-shaped heads on thin snake-like bodies bopped up and down in unison and sang lustily.

"Who are they?" asked Tarquin.

"They're the Three Celsi," replied Calbhach. "A Maloval singing group from Thane, Tharg's sister planet."

Rhiordan got up and, with Finbar acting as ladder, climbed onto the bar to collect the drinks.

"Let's go and see Oleg. He'll want to say hello to you." Calbhach poleaxed a drunken Blagburter who had come too close to him. "No sense, no feeling," he mumbled, stepping onto the comatose Blagburter's back and down the other side.

They arrived just as the leader of the Maloval singers slunk forward, beer in claw, and belched loudly. She wiped a dollop of froth from the corner of her cavernous mouth and, tipping the tankard, gulped down a litre of Bender Ale.

"This will be special," said Calbhach, nodding expectantly.

Oleg rolled his fingers down the keys and the saloon bar hushed. He hit a major chord and held it, waiting for the singer.

"First I was afraid ..."

Her voice rolled across the saloon floor like the moans of a disgruntled wildebeest shaken from an afternoon siesta.

"I was petrified ..."

She hit a bass note and the saloon shuddered, glasses danced, and the reverb rumbled painfully in Tarquin's chest. Another flourish on the piano from Oleg and the singer's companions slid to the front. A heavy staccato beat thudded from the dwarf on the electronic drums, and the singers mewled, undulated and slithered together like amorous boa constrictors.

The crowd loved it, accompanying the beat by crashing tankards on the tables and clapping their hands, mandibles, claws and paws. Calbhach and the leprechauns sang along heartily, taking turns to jig with Tarquin and Jeremiah. D'Arcy reached up to high-five a passing Blagburter waiter, but missed.

The impromptu concert lasted a full hour before Jeremiah pulled Calbhach to one side. As the final bars of the last song faded, Jeremiah and Tarquin followed Calbhach and the others to the back of the saloon, where they waited for Oleg by the painting of a Trundogan racing whippet called Whipper Snapper.

"Okay, Oleg's on his way. Let's get to the Willerby," said Calbhach after a couple of minutes, stepping into the painting. Soon they were all standing in a shady courtyard in one corner of which, atop a pile of bricks, was the Willerby Vogue caravan.

Tarquin smiled.

It was his home from home.

After a loud and expletive-enriched reunion with Tarquin, Oleg went to the Vogue's control room while the leprechauns set about making a stew. Calbhach, Jeremiah and Tarquin sat at the table in the dining room discussing Tarquin's clues.

"Remember? Remember what?" said Calbhach, turning the key in his hands and looking at Tarquin.

"Remember, remember, the fifth of November,

Gunpowder treason and plot.
We see no reason
Why Gunpowder treason
Should ever be forgot,"

recited Tarquin. "I can only assume my father hid the Book of Dreams somewhere in Parliament, but I don't remember him ever mentioning the Gunpowder Plot."

"So, this could be the front-door key to the Houses of Parliament," said Calbhach, scratching his head.

Tarquin nodded.

The rest of the leprechauns arrived with the hot food and soon, their bellies full and too many drinks inside them, the leprechauns were cracking jokes, singing and larking about.

"Seebee," said Jeremiah, above the clamorous leprechauns, "as long as we keep calm and carry on, nothing can go wrong."

Chapter 15

A Night at the Bloated Shagganat

Captain Gruilash Vandergaard did not appreciate being mooned, locked in a hyperjam for eighteen hours or asked to recite love poetry to a space pirate. So, when the amended order came to rescue Lieutenant Granwold Burbart and Prince Solace Ruttfarter from the Bloated Shagganat in Sleazeeze, he thought only of revenge. He would personally lead the Griddlebacks' Tactical Armed Response Teams and, by the end of the day, have the heads of those responsible for insulting him marinating in his galley's collection of pickle jars, along with the heads of all the other unfortunate aliens who'd crossed him during his thirty-year military career. He placed the four Griddleback battlecruisers in a geostationary orbit around Tharg, and had the TART assault vehicles prepared.

Seamus dolloped a steaming ladleful of Irish stew into a bowl.

"Georgia mistrusts Pollux and Castor. She chose the Bloated Shagganat nightclub and theatre for the handover, knowing it will be heaving on a Saturday night." He passed Alice the bowl and set about preparing one for Archie. "As will be many of the clientele."

"She's not daft," added Big Joe, going to the cutlery drawer and collecting knives and forks. "She knows she has to hand over the leathery filth, but she's going to make it as painful and embarrassing for the Griddlebacks as she can."

"She's friends with the nightclub owner," Merv contributed. "Anything could happen."

The clurichauns took their places at the table with Archie and Alice and started eating.

"They invaded her planet and shot her people," Seamus reminded them. "She had to watch them ridicule her president and royal family, and then make them recite love poetry before killing them."

"How did she escape?" said Archie.

"She was lucky, only losing an eye." Seamus speared a dumpling. It was an unfortunate gesture, just then.

Alice winced. "She told us she lost it in a duel."

"Yes, she did, sort of," said Dave Moriarty, ripping a piece of bread in two. "Griddlebacks held her and her sister in cages. Somehow, they escaped and stole a Griddleback ship, but her sister was shot and recaptured. Her fate is unknown. Georgia lost an eye trying to save her. She managed to launch the ship and escape. If her sister's dead, Georgia's rumoured to be the last of her race." He grimaced. "She hates Griddlebacks. That's why she agreed to this trip. Help Rigsworth, yes, but, if the opportunity comes along, she'll avenge her sister and the royal family. Now that she's got the evidence Rigsworth needs, tonight is all about revenge."

Seamus said, "The older Griddleback we captured is Lieutenant Granwold Burbart. It was his ship she stole to escape. Georgia believes he killed her sister." He finished by drawing a finger across his throat. Paddy, Dave and Merv nodded, wiping their plates clean with crusts.

Later in the evening, after the clurichauns had run through their repertoire of bawdy songs and flatulist punctuation, Georgia arrived in the lounging area.

"Archie, Alice, tin man, here's another item from the future. I call it the Wrogley gum gun." She held up a bronze-coloured machine-gun with silver fins, a round magazine and the word DISINTEGRATOR written along the side.

"It looks like something out of a 1950s science fiction movie," said Archie with a chuckle.

Georgia smiled. "And that's where the similarity ends. When fired, it draws matter and antimatter into this round chamber and mixes it, before adding a colour polymer from cartridges loaded here. Pull the trigger and it fires a glutinous wad at your victim. You can choose any colour you like but, for me, pink goes well with Griddleback green."

The clurichauns chortled.

"Think of it as firing an incredibly sticky ball of hot, molten bubblegum that sets as hard as titanium, but with the flexibility of rubber." Georgia handed the gun to Archie, who bemused everyone with an imitation of a 1920s Hollywood gangster.

"Why does it say 'Disintegrator' on the side if it doesn't do any actual, you know, disintegrating?" Alice said.

Georgia raised an eyebrow. "Purely for purposes of intimidation," she said.

Then she clapped her hands.

"Okay, we have two hours to prepare. Screwball, take the team to the stores and kit them out with Wrogleys. We have a fancy dress ball to go to."

This year the warm-up acts at the Bloated Shagganat's Annual Fancy Dress Ball were The Amazing Angelinas, a Shagganat dance troupe of indeterminate gender, and the popular Tricky Dicky and his Dancing Cullions. The Shanklin O'Macy Braigetori Big Band, an ensemble of cluirichaun flatulists much admired by young Zargothian nouveaux riches and Georgia's wrecking crew, would finish the evening. The other headline act was Aquos, a juggler from the planet Aquaenos.

Compèring the show was Georgia's good friend Tresore Munroe, the club's owner, a colourful, camp Frenchman who had emigrated to Sleazeeze; he'd been running the nightclub for over twenty years. Blessed with a barbed and caustic wit, Tresore and his partner, a rescued and modified droid called Izal Medicated—the butt of many of Tresore's jokes—always guaranteed a lively, fun night out.

Georgia led her raggletaggle troop, with the clurichauns carrying the two unconscious Griddlebacks in sacks, around two oversized Blagburter doormen who were sifting the milling crowd at the front of the building. Reaching a side street, they made their way through the garbage towards the stage door at the end of the alley. The door was open, so without further ado they carried their prisoners inside.

Tresore, wearing a gold lamé jumpsuit, stood with his back to them, nervously whisking an orange feather boa back and forth across his tanned face, desperately trying to coerce the Shagganat dance troupe into a dressing room. Izal, in his pink lederhosen and white ten-gallon hat, watched motionlessly, a picture of cherubic innocence.

Georgia coughed.

Tresore spun round. "Dahliiingggg," he effused, holding out a limp hand. "I just cannot go on. These people have no joie de vivre."

Georgia took his hand and they air-kissed each other.

"You look busy, so if it's okay we'll dump the trash." She pointed to the corridor where the dressing rooms were.

Tresore nodded agreement, and they carried their prisoners past him towards the rooms.

"Just keep the feelth away from me," the club owner squealed, looking as though he were chewing broken glass.

Georgia at the front, the motley crew went along the corridor until they reached the last door. In the centre of the room were two wicker hampers.

"One in each," she said, opening the baskets. "The baskets will have to be moved to the stage just before the performance starts. Tresore will organize it."

After the Griddlebacks had been dropped unceremoniously into the hampers, Georgia pushed two silver buttons on their belts and closed the lids.

"Time for some costumes."

At the back of the dressing room was a door into another room, full of clothing. They rummaged through racks of costumes, picking out masks and a variety of disguises.

As Alice picked among a pile of dresses, she turned to Liam. "What was it that Georgia pushed on the Griddlebacks' belts?"

"Homing devices. She wants the Griddleback rescue party to know where these two are," said Liam. "Pretty boring, really."

Georgia found two Galactic Police uniforms, one for her and the other for Archie. Fifteen minutes later, a nurse, several space cowboys, two doctors, a Zargothian Advocate, and one penal inmate stood before Georgia. A lot of these individuals were unusually short of stature.

"That will do nicely," she said. "Walk about, but stay in pairs and keep your Wrogleys primed and hidden. I expect the Griddlebacks will come with a surprise or two."

Slipping unnoticed into the foyer, the gang mingled with arriving guests and enjoyed the music. The musicians, a group with diverse interplanetary origins, sat in four gilt cages suspended on gold chains from a pink vaulted ceiling.

It wasn't long before the clurichauns found a bar and were downing pints of Bender Ale.

After his third pint, Shamus saw Archie walk by with Georgia and, on the pretence of needing a quiet word, prised him away from the space pirate. As Georgia went off to check the layout of the main club entrance, Shamus led Archie to the bar.

"What yer reckon on this?" The clurichaun handed Archie a shot glass full of a steaming, effervescent yellow liquid. "It'll put hairs on yer chest."

Archie sniffed it suspiciously. He was pleasantly surprised to find it smelled of nothing more threatening than honey.

He ventured a sip, and his eyes lit up.

He took a mouthful, and then downed the whole glassful.

A moment's pause.

Then Archie went rigid, goggling at the ceiling.

Like a cuttlefish doing a mating dance, his nose flashed all the colours of the spectrum before his body relaxed and he belched a plume of flaming blue gas into the air.

He giggled—he was hooked.

Archie managed to sink another two drinks before Georgia returned. Seeing the teenager's inane grin and the sight of a wad of money passing quickly through clurichaun hands, she knew what had been going on. They were taking bets on what colour Archie's nose would be when he finally keeled over.

Her face angrily set, she slapped the clurichauns around their various heads, deploying expletives the like of which even their own mothers didn't know, and managed to rescue Archie just in time before he downed the fourth, "toppler" drink.

Archie was unaware of her intervention, awestruck as he was by the thousands of colourful winged beasties that were flying around—and through—his marshmallow head. After three Brocca Bogglers—a notoriously addictive hallucinogenic drink, and banned on most planets—Archie felt no pain.

A voice sounded over the music. "Mesdames et monsieurs, the performance will begin shortly. Please take your seats."

Georgia guided Archie to his seat—or, rather, poured him in that direction. He promptly slumped and fell asleep, snoring loudly. The clurichauns took seats close to the doors at the back of the theatre. Alice and Liam sat in the middle, and Georgia and Archie were two rows from the front.

The lights dimmed and the curtains opened to reveal a desert island. In the centre of the island were the two wicker hampers from the dressing room.

Tresore emerged and, with a devilish grin, introduced the first of the warm-up acts.

The lights dimmed and the pit orchestra fired up anew. Ten burly Shagganats in red ballet tunics and bright pink tutus lumbered onto the small stage. It was like asking a bloat of hippos to stand together on a tea tray. Having arrived late from their home planet and missed rehearsals, they had no idea the stage was going to be far too small for their act. Forlornly, they tried to give each other space, but this just added to the debacle as their chorus-line routine turned into a bad-tempered bread line.

Next they tried a high-kicking number, but within moments this had degenerated into a desperate free-for-all with legs, arms and snouts crashing into each other.

But, like true professionals, they stuck to their task, the old adage that "the show must go on" uppermost in their small but determined minds. The prima ballerina—a large, bustling slab of energy, sweat and cellulite—moved to the centre of the stage and attempted to pirouette. Immediately wobbling out of control, she grabbed two of her companions and all three plunged headlong into the orchestra pit, wiping out the entire wind section and an unattended double bass.

Doggedly, the rest of the troupe struggled to the finale, but then fate once more conspired against them. After they'd created a base for their pièce de résistance, a winsomely bulging corporeal pyramid of dancers, the middle supporting Shagganat collapsed under a particularly venomous forearm smash and dragged the whole pack of cards down, leaving the Shag pyramid more of a Shag pile.

The audience howled for more, assuming the bedlam was deliberate and all part of a slapstick act. A handful of inebriated guests helped the three Shagganats up out of the orchestra pit and back onto the stage, where the newcomers in their excitement threw themselves into the heart of the seething mass.

Tresore rescued the routine by mincing into the chaos and throwing Izal on top of the pile, declaring him the Izal On The Cake.

At which point, to the thunder of riotous applause, the curtain came down. Tresore flounced on stage with Izal, cracking jokes and insulting the audience before introducing the next act, Tricky Dicky and his Dancing Cullions.

As the lights dimmed, Tricky Dicky strolled to the front of the stage and dropped his trousers. The audience erupted with coarse laughter.

Dicky's performance was short but full of action: backhands, forehands, the occasional smash, all accompanied by Tresore's ball-by-ball commentary.

After a few minutes, Tricky Dicky bowed to the audience, scooped up his cullions and waddled off stage to another standing ovation. It was turning out to be a night to remember.

With no announcement and no lights, Aquos slithered slowly to the middle of the stage, drew himself up and stood motionless. Only the gills on the side of his scaly yellow chest moved, fluttering excitedly. He gave an attention-grabbing screech as a floodlight illuminated his insane "You have no idea what's coming next" smile.

With all attention on him, and to the accompaniment of the pit orchestra, he careered about the stage shrieking, his three bulbous red-and-green eyes revolving wildly in their sockets like emergency lights on a speeding fire truck. Each time the music came to a crescendo, Aquos glissaded to the centre of the stage, squeezed out a tennis-ball-sized eye, and left it bouncing there, still attached to its socket by a translucent optic nerve.

Once all three eyes were loose, he hauled on the rubbery optical nerves and juggled the balls, occasionally bouncing an eye off the flinching head of someone in the front row. The stunned audience broke into laughter and roared their appreciation.

Eventually Aquos stopped juggling and, to a roll on the drums and the gasps of the audience, calmly swallowed his own eyeballs, one after the other. Using his neck muscles, he raced the eyeballs up and down his metre-long throat, like lifts on the side of a building, and then, accompanied by a crash of cymbals, expelled them from his mouth onto the laps of three people in the front row. Bowing appreciatively, he left them there, covered in yellow slime, just long enough for the shrieks of the luckless recipients to become ear-splitting, then reeled them in. Finally he pulled each eyeball back into its socket with a loud, squelching plop before slithering offstage to a standing ovation.

The lights in the theatre came on and the excited audience headed for the bars.

During the interval Georgia, with Alice's help, dragged Archie backstage and tried to sober him up. Progress was slow, and fifteen minutes later, when the bell rang to announce the start of the second half, they hadn't made much of it. Leaving him asleep on a bed in Tresore's dressing room, they went back to their seats.

The second half started with yet another drum roll. The pianist played the opening bar of the club's signature tune and a single white spotlight opened on Tresore, dressed in a luxuriant gold evening gown, standing at the edge of the stage.

"And now," he said, "a blast from the past. In fact, a Zargothian flatulist's dream, Ladies and gentlemen, I give you … the Shanklin O'Macy Braigetori Big Band!"

Wearing black uniforms, respirators and hoverpacks, Captain Gruilash Vandergaard and his men dropped silently from their assault craft and flew over the crowded streets of Sleazeeze until regrouping high above the Bloated Shagganat, like vultures circling a meal. Gruilash's plan was to secure the building, enter it by force and isolate the customers and the kidnappers, then rescue Granwold and Ruttfarter.

Gruilash checked the position of Granwold and the prince via their homing devices. He signalled to his team and, pairing up, they descended with military precision to the roof of the nightclub.

With an ear-splitting crash, two Griddlebacks came through the auditorium windows and hung above the audience, pointing their phasers in menacing fashion. Two more burst through the doors at the back of the auditorium while four others floated easily across the stage and paused. Gruilash entered through the main doors and hovered close to the stage, looking at the audience cowering in their seats.

Izal comforted Tresore.

Georgia, sitting back in her seat, simply smiled.

"Silence!" shouted Gruilash, firing his phaser into the air. A mass of plaster and wood plummeted to the floor.

"Where are they?" he shouted, nodding to one of his subordinates.

Two Griddlebacks dropped to the auditorium floor and pulled a young Zargothian male from his seat. They dragged him to the stage. Gruilash landed beside him and put the muzzle of his phaser into the folds of flesh around the Zargothian's neck.

"Where are they?" he shouted, digging the phaser in hard so that the Zargothian yelped in pain.

"I asked, where are they?" Gruilash repeated, checking out the faces in the audience.

Georgia leant forward and spoke into her communicator. "Let's boogie, boys."

Getting to her feet, she shouted at Gruilash, "You want them alive, then drop all your weapons."

The audience turned to look at the tall, red-headed Police Officer standing confidently in their midst.

With the Griddlebacks' attention momentarily drawn to Georgia, the clurichauns fired from their positions, splattering the hovering Griddlebacks with gum so that they were entombed like flies in a spider's web. The heavy aliens' hoverpacks spluttered and died, and the Griddleback troopers crashed loudly to the floor.

The Griddlebacks at the rear of the hall flew forward to the rescue of their comrades … and straight into Big Joe and Seamus, who wasted them. Two pink ant-hills with legs and arms glued themselves to the auditorium floor, their weapons and hoverpacks rendered useless by the Wrogleys' goo.

The Shanklin O'Macy Braigetori Big Band, all sixty of them, came onstage from both wings and pointed their Wrogleys at Gruilash and those few Griddlebacks who remained upright.

Gruilash cursed aloud and dropped the babbling Zargothian. Suckered, yet again.

Georgia strode confidently to the stage, a cheroot clenched between her teeth. She acknowledged Shanklin, and then turned to Gruilash. Rolling the cheroot to the side of her mouth, she looked into his cold eyes.

"God, you're ugly." She blew a cloud of acrid smoke into his face. "Drop your weapons."

Gruilash shook with rage and his mouth curled in a silent snarl. He signed to his troops onstage that they should let their weapons fall. He himself was the last to obey his own order.

Georgia turned and walked to the front of the stage. She raised her arms high into the air and looked at the milling audience. No one had left the auditorium, although several small children were wailing that they needed to, real bad.

"Welcome to the Bloated Shagganat!" Georgia yelled, beckoning to the audience that they should participate.

She looked back at Gruilash. "Do you have something to tell this fine audience, you fat ugly toad?"

Gruilash snorted and plucked a piece of paper from his armoured jacket. He snarled, "Shall I compare thee to a summer's day?" he snarled.

"Can't hear you, slimeface. Speak up!" Georgia walked across to him and cupped her ear theatrically towards his snout. The audience erupted with laughter and applause.

Gruilash hissed and spat a cloud of acid at Georgia. With catlike agility she ducked, turned, and grabbed his throat with both hands. Once more the audience cheered. This was better than the Shagganats, possibly even better than Aquos.

"Do that again and you and your colleagues are roadkill," Georgia growled. Undaunted by his simmering hatred, she calmly let go of his throat and gave his snout a hard flick.

His eyes filled with more rage than ever, he slowly began the recital again:

Shall I compare thee to a summer's day?
Thou art more lovely and more temperate:
Rough winds do shake the darling buds of May,
And summer's lease hath all too short a date;
Sometime too hot the eye of heaven shines,
And often is his gold complexion dimm'd;
And every fair from fair sometime declines,
By chance or nature's changing course untrimm'd;
But thy eternal summer shall not fade,
Nor lose possession of that fair thou ow'st;
Nor shall Death brag thou wander'st in his shade,
When in eternal lines to time thou grow'st:
So long as men can breathe or eyes can see,
So long lives this, and this gives life to thee.

As the last line echoed around the auditorium, Shanklin and several of his band members took out their Wrogleys and covered the remaining Griddleback troopers in gum, immobilizing them and pinning them to the stage. Gruilash was spared the indignity of gum entombment, but worse was to come.

"Strip," said Georgia, her .44 Magnum pointing at his head. She was quite clearly unmoved by his rendition of the great Shakespearian sonnet.

"I am Captain Gruilash Vandergaard of the battlecruiser Tarakan III. I take my ceremonial robes off for no one," he said defiantly.

Georgia fired a round into one of the trunks, shredding it in a cloud of vapour.

"Did you know Granwold well?" she said, looking at the hole in the stage where the trunk had stood, then smiling evilly at Gruilash. "Get me the prince."

The unconscious prince was raised from the remaining trunk and propped against its lid. Georgia pointed her Bosun at him, and then turned again to Gruilash. "Strip."

Gruilash didn't move, just stared. Their eyes locked, and each felt the other's loathing. Four hundred aliens and a passel of humans held their breath.

Georgia fired her Bosun at the prince, hitting him in the leg and sending him tumbling backward.

Awoken, he screamed in pain.

The audience screamed in shock.

"Strip," yelled Georgia at Gruilash, spitting the cheroot from her mouth, "or I will kill him. Yes, I'm mad and pissed enough to start a war!"

Gruilash's jaw quivered and he began to undo his gun belt and body armour. The audience watched in aghast silence, realizing the enormity of what they were witnessing.

Letting his black, ceremonial underjacket slide to the floor, Gruilash stood naked but with a certain dignity in front of Georgia, his spirit unbowed, his will unbroken. Laughing cruelly, Georgia kicked his clothing and body armour into the wings before turning to the audience and walking to the front of the stage. She clicked her fingers and a Wrogley gun soared through the air. She caught it, and locked several goo cartridges into the breech.

"I just wanted to see if your ego matched your physique—clearly it doesn't," she said, turning and firing a barrage of goo at Gruilash so that he was anchored naked to the stage.

The audience got to their feet and bellowed approval.

"That's all, folks—the show's over!" cried Georgia, exiting stage left as Tresore ordered the curtain down.

The clurichauns removed the guns from the Griddlebacks before joining Georgia backstage. Seamus, Liam and Big Joe grabbed the prince, while Shanklin, along with his Big Band, went out through the theatre's rear exit. Georgia and Alice went to Tresore's changing room to collect Archie, and then met up with the others at the back of the alley, before disappearing into the night.

All had gone according to plan. A staged diversion outside the nightclub had kept the remaining Griddlebacks occupied long enough for everyone to escape. Not only had they captured a member of the Griddleback royal family, they'd gummed an elite Griddleback unit and made their senior commander disrobe in front of an audience of four hundred. The ebullient clurichauns, along with Shanklin O'Macy and his Big Band, reached Prometheus and boarded her, while Georgia, Archie, Alice and Liam went to Pandora.

They fired up the spaceships and disappeared.

As they hovered over France, waiting for the opening of a wormhole back to 2340, Alice cornered Georgia on the bridge.

"That was a Shakespearean sonnet he recited, not love poetry from your own planet!"

"Did you really think I'd let that animal abuse my people's poetry?" snarled Georgia.

"And you killed an unarmed creature in cold blood back there," Alice said, shaking.

Georgia took a deep breath and smiled. "If I did, he deserved it."

"That may be so, but you can't just shoot helpless people. It's inhumane."

Georgia smiled more widely, took out a cheroot and placed it in the corner of her mouth.

"'Inhumane'," she said. "Interesting choice of word."

"Yes, he may be evil and a killer, but we become as bad as them if we resort to murder."

Georgia lit the cheroot and took a long drag on it, her eyes not moving from Alice's.

"He's not dead. I had him moved to Pandora during the interval. He's locked up down below, and has a lot to tell us."

On Prometheus, the party was just getting started. Shanklin O' Macy and his Big Band were going through their flatulist repertoire, a mixture of wind and bare brass instruments.

"It don't get any better than this," said Screwball above the music, playfully whacking Paddy on the nose with a rolled-up colour supplement he'd found on the floor of the lounge. Seamus and Merv swerved past him and thudded into Big Joe and Willard, sending a round of drinks crashing to the floor. For a second they looked at the mess, then squared up to each other … then fell about laughing.

"Break out the Brocca Bogglers!" shouted Paddy, forcing his way to the ship's bar. Thirty minutes later, seven partially inebriated clurichauns rolled about the room, grappling with any members of the Shanklin O'Macy Big Band who wanted to fight, while playing fiddles and singing bawdy songs.

As the evening drew to a close, and the snoring of the clurichauns grew steadily louder aboard Prometheus, things were generally quieter on Pandora.

"Why didn't we give the prince and his companion back at the nightclub?" Archie asked Georgia, helping himself to a sandwich.

"I need to find out a few things about them. I use what we call mind-mapping," replied Georgia, taking a small, silver rectangular box from a cupboard and walking toward the exit. "Come on, you two. You'll find this interesting. Liam has already set up the Griddlebacks in the laboratory."

They walked down a brightly lit corridor towards a steel door. Georgia opened it and led Archie and Alice inside.

Laid out on two tables were the Griddlebacks, Granwold and Prince Ruttfarter, naked but for their ceremonial undergarments. Their battle armour lay in a pile on the floor and their personal items on a third table. Encapsulating their heads were translucent spheres filled with bubbling gel. Tubes and wires from several banks of machinery entered the spheres and pressed against their eyes and mouths.

"Ughh," said Alice, grabbing Archie's arm. " What the hell are you doing to them?"

"Mind-mapping their last five Earth years. Unfortunately, the process is painless." Georgia walked over to a console and placed the silver box into a slot there. She typed at a keyboard and a large screen on the wall above them flickered.

"Let's see what they've been up to recently," she said, taking a chair and crossing her legs.

Alice and Archie pulled up seats of their own and joined Georgia in watching the screen.

She fast-forwarded through their prisoners' last five years, occasionally slowing the replay to examine something in more detail.

Granwold's life was full of death, destruction and warfare. Rapacious brutality characterized his every action. When Archie threw up, Georgia shifted to Prince Ruttfarter's memories instead, untainted as they were by involvement in murderous rampages across galaxies. The prince's last five years were filled with royal functions, meetings and unimaginable opulence.

Continuing the fast-forward, they witnessed the start of a meeting a year ago between the prince, his father the king and dozens of high-ranking military officers. Georgia slowed the playback and turned on the translator. The guttural snorts, growls and rasping hisses became intelligible as English.

"It was your son's idea," said a Griddleback general, standing at the head of a table occupied by other senior military figures.

"We kidnap and kill any of Earth's music groups that are named after animals. We work our way through western human history, starting with the Beatles in Earth year 1963. Then we take out the Animals, the Monkees, the Byrds and Steppenwolf, before moving on to the Scorpions, Snoop Doggy Dog, the Pussy Cat Dolls and finally Atomic Kitten and T. Rex." The general smiled. "We'll add more when and if the opportunity arises. Ruining western musical heritage will devastate the young and influential humans. No one will be safe. There'll be civil war and, while they fight amongst themselves, we'll bring the filth to their knees."

Georgia turned to Archie and Alice. "When I've finished downloading all this, you'll have to get these two Griddlebacks into custody and bargain for Jules's release. Jules needs to know about their vile scheme."

"Us?" said Archie.

"Yes. I have a bounty on my head. I can't arrive at a police station on Tharg with these two and risk getting arrested!" She smiled at the two teenagers. "On second thoughts … You found me through that fat Zargothian lawyer Smodius, didn't you?"

"Yes, but—" said Archie, looking to Alice for support.

"We'll leave them with him," said Georgia, "and save you the job of negotiating Jules's release."

They cloaked the ships and set coordinates for the Zargothian Colony on Tharg. Despite Archie's and Alice's reservations, Georgia decided the best way was to deliver the prisoners, along with Liam, directly to Smodius's office, plus a copy of the mind-mapping cube taken from the Griddlebacks and the remains of the two droids.

It didn't take long to break into Smodius's office and deliver the packages. The job done, Alice and Archie said goodbye to Georgia and her wrecking crew, picked up their Sinclair (at no little expense) from Burt Dangle, and prepared for the journey back to Earth. Archie carefully hid in the Sinclair the copy of the silver mind-mapping cube that Georgia had given him.

Had you been visiting the offices of Munchfumble, Scrumble & Twee that Thursday afternoon, the sight of two cursing, naked Griddlebacks, hog-tied and lying on the outer office floor as Liam bored them to tears, would be one that remained with you for a very long time.

CHAPTER 16

THEIR DAY IN COURT

Despite Prince Ruttfarter and Granwold having been returned to the Griddle-back Ambassador on Tharg and Smodius privately disclosing the mind-mapped information he possessed, the court case against Jules Rigsworth and the leprechauns went ahead. Whether it was pigheaded bravado or foolishness on the part of the Griddlebacks, or part of an unknown plan, Smodius was gravely concerned. It made no sense for the actions of the prince and his aide, Granwold, back in 1773 Boston to come out in court. The case would show the Griddlebacks doing exactly what they had accused Jules Rigsworth of doing: meddling with Earth history. In addition, the mind-mapping would demonstrate a litany of murders and tortures of not just humans but people from other civilizations.

The opening arguments were to be heard in the Centre Court of the Presidential Building. Presiding over the court was Judge Freelash E. Pompitulary-Ginglebaum III, a Zargothian High Court judge of immense age, weight and socio-political standing.

Smodius moved imperiously over the Presidential Building steps, flanked by his defence team. Occasionally he looked up from his visipad tablet and nodded regally at the clerks and lawyers who bowed reverentially to him as he floated along the hallowed corridors towards the Centre Court's imposing doors. This was his circus, and he was headlining.

He rapped his cane on the court doors. They opened and he swept in, his retinue in his wake. The public gallery—where Alice and Archie, freshly arrived back from Earth, sat in the front row—swayed forward like long grass to witness the arrival of the great attorney.

Advocate Drisilus S. Toadfimble, the prosecution lawyer, looked up from his brief and acknowledged Smodius with the formal Zargothian greeting: hands waving above the head and a loud cluck. Smodius returned the compliment. The two teams decamped to opposite ends of the bench to set up shop, and made a point of looking busy, the junior members of each team sizing each other up as they waited for Judge Pompitulary-Ginglebaum III to enter.

Jules was next to arrive, brought from the holding cells under the court and seated in the dock.

Smodius acknowledged Jules with a nod, then scanned the jury. He was pleased. The selection process had been long and arduous, but he was confident he'd achieved the best outcome. Griddlebacks had bullied many planets into signing up to their alliance, but Smodius's team had limited the number of Griddleback apologists to two out of a jury of ten.

The court ushers rose and Judge Pompitulary-Ginglebaum III entered. All the Zargothians waved, clucked loudly, and let rip with the noise of a hundred deflating balloons.

"Be seated," said the judge sombrely before throwing his purple raiment extravagantly over his hoverthrone and sitting down with a loud rasp. Turning to the jury, he was about to address them when the clerk of the court bowed and handed him a visipad tablet.

The judge's large donkey-like ears twitched and turned backwards as he read the message. Then he scanned the courtroom and fixed his eyes on Drisilus.

"What is the meaning of this, Counsellor?" he barked gruffly, peering down his nose at the rotund and sweaty advocate.

Drisilus looked bemused and glared at his team for direction.

"I'm talking to you, Counsellor," roared Freelash. "Not your harem!"

Sycophantic laughter rippled through the public gallery.

"Your Honour, I am unsure exactly to what you refer."

"Pray, let me read to you, then," said Freelash, sighing loudly and visibly annoyed.

"'In the matter of the President of the Galactic Confederation versus Julius Ulysses Rigsworth, we, the Griddleback Nation, rescind all charges.'"

The judge glared at Drisilus, who was now pale and twitching. "Do you have anything useful to say, Counsellor?"

"I'm sorry, your Honour"—Drisilus patted his leaking brow—"but it does appear that you hold all the cards." He lowered his throne deferentially to the floor and bowed his head.

Judge Freelash took a deep breath and addressed the dock. "It never ceases to amaze me, the intrigues and deals that are struck inside this building's corridors before a case reaches these courts, but never in my time on this bench have I witnessed such a late stay of action. Jules Ulysses Rigsworth, you are free to go. Case dismissed."

Alice and Archie leapt from their seats and pounded the air with their fists. Jules stood in the dock, smiling. Smodius stayed by the bench, looking at his friend. Something wasn't right. It made no sense. Why would the Griddlebacks go so far down the road to trial and then capitulate? What was the point?

Archie and Alice arrived on the floor and worked their way through the crowd to where Jules was standing in the dock beaming and saluting the gallery.

"Incredible!" was all Archie said to him before a blast of energy hit Jules full on the chest and sent him cartwheeling backward into the wall of the dock, where he slid groaning to the floor.

Pandemonium ensued. People screamed and ran in all directions. Smodius cursed loudly and rose in his chair, just as a court usher pointed accusingly at a cloaked figure walking calmly towards the rear of the courtroom.

"After him!" yelled the usher.

Rickie Riggle, a young but excessively corpulent Blagburter on his first day as a recently trained clerk of the court, heaved himself onto the back of a bench seat like a walrus onto a beach, and lumbered above the mayhem toward the figure. The line of seat-backs creaked under his considerable weight, but they held firm. With a good head of steam, all was going well and he was gaining on the unsuspecting figure when his oversized boot caught the very last seat-back and he went tumbling.

Rickie hit the floor and rolled at speed toward the assassin, finally crushing the figure against the wall with a sickening squelch.

Dazed, Rickie looked around. A crowd of people gathered by the mess on the wall, staring at the remains of the droid and a phase pistol. The chief usher arrived, took one look at the mess and grabbed Rickie's hand before shaking it vigorously.

"They'll be a medal in this for you, I'm sure!" he said excitedly, clinging to Rickie's club-sized hand like a demented rottweiler.

Back in the dock, Jules Rigsworth lay in a crumpled heap.

"Jules! Are you okay?" shouted Archie, running up the steps and into the dock. He grabbed at Jules's head.

To his horror, the head flew into the air like a cork from a bottle. Torrents of green goo and gelatinous wads of crimson erupted from the torn neck, covering Archie. Where the head had been was now a twitching bird's nest of differently coloured cables.

"Yuck!" cried Archie, transfixed, watching Jules's head bounce, spin and roll down the steps of the dock and under the court's front bench. He wiped the goo from his face and scrabbled to retrieve the head.

A hand yanked him back.

Archie looked up to see Professor Tommy Cramdunkle, incongruously smiling.

"Stercus accidit," he said, pulling an open-mouthed Archie from the floor.

The professor deftly removed a thin ring from the droid's neck stump and pocketed it before turning and winking at one of his medical interns, positioned in the gallery above the dock. A blinding flash and the sound of rolling thunder rose from the witness box, making everyone turn to look.

From within a cloud of blue, hissing steam emerged Jules Rigsworth, wearing a guard's uniform and sitting on a white ceramic toilet, grinning. Like a mark of office, he wore the toilet's seat around his neck and held, one in each hand, a toilet roll and a chain pull.

Jules giggled, mouthing the word "oops" at Judge Freelash before waving the toilet roll above his head. The roll unravelled, papering him like a poorly embalmed Egyptian mummy.

He tried to cluck. Unfortunately, with little or no feeling in his drooling mouth—like being at the dentist after having several fillings—his cluck became a wet raspberry. Judge Freelash, who until now had sat in passive bewilderment at the events in his courtroom, rose in his hoverchair, pointed at Jules and looked about to erupt. Jules just yawned, rolled his eyes and fell backward, passing out at the bottom of the witness box, exhausted by the effort of time-hopping and performing a Zargothian greeting.

Unsurprisingly, Judge Freelash did erupt.

"Seal the court!" he bellowed, waving at the crowd now gathered in front of his bench. "Sit down, all of you!"

He turned towards the immobile figure of Jules and snarled and growled at him like a rabid dog. "I want him revived." He pointed at the box. "I want everyone in my courtroom attentive and seated! And"—the judge paused, his ears went backwards, and again he pointed at Jules—"I want his head on a plate!"

Smodius and the jury took their places as the courtroom gallery filled up once more. Everyone looked bemused except Archie, who was too covered in slime to look anything at all.

Six Blagburter ushers closed the doors and stood guard. Jules was speedily revived and plonked back on his toilet, facing Judge Freelash.

"Wow, that was waaaay cool!" he shouted, gazing boggle-eyed at his surroundings.

"Silence!" roared the judge, glaring at him.

Seeing Freelash, Jules hurriedly stood up and began waving his hands above his head.

"Don't even think about greeting me again," said the judge.

Jules sat back on the toilet with an expression of utter confusion.

Smodius covered his eyes and shook his head. He knew where this was going. He had to act.

"Your Honour," he said, rising in his hoverchair and addressing Freelash, "my client has been threatened by the entire Griddleback nation. You yourself just witnessed the destruction of a decoy by an assassination droid sent to kill my client. Don't you think it's time he was allowed to go?"

Freelash glared at Smodius. "You're going to tell me there is no law to hold him, aren't you, Counsellor?"

Smodius looked conciliatory, but with an undeniable hint of smugness. "If you feel Mr Rigsworth's behaviour today warrants punishment, you could always bind him over."

Freelash wobbled his jowls in deliberation.

Eventually he turned to Jules. "Clearly someone doesn't like you, Mr Rigsworth, and, from your ridiculous performance in my courtroom, I can understand why. However, as your learned counsel would point out given the chance, I have little legal ammunition to fire at you as the case has been dismissed. I could give you a custodial sentence for contempt, but I'm sure your learned counsel would clog up my court docket with petitions to appeal and, likely, win them. I therefore bind you over for a period of three years. Do you think you can manage to keep out of galactic trouble for that length of time, Mr Rigsworth? I really, really don't want to see you, or anyone associated with you, ever again."

Jules rose slowly from the toilet and spoke. "Yes, of course, your Honour."

"You may go." Freelash turned to the courtroom, "Please," he said in a loud and commanding voice, "leave my courtroom in an orderly fashion, or I'll instruct my ushers to sit on you."

With a short but eloquent burst of eructation, Freelash nodded approvingly at Rickie Riggle, who gushed, shrugged his shoulders and rotated his eyes to the applause and flatulence rolling around the room.

Jules made his way to the bench and Smodius. "We meet again," he said, standing before his friend.

"I thought it unusual that you contacted me, especially after what happened the last time we met."

"Yes, that was unfortunate. But is there anyone better?"

"When all else fails," said Smodius, shaking his ears and looking down his long nose before ripping loudly, "humans rely heavily on flattery." He wagged a cucumber-sized finger in Jules's face. "You live in a dark world, Jules Rigsworth, full of smoke and mirrors. You are a brigand, likening yourself to the Scarlet Pimpernel of old, and taking unnatural and obsessive delight in sailing close to the wind. I may not be your safety net forever." He ripped again and gave Jules a rueful smile. "Take care, old friend."

"You too," said Jules with a grin as Smodius raised his throne, shepherded his entourage about him and sailed regally from the courtroom.

"How the blue blazes did you know?" asked Archie, turning to Tommy, who stood next to him.

"Because Smodius contacted me and told me of his concerns. We and my interns made a plan," said Tommy cheerfully. "I'll explain everything once we're out of here."

Sitting in Tommy's office, enjoying a mug of tea and cake, Archie and Alice waited for the promised explanation.

"You want to know how we swapped Jules for a bot?" said Tommy.

Alice nodded. "Of course we do! You had us scared to death."

Tommy leaned back in his chair and began to speak. BIFS had picked up news of the hiring of an assassin droid in Sleazeeze for a special job at the Centre Court in Tharg. It soon became clear that the most likely target was Jules, and the time for the hit was when he stood in the dock. Smodius had contacted Tommy, concerned that the Griddlebacks had not withdrawn their case. That, coupled with the hiring of the droid, confirmed to Smodius that the assassination would happen in court.

"Therefore," concluded Tommy, "we needed to stop Jules from appearing. Held in solitary confinement in the penal colony, he was taken twice a day to a yard for exercise. Smodius used his connections and a large number of tokens, and had Jules switched earlier today for one of my medical droids. The droid, wearing a personality ring to look exactly like Jules, was returned to solitary confinement in his place. Jules himself was hidden in an old abandoned toilet block for several hours until the trial was underway. After the assassin was caught, Jules was teleported into the witness box. Unfortunately, rather more was teleported than we'd intended, so he came complete with his, er, throne.

"And the rest you saw," said Tommy with a grin.

CHAPTER 17

REMEMBER, REMEMBER

Loaded with food and ammunition, the Willerby Vogue caravan stood ready for the journey to 1605. Feeling nervous about what lay ahead, Tarquin watched from the cockpit door as Oleg attended to the controls. The mad Russian was poring over Mrs Beeton's books of Needlework and Household Management, his Look-Sees protruding from his head like an insect's antennae. He muttered something under his breath, picked up a calculator-like device and tapped on it feverishly. Numerals and calculus flew across the screen on the front wall of the cockpit.

A loud noise made them both look towards the caravan door. The Brothers Grimm had thudded the side of the caravan with the keg of Bender Pale Ale they'd brought. They lifted it through the doorway and disappeared down the corridor into the caravan's storeroom.

The rooms branching off the corridor were a hive of leprechaun activity. Tarquin had overheard Calbhach giving out the orders: Rhiordan and Ardal were sent to the armoury to secure and prepare weaponry while, in the dressing room, Finbar and D'Arcy were laying out enough seventeenth-century period clothing for everyone.

Back in the cockpit, Oleg had put the calculator aside. He pulled his Look-Sees over his eyes and began pushing a series of buttons on the caravan's dashboard. The screen lit up again, this time showing not maths but a view of the cellar under the Houses of Parliament. It looked large enough to accommodate the caravan. The date—4 November 1605—flashed across the screen. Apart from rats and mice, there was no sign of life.

Grinning, Oleg pulled off the goggles and gave a thumbs-up to no one in particular.

"All aboard," shouted Calbhach, stepping into the cockpit.

Tarquin's heart raced as he stood waiting for the leprechauns to file past and take their positions.

The cockpit area was small and, with the additional seating, somewhat cozy. Tarquin moved carefully through the cramped aisles, apologizing each time he hit a bony knee or tripped on a boot. Reaching the front, he took the seat directly behind Oleg. He pulled the harness across his chest and midriff and tugged hard, securing the spider's web of leather tightly. He'd spent his last trip watching Oleg ride the BRONCO at the other end of the caravan. He hadn't ridden in the cockpit before.

A mix of pulsating lights, string, organ pulls and brass levers fanned out from the flight console, and strung across the vaulted dome was a washing line, at one end of which, neatly pegged, were several pairs of thick wool socks. Further along were half a dozen bathing caps and what looked like several pairs of his Uncle Harold's underpants.

To Tarquin's right sat D'Arcy, his hairy legs dangling over the edge of the seat— two chicken legs protruding from oversized khaki shorts, all wrapped in orange wool that disappeared inside large, hobnailed miner's boots. To his left were the Brothers Grimm, Finbar and Brennan, sitting bolt upright in their life vests; they had their eyes closed and, to Tarquin's unease, hummed a long, monotonous, chest-rumbling note. In front of him was Oleg, his massive frame squashed into a wicker aircraft chair. Alongside Oleg sat Calbhach, perched on several tatty velvet cushions, his hands just able to reach the Willerby's controls. Clenched tightly between his teeth was his favourite briar pipe.

Heath Robinson would have been proud.

"Okay, dialectics time," said Jeremiah, entering the cockpit clutching half a dozen syringes. He'd been busy in the back of the Vogue mixing and preparing language-helper potions for everyone. Brennan, first to be injected, let out a mournful cry.

Tarquin closed his eyes and thought of Rhia. Soon he heard Jeremiah next to him. He was next.

"Arrggh," squealed Tarquin, feeling the liquid rush inside his head. "Do we really need to speak in seventeenth-century English?"

"I knows you don't like it, but what happens if we lose you?"

Jeremiah was right. Tarquin was just letting off steam. His second injection passed off without incident.

The syringing completed, Jeremiah injected his own ears, sat down in his paisley armchair at the back of the cockpit and buckled up.

Preparations for the journey completed, Oleg leaned towards Calbhach. "If we miss the returning wormhole at 3am on the fifth, the next one is five days away."

"I know," replied Calbhach. "I know."

Tarquin heard their conversation and moaned. His gorge rose slowly into his mouth. Every time he had missed a returning wormhole, trouble happened.

"Wormhole appearing in two minutes," said Oleg, a hand above his head, counting down on his fingers as he watched a row of numbers descend on the screen before him.

"Leaving in, five–four–three–two—"

The noise of a dozen wailing guitars filled the cockpit and the caravan shook, spun, flipped upside-down and rolled repeatedly. Tarquin's stomach mirrored the movement of the ship, and could feel himself turning green. It didn't help that the leprechauns were shrieking excitedly and waving their stubby little arms above their heads like children on a rollercoaster.

Amid the mayhem, Oleg and Calbhach threw levers, pressed buttons, and pulled and pushed oversized wooden organ stops with the precision of two synchronized swimmers.

Five minutes into the ride and the caravan lurched sideways and abruptly stopped. The juddering halt caused the floor mountings on Calbhach's chair to creak and then break, releasing him. The chair rose gracefully. The caravan had entered a zone of zero gravity. There was now an addition to the flotsam and jetsam floating around the cockpit's dome: Calbhach, cursing high above them, little legs kicking furiously.

"Get me down, yez Celtic wasters!" he yelled as he floated above a field of outstretched hands. The Brothers Grimm grabbed at a trailing bootlace as Calbhach floated past, but missed.

Oleg was frantically pushing and pulling a line of organ stops, glancing every few moments at the screen. He thumped his hand on the console.

"Got it!" he shouted, and, with a sickening crunch, the chair fell to the floor. In the middle of a pile of splintered wood, Calbhach sat whimpering. He tried to get up but just then the caravan lurched forward and gathered speed, sending him flying backwards and out of the cockpit.

"Crash positions," shouted Oleg, still staring at the series of numbers descending at crazy speed on the console in front of him. "Brace yourselves!"

He himself grabbed the side of the dashboard as the ship twisted and turned, sending bits and pieces of clothing and machinery flying about the caravan again and the unconscious Calbhach tumbling back into the cockpit. Fortunately, Brennan and D'Arcy grabbed his legs as he passed between their seats and held him tight.

The rolls, dives and flips petered out and the caravan slid upside-down into 1605, materializing within an unlit cellar under the Houses of Parliament before crashing into a wall. There was silence, and the lights went out. The cockpit filled with the kind of language generally found only on lavatory walls.

"Don't anyone move while I assess the damage," said Oleg, craning his neck to look downward at the four metres or so between him and the caravan's domed ceiling. Tarquin saw the fear on his face.

Carefully, Oleg released his harness and, using the leather straps, swung like a gibbon before letting go and tumbling down onto the ceiling. He skittered across the surface before finally managing to bring himself to a halt. He looked up into a score of eyes staring back down at him from the inky blackness, like bats roosting in a cave.

"Hang in there! I'll be as quick as I can." He crawled from the cockpit and disappeared down the corridor and into the engine room. The lights flickered and came on.

Oleg reappeared a few minutes later. "Okay, it's safe. Everyone out."

Unbuckling their harnesses, the leprechauns swung and dropped to the ceiling and crawled from the cockpit into the lounge, dragging Calbhach with them. Tarquin released his harness and, with Oleg's help, lowered himself down to sit quietly on the ceiling, waiting for his stomach to join him.

"You okay, young'un? You looks a bit manky," said Jeremiah, crawling over and peering at him. Jeremiah's Hai Karate aftershave only added to Tarquin's discomfort.

"I really do prefer chair travel." Tarquin, holding his midriff, wondering if it would ever forgive him.

"We must have hit some turbulence coming into 1605," said Jeremiah. "At least you didn't Jackson Pollock."

The mention of Pollock was the final straw. Tarquin's eyes rolled skyward and, clutching his stomach, he leaned forward and retched. His lunch made an unwelcome splattering reappearance.

"There, there, young'un," said Jeremiah, tapping him lightly on his back as he heaved again. 'Let's get yer to the lounge and sits yer down. I'll come back to clean up."

Jeremiah helped Tarquin stagger from the cockpit and sat him down with a bucket.

Oleg appeared in the room, shaking his head. "It's fixable. But I'll need several hours."

"What happened?" asked Jeremiah.

"Strange," said Oleg thoughtfully. "It seems we hit a pile-up of wormhole debris. The drive ruptured—lucky I have a spare. This has never happened before. Someone left it there deliberately." He disappeared for a moment, and then returned with a bag of tools. "Hang on to something, everyone, while I right the ship."

He left again and, soon afterwards, the caravan slowly rolled and settled upright. There were cries of anguish as various leprechauns were hit by sliding debris. Tarquin thanked his lucky stars he hadn't yet made use of his bucket.

A little while later Brennan sat in the lounge holding a bottle of smelling salts under Calbhach's nose. When the leprechaun finally awoke his colourful curses rang through the ship. None the worse for his experience, he was soon organizing his team into tidying the caravan.

Tarquin slowly drank a pint glass of Jeremiah's all-purpose elixir and felt a lot better.

"Okay," said Calbhach, calling everyone to order. "While Oleg fixes the ship we'll look for the door lock to fit the key." He jerked his jaw from side to side as if it was loose. "Let's get dressed."

They trooped into the dressing room and rummaged through the period clothing, which was now lying higgledy-piggledy in a heap. Tarquin selected a fetching black tunic and cloak, plus a wide hat. Satisfied, he headed back to the lounge, leaving Jeremiah and Calbhach trying on different jackets. Inside the dining room, all eyes were on D'Arcy.

"What?" said D'Arcy, buttoning his tunic. Someone tutted.

"Jeepers! You know it's 1605, don't you," said Calbhach, entering.

"Of course."

"And we are on land, not sea," added Finbar.

"Well," said D'Arcy, fidgeting with his collar, "admirals have to go on land sometime."

Jeremiah was the last to arrive. He looked D'Arcy up and down. "Where the hell did you get Lord Nelson's uniform?"

D'Arcy crossed his arms and huffed. "I ruddy nicked it. Where else would I get it?"

"Nicked or not, Lord Nelson isn't around for another century," said Calbhach. "Take it off and dress like everyone else."

Muttering darkly, D'Arcy vanished back into the changing room.

"Are you sure it's Nelson's uniform? It looks very small," said Tarquin, taking off his hat and adjusting his periwig.

"D'Arcy's a master tailor and does the alterations himself," said Brennan. "I think he nicks them just so he can see how they're made."

"Turned up at Charles II's coronation dressed as Oliver Cromwell," said Rhiordan, putting on a hat that dropped over his eyes and ears.

"Nearly caused another ruddy Civil War," added Finbar, checking he had enough shag for his pipe.

"He's got a height complex. He wears uniforms to make himself look bigger and more important," said Calbhach.

To a round of applause, D'Arcy walked back into the dining room wearing plain breeches, a waistcoat and a felt hat.

"Right," said Calbhach, climbing onto a Bender Ale keg and hailing the group. "I've made a copy of the key for each of you, so take yours with you and try every lock you find. Wear your personality rings, but don't turn them on. Hopefully you won't need the rings. No one's going to see your ugly mugs under those wigs and hats. Put on your night goggles and carry your lanterns, just in case we need to go local. And remember, though Oleg will be monitoring you, he also needs to fix the ship. All in all"—he looked at the anxious faces around him—"let's be careful out there."

Despite the slavering tongues of thirty baby Rinchkats fighting for his attention, Berbitedge Sludge was a contented father. His five concubines had gone out for a celestial pond cleansing and he was babysitting his brood of kats.

He loved his brood but, even so, he also loved his Friday nights alone. Ululating quietly—not to wake the three kats sleeping on his head—he prepared for Fight Night, his favourite programme on the Human History Channel, presented by his hero, Dorky Dewis.

Armed with a bucket of ale, a Vissy Viz "Special" dinner and a bag of cellulose, he slipped neatly into his shell. Removing the three sleeping kats from his head he placed them into their rubbery shells, passed wind and turned on the Vissy Viz screen.

"This is an epic," said the presenter, flashing a toothy grin. "Tonight we have another royal event, a special bout all the way from …" He gave his trademark pause for effect. "Human year 1605, in little ole London, England!"

Berbitedge had no idea what "royal" meant, but it usually involved fine clothes, guns, women, and lots and lots of grappling.

Standing by the door, Tarquin looked down on what appeared for all the world to be a group of ebullient garden gnomes dressed in a smorgasbord of oversized tunics, ill-fitting hats and musty wigs, and prayed they'd find the room quickly. Whatever the leprechauns might think of their disguises, any guard who clapped eyes on them was instantly going to know there was something horribly amiss. On the other hand, the caravan in the cellar was a bit of a giveaway, too …

With watches synchronized, the leprechauns left in two groups of three and four. Last out were Jeremiah, Tarquin and Calbhach, heading north towards an oak door at the far end of the cellar. The brick walls ran with water and the pungent smell of rotting vegetation reminded Tarquin of the Tower of London. Walking on the uneven floor in poorly fitting thigh boots made his ankles throb before he'd gone more than a few paces.

Reaching the door, Jeremiah tried the lock with his key, but no luck. Calbhach pulled out his lock-picking kit. Pushing open the door a few seconds later, they surveyed the area revealed by their night goggles.

Satisfied it was empty, they moved along a two-metre-wide passage hewn from stone towards a stairwell. Calbhach climbed the first couple of steps and then beckoned the other two to follow. Slowly, they worked their way up to a vaulted chamber.

Huddled together, they peered over the top of the last step. In front of them was a long cathedral-like aisle with rows of seats banked up on either side. Tarquin stopped to pull his boots up. He caught sight of the benches and went over for a closer look.

"You know where we are!" he said, excitedly, turning around, but no one was there. His heart raced. He tried his communicator.

"Oleg! Come in, Oleg!" he whispered urgently, hoping the Russian was paying attention to his console.

No answer.

Shivering, he hastily retraced his steps, in the hope of finding his colleagues. He reached a dead end and realized he was lost.

How could he be lost? He'd gone in a straight line from the top of the stairs to the nearest bench. He'd thought Jeremiah and Calbhach were right behind him …

Trying to remember the route back to the caravan, he walked for ages, not sure what to do, until he found a stairwell and quickly descended, hoping to find at the bottom the door to the cellar. Instead he saw a long, high corridor, five or six metres wide, running left to right. To the left, in the distance, were several wooden barrels and hay bales. To the right the corridor disappeared into darkness.

"Oleg, Oleg," he said into his wrist communicator.

Again nothing.

Cursing, Tarquin set off down the left-hand corridor towards the barrels.

He'd just reached the first barrel when, out of the darkness behind him, there echoed the sound of heavy footsteps.

Panicking, he looked around for a hiding place. About thirty metres down the corridor on the left there was a door.

The crunch of metal on stone grew closer.

Tarquin hurried forward and, reaching the door, pushed against it.

Locked.

More out of desperation than hope, he tried his key and, to his amazement, the door opened.

He'd found the cellar!

Once inside, he grabbed his visipad and sat against a barrel, hurriedly searching for a picture. Glancing up, he could see through the crack in the door half a dozen soldiers appear out of the darkness in the distance, carrying lanterns and walking toward the cellar door—this door—the light from their lanterns drawing grotesque shadows on the wet walls.

A bearded man in a felt hat filled the visipad and Tarquin sighed. He hurriedly fed the image into the morph ring around his neck, threw his cloak across his shoulders, pulled his hat down across his face and pocketed the night goggles. Holding the unlit lantern close to his chest, he waited, feeling his face seem to ripple and stretch like warm chewing gum. Large tufts of ginger hair erupted from his jaw line and meshed into a beard and moustache. Just as the transformation ended, the spill from the advancing soldiers' lanterns lit up the corridor.

"Who goes there?" shouted one of the men outside the door.

"John Johnson," shouted Tarquin. "My oil's gone."

He pushed open the door, waving his lantern.

"What is with the strange voice, Fawkes? It's only us," said the thin man leading the group.

"Should we put the remaining barrels in the cellar?" asked one of the men.

The leader nodded. The soldiers' lanterns illuminated the vast cellar as the men entered, and Tarquin saw it was piled high with barrels and pieces of broken wood.

"Are you set, Guido? Parliament sits tomorrow."

"We have a problem, my lord." Two men dragged another into view. "He says he's John Johnson."

Tarquin looked at the man and his stomach flipped.

"Interesting," said the thin man. "Bring him into the light."

Facially, it was hard to tell them apart, but the other Johnson was more heavily built and looked much older.

The thin man stared at them in turn and stroked his beard. "Very interesting. Two Johnsons—or rather, two Guy Fawkeses."

He walked up and down examining them closely. "Little and large."

He stopped in front of the older Fawkes. "One of you is a papal hero, and the other must be a government spy."

He moved to Tarquin and placed the tip of his sword under the boy's chin. "What is your name?"

"Do you expect me to talk?" spluttered Tarquin, praying that help would arrive soon.

The thin man leered at him. "No. I expect you to die."

Tarquin gulped.

The thin man laughed at his own joke and stood back to take another look at the two of them. "Which one of you is prepared to kill the king, and die doing so?"

The older Fawkes took a deep breath and threw out his chest. "Like you, my friend, I'm ready to die for the papal cause."

Tarquin turned cold.

"Good!" shouted the thin man. "It's settled."

He pressed the cold metal of his blade hard into Tarquin's neck, almost drawing blood. But then, to Tarquin's surprise, the man turned and pointed his sword at the older man.

"Tie up this papal dog!"

"My lord—!"

"Silence, traitor!"

Fawkes was knocked to the ground, and efficiently bound and gagged.

The thin man turned back to Tarquin and smiled. "You're Cecil's famed spy, sent to befriend Fawkes aren't you? He said you might show yourself. Love the disguise. Had me fooled in this light, until the real Fawkes appeared. What's your name?"

Tarquin's mind went blank. "Yes, yes, I am …" All he could think of was sitting down and drinking a calming cup of tea. "My name is Brooke … Brooke Bond. Son of … James."

"Good fellow, Brooke," said the thin man, slapping him hard on his back. "Tell Lord Cecil we have Fawkes and we'll blow up him—and Parliament—tomorrow as planned."

Tarquin nodded, his heart pounding in his chest. He walked hastily past the troops and back down the corridor towards the stairs.

He seemed to have got away with it.

But then suddenly …

"Aaaaargh!" cried the thin man, his lantern exploding in a ball of fire on the stone floor.

Another lantern exploding, another scream.

Tarquin hugged the wall.

The remaining soldiers drew their swords and backed down the corridor, thrusting their lanterns and swords wildly into the shadows. Dark, angular shapes appeared on both the walls and slowly, one by one, the lights went out.

Trembling, Tarquin fumbled for his night goggles.

"Bloody hell, they're full of gunpowder!" came a rasping Celtic voice. Tarquin saw four shadows, one huge and three midget, by the barrels the men had left outside the room and realized Jeremiah, Calbhach and the Brothers Grimm had arrived from the other end of the corridor.

"You okay, Seebee? Sorry we took so long. Jeremiah saw a statue and took us off to look. You'd gone when we got back."

Jeremiah reached Tarquin and took a penlike instrument from his medical kit.

"Thanks," said Tarquin, "but I'm fine. No need for the magic pen. How did you find me?"

"Uncle Oleg, our guardian angel. He saw lifeforms around you and guided us in."

"I tried calling him," said Tarquin, pressing the morph ring around his neck.

Jeremiah nodded. "He could hear you, but your receiver's faulty—probably damaged during the landing."

"Crikey," said Calbhach, from inside the cellar. "There's enough gunpowder to blow up—"

"The Houses of Parliament," said Tarquin, "and the Book of Dreams is somewhere inside!"

A howling wind came from the end of the corridor near the stairs and an icy blast flew along the passage, knocking everyone off their feet. In the distance, the clatter of a hundred horses' hooves erupted.

"What the—?"

The leprechauns, Tarquin and Jeremiah scrabbled across the stone floor and dived into the cellar. A hundred cavalrymen on grey stallions galloped past, five abreast, followed by a hundred more, disappearing through the wall ahead of them. The noise was deafening. Sparks from the horses' hooves lit up the corridor and set several bales of hay alight as the horsemen disappeared through the wall. A Gordon Highlander, hanging onto the stirrups of a rider, lost his grip and flew sideways, landing with a groan on a pile of straw by the cellar door. Another fell, tumbling headlong, and smashed through a barrel left by the soldiers.

At last all the cavalrymen were gone.

Slowly Calbhach pushed open the cellar door and stepped out. "What the hell just happened?"

"No idea," said Jeremiah, "but they weren't from here." He began stamping out burning hay. If the flames reached the gunpowder they'd all be blown sky-high.

"Er, Calbhach," said Brennan, pointing at an angry, straw-covered Gordon Highlander walking towards them with his sword raised.

"Aeeeeeye for Scotland and the Duke!" screamed the Highlander, charging wide-eyed and flailing his sword wildly. He was upon Calbhach and Brennan so fast there was nothing anyone could do.

As the sword descended, Calbhach spun calmly, side-stepped the blow and fired one shot into the side of the Highlander's chest. The man dropped like a stone, flattening Brennan, whose muffled curses echoed loudly in the vast cellar.

The other two leprechauns yelled and punched the air before breaking into an impromptu jig. Finbar pulled Brennan free and Calbhach tried to high-five Jeremiah.

"Who's da leprechaun, who's da leprechaun?" the Brothers Grimm chanted, thrusting their stubby fingers at Calbhach.

Tarquin and Jeremiah left the jigging and went over to look at the comatose Highlander.

"Waterloo," said Tarquin, examining the man's uniform. "Those soldiers on horses were Scots Greys."

"How'd you know that?" said Jeremiah.

"I used to collect lead figures and paint them. This is going to sound crazy, but I think we just witnessed the Charge of the Scots Greys down a Houses of Parliament cellar corridor in 1605!"

"As long as they don't come back," said Brennan, pulling straw from his beard and stretching his neck. The leprechauns checked the second unconscious Highlander, then carried both men into the cellar and tied them up.

"Crikey! What about Fawkes and the others?" asked Tarquin, looking back along the corridor. Jeremiah took Brennan and Finbar to investigate.

"Oh, no," said Jeremiah. "They're … they're all dead."

"How?"

"Trampled by the horses I must suppose."

Tarquin thought of all the bonfire nights that would never be. The hot dogs, tea, firework displays and home-made cakes. Not to mention the groups of boys roaming the streets of England dragging a paper-filled effigy of Guy Fawkes in a cart and demanding a penny for the Guy.

Jeremiah returned to the cellar carrying Fawkes's hat. He gave it to Tarquin. "No sign of his body. All we found was this. Add it to your collection."

A sense of relief spread through Tarquin as he took the hat. He smiled and looked at Jeremiah. "Fawkes must have escaped!"

Then his expression changed. "One of the soldiers said they were going to blow up Fawkes and Parliament with the gunpowder. He called me Cecil's spy. That doesn't make sense! Fawkes was discovered and put on trial. It was a plot by Catholics to blow up the King!"

"Well, something's brewing," said Jeremiah.

"Wait a moment." Tarquin pulled out his visipad. "They mentioned Robert Cecil, the king's adviser. This is what was written about him after his death:

The King's misuser, the Parliament's abuser,
Hath left his plotting, is now a-rotting.

"Why would Cecil create a plot to blow up the king and Parliament?" said Jeremiah.

"Power, prestige, who knows? But, with the king and his court gone, the country would be open for a coup d'état and Cecil would be centre frame to take over."

Jeremiah snorted. "That's pretty fanciful stuff."

Tarquin pointed to his visipad. "It's only four years since a certain Robert Devereux was executed after attempting a coup, and guess who came up smelling of roses?"

"More to the point, what happens when these soldiers don't return?" asked Finbar.

"They'll send a search party," said Calbhach. "Come on, let's hide the bodies."

As they laid the corpses in the cellar, Brennan picked up several knotted ropes.

"Look," he said. "The Scottish soldiers—they're gone!"

"They can't have escaped. We'd have seen them," said Calbhach.

Tarquin was equally puzzled. "Could they have simply disappeared back to their own time, like the cavalry must have?"

"Well," said Jeremiah, "that's a mystery we're going to have to leave unsolved. We need a new fallguy fast, for any search party to meet."

"A fall Guy," said Tarquin.

Jeremiah sniffed. "I was hoping you weren't going to say that."

Calbhach piped up. "Fawkes was a big man!"

Slowly, everyone turned and looked at Jeremiah.

"What, me? No way, I look nothing like him."

Calbhach jumped up and tapped the morph ring around Jeremiah's neck. "You don't need to."

"Oh, bejeebies …"

Jeremiah sat in the corridor, waiting.

"There's someone coming, left-hand side," said Oleg on the communicator.

Jeremiah reacted immediately. "Quick, get ready."

Taking up positions in the cellar, the others watched as the big wrestler, now looking like an overweight Guy Fawkes, put on his hat.

"Fawkes, is everything set?" A man appeared out of the gloom, walking towards Jeremiah. Another followed.

Jeremiah nodded.

"No visitors?"

"Yes, some soldiers. But I hid them in the cellar."

The man's eyebrows meshed. "You hid them? They came to help you move the powder!"

"Well, er," said Jeremiah, scratching his false beard.

The two men stepped back and rested their hands on their swords.

"Is everything set?"

"Heavens to Betsies!" cried Jeremiah, jumping up and grabbing the men by their coat-fronts. "You don't half ask a lot of questions."

"I'm your friend!" spluttered one of the men, his eyes bulging, unable to speak properly as he dangled a metre off the ground.

With a look of furious indignation, Jeremiah slammed them both into a hay bale, knocking them unconscious, and then sat on them.

A million light years away, Berbitedge Sludge leapt from his shell, tendrils flying, as he hollered and mimicked, as best he could, a leprechaun jig.

The two men awoke to find ten pairs of eyes looking at them.

"Circus midgets!" cried one, falling off the bale and crabbing across the floor before thudding into the wall.

Calbhach growled. Only Jeremiah's restraining hand stopped the leprechaun from belting the man.

"Who are you?" asked Tarquin, looking at items taken from the men's pockets while they were unconscious.

"I am Lord Monteagle. We were just checking on the cellars."

Jeremiah, still looking like Fawkes, moved forward and shook his head at the man sitting on the bale.

"You should be stopping me, not helping me blow up the king!"

The man's face went pale and he dropped his gaze. "If I tell you, will we live?"

"Of course," said Calbhach, leering at him. "We circus midgets only eat humans on Wednesdays."

"We were sent to find Fawkes and the soldiers. Make sure that all was ready," said Monteagle, looking at his companion. "The soldiers were to help Fawkes finish setting the gunpowder."

Helped to their feet, the men were given water and continued telling their story. After the blowing up of king and Parliament, Catholics would be blamed and, in the confusion, Cecil and his sympathizers would step in to save England from its Papist enemies—a coup by any other name.

"We're looking for a book hidden in the cellar. Where is it?" asked Tarquin.

The two men looked at each other. Again it was Monteagle who spoke. "Fawkes found a book when he was stacking the powder barrels. I stole it and passed it on to Cecil."

Tarquin groaned and slumped against the cellar wall. "Why is everything so ruddy complicated?"

"We need the wisdom of Solomon," said Jeremiah.

"He wasn't that sharp," replied Brennan, shaking his head.

Tarquin shoved himself upright and gazed at Monteagle.

"You're going to take us to Cecil."

"He'll kill us after this!" the lord cried. "We speak through an intermediary, and only in a coaching inn near Ware."

"Cecil's too clever to be personally involved," said Jeremiah.

"Though I did hear talk of a meeting at his manor, Theobalds House, tonight," said the other captive, eyeing Brennan's sword as the leprechaun swung it threateningly before him.

Calbhach beckoned Tarquin and Jeremiah. "Okay," he said in a low voice, "we're going to crash his meeting and give him a good old-fashioned leprechaun how-de-do."

Jeremiah went back to the two men. "Best get away from here as fast as you can. There'll be no big bang, today or tomorrow."

The men turned and, lanterns held high to guide their way, ran as fast as they could.

Jeremiah, Tarquin and the leprechauns hurried back to the Willerby Vogue. Once inside, the leprechauns scampered to the kitchen to prepare a stew. Work and excitement had made them ravenously hungry. Calbhach went to input coordinates into the flight computer for Sir Robert Cecil's home, Theobalds House.

Tarquin and Jeremiah found Oleg inside the engine room.

"I've replaced the drive, but we may experience a little discomfort when we set off. She's a bit shaken about, but she should hold together," the Russian said, smelling like a drain and covered in gaffer tape, bits of wire and brown, effervescing sludge. "The good news is that I've got the cloaking working again, so we can hedge-hop!"

Tarquin saw an anarchic smile flash across Oleg's face and felt his stomach lurch.

'Not to worry, young'un," said Jeremiah, seeing Tarquin's pale face. "Local travel really isn't as bumpy as people say it is."

Later, Calbhach called everyone together in the lounge. Over several fortifying bowls of Irish stew and a few medicinal Bender Ales, they formulated a plan. They would materialize, cloaked, inside the great hall at Theobalds House, confront Cecil with their knowledge of his plan, and extort from him the Book of Dreams under threat of informing the king. And they would "persuade" Cecil to abandon his plan to blow up Parliament.

"What are you doing in my house?"

Tarquin started. Standing at the far end of the room was a slightly built, crooked man, almost dwarfish, with reddish hair and a tawny beard.

Jeremiah clapped his hands. "Cecil, my boy," he said with a smile. "We're your worst nightmare!"

Robert Cecil shuffled forward and looked at the faces before him. A faint smirk flashed across his pale face and his watery green eyes sparkled in the moonlight that poured in from the large windows. "You have a story to tell me?"

The clatter of footsteps broke the silence and half a dozen armed men appeared in the doorway behind him, pointing their guns at Jeremiah and the others.

Cecil raised his hand and looked at the big man. "I don't believe I'm in any danger, am I?"

Tarquin felt the hair on his neck rise as he watched Cecil coolly size each of them up.

"You have a book that we want," growled Calbhach.

"Hah! A circus midget. This gets better and better."

Before Calbhach could react, Jeremiah grabbed the leprechaun's collar and held it tightly. "Relax, tiger."

An irascible sneer spread across Cecil's face. "A book, you say?" He flourished a hand theatrically in the air. "The room's full of them."

"The book that was found in the cellar below Parliament," said Tarquin.

Cecil's icy stare returned. "Enough of this."

He clicked his fingers and the armed men moved into the room, fanning out.

"This is not a good idea, Sir Robert," said Tarquin, seeing Calbhach and the rest of the leprechauns slowly reach for their Bosuns.

Too late to stop them …

All at once the soldiers collapsed unconscious to the floor. Only Cecil remained standing, his face pale and his body trembling, his sneer gone.

"Now," said Calbhach, moving toward Cecil and kicking him hard on the shin. "This circus midget wants you to do something for us."

Cecil howled, swearing loudly as he hopped on one leg.

Calbhach kicked his other shin and Cecil fell to the ground.

"My colleague's going to ask you something," the leprechaun said, baring his gold teeth and hissing loudly. He followed as Cecil desperately hauled himself across the floor until his back was against the wall.

"What do you want from me?" cried the most powerful man in England piteously, waving his hands in front of his face as Calbhach, Brennan, Ardal and the others closed in on him.

Tarquin popped his head over the wall of leprechauns and smiled. "Hi, Sir Robert. Let's start over again, shall we? My name's Tarquin, Tarquin Jenkins, and I'd like you to listen very carefully to what I'm going to tell you."

Cecil nodded, "Just keep these creatures from me!"

"That's up to you," said Tarquin. "If you don't give me the answers I want, my friends will hurt you, your family, and your family's family. Then they'll start on your domesticated animals."

"Are you sent from Satan himself?" cried Cecil, cowering even more closely against the wall.

"Yes, Sir Robert. Yes, we are. Now, where's the book Fawkes gave you?"

Cecil pointed to his desk. "In the drawer."

Jeremiah moved swiftly to the desk, yanked open the drawer and grabbed up a large leather-bound tome with metal clasps, a mysterious wooden baton and several other, smaller books, including what looked like a diary.

"Got it!"

Tarquin smiled. "We know all about your plot and, frankly, Satan doesn't like it. We're going to go now, but our lord and master"—Tarquin pointed dramatically to the floor—"is watching you … There'll be no blowing up Parliament!"

"Let's go!" shouted Calbhach as more footsteps approached.

The interlopers rushed from the room and into the hall, where the cloaked caravan sat waiting.

"All aboard!" crackled Oleg's voice through the caravan's speakers.

They piled in and raced to the cockpit. A line of numbers descended on the screen in front of Oleg.

"Buckle up!, Wormhole opening in 5–4–3–2–1."

Tarquin locked his belt just as the caravan shook violently, fell over, rolled several times, spun, and then soared dizzyingly upwards.

On their way back to 2340, Calbhach received a message from BIFS headquarters. Jules Rigsworth had been cleared of all charges, and wanted to see the travellers when they got back.

When Jeremiah heard the news, he punched his fists in the air and went berserk, racing up and down the ship and dancing a routine that had the leprechauns joining in, all trying to replicate a dance that soon became known as the Jerky Jeremiah.

"A night at the Yelts Inn wouldn't go amiss," the big man shouted above the clapping and Celtic fiddle music, ending his routine by spinning on his backside with his large feet pumping in the air.

Chapter 18

Finding the Amulet

By the time the Willerby Vogue had landed in 2340 and its engines had rumbled to a stop, Jules was already knocking on the caravan door. Archie and Alice were with him.

"Calbhach!" he shouted as the door opened and a tsunami of arms, legs, and hugs enveloped him. "Good to see you all!"

The crowd moved as one joyous mass towards the lifts. Droids, humans and aliens lined their route, clapping and cheering. Arriving at Jules's office complex, they agreed that, after freshening up and finding a change of clothes, they'd all meet back at the lifts at 7pm and go to the Yelts Inn for a debrief, followed by food, ale and a celebration.

Before leaving for his room, Tarquin grabbed Jules's arm. "You saved my life, but you need to know what's happening. We have to talk."

"Okay," said Jules. "Have a shower and be in my office in an hour."

Tarquin shook his head. "No, we need to meet somewhere unexpected." He pointed to his ear, and mouthed the words, "I think someone's listening."

"Any ideas where we could go?" whispered Jules, looking perplexed.

"The room with the books."

"See you there in an hour."

"I'll bring Jeremiah and Calbhach with me," said Tarquin, still sotto voce. "They're involved too."

He turned and, knapsack on his shoulder, headed for his room.

Jules was last to reach the repository.

Jeremiah closed the door behind him as Tarquin looked around at the empty room before taking the leather-and-metal-bound tome from his knapsack.

Jules read the silver inscription on the cover. "You found the Book of Dreams!"

He took it from Tarquin and tried to open it.

Jeremiah held him back. "Careful, Jules. Best check first for traps and funny things."

The big man took out an instrument that looked more eggwhisk than trap-spotter. The others watched, open-mouthed, as Jeremiah hopped and danced like an aboriginal rain-maker around the book, waving and thrusting the eggwhisk at it.

Finally he gave the book a last tap with the whisk. "Looks okay to me," he said, standing back. "Over to you, Calbhach."

Jules gingerly gave the book to Calbhach. Carefully, the leprechaun put it on a collapsable table.

A blackened clasp shaped like two interlocking fists sealed the covers. In the middle of the union was a keyhole. Calbhach tested the clasp but, as anticipated, it was locked.

"There's not much I can't open," he said, "but dis is very old and tricky, very tricky, with lots of ta dummy mechanics." He glanced up at Jules and added, "But it's doable."

Opening the Gladstone bag by his feet, he took out an embossed leather tool bag and rolled it open on the floor.

"Those are beautiful," said Tarquin, looking at the dozens of small bone-handled instruments pouched in the leather roll.

"Tuatha Dé Danann locksmiths hand their tools down from generation to generation," said Calbhach, selecting several instruments.

A few minutes later he had the clasp open. "Dere we go, for sure!"

Jules lifted the leather cover. The first thing visible inside was a square of folded parchment. Tarquin took it out and opened it, then read the message aloud:

Dearest Tarquin,

Much has happened since I left the journal with Samuel Pepys. The amulet was found before I could get to it, but I hope all is not lost. The current owner has no idea of its power or how it works, so I have left it with him. There is also a Frenchman searching for it, and he, by contrast, may understand its true nature. You must get to it before him. You will also know that the Griddlebacks and the Leche are after the amulet.

Read the Book of Dreams. Learn everything about the amulet, and keep the book safe. It is the only key to using and destroying the amulet. Without the book, the amulet is a mere trinket.

I left a codex with the book. Find what you need, then use the cookbook and needlecraft book.

Love,

Dad

P.S. Science wasn't your strong point, but you'll get it right in the end.

Tarquin smiled. "No, science has never been my strong point, but I know whose it was!" He turned to Jules. "Who does my father mean by 'a Frenchman'?"

Jeremiah turned pale. "Seebee, you've met him."

"Me?"

"On my boat."

"The hairy old naked geezer?"

Jeremiah nodded. "Loopy Nostrils."

"He knows about the amulet!"

"Yes. It would explain why he appeared on the Silvery Moon. He wasn't just lost, like we thought. He was looking for it."

Tarquin took the baton from his knapsack. Since their return, he'd examined it more closely. It was an interlocking wooden puzzle.

"Codex Atlanticus," he explained to the others, realizing that this was no explanation at all. He turned some of the wooden segments.

"Let me open it," said Calbhach, sticking out a hand.

Tarquin smiled. "I'd love you to do that, but it's a red herring, a party trick of my dad's. The answer is in the last paragraph of his note, where it says, 'You'll get it right in the end.'"

Tarquin looked at the baton's two ends. On one was the faint mark of an arrowhead. He placed the puzzle horizontally on the table with the arrow pointing to the right.

"How many words are there in the last paragraph?"

Jules counted. "Fourteen."

"Are you sure?"

Jules read out the words again. "P.S. Science wasn't your strong point, but you'll get it right in the end."

"My father tried to trick me with this once before. The 'P.S.' counts as two, so fifteen is the answer we're looking for."

Tarquin inspected the puzzle anew. There were seven interlocking hexagonal pieces of wood, one larger piece at each end and five smaller ones in the body. He counted up each hexagonal from the bottom and down again until he got to number 15, which was the centrepiece. Carefully, he turned the puzzle one revolution right.

"Okay, Calbhach, if I hold the centre hexagon, can you pull the other pieces away, starting with the endpiece on the right."

Tarquin gripped the middle piece of wood firmly while Calbhach eased the endpiece off.

"Now the smaller ones on the right," said Tarquin.

Calbhach teased the two pieces away.

"Now repeat the process on the left."

Calbhach did as instructed.

Tarquin removed the last remaining hexagon by drawing it slowly along the baton from the right, before passing the piece to Jules.

"There should be coordinates etched into the wood on the inside surface. Use the cookbook to find them."

Jules took out his glasses and peered at the hexagon. "Well done, Seebee! You're right—I can see the markings, I'll check them."

He produced his pocket versions of Mrs Beeton's two books and began comparing the markings on the hexagon to their contents.

"How'd you know all this?" asked Calbhach.

"My dad was always playing with puzzles. He took drawings from Leonardo and made a puzzle just like this for my birthday one year. When I saw this version and the clues in his letter, I knew what he wanted me to do."

"Why not simply break the thing to get the message?"

"It's designed to burst into flames if you don't remove the hexagons in the right order. My dad used to stick a fire cracker inside. Try it if you like." Tarquin grinned as he passed the tube to Calbhach. "I wouldn't if I were you, though."

The leprechaun sniffed it. "You're right—except this is packed with old-fashioned gunpowder, not just a puny firecracker. It would blow your hand off if it exploded!"

"Oh, my goodness …" said Jules.

The others turned to look.

"You okay?" said Calbhach.

Jules nodded, pointing at the books. "We have to go to Leonardo da Vinci's home in Florence. History tells us that he was there on 18 October 1503. I have the coordinates." Sounding increasingly concerned, he continued. "But there's a problem. The best wormhole for the trip opens tomorrow. It'll take us to a bakery opposite the house— but it stays open for only five hours!"

Tarquin shook his head. "Oh, no. Not another bakery!"

"How long to wait before we can get back if we miss the deadline?" asked Calbhach.

"Fifteen days." Jules looked around the room, noting the concern on his friends' faces. "I'll book the Raggedy Rook room in the Yelts Inn. We can discuss a plan with everyone before we celebrate. See you there in a couple of hours."

He turned to go, but found Tarquin standing in his way.

"Can I have a chat?" said Tarquin. "Alone."

"Of course."

"See you later in the Yelts Inn, Seebee," said Jeremiah, following Calbhach from the repository.

Tarquin picked up the Book of Dreams and looked at his uncle. "You saved my life, but I got Rhia killed."

"Tarquin—"

"No buts," said Tarquin, opening the book. "Once we find the amulet I'm going to use the knowledge from this book to go back to Steeple Snoring and right a terrible wrong."

Jules watched his nephew shake with emotion, and tears well up in his eyes.

"Uncle Jules, I have to …"

As Tarquin's head bowed and he began to sob, Jules stepped forward and put his arms around him.

"I know, Seebee, I'd want to do the same. Nothing wrong in that. But I can't let you read the book." Jules drew away from Tarquin and looked into his eyes. "It's too dangerous to take on alone. I'm locking the book away until we have the amulet." He took the book and put it under his arm. "Trust me."

Tarquin reached for the cricket bat around his neck.

By the time Archie, Alice and Tarquin arrived in the Raggedy Rook room, the leprechauns, Jules, Jeremiah and Oleg were already sitting around a circular table in the centre of it.

"Take a seat," said Jules.

As they found chairs he booted up a tablet. "I've asked an old friend of mine to join us. She and her colleagues have a particular set of skills we need."

The screen filled with the image of a long-haired, red-headed woman, smoking a cheroot. "Georgia Blade!" exclaimed Archie, turning to Alice.

Several of the leprechauns, including Calbhach, growled and gave the screen a one-fingered salute.

"Yes, it's me, humans," said Georgia, pulling on the cigar. "And … others."

Jules watched his friends' reactions to the sight of Georgia.

"I bet she's got those filthy clurichauns with her," muttered Calbhach, taking his pint and downing it. Finbar and D'Arcy followed suit. The muttering continued among the leprechauns, and most of it was of a nature to peel the paint from the walls, if most of it hadn't peeled already.

Tarquin was perplexed. From what he could see, this Georgia Blade woman looked rather, well, hot. Obviously Archie thought the same, because he was trying so very hard to look indifferent in front of Alice.

"That's enough!" shouted Jules eventually, clapping his hands. "I know only too well that leprechauns and clurichauns like nothing better than ripping each others' throats out, but we need you all if we are to find the amulet and stop the Griddlebacks and the Leche."

"What's in it for us?" said Georgia.

"It's all about money with you and your filth!" shouted Calbhach, standing up and shaking his fist at the screen. "Earth is under threat and there's an amulet out there that, in the wrong hands, could destroy us all, and yet you want to discuss a reward?"

Jules rested his hand on Calbhach's shoulder. "Georgia, our spies have information that might interest you. Your sister may still be alive. We think the Leche have her in captivity."

Georgia dragged hard on her cheroot and leaned forward. Her eyes were ablaze and her lips quivered. "How do you know this?"

"Your mind-mapping of Prince Ruttfarter gave us a lead."

"I'll help you," said Georgia, stubbing out the cheroot in the palm of her hand. "But promise you'll use all your resources to help find my sister when this is done."

"Deal." said Jules. "I'll take Georgia, Archie, Alice and the clurichauns to stop the Griddlebacks from kidnapping the Beatles. We'll start from the Bingley Five Rise. Calbhach will lead his leprechauns along with Jeremiah, Tarquin and Oleg to Italy and fetch the amulet."

Jeremiah checked his Look-Sees. The jump area in the Florence bakery had proved to consist of a dark, wide corridor, and was luckily empty. The leprechauns and Oleg would remain in the caravan to monitor the progress of the two humans, ready to help if required. Jeremiah and Tarquin, wearing clothing of the period, each took a small bag and a Bosun.

They opened the caravan door.

"Doesn't look like a bakery to me. More like a dungeon," said Tarquin, stepping onto a stone floor and looking around.

"Smells like an abattoir." Jeremiah coughed as the pungent stench of excrement and rotting meat filled his nostrils.

Making their way along the corridor, they picked through the slimy, rubbish-strewn floor. Squealing rats startled Tarquin.

"Beatus! Beatus!" came a cry from the semi-darkness.

Tarquin and Jeremiah hugged the wet wall and turned on their night-vision goggles; seen through the goggles, the blackness turned to a sickly green. They could now see, hung by chains on the wall, a human form, its thin legs and feet dangling. Its head turned, staring wide-eyed in their direction.

"Oh, crap," said Tarquin, tugging at Jeremiah's sleeve. "It's Loopy Nostrils! What do we do?"

"We can't leave him locked up down here. We must help him," sighed Jeremiah.

"He'll slow us down—"

"Yes," said Jeremiah, "but no one deserves to be left chained up in this hole. We can take him back to the caravan. He's still wanted by Jules."

"Okay, let's do it."

Jeremiah followed Tarquin to where the man was hanging.

"Beatus, beatus," moaned Nostradamus.

"Keep your noise down and stop calling me that. I've no idea what it means," said Tarquin as Jeremiah worked to unlock Loopy Nostrils's chains.

"It means you're blessed. Nostra thinks you're special," whispered Jeremiah. He chuckled. "I think you're special, too, but in a different sense."

Soon enough, Jeremiah was successful and the chains fell asunder.

Nostradamus dropped to the ground, babbling, and hopped about like a frog, rubbing his chafed wrists, his eyes the size of duck eggs. Pointing at Tarquin he shook violently and shrieked, "Maximas tibi gratias ego!"

Before Jeremiah could grab him, he'd scurried off down the corridor.

"Oi! Where you going?" shouted Jeremiah. He shook his fist at the disappearing bag of bones. "There's gratitude for you."

"Now the whole of Italy will know we're here," grumbled Tarquin, moving rapidly alongside Jeremiah down the corridor in the opposite direction. "We shouldn't have let him go. Remember, he's looking for the amulet too," he added, watching a line of rodents the size of small cats run along the wall of the dungeon.

"He's the proverbial bad smell in the house, bloody hard to get rid of, so if he gets out of here I have a feeling we'll see Loopy again."

They moved up to the ground floor, listening for movement. Thankfully, the building seemed empty. Eventually they found the door to the street and, checking that no one was guarding it, stepped out into the sun.

"There's Leo's house. Let's get inside." Jeremiah began walking towards two open iron gates. He and Tarquin ambled through and on up the path to the front door, then slipped inside.

"More time-travellers, I presume."

They spun around. Half a dozen men stood brandishing cudgels, swords and daggers.

"Come to steal my art, have you?" said a middle-aged fellow, walking stiffly towards them. Leonardo da Vinci. He was very ordinary-looking for one of the greatest geniuses of human history.

"What is this?" said Leonardo, as one of his men grabbed Jeremiah's head and pulled it back. Leonardo thrust under Jeremiah's nose the aeroplane picture that Nostradamus had pilfered from the Silvery Moon.

"No idea."

Leonardo turned to Tarquin and sneered. "If you don't tell me, boy, I'll have your friend dismembered in front of you."

Tarquin pulled against his captors but they held firm. He looked at Jeremiah then at Leonardo. "It's a horse carriage," he gasped.

"Yeah, right," said Leonardo, scrutinizing the picture.

"A hundred horses are needed to pull it."

Leonardo waved the picture in his face. "The lunatic Frenchman said it flew in the sky and made a terrifying noise!"

Tarquin laughed and shook his head. "French pigs might fly. Whoever heard of a carriage in the air?"

Jeremiah joined in the laughter until Leonardo snapped his fingers and, staring straight at Tarquin, said, "The Frenchman drew many things and told me incredible stories. You are lying. You and your companion are from the Devil's future." Leonardo drew his sword, pointed it at Tarquin's heart and turned to Jeremiah. "Isn't that so?"

Tarquin saw the fear in Jeremiah's eyes. "Yes, yes, we are from the future," the big man gabbled.

Leonardo's men genuflected and kissed their crucifixes. Leonardo himself didn't move. "How did you get here?"

As Jeremiah hesitated, Leonardo pressed the sword into Tarquin's chest.

"In a box—a large, upright, rectangular blue box," said Jeremiah.

Tarquin read Leonardo's mind. The thought of this genius using their ship to travel through time was too much to comprehend.

"Take me to this box," said Leonardo, sheathing his sword.

They left the house, crossed the road and entered the bakery where the caravan was. Going downstairs, they rounded the corner and found Calbhach standing in front of the caravan, growling.

"A circus midget! This gets more interesting by the minute," said Leonardo, laughing and pointing his sword at Calbhach.

"I swear, I'll batter da next bloody human who says I'm from da circus," said Calbhach, waving his hand in the air.

Bosun light pulses lit up the corridor and Leonardo and his men slumped to the floor.

"Bloody neanderthal," said Calbhach, walking over and kicking Leonardo hard in his rump.

Tarquin sighed heavily. "Thanks, Calbhach. I'm not sure how we would have got out of that one."

Calbhach nodded as the rest of the leprechauns appeared from the shadows.

"We still don't have the amulet, and the clock is ticking," said Jeremiah.

Calbhach regarded the prone form of Leonardo. "I think a little chat in da caravan is in order."

Tarquin saw a malicious sneer spread across Calbhach's face. "Don't harm him. He's still got a lot of creativity left in him."

"I'll give him ruddy 'circus midget'," said Calbhach under his breath as he dragged Leonardo by his boots into the caravan, clearly enjoying the thud, thud, thud of the artist's head as it hit the lip of each stair.

Leonardo's equally unconscious thugs soon followed, dragged into the caravan and then tied up.

Calbhach emerged from the interrogation flexing his arms. "The idiot gave it to a model's husband as payment for a debt!"

"Did he give you a name?" said Jeremiah.

Calbhach looked down at a piece of paper. "I t'ink it's Lisa Gherardini del Giocondo. Sounds like a type of posh chocolates to me. Her husband is away on business so she's going to visit Leo this afternoon in his apartment for coffee and sketching."

The leprechauns broke into bawdy laughter. Puzzled, Tarquin looked at Jeremiah, who rolled his eyes.

While they waited in Leo's apartment for Lisa's arrival, Tarquin saw half a dozen books lying on a table and went to look at them. He signalled to Jeremiah.

"Nostra's books."

Jeremiah, still keeping his eye on the door, went over to look.

"Your copy of Scouting for Boys," said Tarquin, handing him the volume. Jeremiah quickly went through the rest of the pile. There was a first edition of Tolstoy's War and Peace, two handwritten manuscripts entitled The History of Cardenio and Love's Labour's Won, and what looked suspiciously like the Magna Carta.

"He has travelled, has old Loopy," said Jeremiah, scratching his head before pocketing Scouting for Boys and the presumed Magna Carta and stuffing the two manuscripts and the Tolstoy into his backpack.

A noise came from outside the door. Hastily, they took up positions around the room.

A key turned in the lock and a woman walked in.

"You're kidding," said Tarquin, rather too loudly.

"Who's there?" she asked.

The leprechauns and the two humans came out of hiding.

"We're not going to harm you," said Jeremiah, holding out his hand. "Are you Lisa Gherardini del Giocondo?"

Terrified, the woman turned to run, but Calbhach and Seamus barred the door. She started screaming so Jeremiah covered her mouth and held her tight.

"We're not going to harm you," he repeated. "We just want to talk."

She continued to thrash wildly in his arms.

"Will you keep quiet, woman!"

Eventually she tired, stopped fighting and nodded. Jeremiah slowly uncovered her mouth.

"I'm very sorry to have frightened you, but are you Lisa Gherardini del Giocondo?"

The woman nodded.

"We want the amulet your husband gave you. Do you have it?" asked Tarquin.

Lisa hastily removed it from around her neck and threw it on the floor. "Take it. I never liked it anyway."

Tarquin picked it up and looked into her hazel eyes. "Thank you. I am truly sorry we scared you."

His quiet tone seemed to calm her. Gently, he took her hand. "One day, you'll live in a palace and the whole of Paris and the world beyond will come to admire you."

"Me?"

Tarquin nodded.

Her eyes grew large. "I ... I don't understand."

"Time to go," said Jeremiah.

"There's five minutes to take-off and we have visitors," shouted Finbar, seeing several men running across the courtyard towards the building. Tarquin leaned forward and kissed the trembling model on the cheek.

"Goodbye, Mona Lisa."

She gazed quizzically at him as he made his exit. A faint, enigmatic smile crossed her face.

"Goodbye, strange foreigner."

She closed the door behind him.

The intruders rushed downstairs and across the street to the bakery. They'd only just jumped into their seats when the wormhole began closing.

"Where's Leonardo?"

Calbhach looked at Oleg. "I thought …"

Oleg shook his head.

"Quick, boys, ditch them!"

The leprechauns made a mad dash to the ship's holding pen and released the door. Leonardo and his friends stood in the pen, motionless.

"Out, run, get out!" shouted the leprechauns, chasing them towards the caravan door. When the last two men fell on the floor, pushed unceremoniously from the caravan, it wobbled.

"Quick!" cried Calbhach, dragging D'Arcy by the ear back to the control room. "Run!"

The Brothers Grimm leapt into the laps and open arms of Rhiordan and D'Arcy, who had sensibly strapped themselves into their seats. Jeremiah scooped up Calbhach, and also managed to grab hold of Tarquin's hands.

"Yeeeeehaaaaaa," cried Oleg, as a classic riff from an electric guitar rent the air and the caravan climbed steeply, leaving sixteenth-century Italy behind.

On the way back to 2340 they had to wait for three hours for a connecting wormhole to open, so Tarquin slipped away unnoticed and found an empty bedroom in the Vogue. Shutting the door, he sat on the bed with the amulet. They now had everything he needed to make the journey back to Steeple Snoring in 2015 and save Rhia. He lay back on the bed and gazed at the ceiling, thinking of her smile, her dimples and her swishing ponytail. What stuck in his mind most of all was the glint in her eye when he spoke of his father leaving clues throughout history to a magical amulet. He looked at the amulet. It was round, about the size of a jamjar lid, and made from a dull silvery metal. In the centre was a blood-red, translucent oval stone set in gold. Carved into the metal around the stone were shapes, diagrams and ancient Nerydire texts that Tarquin could read, but made little sense of; a series of mythological fables was his best guess.

There was a knock on the door. "Tarquin?"

"Yes?" he said, jumping off the bed and hiding the amulet.

Calbhach opened the door and studied him with a concerned look on his warty face. "You okay? You disappeared. We couldn't find you. Want to eat? We're about to make a stew."

"Of course," said Tarquin, slipping the amulet into his pocket. "I'm on my way."

A while later, with the Willerby hovering over the 1936 Olympics in Berlin, Jeremiah and Tarquin watched Jesse Owens take gold in the 100 metres. The leprechauns had made one of their epic stews.

"So," said Jeremiah, "Leonardo de Vinci may not have been the genius history tells us he was."

"What do you mean?" Tarquin respomnded.

The big man took out a notebook he'd found on Leonardo's apartment floor and gave it to Tarquin. "Look familiar?"

Tarquin flicked through the pages and smiled. "They look just like Leo's inventions!"

"I reckon Loopy Nostrils went looking for the amulet, got trapped by Leo, and told him all about his time travels."

"I've really gone off Leo," said Tarquin, ladling stew into his bowl.

"Still, can't deny he's a great painter," replied Jeremiah. "And he has good taste in women."

"I hope Loopy got away, I'd hate to think he's trapped in the sixteenth century."

The hours passed quickly until they landed in 2340 and set off for their accommodations.

RECKITT VANGELOS AND THE SPECTRES OF CALI

"Shall I compare thee to a summ—aahhhggg!" screamed the male Leche as Gruilash Vandergaard fired a single shot into his arm. Immediately, six Leche guns trained on Gruilash.

"It was just a friggin' joke!" shouted an emaciated leather-clad blonde. Her voice echoed in the vast underground chamber as she rushed to the side of her screaming companion. He was writhing on the floor in a pool of pale yellow blood. "You didn't have to friggin' shoot him!"

She got up and walked menacingly toward Gruilash, her molecular-disruptor gun pointed at his head.

In her fury she came too close. Gruilash's leathery fist crashed into her face and, blood pouring from her nose, she folded like a paper serviette.

Gruilash snarled, bile steaming and frothing around his snout.

He turned to look into the vapid face of Reckitt Vangelos. "I don't ever do humour."

Reckitt nodded, and the Leche lowered their guns. The company of Griddlebacks did the same.

"Wise choice," said Gruilash, holstering his weapon. "Now, let's move on."

A Griddleback stepped forward and handed Reckitt a backpack.

"Fill your boots," said Gruilash, causing laughter to spread among the Griddlebacks.

Reckitt looked inside the bag and hissed in eager anticipation. His pale blue eyes shone as he licked his canines. He began pulling half-litre bottles of blood from the bag and passing them to his colleagues.

"There's plenty more … if you're interested," said Gruilash, watching the skeletal figures rush to feed. "Animals," he muttered, spitting phlegm on the ground, where it fizzed and boiled.

"What are they?" asked his lieutenant, covering his snout and smarting at the smell of human blood.

"Bipedal, hematophagous primatoid leeches. We're going to use them for a bit of hirudotherapy."

The lieutenant shot Gruilash a puzzled look. He was not from an educated clan, nor had he seen Leche before.

Gruilash shook his head. "When these animals catch Redhair and her humans, they'll drink them dry."

The lieutenant smirked. This was language he could understand.

Gruilash turned back to the Leche and waited for them to finish gorging.

Sated, Reckitt wiped blood from his lips and ran his fingers through his blonde, shoulder-length hair, shaking as the warm human blood coursed through his body.

He turned to Gruilash, the icy blue pupils now flecked with crimson. "Why the call?"

"I've found Redhair."

Excitement spread through the Leche.

Reckitt's lips were rouged with blood. "And …?"

"I thought we could come to a business arrangement," said Gruilash.

"I want to slit her throat and mount her head on my hoverbike," snarled a pallid stick of a Leche, drawing long, bony fingers viciously across her thin, sallow throat.

Gruilash laughed. "You can have any part of her you like, except her head. I have a pickling jar waiting for that."

The thought of Georgia Blade's head finally marinading in his kitchen made him chuckle, and he snorted a long stream of hot bile.

"And for us?" asked Reckitt.

"The usual."

"We want fresh. No putrid corpses this time."

"She's travelling with fat, bloated dwarfs … plus Jules Rigsworth and two human youngsters," said Gruilash.

Reckitt's eyes flared. "How young?"

Gruilash leered. "Teenagers. Just think of all that tasty young blood, crammed full of hormones …"

"What do you want from us?" said Reckitt, licking his pale lips.

"Your unquestioning brutality."

"We'll need equipment." Reckitt was trying to control his feelings. The thought of teenage human blood made him emotional.

Gruilash snapped his fingers and three Griddlebacks moved forward carrying a large chest. "Lieutenant Raiken and ten of my men will accompany you."

Reckitt nodded agreement, and the Leche descended on the chest, pulling out the guns, grenades and ammunition it contained.

"You'll need a vehicle to drive there," said Gruilash, looking disdainfully at their assortment of custom chopper hovercycles. "I have just the thing."

"Where are we going?" asked Reckitt as he followed Gruilash over to a large open space.

"Liverpool, England, 1963. We're changing history and arranging an ambush for Redhair and her friends. We dangle the Wopplefop, you do your job, we do our job, you get the teenagers and dwarfs, we get Jules Rigsworth. Lieutenant Raiken will fill you in on the details of the plan."

The Griddleback leader pressed a button on his communicator and a droid-driven Police Ford Transit MK II van appeared from the back of Gruilash's sleek, silver-grey battlecruiser.

"It's a Black Maria police van. It'll help you blend in." The van stopped in front of Gruilash and, taking the keys from the droid, he threw them to Reckitt.

"It'll be tight, but you should be able to get it into your ship."

Chapter 20

The Fab Five

"Who's the wormhole guardian at the Bingley Five Rise in 1963?" asked Jules, hunting for the plans of the Bingley lock-keeper's cottage on his paper-strewn desk. Dorothy, his long-suffering assistant, held out a three-page CV.

"Wing-Commander Doughton Dogberry Botley, DFC and Bar, retired. Battle of Britain veteran, ladies' man, fiftyish, never married," she said in her best Judy Garland voice. "Answers to the name of Dogberry, for some inscrutable reason."

Jules chuckled. "Batty Botley! Well, I never." He stopped rummaging for the plans, took the CV, and sank into his beloved Chesterfield before flicking through the pages.

"Good old Batty. This will be right up your canal," he said reflectively, taking a sip of Earl Grey tea.

Dorothy found the plans on the floor and placed them on the table next to him. "I'll go and get some more hot water for the pot," she said, leaving the room.

Jules sank further into his chair and hummed a medley of war-film tunes. Shaping a pair of goggles with his fingers in front of his eyes, his elbows level with his head, he rolled from side to side and murdered the last few bars of his favourite movie theme, just as Dorothy reappeared with a hot-water jug.

"Right then." Jules dropped his pretend fighter-pilot goggles and jumped from the chair. "Stick an advert in the Times for 29 July 1963 … And, I quote …"

Dorothy quickly put the jug on the desk and took a dictation device from her pocket.

Jules stood looking skyward. "After a long and painful illness, we are sad to announce the passing of Aunt Sophronia. Her funeral will be held on 2 August 1963. All who knew dear Soppy are invited to attend."

Dorothy finished recording and cleared her throat. "What address should I give for the funeral?"

Jules smiled. "Good gracious, Dorothy. We don't want anyone to turn up!"

Dorothy looked perplexed for a moment and then a big cheesy grin spread across her face.

"Don't worry about a location," Jules said. "What time are we meeting in the BIFS spaceport?"

"In two hours."

"Let's get this party started."

"Wormhole opening in an hour. Let's move, people," shouted Jules, striding through the spaceport, carrying a brown cardboard shoebox, a battered saxophone case and a pocket-size copy of Mrs Beeton's Book of Needlework.

He headed towards Prometheus and Pandora. Both ships had shed their disguises so that he saw, instead of a truck and an RV in front of him, two medium-sized, silver, streamlined spaceships parked alongside the far wall of the hangar. Opposite them stood the 1960s vehicles the ships were going to carry: a Mr Whippy ice-cream van, a Bedford milk float, a dark blue Police MK II Jaguar and an array of Frisky Family Three microcars, Heinkel bubble cars, Trojans, Messerschmitts and Peel 50s.

Georgia Blade, wearing the green uniform of a 1960s Aer Lingus stewardess, her flaming red hair pinned beneath a pillbox hat, lounged against Prometheus's door. She was talking to her clurichaun wrecking crew and, as always, smoking a cheroot. Alice and Archie stood close by.

"Did you hear the details of where we're going?" Alice asked Archie.

"Jules told Georgia that we're landing in a cave-like area underneath the Bingley Five Rise."

"The what?"

"A series of lock gates. The BIFS northern safe area in England lies underneath them. Jules says it's perfect as our base camp for going into Liverpool. The lock-keeper's an old wing-commander called 'Betty' or something. A wormhole guardian, like Jeremiah. Should be a piece of cake."

"Nothing's ever straightforward with Jules," observed Alice.

Just then Jules walked to the centre of the hangar and placed his packages on the floor. "Okay, everyone, gather round."

He opened the shoebox and started taking out Timex watches and pouches of banknotes and coins. "When we get to 1963, I'll tell you what to do with the watches," he said as these items were passed around. "Keep the money with you in case we get separated in Liverpool. There's enough there to feed and house you for a day or two. Now, larger vehicles inside Pandora; the smaller ones go into Prometheus." He glanced at his watch. "Georgia, get your team into gear. Less than an hour before the wormhole opens.

"In case you haven't heard," he added, "we land beneath the Bingley Five Rise, a set of five locks on the Leeds and Liverpool Canal near Bingley. The lock-keeper in 1963 is one of the BIFS's finest guardians, retired Wing-Commander Doughton Dogberry Botley. He's old school and lives a solitary bachelor's life."

Archie couldn't help noticing the smile on Jules's face. It worried him.

Once the vehicles had been loaded into the spacecraft and everyone strapped in, Jules pulled on his Look-Sees and gave the thumbs-up sign from Pandora's bridge.

The countdown began.

"Two—one—zero …"

Accompanied by a swirling cacophony of strings and horns, the two ships disappeared in a vortex of steam en route to Bingley, 1963.

The journey to the 1960s included an hour's wait hovering invisibly over the Suez Canal workings in 1868 and a thirty-minute white-knuckle ride along the Dust Rings of Friem in the Goldilocks universe.

In 1963, waiting in the subterranean chamber below the five locks in the village of Bingley, was the enigmatic Wing-Commander Doughton Dogberry Botley. As he relaxed in his "acquired" Downing Street guard chair, he was a symphony of sartorial elegance in his frog-fastened cashmere smoking jacket, Trone d'Amour cravat, silk pyjamas and paisley slippers. Beside him was a large oak dining table laden with food and several wax-encrusted silver candelabra. Behind the table, Indian incense burned slowly in two large brass urns, its sweet and spicy aroma filling the cave.

Dogberry drummed his fingers on his knees and waited. Every few minutes he looked at his pocket chronometer and peered into the darkness of the large circular cave ahead of him.

It wasn't long before the cave's temperature dropped and a ball of steam the size of a grapefruit appeared. Placing a monocle over his left eye, he puffed lightly on a calabash pipe and, as the ball grew ever larger, poured himself a cup of mint tea from a Meissen Chinoiserie teapot. He reached to his left and took an umbrella from an upturned artillery-shell casing. Putting down his teacup and with his pipe clenched between his teeth, he rose, opened the umbrella, and placed it above his head. He walked towards the weather ball just as the rain started falling in the arrival area.

Pandora came first, emerging from a squall, and then Prometheus, along with a clap of thunder and a spike of lightning. The weather fronts receded and slowly disappeared, leaving the glistening vehicles standing alongside each other in front of him.

A door opened in Pandora and Jules jumped from the cab, followed by Archie and Alice.

"Jules! How the devil are you?" shouted Dogberry, putting his pipe into his pyjama-top pocket, lowering his umbrella and shaking it.

"Batty!"

The wing-commander smiled and extended a hand. "I saw the advertisement."

"Good to see you, old boy. Yes, I thought you'd like the wording," said Jules, as Archie and Alice joined them.

"And you must be Archie and Alice. Jules has told me a lot about you." Dogberry smiled. "Pretty smart chaps, according to him!"

"If Jules says we're smart then I suppose we must be," said Alice, grinning. "Pleased to meet you, Wing-Commander."

Dogberry smiled below his bristling handlebar moustache. "Welcome to the Bingley Five Rise. Dogderry's the name. I don't do titles." He looked around, eyes glinting. "And where's that Fay Wray, Mata Hari, scarlet woman?" he asked, with another twirl of his moustache.

"I'm here, daaarling,"

Dogberry growled, and his monocle dropped; he caught it skilfully in the palm of his hand.

Georgia undulated towards him on heels impossibly high, with the clurichauns in tow. Slowly she removed her kid gloves, one after the other, as if they were silk stockings.

"Gadzooks," said the wing-commander, clenching his pipe doughtily between his teeth.

Languorously, Georgia winked at him. The ends of his moustache went north and his eyes bulged.

Jules shook his head and moved between them. "More tea, old boy?"

Dogberry blinked, looked at Jules and took the proffered cup. "Of course. Not sure what came over me. Mouth is suddenly parched, can't think why."

Georgia blew Dogberry a kiss and sauntered towards the table, lithely taking a seat opposite Dogberry's. The handle of his teacup snapped.

The clurichauns took seats either side of Georgia.

"Please eat. Time travel is such hungry business, I know," said Dogberry.

"A little something Mrs Figglebottom and her Lyons Tea girls put together?" asked Jules as they all started to tuck in.

Dogberry nodded. "Wonderful woman."

The clurichauns set about the food like pigs at a trough. Unperturbed by her charges' behaviour, Georgia poured herself a large cognac and pushed a salad around her plate.

"Dogberry," said Jules, cutting a leg from a turkey, "you didn't, did you?"

"Marry Figglebottom? Oh, no, I just borrowed her."

Jules shook his head as he scooped up a spoonful of cranberry sauce. "You can't go borrowing people! The Confederation will arrest you."

Dogberry looked dismissively down his nose. "Let them try, old boy. Just let them try."

As they demolished the fine spread, Archie turned to Alice and whispered, "Does this remind you of anything?"

Alice looked at the table, and then around the room. "No."

"Alice, you're in Wonderland."

Alice sniggered, spilling her tea.

"Everything okay, Alice?" said Jules.

"Yes, fine, thanks. But I'm still not entirely clear why we're going to Liverpool."

Jules crossed his arms, his eyes flared with manic delight and he stroked his goatee. "How many Beatles were there?"

Alice looked at him warily. "The Fab Four, of course." She glanced at Archie for confirmation.

"Nope," said Jules. "There were five Beatles. John, Paul, Ringo, George … and Terry."

"'Terry'?" chorused Alice and Archie.

Pulling a yellowing newspaper from his pocket, Jules gave it to Alice. "In the Liverpool Evening Echo, dated 4 August 1963, it says five, so it must be true."

She looked at a picture of five mop heads under the heading "The Fab Five Play Their Last Cavern Gig Tomorrow!"

"Yep," said Jules. "Mersey Terry, the saxophone-playing fifth mop-haired Beatle. We've nicknamed him Mop Bot Terry."

Alice looked spooked.

Jules continued, "Terry joined a couple of weeks before this picture was taken. Musical history is now being made by the Fab Five."

Picking up a bone china saucer, Jules unexpectedly—and with consummate skill—spun it on its edge.

"Why did the Griddlebacks do this? What's the point?" asked Archie.

"That's what Griddlebacks do. They play with Earth's history, trying to change it," replied Jules.

"That's illegal, isn't it?" said Alice, "I mean, adding people to history and changing it?"

"Indeed. Law 353/012 of the Confederation Interplanetary Charter on History & Time specifically forbids it. But"—Jules pursed his lips—"it's never stopped them before, and I have to admit it's rather clever." He started spinning a second saucer, this time counterclockwise. "Altering a country's culture, politics, sport and religion can have a bearing on the whole planet. Adding people to history can affect a timeline as much as killing people can."

Alice passed the paper to Archie. He looked at the pasty-faced Terry and shook his head. "How do they make a droid so lifelike that it fools people?"

"They're not droids like the ones we use in 2340. Griddlebacks create clones from flesh and titanium. They manipulate DNA to create a living, breathing and anatomically correct clone of the person they want to replace, or simply design someone new. It's a shell on a metal frame, without a consciousness as we understand it. The Griddlebacks add the rest."

"Why do they bother meddling?" asked Alice. "It must cost money and lots of time to do it properly."

Jules shrugged. "They're in it for the long haul. Because of the protection Earth gets from being part of the Confederation, analogous to NATO and the United Nations in your own home time, they can't conquer and trash Earth like they do other planets. So they meddle with Earth's history, hoping to profit from sending it down dark alleyways." His smile evaporated. "If they can help mankind to destroy Earth, they profit. No one is going to bother stopping them from pillaging a barren planet. To resist them, the BIFS and various of our allies monitor Griddleback and Leche incursions into Earth's culture, religion, politics and sport. We then try to unravel them quietly. It's a game of cat and mouse, played for the most part beneath the Confederation's radar."

"I think Beatles music with a saxophone could be really cool. Remember Gerry Rafferty and 'Baker Street'? Is it that bad to let musical history take a new course?" said Alice.

"Admittedly," Jules said with a nod, "meddling with the Beatles in 1963 may seem like small beer. Nevertheless, we have good evidence, as you know, that they intend to kill or maim all the musical groups named after animals. We can't ignore this."

Jules looked around the table. "History isn't fixed. Think of it as a slow-setting jelly. If we ignore the meddling, eventually the jelly sets, creating a different foundation for a series of future events. Changing history creates ripples that can turn into a tsunami of change that becomes impossible to unravel. Think of a long line of dominoes standing on end. It just needs one falling domino to set the rest off."

"And, on the bright side, one person to stop the rest of the chain falling," said Archie.

Jules surveyed the faces around him. Even the clurichauns had stopped gorging and started listening.

"When time travel began, many thought it an opportunity to change Earth's darker parts of history and eliminate the suffering of millions. We stopped Hitler's birth a dozen times, but in each instance something similar or worse happened. We learnt a valuable lesson. Changing the grimmer aspects of human history caused new, unimaginable events. Through our mistakes we realized that history, like nature, is its own maintainer of the status quo."

The silence around the cave was palpable. Jules lifted the case from the floor. "Archie, I see from your file that you played a mean sax at university. Get practising."

He passed the case to Archie. "You'll find a learning helper in the caravan, and I've prepared an Edubed file. For one night only, you're joining the Beatles!"

Jules grinned manically, and then turned to the wing-commander.

"Did you round up the Mollies? We're going to need all the help we can get."

Dogberry's eyes flared and his moustache jigged excitedly. "Let the games begin," he said, grinning. "Eyes right!"

Taking a whistle from his jacket, Dogberry blew it hard. A door in the cave wall to the right of the ships opened and accordion music began dancing around the cave. Through the door walked eight men with night-camouflage-blackened faces, each carrying a long black stick and dressed in heavy canvas trousers, neckerchiefs, waistcoats, hobnailed boots and bowler hats. They moved slowly towards the table. Behind them, entering through the same door, came five musicians playing an assortment of instruments and wearing long coats, green sashes and hats covered in thick green foliage.

The eight black-clad men lined up in front of the table, the musicians behind them. Then the men began to dance, hopping, twirling and wheeling around the floor to the accompaniment of the strange, hypnotic music.

Dogberry closed his eyes. He tapped his fingers to the rhythm of the hobnails on the stone floor and rocked back and forth, lost in the music.

"These are the Mollies? And you say they're going to stop the Griddlebacks?" asked Archie.

A faint smile crossed Dogberry's face as he continued to enjoy the music with his eyes closed.

"Wing-Commander," said Archie, raising his voice in an effort to attract his attention. "Wing-Commander!"

"Yeeeeeeooooooo," came a piercing scream.

All eyes shot to the door in the wall. With fists clenched, the clurichauns rose to their feet. Georgia signalled them to wait.

A man in a tracksuit, waving a samurai sword, hurtled toward the wheeling dancers. Another sword-flourishing tracksuited man burst through the door and flew across the floor, followed by two more.

"Wing-Commander!' shouted Archie, pulling at Dogberry's arm.

Dogberry didn't move, nor did he open his eyes. He pointed a finger at the dancers. "Watch and learn," he said calmly. "Watch and learn."

As the four tracksuits closed in on the table, the Mollies moved into line and, with military precision, dropped onto one knee, pointed their sticks at them. The sticks pumped a barrage of pink goo at the attackers that covered their legs. The swordsmen skidded to a halt, stuck to the floor. They tried to wade through the sea of pink treacle, but to no avail.

Two more screaming tracksuits raced across the cave floor and, once again with the minimum of fuss, the Mollies encased them in pink, glueing them to the floor, where they swayed in frustrated impotence.

Spontaneous applause echoed around the cave. Dogberry opened his eyes and stood up, clapping and pointing towards the musicians and dancers.

"Please welcome, ladles and jellyspoons, the Wrogley gun–carrying Mersey Mollies!"

"Ninja Morris Men!" shouted Jules, laughing loudly. "Now that's original!"

The dancers and musicians formed a line, took off their hats and bowed before turning and spraying the tracksuits with a liquid that dissolved the goo. They all trooped back out through the door they'd entered by.

Jules grinned. Even the clurichauns looked impressed.

"Your hidden weapon," said Jules to the wing-commander with a broad grin. "We'll give the Griddlebacks and Leche a little Mollie musical culture. They won't know what hit them."

After an above-ground whistlestop tour of the Bingley Five Rise, Dogberry brought them back to the cave system and showed them to their sleeping quarters, built into the cave walls. Alice put her knapsack in her room and went to find Archie. She found him sitting on a sofa in a lounge area.

"Don't you find this all very weird?" she said, sitting down beside him.

Archie nodded, looking at the papers Jules had given him. "Tell me about it. Remember, I've got to learn the saxophone parts on 'She Loves You', 'Please, Please Me' and 'Twist and Shout' … by tomorrow!"

"I wonder when we'll hear anything about Tarquin finding the amulet. Why is it so important?"

Archie looked up from his music. "It's a very powerful talisman that has the ability to alter time. Many others, including the Griddlebacks, are hunting that amulet."

"What's so special about it?"

"I'm not sure, but it allows you to travel through time much more easily, altering it as you go. That's why everyone wants it."

"Why Tarquin?" said Alice.

"Jules told me that Tarquin's father and mother were important secret agents with the BIFS. His father left him clues to the amulet's whereabouts hidden throughout world history. He wanted to make sure Tarquin was the only person who could find it and learn to use it."

Early the next morning they gathered in the cave around a table now laden with scrambled egg, muffins, toast, bacon, sausages, mushrooms, black pudding and pots of tea. The smell of hot bread and sizzling bacon had the clurichauns salivating like Pavlov's dogs. Mrs Figglebottom and her girls—Emma, Cathy and Tara—had prepared them a wonderful full English breakfast. Dogberry was having a lie-in, but everyone else, including the Mollies, the musicians and the men in tracksuits, took their places and started stuffing themselves. Only the noise of contented munching and the occasional ripping belch from one of the clurichauns disturbed the cave's tranquillity.

After everyone had finished eating, Jules called them to order. He paused and looked at his 1960s Timex wristwatch. It was exactly 8am.

"Everyone, please synchronize your watches. The time is now … 08:01."

The assembled gathering did as instructed.

"Before we depart," said Jules, "I have one more surprise."

He wiped his lips with a serviette, raised a hand and counted down from five on his fingers. With one finger remaining, he pointed theatrically to the landing space in the middle of the hangar. A sputtering ball of inclement weather appeared a couple of metres above the floor and expanded slowly. Once it had reached the size of a house, it crackled with lightning. There was a deafening clap of thunder that made some of the gathering cover their ears. Dark rain clouds rumbled, and lightning forks effervesced from within the ball, bouncing on the cave floor.

Hidden within the expanding clouds, a Russian helicopter gunship, painted in Soviet air-force camouflage colours of green and grey, materialized. The helicopter grew until it hovered above the floor. Downforce from the whirling twin rotor blades, rain and steam flew everywhere. Taking cover under umbrellas, Jules and the others watched as the weather front dissipated and the helicopter dropped to the floor. The rotor blades slowed and the engine whined, clanked several times, and juddered to a stop. On the sides of the helicopter were armorial crests, the centrepiece of each being an arrangement of Japanese cherry flowers entwined with the words

BRAZIL'S GBH
IKEBANA SPECIALISTS
HAPPINESS HELD IS THE SEED
HAPPINESS SHARED IS THE FLOWER

"Hell–o, comrade Rigsworth!" boomed an amplified voice, laced with a heavy Russian accent, from within the gunship. The helicopter's windows opened and three heads with blonde buzzcuts poked out.

Slowly the watchers collapsed their umbrellas and stood looking at the gleaming machine.

"It's the Russians!" exclaimed Archie, rushing over to the helicopter. "I'd heard rumors you'd liberated a helicopter," he shouted, wiping water from his eyes, "but I'd assumed it was a small commercial thing!" He looked up at the sleek Mi35 HIND helicopter gunship, bristling with ordnance. "Oh, God, they're not live are they?" He turned white and backed towards the table.

"No, Comrade Archie, it is big work, but over done now. We see crocodile ship on visit to Motherland and had to … what you say? … liberate her. We come back today again." The microphone clicked off, the heads disappeared, and the doors opened. Three burly Russians with CCCP emblazoned on their red shellsuits jumped from the craft and strutted toward the assembled gathering, their mass of gold chains glistening in the subterranean floodlights.

"Bloody hell, it's Giorgi, Havel and Boris, all covered in bling!" shouted Big Joe. Joined by the other clurichauns, he ran to greet the Russians.

Jules smiled. It was over a year since he and Archie had last seen the ex-KGB security guards. Georgia and the clurichauns had often bumped into them during their escapades in history.

Soon the greetings were done and the Russians were sitting at the table, digging into newly arrived food.

"Okay, okay," said Jules finally. "Listen up, we have work to do." Gaining their attention, he pointed at the nearest wall. A 3D plan of the Cavern Club in Liverpool and the surrounding area appeared in front of them.

Jules left the table and walked inside the plan. "I got the latest intelligence report this morning. Griddlebacks and Leche are definitely planning something in and around the Cavern Club on the day the Beatles play their last gig there, so we are a go." He pointed with a stick at the club. "Worst case scenario: the death or abduction of the Beatles."

He walked into the Cavern Club hologram and slapped the stick hard against his palm. "The streets in and around the Cavern Club are small, hence we use microcars. Alice will pretend to be autograph-hunting outside the club fire escape. Her job is to get the Beatles over to the Mr Whippy ice-cream van. Boris and Archie will be in the van, parked opposite on Mathew Street, waiting to exchange Archie for Terry. I will be in the police car, with a couple of Mollie musicians, parked in Temple Court, monitoring Griddleback communications. Seamus will wait with the milk float further down on Mathew Street, in case we need a distraction. Inside the club, waiting to help if the Griddlebacks or Leche appear, will be the other clurichauns. Hidden in a garage not far from the Cavern Club will be the remainder of the Mersey Mollies in the microcars, armed with their Wrogley guns, ready to help in case events take an unexpected turn. Georgia and Dave Moriarty will be in Prometheus, cloaked as a removals van, on Mathew Street."

"And the helicopter, where will that be?" asked Alice.

"We can't have too many people in Liverpool at the same time."

Alice looked disappointed. She wanted to see the helicopter in 1963.

"But," said Jules with a grin, "we've found a wormhole, and Giorgi's ready to arrive later in the afternoon, if needed."

He continued, "Taking out Terry and replacing him with Archie will alert his Griddleback minders. I realize it's risky, but we must locate and neutralize them. As soon as they show their hand, Georgia will pinpoint their location and take them and their ship out. Archie then rehearses with the Beatles inside the Club, before telling them he's had another offer and is leaving. Then there were four. Simple."

Jules's expression changed. "The Leche, however, are a separate problem." He tapped his Timex. "These watches change colour if a Leche comes within twenty metres. Don't go near them—leave them to Georgia and the clurichauns."

He walked out of the 3D plan and Georgia stepped forward.

"Leche are insidious, evil creatures. They are very thin and pale-skinned, and they melt into the background. They're masters of disguise. I'll be monitoring your watches. If we detect anything, I'll let you know."

"We don't have any intelligence on the Leche's role, but it won't be good, so be careful out there," said Jules, looking at the gathering in front of him. "Okay, time for more twenty-fourth-century wizardry." He took out a small metal lapel pin—a centimetre-tall replica of a jamjar—and placed it in Archie's lapel. "It's a prototype gadget. An upgrade of the personality ring, but disguised as a badge so as to fit into the 1960s."

He produced a pocket mirror and gave this, too, to Archie before pressing the badge with his finger. To the watchers, it seemed that Archie's face turned slowly into a ball of pink sludge—he looked like so much melting strawberry ice cream. Then, bit-by-bit, Archie's blobby face evolved into Mop Bot Terry's.

"Cool!" said Archie, looking at his face in the mirror.

"You look fab, really, you know, like," said Alice to him in a Liverpudlian accent, trying not to giggle. "Why do we need badges?" she added to Jules as he handed them out.

"We mustn't be recognized," he said. "What we're doing could be regarded as illegal by the Confederation. When you choose your identities, please stick to the list provided. I don't want to see Elvis, Lady Gaga, Katie Perry, Donald Duck or Adolf Hitler outside the Cavern Club. It would complicate things."

Paddy nudged Willard. "We'll tweak dis later," he said.

Willard winked and flashed him a wicked smile.

"Jules," said Alice, pointing at the eclectic mix of microcars, "if we get into trouble we'll be rescued by those?"

Jules nodded. "I'm not likely to give a bunch of marauding Mollies Aston Martins, am I?" He walked towards the cars. "And, besides, the streets are very narrow, so these small cars will do nicely." He paused briefly. "If you need help—and pray that you don't—the Mollies will speed to your rescue."

Jules turned back to the gathering as a whole. "Now, Stage One is to exchange Terry for Archie. Stage Two is to take out the Griddlebacks' support ship. And Stage Three"—he let the words sink in—"is to let Archie briefly enjoy himself rehearsing with the Beatles and then bring everyone back to the Five Rise in time for crumpets and tea!"

Laughter and cheers filled the cave. Jules picked up a sheaf of paper. "Here is the plan with timings." He gave Alice copies to hand out. "No using your tablets—they weren't invented in 1963. We go native. Everything is on paper, and on your watches."

Taking their copies of the timetable, Jules's troops dispersed to make last-minute adjustments to their plans.

OPERATION MERSEY BEAT
Weather conditions: Heavy, torrential rain, light southeasterly wind.

09:00 Clurichauns descend to roof of Cavern Club building and break in. Find owner and staff and tie them up. Await communications check at 10:30.

09:30 Mollies unload Heinkel bubble cars, Frisky Family Threes and Peel 50s into disused warehouse and set up communications base five-minute drive from Cavern Club.

09:45 Status checks with Georgia, Seamus, Archie and the clurichauns.

10:00 MK II Police Jaguar slips into Mathew Street.

10:05 Milk float starts down Mathew Street as backup.

10:17 Mr Whippy Ice Cream arrives on Mathew Street and stops outside Cavern Club, on corner of Boran Lane. Georgia parks Prometheus, disguised as removal van, further down Mathew Street.

10:30 All points communication check.

11:00 Alice to Cavern Club's fire exit door, autograph book in hand.
       DO NOT FORGET BALL-POINT PEN!!!

11:02 Beatles arrive.

11:03 Operation Mersey Beat begins.

Alice stood under an umbrella, shielded from the pouring rain outside the Cavern Club's fire exit on Mathew Street, armed only with an autograph book and—remembered at the last moment—a working ball-point pen. Coming from inside the club she could hear the faint sound of Celtic songs and laughter. She looked down the street. The atrocious weather meant traffic was light.

The Mr Whippy van arrived and stopped across the road. Alice could see Boris and Archie by the van's counter. The plan was simple. Alice would ask the Beatles for autographs and slip a bot control disc into Terry's pocket when he signed her book. Boris in the Mr Whippy van would take control of Mop Bot Terry, make him come over to buy an ice cream, and close him down. Archie would slip from the van and take his place, leaving Boris to hide the droid.

At precisely 11:02, a Commer van turned the corner of Mathew Street and drew up outside the club. Alice readied herself. To her surprise, John, Terry, George and Paul made straight for the Mr Whippy van. Only Ringo stopped outside the club. Alice offered him her autograph book.

"Didn't know we were that famous, like. Who's it for, little girl?" he asked, taking shelter in the doorway from the sleeting rain.

"Er, Lulu," she replied, seeing a poster on the wall.

"Nice name."

Alice smiled sweetly.

"Fancy an ice cream?" she asked, pointing to the others.

"Nah, not my scene."

"Oh," she said, unsure what to do next. "Weather's not good today, is it?" she said, looking over at the ice-cream van.

While Alice spoke about the weather, John and the others had reached the van and were ordering ice creams.

"Two 99s, a Bunny Ear, and loads of hundreds and thousands."

Boris stood motionless. When he'd been a youth in the Soviet Union, the Beatles had been his heroes and now, standing before him, were the revered icons of western liberalism: John, Paul, George and … the other one.

"Oh!" he shouted, overcome with emotion. "You great man! Loved by Oblast 44 School for Young Communist Members." Boris thrust his head out of the van, opened his arms in a huge "The Hills Are Alive" embrace, and roared, "We loves you all!"

The Beatles hastily stepped backwards. Some nutter.

"Shouldn't you be back in the USSR?" said Paul worriedly, seeing the CCCP on Boris's tracksuit top. Archie tried to pull the burly Russian back inside, but in his excitement Boris swatted Archie out of his way.

"Oh, joke is good, big love you today," he said, before bursting into song—"Back in der USSR, Back in der USSR!"—and bouncing up and down, causing the van to rock alarmingly from side to side and send poor Archie crashing against a cabinet and hitting his head, so that he slumped unconscious to the van floor.

"This guy's lost it," said John, pulling his coat about his head. He and the other three ran across the road to huddle against a wall.

Alice and Ringo arrived to see what was going on.

A screech of tires made them all look to the right, towards North John Street, where a Black Maria police van hurtled around the corner in a wall of spray with its blue light flashing and its bell ringing.

"What's going on?" shouted Paul from under his coat.

Alice's watch flashed every colour of the rainbow. "Leche," she muttered.

The Black Maria skidded to a halt in front of the ice-cream van, billowing tyre-smoke and dripping water. The back doors flew open, and Reckitt Vangelos and his Leche brigade, in donkey jackets, skullcaps and miner's boots, looking as if they'd dropped out of a Lowry painting, slipped from the vehicle. Wielding pick-axe handles, they weren't about to order a vanilla brick.

"The van man must have taken someone else's patch," said Alice, cowering under the umbrella with the five Beatles.

"See that police box at the end of the street," said Ringo, pointing. "Let's call the fuzz."

Alice looked at the blue box and hesitated. She was off-plan and needed help. "We might … we might disturb someone inside it?"

"Inside a police box? What do you think you'd find, a sleeping policeman!"

The Leche ignored the cringing Beatles and surrounded the ice-cream van, wading into it with their clubs, smashing the glass and denting the bodywork. On seeing the Black Maria, Boris had locked the door and hidden under the counter with the unconscious Archie. Another siren wailed in the distance and the Leche stopped and looked up. A police Jaguar turned into Mathew Street and headed straight for them. Trundling behind came a milk float with Seamus at the wheel.

"Here comes the bloody cavalry!" shouted Paul. "You know."

Inside the unlit Cavern Club, Merv Mulligan and the rest of the clurichauns worked their way towards the only light on in the building. They spread out, and Merv peeked inside the lit room. Three men sat eating breakfast—the club's kitchen staff.

Never one for turning down a free meal, Merv signalled to his clurichaun brothers and they rushed in and overpowered the men, tied them up and sat down to eat their breakfasts.

Merv belched, and soon the clurichauns were trying to outdo each other in an impromptu belching and farting contest. At the back of the kitchen, Paddy slipped and, stumbling, fell down a flight of steps into a cellar. Cursing and rubbing a large lump on his bald head, he looked around. The bunions on his nose twitched as he inhaled the sweet scent of hops. He smiled and, with an anarchic glint in his eye, called up to the others.

"Er, I t'ink I've found something interesting, lads!"

The lure of beer, peanuts and pork scratchings had the clurichauns jumping into the cellar like passengers fleeing the Titanic. Someone found the light switch and soon they glued themselves to a line of beer kegs. They guzzled pint after pint after pint—the lunatics had found not only the keys to the asylum but a fully stocked beer cellar for the emptying.

By 10:30, the Cavern Club rocked to the strains of bawdy Celtic drinking songs and another farting'n'belching contest. All thoughts of the stake-out had disappeared in a torrent of flatulence, froth, ale, crisps and nuts. They had created their very own—noxious—Mersey Beat.

After dousing himself in ale for the third time, Paddy looked at his jam badge and grinned mischievously.

"Gather round, boys …"

How they arrived at having blue-painted faces and wearing beer towels, tartan curtains with all manner of plastic flora and fauna stuck in their hair, while everyone spoke in pseudo-Australian and Scottish accents, was never determined. Nevertheless, they enjoyed themselves drinking the club dry.

Big Joe had just laid Merv out cold with a right hook when his communicator went off.

"Cavernz Clubsszz?" he said, swaying and listening intently. "Ohhh shizzzzz."

He closed the communicator.

Staggering to the steps leading up to the kitchen, he dislodged the bung in a beer barrel. A torrent of ale descended upon the comatose Merv—who, with a knee-jerk reaction, woke up, opened his mouth and swallowed. It was manna from heaven and, like a rapacious cuckoo chick, he gulped and swallowed until his eyes bulged and beer cascaded from his mouth.

Big Joe reached the stairs and, steadying himself, pointed upward. "Streeeet, kwuichhh!"

The police car skidded to a halt, scattering the Leche. The doors flew open and Jules leapt out with three Mollie musicians.

One of the musicians caught a Leche square on the jaw, lifting him off the ground and sending him crashing into the remains of the Mr Whippy van. Jules followed up with a vicious kick to the next Leche's solar plexus. With the melee in full flow, Alice herded the bemused Beatles along the street towards the arriving milk float.

In the chaos, she managed to slip the bot control disc into Terry's pocket. Well, at least part of the plan was working, right?

At the far end of Boran's Lane, two companies of Griddleback stormtrooper droids, dressed as soldiers from the King's Regiment, jogged down the road, led by Lieutenant Raiken, who had morphed into human form.

Alice saw them coming and pointed to the approaching milk float. "Quick, jump on that!" she yelled at the Beatles.

Without hesitating, they followed her and clambered in among the milk crates, sending bottles flying in all directions. Seamus, after checking he'd got everyone on board, engaged the Trazorgian drive and they roared down Mathew Street, flames bursting from the float's exhaust pipe.

Paul, thrown on his back by the sudden acceleration, looked up into Alice's face. "Hi. Me name's Paul," he said, smiling. "Don't you just love Liverpool!"

A line of microcars driven by the Mollies came around the corner ahead of them and raced seemingly straight at them. At the last moment the microcars swerved past and sped off in the direction of the fracas.

"Diddy cars full of Diddy Men!" exclaimed Ringo, watching them skid to a halt by the police car.

The Mersey Mollies and the remaining musicians leapt out, and levelled their Wrogley guns at the fighting, pumping a withering barrage of pink goo at the Leche and coating them until they resembled plasticine figures. At the same time, the Cavern Club's fire exit doors burst open and Paddy, Merv Mulligan, Hugh and the rest of the clurichauns staggered into the street. They began a meandering charge toward anyone they could focus on, waving and shouting, "Fffweeeedom!"

It would have been a classic pincer movement, worthy of the famous Chinese General Sun Tzu, except that the inebriated clurichauns hammered anyone in range, including the Mollies and their musical accompaniment. Fortuitously, Jules had gone to find Archie in the wreck of the ice cream van, so missed getting walloped.

When Merv caught one of the Mollie musicians with his elbow, two Mollies took exception and ploughed into him. The clurichauns and the rest of the Mollie musicians joined in the scrum, leaving the Leche swaying like jelly in an earthquake.

Lieutenant Raiken and the two companies of Griddleback stormtrooper droids reached Mathew Street.

On board his ship, which was cloaked and stationary above Liverpool city centre, Gruilash Vandergaard laughed and snorted a stream of bile and steam. On the screen before him was Prometheus, disguised as a removal van. The Griddleback flight officer turned excitedly toward Gruilash, his claw hovering above a large, red button. "Shall I destroy it, Captain?"

Gruilash rose triumphantly from his chair, took a Wopplefop out from the food cage by his throne and bit hard, squeezing it like a lemon, draining the creature's blood into his gullet before throwing the carcase into the recycling bin.

"No, wait to see who's going on board, then send a squad to collect them all."

"Very good, Captain."

Gruilash took another Wopplefop from the cage and played with it in his claws, the way a cat plays with a cornered mouse.

"Take us down to the Cavern Club."

When the area around the Cavern Club appeared on screen, Gruilash roared with laughter. The Leche were pinned to Mathew Street and, like pink anemones, were undulating out of the way of their assailants. The Mollies, musicians and clurichauns brawled around them.

"Lieutenant Raiken," said Gruilash through his communicator, "I want this under control, now!"

Gruilash looked again at the screen. "But leave the slime-drinkers—they can rot," he added, sinking his teeth into the animal's neck and swallowing its blood. He licked his sulphurous lips and used the carcase like a napkin to clean his snout. Belching, he nonchalantly waved a hand at the screen. "Send in the clones."

The stormtroopers quickly joined the fight and soon only Merv Mulligan and two Mollies were left standing amongst the swaying Leche.

Out of danger, Seamus slowed the milk float and let it trundle down the road.

"Gotta be a song in there somewhere, John," said Paul, watching the fight in the rear-view mirror.

"It's not a song," replied John. "We're on a flipping magical mystery tour watching a bunch of Birkenhead dockers and them blue meanies kick seven bells out of the police … And what are them pink bazookery things?" Swinging his legs over the end of the milk float alongside Paul, he took out a cigarette, lit up, and dragged heavily on the end. He eyed the scene suspiciously. "All we need is a ruddy yellow submarine to surface and I'd think we were dreaming, like."

The milk float slowed, turned left down North John Street, and headed for the open back of a removal van parked in the road.

"Hold tight, everyone, we're going inside!" shouted Seamus. The milk float lurched and bounced up the ramp, shuddering to a stop at its top. The back of the truck closed, sealing them in.

A bright light flooded the inside of the truck. The milk float was now in the middle of a large hangar. Georgia emerged from a Warhol painting, and sashayed towards them with a tray of drinks. "I am your stewardess," she said, offering the Beatles a drink. "May I on behalf of the crew wish you an enjoyable flight aboard Prometheus."

Georgia smiled, waiting for them to finish their drinks before taking an orange-sized sphere from her pocket and releasing it to rise in the air above them. The light from the sphere pulsated, transfixing the Beatles.

"Do you want to know a secret?" she asked, smiling.

Hexed by the light and drugged by the drink, the Beatles, open-mouthed and wide-eyed, slowly nodded.

"Here comes the sun," said Georgia.

The sphere exploded in a blinding flash, and the Beatles collapsed unconscious. Alice and Seamus joined Georgia in putting the Beatles to bed in Prometheus's cabin area.

"When they wake, their memories will be cleansed of this adventure," said Georgia, laying Paul out on the bed. She left the sleeping quarters and went to the flight deck.

She opened the door and looked straight into the barrel of a Griddleback stormtrooper's gun.

Another Griddleback stormtrooper materialized next to her. His cold eyes lit up when he saw Georgia. "We have Redhair, a human girl, a dwarf, the Scorpions and our droid Terry," he said into his communicator.

"No," corrected a distant voice. "You have the Beatles. We do the Scorpions next week, along with the Eagles and the Byrds. The Black Crowes and the Monkees the week after that."

"Yes, of course, Captain."

While the Griddleback was talking, Georgia carefully flicked a switch on the flight deck.

"Attention! This spaceship will self-destruct in two minutes," said a loud recording of Georgia's voice in both English and the Griddleback language. The stormtrooper looked at Georgia, then at his men, and screamed, "Quick, get everyone off, now!"

A mad panic ensued as a posse of stormtroopers rushed to the sleeping quarters, grabbed the sleeping Beatles, and ran out onto the street to the supposed safety of the far side of the road. They were joined by Georgia and the others. Everyone waited apprehensively for the imminent explosion but, after some minutes, all that happened was that the removal van suddenly disappeared.

Well, everyone except Georgia had been expecting a bang.

The Griddleback officer hissed and turned to her. "You said it was going to self-destruct!"

"I lied. So sue me," she replied.

"Where's Prometheus?" whispered Alice to her.

"Gone travelling."

As they were taken down Mathew Street they could see, all around them, Griddlebacks and droids, dressed as soldiers from the King's Regiment, pouring along the road, organizing roadblocks, putting up radiation-leak signs, emptying buildings and taking up firing positions. Placing a ring around the Cavern Club, the Griddlebacks and their troops successfully blocked all entries and exits. No humans were to be allowed inside, and those found within the cordon were to be sent to "memory cleansing" tents at each checkpoint before being allowed to leave. The area surrounding the club was in lockdown. The official line to explain the lockdown was that there'd been a serious radiation leak inside the Cavern Club.

The soldiers rounded up Jules, the clurichauns, Mollies and musicians and herded them into the middle of the road, where they were joined by Alice and Seamus.

A British Army Land Rover, followed by a Bedford truck, turned onto Mathew Street and stopped in the centre of the street. Gruilash Vandergaard climbed from the Land Rover and, followed by a phalanx of bodyguards in King's Regiment uniform, walked towards the group of prisoners. Sniffing the air, he jerked his head at the disparate group sitting on the ground.

"Bring Redhair to me," he roared.

Back at the Bingley Five Rise, Dogberry's communicator flashed, and he turned to the message on the screen.

It's Archie. I'm hiding. The mission has gone wrong. Griddlebacks captured everyone, including Beatles. HELP! I need somebody!

"Fire up the helicopter! You're needed!" Dogberry bellowed at Giorgi and Havel, who were waiting in the Hind.

The rotor blades on the helicopter started. Dogberry patched Archie into the Hind's communication system. The Russian cavalry was on its way!

A truck turned down Mathew Street, coming from the direction of John North Street. Rumbling past the prisoners and the entombed Leche, the truck stopped next to the Griddleback Land Rover. The back of the truck opened and Georgia Blade was thrown onto the ground, falling at Gruilash's feet.

"It's been far too long since that night at the Bloated Shagganat, Redhair," said Gruilash, grabbing her arm and pulling her to her feet. His hot, sulphurous breath made her wince and pull her head away. "Lieutenant Raiken, transfer the prisoners to your ship. I'll take Redhair with me."

Raiken nodded and signalled to his men.

On board the Hind, Havel was trying to contact Archie.

"Archie, we arrive Liverpool City centre five minutes, da?"

Archie's desperate voice suddenly filled the Hind cockpit. "Griddlebacks are loading everyone onto their ship—hurry!"

"Cloak is on, silent mode, arrive soon. Five—four—three—two—vun."

The weather front cleared, and through the mist Mathew Street came onto the Hind's screen. In the middle of the road stood several overturned microcars, military vehicles and soldiers. The clurichauns, along with the Mollies and their musicians, were being herded onto a Bedford truck.

"Engage," said Havel.

The invisible helicopter sped silently above Mathew Street, its stun guns locked on the soldiers. Taken by surprise, the Griddleback soldiers had no chance to react to the helicopter's first pass. Only the Leche, protected by the goo, Gruilash and the prisoners remained standing. The Hind turned, banked and began a second pass but, as it dropped to the rooftops, a Griddleback battlecruiser appeared in the helicopter's screen, hovering in front of them, barring their path.

"Abort!" shouted Boris, taking the Hind up, out and over the city, and away from the Cavern Club.

The Russians watched, unable to do anything as Gruilash, having escaped the Hind's first pass, was now in the midst of his recovering stormtroopers, supervising the loading of the clurichauns, Mollies and musicians into the truck.

"Giorgi—see Archie, left!" shouted Havel, pointing to a figure that ran into view along Harrington Street and ducked into a car park.

"I see him!"

Giorgi maneuvered the helicopter into the only space available in the car park. Decloaking the Hind, he put it down just as the Griddleback battlecruiser appeared on the horizon.

"Quickly, Archie!" shouted Havel, watching the battlecruiser move slowly towards them.

From the back of the car park raced the boy, fists pumping, boots pounding the wet ground and throwing up a wall of spray. He reached the helicopter and dived through an open door in the side of the Hind just as Giorgi pulled the vessel up, cloaked her, and sped upward and away from the car park, followed by the battlecruiser.

The two ships sped low above the city centre, twisting and turning. Only the Hind's size and better maneuverability allowed it to evade capture.

When the Hind reached the outskirts of the city of Manchester, the battlecruiser turned and disappeared back towards Liverpool.

Havel radioed the situation to Dogberry at the Five Rise.

It wasn't good news: Archie was the only one of the would-be rescuers to have been safely recovered.

CHAPTER 21

MAKING A DECISION

The BIFS duty officer was relaxing in his bathtub when his communication screen buzzed. Cursing loudly, he climbed out of the bath, put on a robe and entered his bedroom. He opened the screen and a hologram of Cybele Rain, the head of BIFS, stepped out, looking very angry. The DO's stomach flipped.

"You, boy!" she said, stabbing a red, taloned finger at him. "Whatever Rigsworth and his damned coterie were doing on Earth in 1963 has gone horribly wrong." The ferocity of her vocal attack belied her small, bustling frame. Shaking violently, she drew a deep, lunging breath before continuing. "One hour ago we received an ultimatum from the Griddlebacks. I've sent it through to you."

The DO had never seen Madame Rain's coiffured hair look so dishevelled.

"The Prime Minister is not amused," she said. "In fact, she's apoplectic." Taking a bottle from her coat, she downed the contents and glared at the DO. "Sort it out. We have denied all knowledge of an operation in Liverpool, for now. We have forty-eight hours before the Griddlebacks go public and we have to answer to the Confederation. Do whatever is necessary—without admitting anything—to smooth this over and get Jules and his team back."

The hologram blooped and disappeared. Relieved, the DO was just turning to the refuge of his bath when the hologram reappeared mere centimetres from his face.

"Ahhh!" he cried.

"And who the hell are Sergeant Pepper, Lulu and Tiny Tim?"

Battered and bewildered by his boss's tirade, the DO shrugged his shoulders.

"If I find Jules is consorting with those damned leprechauns again, I'll have him sanitized!" Rain said, scowling. Another talon jabbed at him.

"Get our boys back!" she screamed before disappearing a final time.

After landing the Hind in 2340, Archie and the Russians were met by the duty officer.

"I've just had an ear-bashing from Cybele Rain," he said before flicking a control switch on a handheld screen and showing them a recording of the Griddleback commander.

"This is Gruilash Vandergaard, captain of the battlecruiser Tarakan III. We have foiled a plot mounted by a nefarious humanoid known as Jules Rigsworth and his followers. Their intention was to kill innocent members of our great nation and our Leche brothers. If we do not have the Jenkins boy here, with the amulet he stole, within forty-eight hours of your Earth time, you will never see them again and we will take this before the Confederation. Here are the coordinates for the exchange …"

"I checked out the coordinates just before you arrived," said the DO. "They want to do the swap for this Jenkins boy and the amulet in a room under a lake in 1891 at Witley Park, in Surrey, southern England."

"How do the Griddlebacks already know Tarquin has the amulet?" asked Archie.

"Because we have a spy in our camp," said Calbhach, walking into the arrival hall with Tarquin and Jeremiah.

"When we got back from finding the amulet, Professor Cramdunkle discovered there was a trace on me," said Tarquin, showing the underside of his arm.

"I say we circle the wagons and sort out what we can do," said Calbhach. "Let's meet in da Raggedy Rook room at the Yelts Inn in an hour."

An air of despondency hung about the meeting. So many of their friends had been captured by the Griddlebacks.

"What about the tag?" asked Archie.

Tommy Cramdunkle took out a petri dish from his pocket and showed everyone its contents.

"This is what we found on Tarquin. It's very sophisticated. Not only does it keep track of the subject's coordinates, it can, under certain circumstances, pick up conversations close by. Oh," he added, "don't worry now. It can't hear anything while it's sealed in the dish."

"We're going to use it to find out who the spy is, before we do the exchange," said Tarquin. "We've prepared a little performance. So no talking, the rest of you. Just watch."

Tommy took the top off the dish and turned to Tarquin. "We need to save Jules Rigsworth and the others who have been captured by the Griddlebacks," he said very distinctly. "What do you mean you will not help?"

"When I have read the Book of Dreams, I am going to use the amulet to save Rhia. Jules Rigsworth will have to wait," said Tarquin.

"But we have only two days? You cannot do this."

"Jeremiah Cavendish says that he will help me. He is going to take me back to 2015, two days after the fire, and I will use the amulet to then travel back to the day of the fire and rescue Rhia Collins."

Tarquin nodded, and the professor put the lid back on the dish.

"Could it be the Time Guardians who planted the trace?" asked Archie. "Georgia said they were the ones who crashed us in 1773."

"They're involved," said Jeremiah. "Great-Aunt Polidori has been buzzing around Tarquin, and left a listening device in his room. I'm guessing she is working with the Guardians. Let's convince her to send them off to 2015, and leave us to save Jules and the others without any surprises."

With Jeremiah carrying travel packs and Tarquin wearing his signature frock coat and a knapsack, they set off for the departure area.

"The quickest wormhole takes you to the Blisworth Tunnel, an easy walk from the lock-keeper's cottage," said Archie, leading the way to the travel chamber. He opened the iron door and the operator pointed at two rusting Edwardian roll-top bathtubs with boxes of machinery riveted to their undersides.

"Disposable time machines," the operator said. "We're on an environmental drive. Just push them into the canal when you arrive. We've increased their rate of disintegration, so they'll dissolve into the ecosystem in about twenty-four hours."

Tarquin stepped into the first tub and sat down, placing the Look-Sees over his face. Jeremiah took the second tub. Despite poor visibility, Tarquin could make out a huge shape sitting on the canal-bank fishing—like a large bear playing with a twig.

He took off the Look-Sees and glanced at Jeremiah. "Who's that?"

"Fishing on the canal? That'll be Dog, my old sparring partner. I contacted him last night. I thought he'd be useful to have around."

Tarquin grinned.

"He's a guard, Dog!" said Jeremiah with a laugh.

"Barking mad," said a voice from the door.

"Calbhach!" exclaimed Tarquin as the leprechaun walked into the travel chamber.

"Aye, I thought I'd be checking on you. Give you something to take with you on your quest." Calbhach rummaged in his overcoat and produced a small silver teapot. "If you need help, just rub—"

"And a genie jumps out and gives me three wishes?" interrupted Tarquin excitedly.

"Get serious. Dis ain't no pantomime. Rub it hard and eight of me leprechaun cousins, who just happen to be in Northamptonshire, will materialize and knock seven shades of crap out of whoever's bothering you, no questions asked, and then take you to safety. If you call them they will come. They'll need feeding, mind. Please don't forget to feed them or you'll have hell to pay."

As he left he added, "Oh, and it also makes a cracking two-mug pot of tea."

Lost for words, Tarquin nodded, sat down in the bath, put his knapsack between his legs and gripped the top. He glanced at Jeremiah, squeezed into the tub ahead of him.

The operator started up the machinery and looked at Tarquin. "Taken the bananas and your last spoonfuls of elixir?"

Tarquin nodded, already feeling queasy. The tubs started spinning. Tarquin closed his eyes and, with fireworks exploding inside his head, thought of Rhia.

"Seebee?"

Tarquin smacked his lips and opened his bleary eyes to see Jeremiah's concerned face a handsbreadth from his own. He made no objections as Jeremiah lifted him gently from the tub and set him down on the canal bank to recover. Dog heaved the baths into the canal, where they slipped beneath the water.

Jeremiah raised Tarquin into a sitting position. "Tarquin, can you see me?"

"Weanut rutter and bam wit a wawberry weesecake pleazzzz …" said Tarquin. With a limp wave of his hand, he smiled inanely at Dog and dribbled. "Whoozz let the dogzz out, woozz, woozf, woof, woof!"

Bewildered, Dog looked at Jeremiah, who merely shrugged. "I reckon's he's having a problem with the travelling. Wouldn't be the first time."

The big man held Tarquin upright as Dog massaged his back. The massage seemed to have no effect.

"Nothing for it but to use me special remedy." Jeremiah took a glass scent bottle from his coat pocket and wafted it under Tarquin's nose.

"Wuurgghhh! Waz is tat?" spluttered Tarquin as he shook fuzziness and the stench of smelling salts from his head.

"You don't want to know, Seebee.'"

"Welemiah!"

"Aye, it's me," said Jeremiah, relieved his protégé was finally waking.

The boy hugged him. "It's so wood to see you!"

Tarquin's speech slowly returned and, one by one, his lights clicked on. Dog and Jeremiah raised him to his feet and together they walked carefully to the opening of the tunnel.

"There's an old lady coming to Steeple Snoring who wants to meet with Tarquin," said Dog.

"Don't tell me—Great-Aunt Polly!"

"How did you know?" asked Dog.

Tarquin smiled at Jeremiah. "Our spy!"

Jeremiah nodded. "Polly's the informer."

After a thirty-minute walk they reached the Steeple Snoring lock-keeper's cottage, where Ingeborg was standing by the gate. Tarquin looked at her face, normally warm and inviting like a fresh-baked apple pie. Today she looked ashen and tired.

"Your Great-Aunt Polidori will be here soon," said Inga.

Tarquin looked furtively around in case Polidori might suddenly swoop from the sky and carry him off.

"Be careful, young'un," said Jeremiah. "Remember to do as we discussed. And, Dog, you look after him."

Dog nodded.

Inga leaned forward to kiss Tarquin on the forehead. "Take care, Seebee."

The Cavendishes closed the cottage door, leaving Tarquin and Dog to walk up to the road.

The weather mirrored Tarquin's unease as the afternoon sun quickly faded and the temperature dropped unnaturally. Dark clouds rolled in from the east and blackened the sky. He felt icy fingers play along his spine, like arpeggios racing down a keyboard. He shuddered, remembering his last meeting with his great-aunt.

In the distance, a dust cloud followed a black dot travelling along the road at speed. Soon Tarquin could hear the sound of hooves. The black dot grew and took the shape of a coach and horses. As the coach got closer, the temperature dropped further and rain poured from the heavens, interspersed with the crackle of lightning. He pulled his frock coat around his shoulders, trying to shield himself against the downpour.

Through the raging storm he could now make out six stallions with large purple ostrich plumes dancing atop their heads. Driving the coach was a man in a wide hat and cloak, his face hidden by a scarf.

As the coach drew closer, the coachman pulled hard at the reins and the horses reared, their wet black coats shimmering in the fading light. The six horses stared at Tarquin, their eyes wild and cold. The breathless driver tried to calm them, but it was as if they knew what was coming.

"George Byron!" bellowed a voice from within.

The door flew open to reveal, glaring at him from the purple velvet interior, swathed in acres of black mourning clothes, Great-Aunt Polidori.

"Come aboard," she commanded imperiously. "Not you, wretch!" she shouted at Dog as he tried to follow Tarquin.

"Where I go, he goes," said Tarquin with one foot inside the carriage.

Her nostrils flared and she growled. "Servants sit with Carruthers, outside."

Tarquin looked at Dog, who shrugged and went to the front of the carriage.

"We have a lot to talk about and not much time," said Polidori. "I'm expected at a funeral."

Her tone was measured, but laced with threat.

Tarquin felt like a condemned man as he took his seat next to her in the carriage, but he had a job to do.

"Don't you wipe your feet when you enter someone's home?" she snapped.

The door slammed behind him and he swallowed hard. He looked down at his muddy shoes. Even through the lace veil, Polidori's wild eyes burnt into his skin.

She thumped the roof of the carriage with her cane. "Carruthers! Move on!"

With a loud yell and a crack of his whip, Carruthers drove the horses at breakneck speed down the avenue of trees.

Polidori looked at Tarquin and tutted. "For goodness' sake boy, show some character! I should have dragged you up myself rather than leave you in the hands of those Neanderthal relatives of ours."

He slowly turned towards her, his heart doing a drum roll. She moved closer and raised her veil. Two hawkish cobalt-blue eyes locked onto him like twin searing searchlights.

"You have, in your infinite wisdom, decided to attempt a rescue of that Welsh lassie and leave your friends to fight alone. Correct?"

"No! It isn't like that ..."

"What is it like, George?" Her voice was strong and authoritative.

"I want to save Rhia, yes," mumbled Tarquin, feeling like a field mouse pinned down by a hungry eagle.

"Speak up, boy. No great-nephew of mine shall mumble. Not if he values his knuckles."

Tarquin took a deep breath. "I want to save Rhia."

He stole a glance at his aunt and felt his stomach flip. He could swear he saw steam venting from her ears.

"You think, just because you can read half that journal and have found the time amulet, you now have the wherewithal to merrily wander through time saving people! Who the Charles Dickens do you think you are?" Her booming voice rattled the carriage windows.

"How ... how do you know all this?"

"Because I am your great-aunt and have lived way beyond your pitiful fifteen years!" she said, bristling.

Tarquin bowed his head and sat in silence.

"Tarquin, look at me."

He looked up and froze. Her hooked nose was no more than a couple of centimetres from his face.

But then, unexpectedly, her craggy face softened. "Can you be certain you can work the amulet correctly?" She peered into his eyes. "Mmm, I see. You really do care for this scrawny little friend of yours, don't you? Well, know this. You have very little time. You realize the Griddlebacks have arranged for the Leche to kill your friends in twenty-four hours, not forty-eight, don't you? They lied to you people not because it gave them any advantage but because they find lying a lot more enjoyable than telling the truth. If you're certain you can use the amulet correctly, go. If not, you save no one by being here in 2015."

"Rhia died trying to save me ... I must do something."

His great-aunt coughed and shifted back against the velvet. "Talk like that didn't build an empire. Stiff upper lip and shoulders back is the way forward. Just have to take it on the chin, keep calm and carry on."

Tarquin wasn't listening. His thoughts were with Rhia. The sudden rapping of his aunt's cane on the floor made him jump.

"For goodness' sake, boy, stop daydreaming!" Her veil was back down and her fearsome autocratic mien had returned.

Tarquin avoided her gaze and looked out at the thick forest rushing past.

"Well, are we now focused on saving your colleagues?"

"No," said Tarquin, pulling his knapsack close. "Rhia comes first."

"You obstreperous wretch of a boy!" shouted Polidori, crunching her bony fingers tightly together with a sickening crack.

Tarquin thought she was about to throttle him and pushed himself back against the upholstery, but she recovered herself and tapped her cane on the roof of the carriage.

"Carruthers, drop Master Jenkins back at Steeple Snoring, then find my ship and set a course for Windsor Castle, England. The second of February 1901. And don't spare the horses!"

She turned back to Tarquin. "Look, you are very inexperienced, and can't hope to save your friend on your own." She produced a smile from somewhere—Antarctica, by the looks of it. "Why don't you give me the amulet and we'll rescue your friends together and I promise we'll both bring Rhia back to life."

"You will save Rhia, won't you?" he said, opening his knapsack.

She nodded, her beady jackdaw eyes tightly focused.

Tarquin delved into his bag and grasped metal.

Polidori held out a pale bony hand expectantly.

Tarquin looked into her cold, calculating gaze and rubbed the teapot as hard as he could.

There was a knock on the cottage door and Jeremiah opened it. "Jimmy Greaves! You okay? What happened?"

"It's a long story," said Tarquin, pulling ferns and twigs from his mud-splattered clothing.

"I see you called the cavalry!"

Behind Tarquin, stood eight snarling, tooled-up, donkey-jacket-wearing leprechauns.

"Yes, I didn't want to, and I waited as long as I could, but the old goat demanded the amulet, so I had no choice."

"Did you give it her?" cried Jeremiah, his face a portrait of shock and fear.

"No, of course not. I've hidden it back in 2340!"

The big man gave out a loud sigh and closed his eyes. "Thank you," he mouthed.

"Is Polidori okay?" asked Ingeborg, rubbing her hands on her kitchen apron.

"Yes, just lost in time for a couple of days. She won't be going to any funerals for a while."

The leprechauns chuckled at Tarquin's joke. Jeremiah and Ingeborg looked confused by it.

"And," said Tarquin, holding up a book, "I found this in her handbag."

Jeremiah shook his head. "The original Journal of Metapheesis Olgiblat Screet, what she took from you, the old bat!"

The leprechauns shuffled on the porch and coughed meaningfully.

"Sorry, I forgot. Inga, we need to feed them."

"Not a problem," she said, opening the cottage door full and letting the leprechauns troop in. "There's a stew in the pantry. I'll get it warmed up." Her eyes boggled at the sight of Dog, who followed the last leprechaun through the door wearing Great-Aunt Polidori's hat backwards on his bald head and twirling her broken swagger stick like a majorette's baton.

Soon they were all sitting around the large oak kitchen table while Ingeborg passed around bowls of stew. The leprechauns ate heartily, going back for second and third helpings.

"I think I convinced her that I'm using the amulet to save Rhia," said Tarquin once the clatter of cutlery had died down to less than deafening levels.

"What about Pollux and Castor? Will she convince them?"

"Let's hope so. She can't go by herself now, so hopefully she'll send them on a wild-goose chase to the tea rooms in 2015."

"Right, get yourself sorted." said Jeremiah, wiping his plate clean with a chunk of his wife's homemade bread. "We've got to go to 2340 and tidy up this mess."

"Here we go again," said Tarquin.

CHAPTER 22

END GAME

Taking a mouthful of tea from his Mad Hatter mug, Oleg swallowed hard and shook his head.

"Bad news. The Time Guardians didn't take the bait. They've followed us to 1891," he said, reading the communiqué on the wall screen in front of him.

"What nonsense is this?" cried Calbhach as he came into the cockpit, followed by the other leprechauns. "They still want us ta send Tarquin to the billiards room under the lake? I don't get it."

Archie, sitting in the co-pilot's seat next to Oleg, shrugged expressively. "That's what they're saying. Tarquin must put the amulet on the table and then leave." He leaned across the dashboard and punched up the directions on the screen. A black-and-white photograph appeared. "This is where we are. Witley Park, Surrey."

"Why?" asked Calbhach, looking up at the screen and dabbing his brow with a large blue handkerchief. "Why there?"

"No idea. We have no intelligence on the venue," said Oleg, taking another slug of tea.

"That's a ruddy large feckin house! Looks a dog's dinner of a building, you ask me," said D'Arcy, standing on his toes and holding on to Calbhach's arm to see the screen.

"You know, they're bonkers," said Oleg, sitting back in the pilot's chair and putting his feet up on the dashboard. "Remember what happened in New Mexico in July of '47? Time Guardians? Lunatics, the lot of 'em!" He began chiseling mud and grit from under his fingernails with a screwdriver he'd pulled from his boot.

"But," said Archie, hoping to draw the leprechauns' attention away from his tray of freshly baked Rogolian pastries, "we have no choice. They want the amulet and we want our friends back. We have to go along with them. Besides, we have the Book of Dreams, and they can't operate the amulet without it."

"Thank goodness they don't know that," said Calbhach.

"If it's the only way, I'll take it," Tarquin said, standing in the cockpit doorway. Everyone turned to look at him. "We have no choice," he continued, rolling the amulet in his hands.

Oleg shook his head. "I'm not sending anyone down there. It looks too dangerous."

"What choice do we have?" Tarquin walked into the cockpit. "Besides, you can check out the billiards room before I go, and rescue me if things go wrong?"

"I don't trust them," said Oleg. "There must be a better way."

He spun around in his chair and looked at people for ideas. No one spoke.

Tarquin smiled at Oleg. "It's settled, then."

"Okay, okay," replied Oleg, "but we'll be watching your every move."

With all eyes on Tarquin and Oleg, Seamus snaffled a Rogolian pastry.

The Willerby Vogue and the Time Guardians' Airstream Bubble materialized simultaneously on the bank of the lake, less than a hundred metres apart. A violent thunderstorm raged around them. Lightning illumined the night sky and outlined the vast, neo-Tudor expanse of Witley Park Mansion, the lake, lawns and ornamental gardens. Oleg covered his eyes with the Look-Sees and surveyed the billiards room.

"Blimey," he said, "it's beautiful!"

What do you see?" asked Calbhach.

"I'll put it on screen."

The view through Oleg's Look-Sees appeared on the cockpit screen. Round and domed, the room was constructed of metal walls and hexagonal glass panes. Hanging from the centre of the dome was a magnificent crystal chandelier. Its warm yellow light flooded the room, making the gold-painted walls, Chinese carpets and yellow flagstone floor glow. Directly below the chandelier was a full-sized billiards table.

There was no sign of life.

Waiting nervously inside the Willerby's transportal, Tarquin held the bloodstone pendant Rhia had given him in one hand and his Bosun phaser in the other. The lights of the Time Guardians' Airstream Bubble flashed on and off on the wall screen in front of him.

Tarquin swallowed hard.

Oleg's face appeared on the transportal's screen. "Okay, Seebee," he said, pushing his Look-Sees back on his head, the lenses pointing skywards like two large brass bedknobs. "There's no one there, time to rock and roll." His face grew bigger on the screen. "Courage is being scared to death and saddling up anyway."

"You're quoting John Wayne now!" sighed Tarquin.

"Sending you to the billiards room in, ten–nine–eight–seven–six …"

Oleg's face disappeared and the screen went black, only his voice remained.

"Five–four–three–two–one …"

Tarquin inhaled deeply, pulled his jacket around his neck and flexed his shoulders. He squeezed the pendant tight and thought of Rhia.

After pressing a sequence of buttons, Oleg pulled out half a dozen organ stops to varying lengths on the dashboard. As Tarquin dematerialized from the transportal, Oleg quietly mumbled something—a prayer, perhaps. The open channel to Tarquin briefly hissed with static and then died.

Silence.

"Seebee, you with me?"

Oleg scanned the dials, levers and flashing lights on the communicator panel.

Calbhach lurched forward in his chair and pointed at the screen. "The Guardians, they're leaving!"

The leprechauns rushed from the cockpit to the corridor window and peered through the rain at the Airstream Bubble, slowly disappearing inside a ball of water vapour.

"Where's Tarquin now?" cried Calbhach, pressing his pomegranate nose hard to the glass.

"Still in the billiards room," shouted Oleg from the cockpit.

"They've just left him there?" Calbhach shouted back.

"Yep," said Oleg,

"What should we do?"

The Willerby fell silent. Calbhach looked at Oleg, then at the screen, then back at Oleg. The lines on his face deepened. He inhaled deeply before thumping his fist on the dashboard.

"Follow that damn ship!" he said, angrily. "They knows where our friends are. We'll just have to pray Tarquin stays out of trouble until we gets back."

Oleg nodded and waved his hands over a small glass instrument panel on the side of the dashboard. A blue hologram rose out of the panel, showing miniature replicas of the Bubble and the Willerby.

Archie jumped out of his seat and helped Oleg push and pull levers and organ stops. After a series of wild hand movements, Oleg jabbed a finger at the Bubble.

"I've got you," he said.

"Well done!" cried Archie, whacking him on the back.

Deftly Oleg typed numbers into his keyboard. Inside the hologram, the Willerby tucked in behind the Bubble and slipstreamed the silver spaceship.

Suddenly Archie looked at Oleg and leapt to his feet. "Oleg, no!"

The Mad Hatter mug bounced off the dashboard's edge and smashed on the floor.

Archie grabbed Oleg's arm. "Let's just monitor them from here. We can try to catch them later. You don't run down a Time Guardian ship!"

The crazy Russian grinned mischievously and calmly patted Archie's hand. "Wy-all," he said, in a low American drawl laced with a heavy, Russian accent, "there are some things a man just can't run away from."

"Oh sh—" groaned Archie, slumping back into his seat and fastening his seat's harness. Behind him, everyone scrambled for seats and hastily buckled up.

Chortling, Oleg continued pushing and pulling buttons and levers, his eyes fixed on the moving Bubble on the screen in front of him. With both hands, he grasped what looked like a red railway-signal lever next to him and waited. Crossing his fingers, he mumbled something in Russian, then turned to look at Archie and the sea of faces behind him.

"Guardians are jumping!" he boomed. His eyes bulged and he threw out his chest. "Let's go fishing!"

Pulling the lever down, he lunged across the dashboard and thumped a large red button before screaming, "Let's go, BRONCO!"

Pushing past Archie, Oleg flew from the bridge and raced down the corridor, chased by Archie and the others.

Reaching the BRONCO room first, Oleg flicked a switch on the wall and closed the airtight door behind him. He rushed to the centre of the transparent sphere and hauled himself up into the suspended bucket seat. Once there, he covered his head with the hairdryer hood. Donning a pair of Look-Sees, he slipped into the chair's seat harness and drew the straps tightly across his chest and abdomen.

Archie and the others could only watch in silent horror from the far side of the door.

Oleg grabbed a gold-coloured mouthguard from a rack above his head and popped it into his mouth. Wriggling his bottom on the seat, he gripped the hand rods fanning out from the chair. On the small screen on the console in front of him appeared a decreasing line of numbers. He flicked a switch and his voice, counting down the numbers, filled the ship.

"Twenty–nineteen–eighteen–seventeen–sixteen–fifteen …"

Archie bit down hard on his knuckles. D'Arcy pulled anxiously at his hair. Calbhach chewed his pipe-stem.

"Fourteen–thirteen–twelve–eleven–ten–nine …"

Brennan grabbed Archie's spare fist and stuck it in his own mouth. Archie thumped him. D'Arcy covered his eyes. Calbhach chewed right through his pipe-stem and absentmindedly swallowed.

"Eight–seven–six–five …"

Archie grabbed Brennan's fist. Calbhach thumped Brennan. D'Arcy groaned.

"Four–three–two–one …"

"Oh, bloody hell!" cried Calbhach. "He's following them!"

The sound of drums erupted into the air and Oleg's chair started bouncing and hopping to a syncopated four-four rhythm. The chair's coiled springs extended and contracted rapidly, wheezing and slurping. Hanging inside the sphere, Oleg bobbed up and down in the seat like a buoy caught in the eye of a storm.

Slowly, the sphere started rolling, building momentum, until, to the sound of a horn section blaring, it soared into the air and bounced like a pinball off the room's rubberized walls.

Oleg clung to the hand rods, his biceps straining as he controlled the sphere. His skin twisted tight around his skull, his mouth puckered, and his eyes bulged to the size of duck eggs. He looked like a puffer fish close to exploding.

Hopping and manoeuvering the caravan along a dozen wormholes, Oleg followed the Time Guardians' Bubble through space and time. The sphere bounded inside the room like a March hare, spinning and accelerating away from the door before catapulting back towards it.

On the wall screen inside the BRONCO room it became clear that the distance between the Airstream Bubble and the Willerby Vogue was gradually increasing.

From inside the sphere, Oleg's cursing became more colourful.

He was losing his prey.

Click!

"Oh, bollards! It's a trap!" hissed Tarquin to himself.

Turning, he saw Gruilash Vandergaard and two of his bodyguards pointing their guns at him.

He looked into Gruilash's cold, reptilian eyes. The Time Guardians had delivered him straight to the Griddlebacks!

"Drop the Bosun," growled Gruilash, waving his gun at Tarquin from across the billiards table. "Put the amulet on the table and slide it to me."

Tarquin obeyed. The light from the crystal chandelier made Gruilash's reptilian skin glow a wet, putrid, sickly yellow.

Click, click!

Gruilash's bodyguards crashed to the floor.

Startled, the Griddleback leader stared at Tarquin. His inner eyelid flashed across his eyes and he blinked.

Behind him, two tall, ghostly white humanoids—Leche—dressed in black-and-purple leathers crept into the room from an adjoining corridor, their guns fixed on Gruilash. One of the humanoids, a female with long black hair, came up behind Gruilash and jabbed her gun hard into the scales of his head, making him snort loudly.

"Drop it," she said.

Gruilash growled and let his gun fall to the green baize table.

"We'll take that amulet, you pathetic excuse for a handbag," she said.

Gruilash picked up the amulet and turned to face her.

"We had an agreement," he said. Bile dripped from his jaw and frothed on the flagstoned floor.

"Oh, yes, our agreement." The Leche female smiled wickedly, then shot him in the thigh.

Gruilash shrieked, dropped the amulet and collapsed to the floor clutching at the bleeding hole in his leg.

"We do not do witticisms, nor do we keep to agreements—especially not with you, not after you betrayed us in Liverpool, leaving us to die!" said the male, laughing as he moved forward to kick Gruilash viciously in the head a few times. He kept going until the Griddleback stopped writhing.

Stepping over Gruilash, the Leche picked up the amulet and bared two fifteen-centimetre scimitar-shaped incisors at Tarquin and snarled. It was the creature that had shot him in the Steeple Snoring teashop.

Tarquin's stomach went south.

"Now, human," said the female, directing her gun at Tarquin and moving around the table. "I'm going to slice off your head, suck out your brains, and ram your ugly head on the front of my turbo hoverbike."

Tarquin gulped. He could think of worse places to have one's head rammed, but not many. Only one, in fact.

He tried to back away, but found himself pressed up against the metal wall of the billiards room, powerless to do anything more than watch as the female strutted towards him, the echo of her heels tapping a slow, ominous rhythm on the flag-stone floor.

She grinned and licked her blood-red lips. Her icy blue eyes showed no emotion as she pressed the barrel of her gun into Tarquin's forehead. A sickly sweet perfume filled his nostrils and he shivered uncontrollably.

"You have no idea the trouble you've caused," she said, drawing a bony-fingered claw down his cheek. She jabbed it hard into his chin, puncturing the skin. "No matter," she said, licking Tarquin's blood from her talon and rotating the barrel against his head, "Time to christen my bike."

Tarquin expelled air and his shoulders sagged. Closing his eyes, he thought of Rhia and his parents.

Whoooosh!

A gust of ice-cold air, followed by a blast of steam and a deafening thunderclap, knocked all three of them off their feet.

Stunned by the noise and the watery blast, Tarquin lay groaning on the floor. A hundred pealing bells rang inside his head. He blinked and rubbed his eyes.

A ball of turbulent weather the size of a skull appeared within the glass chandelier. Growing quickly, it smashed the chandelier and sent thousands of shards of glass bouncing from the table and floor.

Hovering high above the billiards table, the ball continued to expand and become more turbulent. Fearing he was about to be blown to pieces, Tarquin hauled himself to a corner of the room, as far away from the billiards table as he could get. When he reached the wall he sat up.

Gruilash and the Leche lay motionless. The sphere engulfed the table, touched the dome's ceiling and exploded, releasing a dense, thick cloud of smoke.

Tarquin covered his face with his hands. All he could do was watch between his fingers.

From within the clearing smoke appeared a sedan chair, its legs resting on the billiards table.

Tarquin blinked. The pealing bells inside his head continued unabated.

Something moved inside the chair. A head covered in short grey hair popped out, followed by another. Like two old, hungry rats, the passengers looked around the billiards room with their wet, beady eyes and sniffed the air.

Seeing the amulet amongst the glass on the floor, they pointed to it, chattered briefly, and disappeared back into the chair.

Seconds later, one of the travellers, pale and little more than a bag of bones, emerged from the chair, naked apart from a pair of worn army boots and a plumed tricorn hat. Scuttling across the table, he jumped to the floor, picked up the amulet and turned.

Seeing Tarquin, he froze.

He said something, but all Tarquin could hear were the bells.

The wizened man pointed and waved a crooked finger at him, his mouth opening and closing like an over-excited auctioneer's.

"Please," said Tarquin, shaking and holding out his hand. "That's mine."

The man raced back to the table, swung himself onto the baize and, clutching the amulet to his hairy chest, cocked his head sideways and peered down at Tarquin, sniffing him suspiciously.

"Please, you don't understand. I need it," implored Tarquin.

The old man's rigid, frightened expression relaxed and he seemed to smile. Getting down on his knees, he moved to the edge of the table and slowly climbed back off.

Cautiously, he came towards Tarquin and took his hand. He shook it repeatedly, mouthing the same word again and again, but Tarquin couldn't make out what he was saying.

"You give me the amulet, yes?" said Tarquin, trying to get up.

Suddenly the man's frightened expression returned and he ripped his hand away. Now he shouted, gesticulating like an angry baboon, and moved backwards.

Tarquin tried desperately to get up and follow him. "No, wait! I can get you another one!"

The man shook his head before climbing back onto the baize and scuttling to the chair.

Tarquin crabbed his way to the table's edge. He tried to raise himself, but his arms and legs were like rubber and he just slid along the table's side, clutching forlornly at the baize rim before falling to the floor.

A sphere of light grew above the chair.

"Noooo!" cried Tarquin, rolling into a protective ball by the side of the table.

Through his fingers he could see the weather front expand to the size of a hot-air balloon, engulfing the chair and then filling the domed ceiling.

Finally it exploded, sending Tarquin, Gruilash, the bodyguards and the Leche rolling across the billiards-room floor like plastic bags blown by the wind. They tumbled and zigzagged over the flagstones, stopping only when the weather front shrank to the size of a soccer ball and abruptly disappeared.

A final bolt of lightning flashed through the room.

Tarquin uncurled himself and looked up. A letter-sized piece of parchment spiralled slowly down from the top of the dome and landed on the table.

Breathing heavily, he struggled to his knees. He had an almighty headache and the ringing in his ears continued incessantly.

He rubbed his neck and gazed around the room. The Griddlebacks and Leche remained motionless.

Tarquin was next to a leg of the table. Grasping it, he reached up to the string pocket and pulled himself to his feet, leaning against the table.

Taking the parchment from the water-sodden green baize, he peered at it. Once he'd got his eyes properly into focus, he could see the drawing on the parchment. It was a pen-and-ink picture of two naked men standing inside a square and surrounded by a circle. Their arms and legs stretched out, touching the circle.

"It can't be!" said Tarquin to himself, looking at the face in the drawing. "He's had a shave and a haircut, but that's Loopy Nostrils! And Leonardo!"

He turned the parchment over and saw writing in French and lots of coordinates. Amidst the numbers, he recognized the name of Witley Hall.

Tarquin's legs buckled and he groaned, clutching at the table as he slid to the ground and rolled onto his back, still clutching the parchment. Bathed by the pale moonlight seeping in through the domed glass roof, he sighed.

The amulet was gone.

Anger replaced tiredness, and he waved the parchment at the ceiling.

"If I ever get my hands on you, you hairy-arsed kleptomaniacs—"

Cold air rushed into the room and the temperature dropped. Ice formed on the glass and spread out in crazy spidery patterns.

"Not again!" he cried, pocketing the parchment and rolling under the table before pulling himself into a ball and covering his head with his hands and coat. A pressure wave pushed him once again across the floor like tumbleweed until he rested against the metal wall. Gritting his teeth, he pulled his arms tight to his body and shut his eyes, waiting for the inevitable.

Despite the bells ringing inside his head he heard screeches, scrapes, heavy thuds and the sound of splintering wood. Whatever was coming through was big.

Tarquin opened his eyes.

A dark cloud covered the opposite wall. Within it lay the Willerby Vogue on its side, its door open, flapping in the wind. The remains of the billiards table were beside it.

"Thank God!" yelled Tarquin, pulling his coat from his head and digging his nails into the mortar around the floor's flagstones to pull himself toward the caravan. Two heads emerged through the doorway, which was now effectively on the roof of the caravan. Archie and Calbhach climbed out and jumped down onto the floor.

Seeing Tarquin, they ran over. Calbhach grabbed his arm and smiled, mouthing something Tarquin couldn't hear. Archie took Tarquin's other arm and together he and Calbhach lifted the battered boy to his feet and helped him towards the caravan.

Tarquin looked up with an effort and saw a beaming Oleg halfway out of the door.

Wuuummph!

Dazed, Tarquin looked up to see Archie and Calbhach on their knees beside him. *I'm getting fed up of being blown off my feet,* he thought.

Wuuummph! Wuuummph! Wuuummph!

Phaser fire bounced around the metal room, shattering three glass panels near the top of the domed ceiling. Ice-cold lake water cannoned through the holes. One stream of water hit Tarquin in the chest just as he was getting up, and sent him sprawling again.

He sucked in air and grabbed at a carpet to slow himself down.

The shock of the freezing water cleared his head. The ringing in his ears had finally gone, to be replaced by the roar of the water as it poured into the billiards room and swirled around his thighs. Archie and Calbhach had managed to reach the wall, and stood pressed against it as the water flowed past.

Tarquin tried wading toward them. He lost count of how many times he lost his balance and fell into the water, but each time he resurfaced and tried again. Finally, shivering and out of breath, he reached Archie and Calbhach, who pulled him up alongside them against the wall.

Clutching his stomach, Tarquin looked down the corridor. Gruilash, his body-guards and the Leche were gone.

Water swirled around the waists of Tarquin and Archie—and around the neck of Calbhach—pulling them towards the flowing current and thwarting any attempt they might make to reach the caravan.

From the distance came the sound of more phaser fire.

Desperately cold, Tarquin turned more in hope than expectation towards the Willerby, and saw Brennan wading in their direction, dragging three ropes behind him. The leprechaun was secured to a rope held by the rest of the leprechauns, who were standing on the caravan and shouting encouragement.

"We need to leave, now!" shouted Brennan, reaching the wall and swiftly tying the ropes around their waists. He signalled to the caravan. Unceremoniously, and with the proficiency of a tug-of-war team, the leprechauns hauled Brennan, Tarquin, Archie and Calbhach through the water and up the side of the caravan and in through the door.

The door slammed shut. The caravan wobbled and started spinning.

"We're damaged. I can only get the ship to hop!" came Oleg's voice over the communicator. "Hold onto anything you can!"

Tarquin and the rest of the crew tumbled and spun across the caravan floor, ceiling and walls like a load of heavy washing in a dryer.

The caravan materialized on the front lawn of Witley Hall, landing heavily. Its door flew from its hinges, bounced across the lawn and smashed into a statue, decapitating it as the caravan gouged a large scar, rolled and came to rest upside-down.

Despite three leprechauns sprawled on top of him, Tarquin could see through the open doorway. Griddleback stormtroopers poured across the landscape like packs of marauding hyenas.

"Move!" he shouted, as white light bounced across the ground and exploded close to the upturned caravan, driving columns of black earth and rock into the air. Everyone scrambled to their feet and made for the cockpit.

"Where's Oleg?" cried Archie.

The screen in the cockpit filled with the Russian, now standing in the caravan's open doorway wearing cowboy boots, a Stetson hat and a gunslinger's double gun belt.

"What the hell do you think you're doing!" yelled Calbhach, thumping the communicator and trying to get Oleg's attention.

Oblivious to the mayhem around him, Oleg tugged at his hat, settled his gun belts firmly on his hips, and chewed hard on a Cuban cigar. The spitting fire of Griddleback phaser bolts crept closer. Slowly, he took a pair of leather gloves from his waistcoat and methodically pulled them on.

Powering up his guns, Oleg looked down the hill at the oncoming Griddleback tide, rolled the cigar from one corner of his mouth to the other, and sneered, "A man's gotta do what a man's gotta do."

Stepping from the caravan, he drew his pair of Wrogleys.

"It's payday, boys! Come and get it!"

Ignoring the phaser fire arcing and howling all around him, he walked steadily towards the stormtroopers, the spurs on his boots glinting in the moonlight. This was his moment. He was Rooster Coburn, the Ringo Kid and Lieutenant Colonel Kirby Yorke all rolled into one mad loveable John-Wayne-quoting Russian.

Wuuummphhh!

A phaser bolt landed close to the caravan, threw up a wall of earth and buried Oleg.

The sudden roar of rotor blades made everyone in the caravan rush to the nearest window and look to the sky. Rising slowly above the hall, like a giant eagle, was a Russian Mi35 Hind helicopter gunship bristling with rockets.

"The Russians are coming!" shouted Calbhach, punching the air and hugging Archie. The gunship circled the Willerby, pumping a withering barrage of goo at the first wave of Griddleback stormtroopers coming up the hill. Caught by surprise, the stormtroopers were soon encased and stuck to the lawn, where they rocked from side to side like a field of pink anemones caught in a current.

As the remaining Griddlebacks retreated, Oleg rose like a phoenix from his mud tomb and continued after them down the hill.

The Griddlebacks regrouped, and soon a second wave of stormtroopers started up the hill towards the caravan, swarming like ants around their trapped colleagues. Using them as shields, the warriors slowly moved forward.

Jeremiah's voice, amplified through the helicopter's loudspeakers, boomed across the lawn, "Oleg, you daft bugger, get back to the caravan. We're leaving!"

Oleg spat out his cigar and took out a horde of Griddlebacks ahead of him, before retreating up the hill as fast as he could, emptying his guns while the helicopter offered him covering fire.

He was close to the caravan just as it lifted off the ground and lurched left, then right.

Diving headlong, Oleg threw himself at the doorway. Two lavishly bunioned hands reached out and grabbed him, hauling him in just as the vehicle rose like a rocket into the night sky, its exit marked by the sound of a full orchestral musical score. The helicopter followed.

"Close the ruddy door!" shrieked Jeremiah over the communicator. Grabbing a table from the dining room, the leprechauns used it as a door to seal the caravan.

Tarquin lay on the caravan floor in semi-darkness, cold, wet and exhausted. His only thought was of the amulet, tumbling through time and space, held in the sweaty hands of a French lunatic accompanied by a maverick inventor born five and a half centuries before Tarquin himself.

"Tarquin?" came a voice. A shadow moved across his face. Startled, he sat up and looked around.

"Jules!" he cried, recognizing the man who stood smiling at him. "I thought we'd lost you!"

"No chance. Oleg chased down the Time Guardians' Bubble, glooped them so they couldn't escape, and then Calbhach and the leprechauns rescued us."

Shock spread like wildfire across Tarquin's face.

"What about the Beatles? Did you save them?"

Jules grinned and nodded. "Not only were they saved, but they've agreed to do a gig at the Yelts Inn!"

Tarquin's face changed from happiness to confusion. "But, but, how can they go back to the sixties after they've seen the twenty-fourth century?"

"The same way we would have sent you back if you hadn't wanted to join the BIFS. They'll wake up close to the Leeds and Liverpool canal with sore heads and no recollection of recent events."

"That's good news," said Tarquin, getting up. "But most of the rest is bad. I found this in the billiards room."

He took the parchment form his pocket and handed it to Jules. "Nostradamus and Leonardo arrived and saved my life. But they also took the amulet."

Jules looked at the drawing. "Turn it over," said Tarquin.

Jules rolled his eyes. "Bloody Time Guardians! These are the coordinates for the room under the lake. They arranged for those freaks to take the amulet!"

"That would explain why the Guardians left you to the Leche and Griddlebacks," said Calbhach, arriving in the corridor. "They knew Loopy Nostrils and Leo would arrive, wipe everyone out and take the amulet."

Epilogue

A week had passed since their escape back to 2340. The Beatles concert at the Yelts Inn had been a tremendous success, and the band had returned now to Liverpool, none the worse for their adventure. The BIFS were throwing all available assets at finding Nostradamus and Leonardo, even employing Georgia Blade and her wrecking crew as "consultants". The Russians were involved, too, and Jules was working with Georgia to locate her sister on the Leche's home planet. Jeremiah was back on his beloved Silvery Moon, where Inga was making sure he ate properly—or at least ate lots—and Calbhach was giving Alice and Archie lessons in Raggedy Rook. Alice was appallingly good at the game, revealing an innate viciousness that terrified Archie.

Tarquin sat with Archie in Rigsworth's Diner, looking at the menu. Alice's Wopplefop lay happily on its back in its box, purring, its large watery eyes staring at the strange world around it.

"Woz yer want, small human," said the Maganoid Shagganat waitress, taking Flopsy Wopsy from its box before Tarquin could prevent it.

With a bullying leer, the waitress slathered phlegm across her painted lips and deliberately dripped it on Flopsy.

"On my planet we eat dese," she said, rolling her tongue across her lips.

Tarquin didn't flinch. He rose from his seat, looked her straight in the eyes and moved forward until his nose touched her wrinkled snout.

"Put. The. Bunny. Back. In. The. Box," he said loudly.

The diner went quiet.

"I said, put the bunny back in the box."

The Shagganat didn't move. Another dollop of phlegm dripped from her snout and slid down Tarquin's jacket.

"You really should give me some respect," said Tarquin. He poked her nose hard with his index finger, at the same time stamping on her foot.

The Shagganat wailed, dropped the Wopplefop on the table, and grabbed her proboscis between her club-like hands before running towards the kitchen as if chased by a rampaging tribe of Booger Burros.

"Why couldn't you put the bunny back in the box?" Tarquin said to her disappearing form.

"Wow, that was brave!" Archie said, watching the waitress crash through the kitchen's double doors, moaning.

"It was time I stood up to the bully." Tarquin took out the bloodstone pendant he'd been clutching in his pocket and put it on the table before picking up the startled Wopplefop. He gave it a reassuring cuddle, then put it back in its box, sat down and returned to the menu.

"You're going back to save her, aren't you!" exclaimed Archie, looking at the pendant.

Startled by his friend's directness Tarquin looked up.

Archie pointed at the pendant. "That stone was Rhia's. I recognize it."

Tarquin looked furtively around the room, then at Archie.

"Since I've been back, Jules has been letting me read the Book of Dreams in his office. He wants me to learn how to destroy the amulet."

"Yeah, right!" said Archie, shaking his head.

"No, saving Rhia would break a dozen intergalactic regulations …" The faintest of smiles flashed across Tarquin's face. "But I think I know where to find Nostra and Leo …

"And what are regulations, after all?"

What's Coming Next?

After his gruesome death in 2015, Tarquin Seebohm Jenkins can now get back to studying the Book of Dreams, and joining the search for Nostradamus and Leonardo Da Vinci, and the amulet they stole. Trouble is, every Tom, Dick and alien are preparing to do the same...

Excerpt from Book Two

The Steeple Snoring Post Office door flew open and Mrs Roundtree bustled in. "They've found that Jenkins boy in the woods! He's been eaten!"

The post office fell silent. A dozen ordinarily gray faces turned white; a baby cried.

"How, why?" asked the Post Master. "It's been three weeks since he went missing."

"That joyous day," muttered Mrs Hoploosely, but luckily nobody heard her.

All eyes were turned to the new arrival who, having run—well, waddled—all the way down the High Street, was now being comforted by husband Kenneth from his mobility scooter.

Mrs Roundtree gripped the edge of the counter tightly, her face the colour of rhubarb. Wheezing histrionically, she sucked in a deep breath.

"Sergeant Sloth says ..." She sniffed and looked skyward before continuing. "He says ... a sounder of wild boars ate him! The best bits, anyway. They left just enough to recognize him by. The Jenkins boy, that is."

She burst into a flood of tears and collapsed backwards to sit on her husband. He emitted a mournful cry.

Mrs Hoploosely nodded shrewdly. "It's a technical term. She means a pack."

"Are we safe?" The speaker was a very small man in a trilby hat who was stretching up on tiptoes to look out of the casement window. Several customers moved to join him. As they did so the little man inconspicuously eased himself away and made for the door.

"Excuse me, but you look strangely familiar." Standing in the doorway, staring down at him with a visage reminiscent of a pit bull terrier who'd just been spayed, was Mrs Hoploosley. "You're Vladimir Pu—"

"Oi don't t'ink so. O'im jist passin' through ta village." The little man pulled his trilby down over his face, ducked under Mrs Hoploosley's closed umbrella and darted out of the post office.

Walking away along the High Street, he occasionally glanced behind to see if anyone was following him. Once he reached the doorway of the burned-out Enchanted Teapot Tea Rooms, he paused for one last look up and down the High Street.

No one was interested in him.

Smiling, he continued on his way out of town until he reached the double lock and, beside it, the lock-keeper's cottage. In the cottage's front garden was a battered Willerby Vogue caravan, mounted on bricks.

The little man opened the door to the caravan and hopped in. In the corridor just inside the door he found Jeremiah Cavendish, once a heavyweight wrestler who'd been talked of in terms of a world championship, now retired and for many years the Steeple Snoring lock-keeper.

"Calbhach! How did it go?" Jeremiah asked.

"Pretty boar-ing really."

"You've been working on that born mott all morning, 'aven't you?" said Jeremiah with a grin. "Not sure about the disguise, though. Anyone recognize you?"

"Nah, me Putin wus grand," said Calbhach, pressing the ring around his neck. The semblance of Vladimir Putin vanished and a wart-encrusted, bunion-nosed red-haired leprechaun appeared in its place. "You got dat pack of boars back to medieval France?"

"All good," said Jeremiah. "Though one of them took a shining to Rhiordan, which was a bit messy."

Calbhach raised his bushy eyebrows. "For Rhiordan or the boar?"

"Both. We prised them apart eventually. Rhiordan's still sulking."

The leprechaun shrugged off his coat. "Lunch ready?"

"Yes. The brothers Grimm have made something special."

"Chops?"

Jeremiah nodded, looking guilty. "Rhiordan says I can have his."

You can find out more about Tarquin Jenkins and his adventures by following his blog at www.tarquinsjenkins.wordpress.com.